IN THE HOURS OF NIGHT

ALSO BY WILLIAM BRADFORD HUIE

NOVELS
THE KLANSMAN
THE AMERICANIZATION OF EMILY
THE REVOLT OF MAMIE STOVER
HOTEL MAMIE STOVER
MUD ON THE STARS

NONFICTION
THE EXECUTION OF PRIVATE SLOVIK
THE HERO OF IWO JIMA
THE HIROSHIMA PILOT
RUBY MC COLLUM
HE SLEW THE DREAMER

IN THE

A NOVEL BY

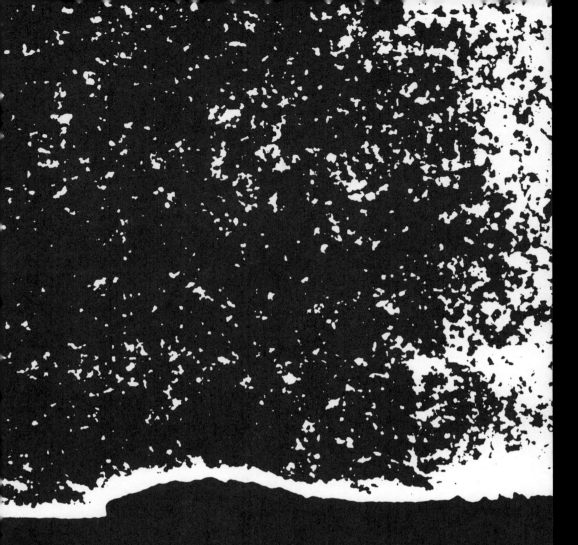

HOURS OF NIGHT

WILLIAM BRADFORD HUIE

DELACORTE PRESS/NEW YORK

Manufactured in the United States of America
Designed by Jerry Tillett
First printing

LIBRARY OF CONGRESS CATALOGING IN PUBLICATION DATA
Huie, William Bradford, 1910–
In the hours of night.
I. Title.
PZ3.H87583In [PS3515.U32] 813'.5'2 75-12640
ISBN 0-440-04367-0

The author was
graciously and efficiently assisted by the librarians
of the Tennessee Valley Authority at Knoxville,
of the Atomic Energy Commission at Oak Ridge,
and of the University of the South
at Sewanee, Tennessee.

To the Memory of
Ruth Puckett Huie

FOREWORD

As I write these words, half of all living Americans cannot remember the years 1946–48. Some of us who can remember do so fondly. We had celebrated the nation's last military victory. We had brought the boys home, and they were in college under the GI Bill. We had created the UN to perpetuate peace. *The Best Years of Our Lives* was the film we liked most. *Peace of Mind* was the book we preferred. After enjoying performances of *South Pacific* or *Mister Roberts,* which gave us war as we liked to think of it, we went to supper clubs and enjoyed Hildegarde singing *"Wunderbar"* and "a song of love is a sad song, hi-lilly, hi-lilly, hi-lo." Then we went home and joyfully impregnated our wives, giving the nation its last "baby boom." We found women delightful in their New Look: narrow-waisted suits with flared skirts down to mid-calf and shoulder-length hair with the ends turned up in "flip" curls. Most of us enjoyed those years.

Only an infrequent scream *In the Hours of Night* disturbed us. This novel is about one such scream.

—WILLIAM BRADFORD HUIE
March, 1975

And he, valorous Ajax,
Who was once my ward and cover
From every flying shaft
And dread in the hours of night,
Now is handed over to his harsh daemon.

—FROM *Ajax* BY SOPHOCLES

I<small>N</small> the late afternoon of Tuesday, April 27, 1948, a United States Navy transport plane glided toward a landing at Washington National Airport. It carried an unusual party of passengers.

The wind was gusty, rain was falling in sheets, and the plane's wheels, on striking the wet asphalt, skidded ten feet before they found purchase. The four propellers, suddenly reversed, fought to brake the roll of the heavy craft, and as the plane slowed it turned and taxied toward the north end of the field, which was reserved for military traffic.

Because of the rain and the black hovering clouds, yellow fog lights had been turned on in the docking area, and these lights gave the area a jaundiced, somewhat unsettling sort of illumination. More unsettling were the military police, whose rubber capes and polished plastic helmets, wet from the rain, glittered under the yellow lights. The police were uneasy. They had banished all civilians, including reporters and photographers, from the area.

As the plane halted and hushed its engines, police pushed a ramp to the door, and a khaki-colored Red-Crossed military ambulance backed toward the ramp. A black Cadillac limousine with a White House license plate backed alongside the ambulance. Police formed ranks which left a guarded path from the foot of the ramp to the ambulance and the limousine. A police lieutenant and a sergeant, each carrying an umbrella, hurried up the ramp as the plane's door opened. Then, while the ranked police stood at attention in the gusty downpour, the passengers emerged from the plane, not one directly behind another but at intervals, and proceeded down the ramp under the umbrella of either the police lieutenant or the sergeant.

First to emerge was a Member of the President's Cabinet, Paul Blanton, who in private life was a partner in a Wall Street banking house. Hatless and bald, he moved confidently on the slippery ramp because he was a yachtsman, trained to hold his footing on a pitching awash deck. He was also a former intercollegiate boxing champion, who still kept in shape with regular workouts. Trying to keep pace with him down the ramp, the sergeant with the umbrella slipped and almost fell. Paul Blanton entered the limousine.

Emergence of the next figure, who was lithe and lean-faced, caused the police to brace rigidly. He wore a homburg and a gray civilian suit, but the police knew he was Vice-Admiral Clarence Evans Potter, head of Combined Intelligence, a wartime director of cloak-and-dagger operations. He hurried down the ramp and entered the limousine.

At this point there was a moment's delay, like a stage wait, and the two men in the limousine looked toward the plane door. Then, at the door, a group of four people appeared, three of them assisting the fourth. Leading the group was an agent of the Federal Bureau of Investigation. His photograph, often showing him with a submachine gun in his hands, had dominated many a front page after he had slain or captured some public enemy. His name was Jack Hardwick, and now his left wrist was handcuffed to the right wrist of, not a public enemy but a public servant: Thomas Francis Castleton, a Tennessean who had been summoned to Washington in 1941 by Secretary of State Cordell Hull, who had handled sensitive wartime assignments and who was now a member of President Truman's Advisory Council.

Holding Frank Castleton's left arm was Dr. Arthur Leo Palkin, a Navy captain and the Navy's senior psychiatrist, and directly in front of Frank Castleton, partially shielding him from the rain, was Lieutenant Mary

2

Sullivan, of the Navy Nurse Corps. With a tissue Mary Sullivan reached up and dried tears from Frank Castleton's cheeks.

It was Castleton, therefore, who was the focus of the group; he was being restrained, isolated, transported, assisted, doctored and nursed by the others. As Castleton was maneuvered through the plane door and down the ramp, the doctor, the nurse, the FBI agent and the policemen with the umbrellas looked like considerate tugs trying to dock a disabled ship in heavy weather. Frank Castleton was a tall slender man: six feet two inches, a hundred seventy pounds, with a sinewy still-athletic frame, though he had just passed his forty-sixth birthday. His sandy hair, graying in the temples, was close-cropped, crew-cut, and in health his face was ruddy, relaxed and friendly. It was the face of an outdoorsman who loved mountains, forests and rivers. But now Frank Castleton's shoulders sagged from sedation; his brow was anguished; his chin trembled. He seemed like a trapped, terrified animal that can't understand what is happening to it, and his eyes were brimming, then overflowing with the tears which his nurse frequently wiped away.

Since dawn newspapers across America had been reporting: A-BOMB EXPERT SUFFERS NERVOUS COLLAPSE! Radio newsmen had added details every hour on the hour: how at 3 A.M. Castleton's wife had telephoned the White House to report that Castleton, while on a hiking trip in the Great Smoky Mountains, had become hysterical . . . how at 8 A.M. the Navy plane had left Washington carrying Secretary Blanton, Admiral Potter, Jack Hardwick, the doctor and the nurse . . . how the plane had landed at Knoxville before noon . . . how Castleton had been taken into custody at his home in Norris, Tennessee . . . and how Castleton was being flown to the service hospital near Washington for treatment and for "the safety of the United States and the Free World."

Radio commentators had kept repeating: "The situation is without precedent in the nation's history. For the last five and a half years—since October, 1942—Castleton has been trusted with atomic-bomb secrets. Reporting directly to President Roosevelt, he watched step by step the creation of the bomb at Oak Ridge, Tennessee, at Hanford, Washington, and at Los Alamos, New Mexico. He once owned some of the land on which the vast Oak Ridge atomic laboratory now stands. If, as reported, he has now become mentally unstable, officers in the combined security agencies doubt that he can be allowed treatment in a civilian hospital, where he could become the prey of an enemy agent. The United States is said to have no choice but to hold Castleton in protective custody, to lodge

3

him in a service hospital and to allow him to be treated only by the highest-ranking service psychiatrist until he regains his stability."

Frank Castleton was a prisoner in handcuffs, not because he had committed a crime but because he was ill and he knew so much. As gently as they could, and trying to fend off the rain, Jack Hardwick and the others guided the tall, trembling man down the ramp and into the ambulance. There Hardwick unlocked the steel cuff from his own wrist, helped Castleton lie down on the cot, then locked the cuff to the cot's metallic rail. Dr. Palkin nodded at him. Unless he was cuffed to the cot, Castleton might try to knock out a window and cut himself with glass. Hardwick sat on a stool at the rear door while Mary Sullivan sat near Castleton's face, wiping his tears. After the ambulance door was closed, Dr. Palkin took a seat in the limousine. Then the ambulance pulled away, led by a police car and followed by the limousine.

As the three-car caravan sped past the Pentagon, Paul Blanton, riding in the limousine with Admiral Potter and Dr. Palkin, lighted a cigarette and tried to relax. He was fifty-two, a powerfully built Irish-American, with a broad florid face and blue eyes set wide apart under his massive bald dome. What remained of his hair was reddish gray, and his mouth was a straight slit which often compressed on a pipestem. Now he felt tired. At 4 A.M. he had been roused at his home in Georgetown and asked to be at the White House at 5. There the President's Chief of Staff, Admiral William D. Leahy, had informed him of Castleton's crackup . . .

Blanton sighed heavily, shook his head, then said to Leahy, "This is very sad news. But I can't say I'm surprised. Frank has worked so hard since the war and been so disappointed that he's become a fanatic."

Admiral Leahy, who was bald, old, angular and hawk-faced, poured coffee for Blanton. "You know him well, don't you?"

"Quite well. We started out together on the bomb in the fall of '42. He was reporting to the President, and I prepared the weekly progress report for Mr. Stimson and the Joint Chiefs. You weren't here then; you were in Vichy."

The admiral nodded and grimaced.

Blanton drained his cup. "Frank and I both visited the bomb laboratories frequently, so we sometimes traveled together. When we visited Los Alamos we both stayed at the La Fonda Hotel in Santa Fe, and we ran into

4

each other a lot there. When I visited Oak Ridge I always stayed at his home, ten miles north of the government reservation, whether he was there or not. I guess I must have spent forty nights in that guest house. I've ridden his horses and used his boats. I know his wife, his children, his parents—fine people. Hospitable, friendly, responsible, well-off . . . the kind of folks who built this country. Frank and his wife have been in my home here in Washington, of course. And you may recall that the President took both Frank and me with him to Yalta." He paused, then added, "Yes, sir, the Castletons and I are friends."

The old admiral's old eyes narrowed. "Will Castleton and his family cooperate with you now?"

A yellow warning light came on in Blanton's mind. He weighed his answer while he lighted his pipe. "They're independent folks. But they're patriots. They know I'm their friend. Oh, Frank and I haven't agreed on everything. My God, if he'd listened to me he wouldn't be in the shape he's in now. We're different kinds of men, and you know he got up the ladder easier than I did. He's emotional—a musician, a painter and a runner who ran in the Boston marathon. Me, I'm a puncher, a realistic old Wall Street alley fighter. Frank's father, Bert, is a rural banker who speaks my language, and his wife, Diane, seems to trust me. So yes, I believe Frank and his folks will try to cooperate with me now."

"They must cooperate!" The admiral spoke sharply. "Frank Castleton's crackup couldn't have come at a worse time. Cold War, Berlin and an election year!" The Berlin Blockade had begun three weeks earlier, on March 31, 1948. "The President is gravely concerned. What Castleton could tell a Congressional committee would convulse this country and might plunge us into war with the Soviet Union."

"No doubt about that."

Admiral Leahy leaned back in his chair and tapped the tips of his fingers together. "Mr. Secretary, the President needs your help with this problem. He'd like you to telephone Diane Castleton immediately and tell her that you're posting a guard at her home and that you'll arrive there before noon. The President wants you to go to Tennessee, convince the Castletons this is the only thing—the right thing—to do and bring Frank here to the service hospital. Take Ev Potter and Jack Hardwick with you. Handle the press, and for God's sake get the story out of the papers and off the air as soon as possible. Handle the outcry in Congress. In short, Mr. Secretary, the President is asking you to take charge of this case as of this moment and make sure that it doesn't give aid and comfort either to the Russkies, or to Tom Dewey and the Republicans, or to Henry Wallace, or to Strom Thurmond."

Blanton felt awful. This was an assignment he didn't want, but it was evident he couldn't avoid it. He had been trapped by his association with Castleton. "Have Admiral Potter and Jack Hardwick been notified?"

Admiral Leahy nodded. "Hardwick is at his office now, reviewing Castleton's security file. Both he and Ev will meet you in the senior officers' lounge at the airport at seven thirty. You'll need a psychiatrist."

"I don't know any."

"We've done some checking. The best man for this job appears to be a Navy captain named Palkin. He'll be reliable because he's ambitious—he wants to be our first Jewish admiral. When my aide called him he said he'd need a reliable psychiatric nurse and suggested someone named Mary Sullivan. Jack Hardwick is checking her Navy file now to see if she can be cleared for bomb information. If she's okay, she'll be at the airport with Palkin at seven thirty."

As Blanton got up to leave, the President walked in. He looked jaunty, with his bow tie and cane, ready for his ritual early-morning walk. He asked, "Is everything understood, Paul?"

"Yes, sir," said Blanton.

"Good. See that Frank gets the treatment he needs. And see that he doesn't hurt us."

AFTER the Navy plane leveled off at 14,000 feet, en route to Knoxville, Jack Hardwick handed Paul Blanton and Admiral Potter, who were sitting together, copies of a digest he had made hurriedly from Castleton's security file. He said, "I thought you might like to refresh your memories, and that you might want the doctor and the nurse to read this as an introduction to their patient."

Blanton read the one-page digest, then said, "Give them copies of it." The paper was transmitted across the aisle, and as the plane flew south over Virginia Dr. Arthur Leo Palkin and Nurse Mary Sullivan read:

On September 3, 1939, at the outbreak of the Second World War, President Roosevelt said in a radio address: "From this day forward the purpose of America shall be to seek for humanity a final peace which will eliminate the continued use of armed force between nations."

Pursuant to this purpose, Secretary of State Cordell Hull began organizing the President's Advisory Council. Three members were to be from the public and the other twelve from Congress and the State, War and Navy Departments. This Council was to advise the President on means to achieve our national purpose of ending international war.

As one of the public members of the Council, Hull proposed to appoint his godson, Thomas Francis Castleton, of Norris, Tennessee; a silent partner in several modest businesses; born April 2, 1902, in Clinch County, Tennessee; academic degree in Fine Arts, University of the South, Sewanee, Tennessee, 1922; Phi Beta Kappa; married in 1925 to Diane Jemison, of Knoxville; one daughter, Susan, born in 1927, and one son, Cordell, born in 1934; net worth $400,000; Episcopalian; Rotarian; Democrat.

The first security check on Castleton revealed this DEROGATORY INFORMATION: In 1934 he was instrumental in securing employment by the Tennessee Valley Authority of two men whom he knew to be members of the Communist Party, USA. Despite this DEROGATORY INFORMATION, on January 8, 1940, Hull announced creation of the Advisory Council with Castleton as a member.

On May 8, 1941, Castleton became an Assistant to the Secretary of State and began spending much of his time in Washington, living at the Shoreham Hotel. On October 20, 1942, by order of the President, he was issued a Q-clearance for access to all records and activities of the Manhattan Project to create an atomic bomb. By Presidential order this clearance was renewed each subsequent year and is presently held by Castleton.

In his government service, for which he has been paid a dollar a year plus travel expenses, his duties have been to assist Hull in creating the UN, to report to Roosevelt then to Truman on the bomb and to advise Roosevelt then Truman on means to end war among nations.

The file indicates that Castleton is heterosexual, drinks very little and takes no drugs, but he indulges in occasional extramarital sex. He has profited enormously from the atomic bomb, and is presently worth about two million dollars. The file reports only one incident of BIZARRE BEHAVIOR. *At 10:20 p.m., October 20, 1942, the date on which subject was granted his Q-clearance for the atomic bomb, he attracted police attention by running and crying along Connecticut Avenue in the vicinity of the Shoreham Hotel. When halted and questioned he explained only that he was feeling low and needed exercise.*

When Blanton and his companions reached Castleton's home, they found Frank sleeping under sedation. Frank's wife, Diane, and Bert, his father, brought Blanton into the study to talk. Neither of them wanted

Frank to be treated under government supervision, but they finally agreed that he might be taken to the service hospital for "examination and diagnosis."

Diane shook her head. "We are consenting to this because we trust you, Paul," she said. "We don't trust the government, but we trust our friend Paul."

Now, in the limousine, through the half-moons formed by the windshield wipers, Blanton watched the ambulance ahead. The caravan was crossing the Potomac, over Key Bridge, heading for the hospital in the Maryland countryside. Blanton snuffed out his cigarette and turned to Admiral Potter and Dr. Palkin, beside him. "I don't like what we're doing," he said. "We should protect the country, but we should also protect Frank's individual rights."

Admiral Potter looked at him sternly. "Our first duty is to protect the United States."

"But this is all illegal procedure," said Blanton. "Frank has never been a member of the armed services. By what right do we seize him and lodge him in a military mental hospital?"

"We have no established right," Admiral Potter conceded. "We are simply acting as we must. The Castleton case was not foreseen by the framers of the Constitution."

"They could hardly have foreseen it," Dr. Palkin observed. "The framers of the Constitution believed that mental illness afflicted only the defective, the illiterate, maiden ladies during menopause and Divine Right kings with syphilis."

"But come on, Doctor," Blanton said, "*you* must believe that the patient should be put first? Isn't that a rule of your profession? I'm not saying that Frank won't get excellent treatment at the service hospital, or that you aren't a reputable psychiatrist. Obviously, you're one of the finest in the country. What I'm saying is that Frank has the right *not* to go to the service hospital and *not* to be treated by you. Every American citizen has the right to select his doctor and his hospital. If he is too sick to select for himself, then his kin have the right of selection. But that right is being denied to Frank Castleton. Surely you, as a doctor, must oppose this?"

Arthur Palkin lighted a cigarette. He doubted that Paul Blanton thought he was one of the finest psychiatrists in the country—if he was good, what was he doing in the peacetime Navy, why wasn't he out getting rich in private practice? But Palkin preferred being in the Navy, and considered himself a fine psychiatrist. He had been in since '42, and he enjoyed teaching admirals that psychiatrists, as well as surgeons, could fit and refit men for battle. At forty-five he was an impressive man with penetrating black eyes. He did indeed intend to become the highest-ranking medical officer in the Navy, the first Jewish-American admiral, because—and he admitted this—he liked the power of bureaucratic rank. After another drag on the cigarette, he turned to Blanton. "I understand your concern, Mr. Secretary. But I approve the security measures we're taking with Castleton. A doctor who is a Navy captain must consider national security as well as individual rights."

Admiral Potter nodded approval, but Blanton seemed exasperated. "That's precisely the point. Frank Castleton has the right to be treated by a doctor who is not a Navy captain." He looked at Admiral Potter and said, "We may have handled the press clumsily. By barring reporters from Frank's home and from our landing areas here and in Knoxville, we exaggerated the story. Now it will attract exaggerated attention in Congress."

"We've done what we had to do," said Potter.

The three men were quiet as the caravan sped along Wisconsin Avenue. Then Blanton asked Palkin, "Doctor, from your brief observation, what's your probable diagnosis?"

Again the doctor hesitated, then answered. "It's apparent that he's demoralized, disheartened, bewildered. He's conscious of having failed to meet his own expectations and feels powerless to change the situation. His environment, which is both the government and his family, has begun to menace him. Those who normally would help him are now unable to do so because they feel annoyed, embarrassed or threatened by his behavior. So he's demoralized to the panic point."

"Can you help him?"

"I don't know. It's a difficult situation. I'm a government psychiatrist, and he's in conflict with the government. He needs psychotherapy, psycho-energizing drugs, and probably electroshock. But no psychotherapist can help a patient until the patient seeks his help and comes to feel that the therapist is loyal to him above all others. Before I can help Castleton I must convince him that while I work for the government I too distrust the government and am pulling for him."

"Well, goddamn!" snorted Blanton. "You just said that you approve of allowing only a doctor who is a Navy captain to treat Castleton!"

"I do approve it. The situation demands it. But, you see, I understand

9

the difficulties. You tell me, now—are you here to help Castleton or to make sure that his behavior doesn't embarrass the President?"

Blanton's brow furrowed. "I'm here to do both."

"And you don't like the assignment," said the doctor. "Well, I don't like it either. Nor does Mary Sullivan." After a pause he added, "Castleton is in that ambulance ahead only because his wife trusts you, Mr. Secretary, to protect him from the government."

Blanton shifted his weight nervously. "Looking at it that way, Frank himself is in the same situation. He's been trying to serve a government he distrusts and is in conflict with."

"That's probably why he's demoralized." The doctor leaned back in his seat and rubbed his hand across his face. "When you think about it, every free man must distrust government. The free men who gathered in Philadelphia in 1783 to create the United States distrusted what they were creating. They no sooner created it than they began trying to protect themselves from it."

Blanton thought about that for a moment, then faced the doctor again. "Well, all right, what's your prognosis? Can Frank get well, or will he remain a problem for himself and his family and the government?"

"That depends," replied the doctor. "A demoralized man needs close friends who are not annoyed by his behavior. Will the government allow Mary Sullivan and me to become such friends to Castleton? Will the government make any concession to him at all? His wife, his son, his daughter . . . will they forgive him the embarrassment he has caused them, and again love and encourage him? His recovery probably depends on whether the government and his family really want to help him, or whether they decide to destroy him."

He was silent for a moment and then said, "This morning, as we flew to Tennessee, I guessed that this case would be unusual. But after visiting this patient's home and meeting his wife and parents, I see that it will be difficult, even dangerous, for all of us who are involved in it. Castleton must have been the only man in that gilded conference room at Yalta who was not a lawyer, a politician, a bureaucrat, a military expert or a captain of industry. He also must have been the only one who plays the cello in a string quartet and creates expressionist paintings. So why did Roosevelt take him to Yalta? He has only an academic degree in fine arts—from Sewanee: a small isolated elitist all-male mountaintop citadel of Protestant Episcopal rectitude. Neither Vice-President Truman nor Secretary of State Hull was told anything about the developing atomic bomb, but Roosevelt saw that

10

Castleton knew everything from the start. Why? Castleton has had a strong positive tie to life, an adequate ego. Now his ego has been overwhelmed; his equilibrium has been lost. His mechanisms of ego defense have failed. To help him we must help his ego regain control. We must help him reestablish his tie to life. We must help him find hope."

Paul Blanton grunted. "Hope, huh? My mother always told me that only a priest can give a man hope."

In the ambulance, Mary Sullivan gritted her teeth in pain. As she was bending over Castleton, wiping his eyes, his left hand had suddenly seized hers. For a moment he had just held it firmly; then, as terror seized him, he had tightened his grip until she felt real pain. She started to ask him to release her, but then she decided to keep quiet. She didn't want to risk embarrassing him, and perhaps he'd soon relax.

Mary Sullivan, by hard work and determination, had escaped from a deprived environment in rural Georgia and made herself into a highly competent psychiatric nurse. Thirty and unmarried, she was a slender, graceful, compassionate woman, ambitious to rise even higher in her profession.

Suddenly Castleton released her hand, gesticulated and muttered, "Please close that curtain."

The caravan had halted for a traffic signal, and the ambulance stood close to a lighted bus filled with high-school students. Each spring Washington was overrun by such buses when graduating classes from every state were brought to the capital for inspiration. The students peered down at the Senate in session. Pressing their noses against the glass case, they read the Declaration of Independence. They looked up at Lincoln and murmured the words of the Gettysburg Address. They stood at the tombs of the Honored Dead. Castleton could see two young faces through the rain-washed windows, and he feared they could see him. Mary Sullivan reached across him and closed the curtain as the caravan picked up speed.

Jack Hardwick, at the rear door of the ambulance, noted Castleton's reaction to the students. Purely and simply, he looked at life with a security agent's attitude. His job was to help men indirectly by protecting their government from their crimes and follies. He dealt in human weakness: Each day he sought it, found it, recorded it. He knew that government servants might endanger their government by making basic mistakes: by

11

questionable financial maneuvers, by association with the guilty, by subscription to doubtful publications and by reckless sexual behavior. Following government practice, Jack Hardwick had reduced these four basic mistakes to their initials: MAPS. It meant: Money—How does the subject acquire and use it? Associations—With what other individuals does he seek common purpose? Publications—To which ones has he subscribed? And Sex—Is the subject hetero or homo? And, by threat or entreaty, can the subject be influenced by a sexual partner?

Several times each day Jack Hardwick spoke the word "MAPS." He never looked at a human face without imposing MAPS on it and silently asking the questions. Indeed, he had attained position by regularly imposing MAPS on his own face and asking himself the questions. At forty-seven he prided himself on still being celibate. Not once had he ever risked having a sexual partner; from puberty his only sexual activity had been with himself. He had never subscribed to a publication or joined an organization. He had never had a penny's income except from a government salary. He invested his savings only in government bonds. He didn't drink, gamble, smoke or blaspheme. Having been born in Washington, where the law denied him the ballot, he had never favored any political party. So Jack Hardwick was the perfect government security agent: absolutely invulnerable, criticized by none, admired by all, feared by everybody—the only American ever to be universally regarded as indispensable. Even his looks fitted him: He looked stocky, solid and relentless.

Jack Hardwick believed that the conduct of every government servant was foretold in his GSF—his Government Security File. Hardwick frequently said to Congressional committees, "A subject's conduct can always be anticipated and predicted within reasonable limits if only the raw material in his GSF is correctly evaluated." As he watched Castleton's anguished face in the ambulance, Hardwick thought, "There lies another Roosevelt mistake . . . one of the last men in America who should have been assigned to report on the manufacture of the atomic bomb."

THE service hospital could be seen for miles as you approached it, like the cathedral at Chartres. A cluster of white buildings crowned a forested hilltop, and the main building, a chalk-white shaft, reached sixteen stories toward the Maryland sky. In the early evening when lights burned in every room of the shaft and a red aircraft-warning beacon flashed from its tower, the shaft looked like an exclamation point blazing up through the dusk. But here the comparison with a cathedral ended, since the shaft stood not for man's hope but for man's despair. The hospital was a refuge for some of the two hundred thousand Americans who had returned from the Second World War still sound in body but broken in mind and spirit.

Two groups of visitors awaited the arrival of Frank Castleton inside the hospital. Thirty reporters and photographers, with cameras and recording equipment, waited noisily in a makeshift press room. And sitting quietly in another room were an attractive young woman and two men in their middle forties. The young woman was Susan Castleton, twenty-one, who had reached Washington that afternoon from college in Baltimore, and the men with her were Keith McDowell, the newspaper columnist, who was based in Washington, and the Reverend Joseph Bramwell, rector of an Episcopal parish in Arlington, Virginia. Susan had known both of them all her life, for they had been classmates of her father's at Sewanee.

McDowell snuffed out a cigarette and spoke bitterly. "The week after Japan surrendered, I begged Frank to leave Washington. The war's over, I told him, now celebrate the victory and go home and make music and paint pictures and climb mountains. Sit on boards of directors and direct business in East Tennessee. But for God's sake don't ever again try to help direct the United States. Because this nation is not going to be directed successfully any more. From now on . . . only frustration and failure. So go back to Arcady, where you belong, and stay there!"

"You didn't expect him to take that advice, did you?" asked Joe Bramwell. "A man whose idol as a college freshman was Woodrow Wilson? A man who admired and worked for Cordell Hull, George Norris and Franklin Roosevelt?"

"If he had taken my advice," insisted McDowell, "he wouldn't be in the condition he's in now."

Bramwell shook his head. "Frank couldn't have done that. You know, I remember our days as roommates at Sewanee Military Academy when we were fifteen. Pasted on his desk then were Tom Paine's words, 'The cause of America is the cause of mankind.' Frank has always felt that he must work, not only for himself and his family, but also for Clinch County, for the Tennessee River basin, for the United States and for the human race. To Frank Castleton the cause of America *must* be the cause of mankind. National and international hope are as necessary for him as family and community hope."

"The only hope for him now," said McDowell, "is that we can raise

13

enough hell to get him out of here. Paul Blanton is no longer Frank's friend. He has become the Pope's field marshal in the crusade against Communism. That beady-eyed bastard Ev Potter would slit his mother's throat if he thought she was a Communist sympathizer. And I don't have to tell you what Jack Hardwick is . . . a Red-baitin' robot. They'll bury Frank in here unless we can smash the door down and take him back to Tennessee."

Susan Castleton shuddered. She felt embarrassed and afraid, and her large eyes were swollen from crying. "I'll always be sorry I wasn't with Mother last night when they brought Daddy home. It seems unbelievable that Daddy could become hysterical. I'll always be sorry I wasn't with Mother when it happened." What was most noticeable about Susan was her unusual combination of lustrous black hair, which reached to her shoulders, and large deep blue eyes. She was five feet nine inches tall, with long legs and thin ankles, and because she walked so erectly on high heels and looked so self-assured, people who didn't know her thought she was haughty.

"Diane can stand up under it," said Joe Bramwell.

"And poor Cord!" continued Susan. "How terrible for a fourteen-year-old boy, especially since he was away at boarding school! Mother didn't want him to be wakened and have to hear it over the telephone. So I called Major Anderson and asked him to go to the barracks and wake Cord and tell him gently, then let Cord call Mother. And of course he called me after he talked with her."

"You'll all be together here tomorrow," said McDowell.

Susan dried her eyes again and sniffed. "Daddy'll get well quickly if they'll just talk with him, and let him rest, and, above all, let him get outdoors."

Joe Bramwell smiled. "When I think of Frank and how he loves the outdoors, I think about when we were freshmen at the university in the winter of 1918–19. You remember all this, Keith, I know, but Susan will permit an old fellow to reminisce. About twenty of us, including Frank, Keith and me, with our matron, we lived in Magnolia Hall, which was a big old L-shaped two-story frame house, like the summer houses at Monteagle. Magnolia Hall was heated with open grates in which we burned that poor-quality coal mined up at Tracy City. And, Lord, those winters were cold on the Cumberland Plateau! Frank and I slept on the second-story porch. That is, I slept out there until the freezing nights came, then I moved inside. But not Frank! He slept out there every night, even during snowstorms, covering himself with blankets, then with a tarpaulin. I went out there on that porch many a morning and found Frank asleep under five or six inches of snow. He'd be warm and dry, and when I woke him he'd jump up and take a snow bath. We'd call him Polar Bear."

"When I was five," said Susan, "I can remember Mother and I going with Daddy into the mountains on horseback. I can see us now, Mother and I trying to go to sleep in our sleeping bags and Daddy at the campfire picking a guitar and singing 'Shenandoah.' "

Paul Blanton walked through the doorway and hugged Susan, who kissed him on the cheek and introduced him to Joe Bramwell. Blanton shook hands with Bramwell but only nodded to McDowell. "Frank's quiet," he said. "He's being settled in his room here in the main building. Now I'd like for . . . for all three of you to come with me while we answer some questions for the press."

He led them to the makeshift press room, where they all got settled. Blanton and Dr. Palkin stood facing the seated reporters and photographers, and Susan and Joe Bramwell were seated behind the two speakers. McDowell sat with the reporters. A Navy public-relations officer introduced Secretary Blanton.

"Ladies and gentlemen," Blanton began, "we have little further to report at this time. You know that Mr. Castleton became ill last night, and that today we flew to Tennessee and brought him back with us. The patient rested under sedation, and he is now lodged comfortably in this hospital, being treated at the direction of Dr. Palkin. We anticipate a prompt and complete recovery."

"Is he a prisoner?" was the first question.

"Certainly not. He is, of course, lodged in a secure area, as are many of the patients in this hospital."

"Whose idea was it to bring him here?"

"The decision was made by Mrs. Castleton and me."

"Then he's here at the request of his wife?"

"Yes."

"Where is Mrs. Castleton now?"

"She felt that she should remain at home until she could be joined by her son, Cordell, who was en route home today from Sewanee Military Academy. They will arrive tomorrow. The young lady with us now is her daughter, Miss Susan Castleton, who came by train from Baltimore, where she is a college senior."

"May we question Miss Castleton?"

"Not now. Perhaps tomorrow."

15

"The son? Is he named for Cordell Hull?"

"Yes. Cordell Hull Castleton. Beginning in 1907, I believe, the Castletons helped send Mr. Hull to the House, then to the Senate, where he was serving in 1933 when he became Secretary of State."

"Suppose Mrs. Castleton decides tomorrow to move her husband to . . . say, the Menninger Clinic? Will she be allowed to do so?"

"Certainly."

"But, Mr. Secretary, isn't it true that the reason Castleton is in this hospital is that for six years he has held a Q-clearance in atomic weapons? Isn't that why you took Admiral Potter and Jack Hardwick with you to Tennessee?"

"Well, he does hold such a clearance, and that is a matter of proper concern to the security agencies. But the press is exaggerating this point. Several hundred Americans have such clearances. Mr. Castleton is only one of many such individuals."

"But he is the only one who has cracked up?"

"That may be true."

"The decision to drop the bomb on Hiroshima—I believe that you, Mr. Secretary, helped make it, as did Castleton. Isn't it true that he was a vigorous advocate of dropping the bomb in a manner to kill or maim the maximum number of people?"

"The initial decision to drop the bomb was made by President Roosevelt, the final decision by President Truman. A number of us, including Mr. Castleton, were asked for our opinions, and it's true that he favored dropping the bomb for maximum effect."

"Isn't it true that Castleton saw the bomb fall—"

"No," Blanton interrupted, but the reporter went on. "—and that soon afterward he visited Hiroshima?"

"No, he didn't witness the explosion. He was on Tinian when the *Enola Gay* took off with the bomb. Three hours after the explosion he flew over the blasted area. After the Japanese surrender he visited Hiroshima as a member of our evaluation team."

"Will his Q-clearance be canceled as a result of this illness?"

"No. We expect him to recover and to continue serving President Truman as a member of the Advisory Council."

"Mr. Secretary, regarding what is said to be a friendly relationship between Castleton and Truman—an AP report from Tennessee quotes the two men who were with Castleton when he cracked up as saying that, in his hysteria, he kept repeating, 'If only Roosevelt had lived, if only Roose-

16

velt had lived.' What does that indicate to you, sir?"

"Only that Mr. Castleton was one of many millions of us who deplored President Roosevelt's untimely death three years ago."

"But there is a further report that Castleton favors the Dump Truman movement. Allegedly he opposes the President's nomination and election this year. Is that correct, sir?"

"I doubt it, but I don't know."

"Since you are heading the effort to finance Truman's campaign for reelection, if Castleton does in fact favor dumping Truman, then you and he are in political conflict, aren't you? And he is in bitter conflict with the Administration to which he is an adviser?"

"I'm not aware of any such conflict. If it exists, it has no bearing on our effort to restore Mr. Castleton to health."

"Castleton is listed as a contributor to all four campaigns to elect Roosevelt President. Has he contributed to the Truman campaign fund?"

"Not yet, to my knowledge. That doesn't mean he won't."

"Regarding former Vice-President Wallace, who is now a third-party candidate against Truman and who allegedly is supported by Communists and their sympathizers—reportedly Castleton and Wallace were once and perhaps still are close friends. Is that report true, sir?"

"There may be some truth in it. Back in the thirties, when Wallace was Secretary of Agriculture, he often visited the TVA area. Since Mr. Castleton was an ardent supporter of TVA, the two probably met. I'm not aware that they have been associates in recent years. And now," Blanton hurried on, "since there is nothing more I can add, perhaps Dr. Palkin will answer a few of your preliminary medical questions."

Dr. Palkin stepped forward and said, "I haven't examined this patient; I have only observed him briefly, so I'm not going to be able to tell you much. From listening to your dialogue with Secretary Blanton, I feel that you are exaggerating the possible political and military aspects of this case. Psychic disturbance is not unusual in the United States in 1948. We now have more mental than physical suffering. This patient is forty-six years old —at the climacteric—and anxiety at his age is not uncommon. So it's quite likely that his symptoms are not related to his government service. He is only a man—a husband, a father in a complex society—so he's as vulnerable as the rest of us."

"Have you observed any evidence of paranoia?"

"No. The patient doesn't appear to feel that he is being derided or persecuted."

17

"Is he hallucinating? Or suffering from obsessions or delusions?"

"No. There is no evidence of bizarre ideation. He has knowledge of himself and understands what is happening around him. Last night his ego was temporarily overwhelmed by anxiety, and he panicked. He is suffering a painful disorder, but it is one which can be relieved."

"What about guilt, Doctor? He wanted to maim the maximum number of women and children at Hiroshima. Then he looked into the faces of his victims. Maybe last night in the Great Smoky Mountains those faces came back to haunt him and drove him into hysteria. Would you say that he may be suffering from bomb guilt?"

"Let me put it this way. In all of us the superego tries to control the ego by imposing feelings of guilt on it. Whether this patient has an excessively demanding superego can be ascertained only by psychiatric examination."

The reporters wanted to ask more questions, but Dr. Palkin held up his hands. "Please, there is nothing more I can say."

"Will you issue daily reports on his treatment and condition?"

"Certainly not. Mental illness can't be reported on like physical illness. Thorough psychiatric examination takes days, possibly weeks. We must examine not only the patient but also members of his family and others with whom he has sought to achieve various goals. There is nothing to report from day to day except a continued effort to understand and to restore morale. So please don't call me and don't come here expecting to question me. This hospital must be a sanctuary for Frank Castleton, where he meets only those who are sympathetic with him and in whom he can confide."

"I'm sorry, Doctor," one reporter said, "I can't cooperate with you in maintaining sanctuaries. My editor will want frequent and detailed reports on what Thomas Francis Castleton is saying, and to whom, and on how the government is treating him. So I'll be coming here, Doctor, and I'll be after you. That's called freedom of the press."

AFTER the press conference Dr. Palkin brought Susan Castleton, Joe Bramwell and Keith McDowell into a side room and told them that he wanted to talk with each of them during the next two or three days. Then he tried to excuse himself. But Susan and Bramwell insisted on seeing Frank Castleton before they left the hospital, so the doctor walked with them down the corridor to his office, where he

18

asked Joe to wait in his outer office and led Susan into his inner office. He seated her on a sofa, then drew up a chair and sat facing her. The press conference had shaken him. Never before had he treated a patient in which the national press was interested, along with Congress, the security agencies, the Cabinet and the President himself. Obviously the case could help his career, but it could also ruin it. He had to proceed cautiously.

"Susan," he began, "I know that all this is frightening and embarrassing for you. When there is time I want to talk with you at length. Now, before I can allow you to visit your father, I must ask you to describe very briefly for me his life as you see it."

She leaned forward, her hands in her lap. "My father believes that a man has the double mission in life of cultivating himself and improving the world. So the years from 1933 through 1945, from the time I was six to the time I was eighteen, were wonderful years for him. You see, he was doing just those two things, and doing them well."

"What made him think he was improving the world?"

"First, well, because he worked to improve the Tennessee River basin. We live on the Clinch River, you know, which is one of five rivers which flow out of high mountains to form the Tennessee. In those mountains winter snow and spring rainfall are heavy. So my grandfather foresaw the TVA—the building of dams on the mountain tributaries to store floodwater in the spring and thereby eliminate downstream flooding. The stored water could be released in the dry summer and fall months to provide a year-round constant flow in the Tennessee, and to generate electricity in the process of release. Then dams could be built on the Tennessee to maintain a year-round navigable depth and to generate more electricity for homes, farms and industries. The river system could just do so much, you see. It could revitalize the farm land, the forests and the poor people who lived in a region that stretches over portions of seven states and is as large as New England."

"Your grandfather foresaw all that?"

Susan nodded, wiping her eyes. "And my father worked to realize it. When he was fifteen he spent the summer in the mountains with the Army Engineers, looking for the best dam sites on the tributary rivers. When he was seventeen he went with Mr. Hull to meet President Wilson, and the President told him about the great dam then being built at Muscle Shoals, Alabama, on the Tennessee, and about the day when the revitalized Tennessee region would be the model from which to revitalize all the poor eroded hungry regions of the world."

19

Momentarily Susan choked and lost her voice. Then, her blue eyes glittering through the tears, she went on. "In the summer of 1920, after his sophomore year at Sewanee, Daddy paddled a canoe, all by himself, the entire length of the Tennessee, to Paducah, Kentucky, where it flows into the Ohio. Six hundred fifty miles! He thought he was kin to every poor creature who was trying to scratch out a living along that river. I think he learned a lot from that trip. In 1921 he went to Washington to meet Senator Norris, who had introduced a bill to create the TVA to complete the dam at Muscle Shoals and build twenty other dams."

The doctor smiled. "I remember all that. I was in school in Michigan."

"Then you know how Daddy suffered during the Republican Reaction. He celebrated in 1927 when Congress passed the Norris TVA Act. Then he cried when President Coolidge vetoed it. He celebrated in 1931 when Congress again passed the Act, and he cried when President Hoover vetoed it. But he also found hope in 1931. With Senator Hull he went to Warm Springs, Georgia, and met the Governor of New York, who said he'd sign the TVA Act if he could become President. From that day Daddy's hopes, and all the money he could raise, were with Roosevelt."

Dr. Palkin got up, poured a glass of water and brought it to Susan. "It's strange, you know. While I was in your home today," he said, "I had an incredible sense of history. I saw all those photos of Roosevelt and Norris dedicating dams and visiting model farms and forests. I saw the pen Roosevelt used to sign the Norris TVA Act. And I looked closely at some of your father's remarkable paintings of the rivers, mountains, lakes and the dam sites before and after the dams were built."

"He thought TVA was the most hopeful development in the world," said Susan. "And during the years 1933–43, while the dams were being built and the land repaired, he wanted his wife and children to feel part of it. That's why I know so much about it."

"Now tell me . . . when he began helping Hull and Roosevelt in the war, did he still think he was improving the world?"

"Oh yes, he felt sure he was. He thought the war would be the last war, after which more TVAs would be built in America and throughout the world. He was pleased when ten more TVA dams were completed immediately to provide electricity to make aluminum for the bomber fleets. Then came the Oak Ridge project. Daddy knew it was the atomic bomb, but of course he didn't tell us that. All we knew was that it needed one-sixth of our county—fifty-four thousand eight hundred acres—and seventy-five thousand people would work there, and it would use more electricity than all of New England. You see, had there been no TVA, there could have been no bomb, because only TVA could supply the amount of power that Oak Ridge needed."

"That's when your father's disappointments began?"

"Yes. He was appalled by all those strangers pouring into our county. He was hurt by the deaths of Senator Norris and the President, and by the illness and forced retirement of Mr. Hull. He worried about being away from home so much, especially when Mother and Cord were there alone after I went off to college."

"When did you and your mother begin worrying about him?"

Susan dropped her eyes and reflected. "Oh, I don't know. I guess a little more than two years ago—Christmas, 1945. He had come back from visiting Hiroshima, and he couldn't relax at home, not even for Christmas! He couldn't make music or dance. You see, we're such a celebrating family, and when we couldn't celebrate Christmas it depressed all of us. Then Daddy told us that for the next few months he'd have to spend a lot of time in Washington."

"Did he tell you why?"

Susan sighed deeply. "He couldn't tell us, because it was about the bomb. He hates all the secrecy about the bomb, just hates it. He told us to remember a quotation from Whitman: 'the goal that was named must not be countermanded.' Later he told me that the war had only begun, the war to prevent America from becoming another Rome and having armies all over the world."

"His anxiety has progressively increased?"

"Oh, it was awful, Dr. Palkin. Month after month he has grown more tense, his face tighter, his eyes brighter. He has come home and tried to live normally, tried to hike and paint and play the piano or the cello and read and interest himself in the businesses he owns parts of. But always, after three or four days, he has gone back to Washington for a week or more. A year ago Mother decided that he had found a woman in Washington he couldn't stay away from."

"Is there a woman? Do you mind if I ask you this?"

Susan answered promptly. "There probably have been several, but they aren't awfully important in all this. He is afflicted with a terrible sense of urgency—that's it—urgency. The last time I saw him—at Easter—he seemed like a man who knows the house is on fire and is not allowed to warn even his own family."

"And there has been conflict between him and your mother and you?"

21

Susan's eyes widened, and the pitch of her voice rose. "Well, of course there has! We've tried to bring him to his senses! We've begged him to put out of his mind whatever is bothering him. All he can think of now is saving the world, and that's foolish. He's only one man, and he has no power. When the war ended he should have come home like other men and resumed his normal life. Instead he has given up on his talents, and harmed himself, and all of us. Four months ago Mother quit sleeping even in the room with him."

The doctor got up and walked to the window. The rain had stopped, but the trees and shrubs on the lighted hospital grounds were still dripping. "Susan," he said, "most of the patients in this hospital are here to get away from wives and daughters who have been annoyed and hurt by their behavior. So why do you want to see your father now? Can you help him? A forty-six-year-old man suffering from anxiety is as vulnerable as a child. If you walk into his room now, won't he feel that you have come to blame him again for acting the fool and hurting himself and his family?"

"But if I don't go to see him tonight," asked Susan, "won't he feel that I'm not concerned about him, and won't that hurt him? I only want to see him long enough to tell him that I love him and am pulling for him."

"Well, that's a good reason." Dr. Palkin went to his desk, picked up the telephone and asked that Mary Sullivan be summoned to his office. Then he turned to Susan. "All right. But you must do exactly as I say. You can't see him alone. His nurse will go with you and stay with you during the few minutes you are with him. At this point, I'm sorry, but we have to watch his reactions to everyone who visits him. Remember you're there only to help him. So dry your tears; don't mention his being ill. Just kiss him, smile and recall some happy incident for him . . . some family celebration back when he was still hopeful."

The doctor then asked Susan to wait in his outer office for Mary Sullivan, and he asked Joe Bramwell to come into the inner office.

THE Reverend Joseph Eggleston Johnston Bramwell, named for a Confederate general and descended from several generations of South Carolina ministers of the gospel, was the handsomest clergyman in the Washington area. Bronzed and lean from playing tennis, at which he was a country-club champion, he looked agile, healthy, wholesome and filled with blessed assurance. He had the sort of straight chestnut hair which seldom thins or grays early, and he parted it perfectly on the left side. His voice was warm and dramatic, and his parishioners, especially the ladies, adored him. He strode into the office and spoke without sitting. "Doctor, I only want to pop in and show Frank that I'm here, ready to help, and I'll say a prayer with him. I can go right along with Susan."

"Please sit down," said the doctor. The tone of his voice was not unfriendly, but it was authoritative. "I want your help, and when there's more time we'll talk. But I prefer that you not see Mr. Castleton until I have examined him."

"You think I might hurt him?"

"I can't answer that until I examine him. And I must ask you, I hope you don't mind—have you ever been checked for security?"

Bramwell was astounded. "There's been no reason for me to be checked! I've never been employed by the government. During the war I did volunteer work for the USO and the Red Cross, and I helped minister to President Roosevelt at the White House. The government must have conceded my loyalty."

"Well, I can't concede it," said the doctor. "Before you can see Mr. Castleton in this hospital, the security agencies must be satisfied."

"That sounds unbelievable!"

"I'm surprised that it surprises you, Reverend. You read the papers today. You heard the press conference a few minutes ago. You live here in the Washington area, so you must be aware of the widely known chairman of the House Un-American Activities Committee, J. Parnell Thomas. Hysteria is epidemic—the whole country is afraid that some Red sympathizer will deliver the bomb secret to the Russians. The new fear is that Castleton may already have delivered it, or that some undiscovered Red sympathizer will get to him, get the secret from him and deliver it. Surely you've thought of this?"

"Well, but I never dreamed it would touch me."

"You're an associate of Castleton's, therefore it touches you." A buzzer sounded on the doctor's desk, and he picked up the telephone, saying he'd be there in a moment. Then he shrugged and smiled faintly at Joe. "This is no major problem. You can be cleared in a day or so. You aren't a Red sympathizer, are you? You never contributed to the defense of the Scottsboro boys? You never subscribed to the *New Masses* or the *Daily Worker?* You never recommended Party members for government employment? And that little pro-Red school down there in the mountains near Sewanee —what's it called?"

"Highlander Folk School."

"You never raised money for it or attended one of its seminars?"

The doctor and Joe got up and walked into the outer office, where the doctor introduced his visitor to Mary Sullivan, then told the nurse to take Susan in for a brief visit with her father. Joe sat down on a couch, and after Susan and the nurse went out Dr. Palkin excused himself. Joe sat alone and thought. He felt deeply distressed.

T HE three physical calamities which terrify a man when they strike him are heart attack, paralytic stroke and vertigo. Of these calamities, vertigo can be the most terrifying. Because if it has resulted from something serious—say, from arteriosclerosis having slowed or stopped the flow of blood through the capillaries of the inner ear —the victim cannot hope to recover from it; he can hope only for respites as he reels, spins, staggers and whirls out his life.

Frank Castleton was not suffering from physical vertigo but from a sort of mental vertigo. Physically he felt oriented. He knew he was standing before a window looking out over the Maryland countryside toward Washington. He knew he was wearing bedroom slippers and blue cotton pajamas, and that he had to hold up his pants with his left hand because Mary Sullivan had taken the drawstring to make sure he didn't strangle himself with it.

Physically he felt supported. He felt concrete under his feet; he could see and feel the furnishings of his room: a low foam-rubber bed, a table, and two chairs, all of them bolted to the concrete floor. In the bathroom was a shower, a basin and a toilet with only its porcelain rim for a seat. In a smaller connecting room was an electric refrigerator with no ice trays in it, only paper cartons of water, milk and orange juice. In that room were two stools and a table on which meals could be eaten, and those stools and that table, too, were bolted to the floor. Also in that room was another window, and a locked door which opened into a corridor. All light bulbs were recessed behind unbreakable plastic. Nowhere was there anything sharp or anything that could be detached or broken and used to hurt himself or anyone else. The screens in the windows were heavy corrugated steel mesh, and they were locked in. So physically he felt held up and rooted to one spot.

Mentally, however, he felt unsupported and out of place. There were periods in which he felt he was reeling, spinning, staggering and whirling through space, without direction or destination. He remembered Disney films in which Mickey, Donald and Pluto run off precipices but don't fall: They hang in space, legs churning, trying to find support. There were periods when he felt he had quit spinning and whirling, and was only drifting in space, trying to locate position and establish direction by focusing his mind on a particular memory. He could feel his senses stretch and strain, trying to fasten on a memory and bring it into focus, trying to light it so he could see it clearly and find a bearing with it. And when his mind wouldn't focus, and the memory escaped, he surrendered to terror.

Then came respites when, even though he was still drifting, he could focus on memories. He could see them more clearly than he had ever seen them—brilliantly lighted, marvelously detailed. While these memories were in focus he felt located and therefore less terrified. But as the fear receded, he was left with the feeling that he was forever alone in a limitless universe which he could not affect, which didn't care or even know that he existed.

The only comforts in the suite had been sent by his wife via his nurse. They were three books she knew he valued: *The Collected Poems of W. B. Yeats, Selections from Browning,* and *The Book of Common Prayer,* including the Psalter. Castleton picked up the Yeats collection, and was trying to read from it when he heard a key in the lock of his door and Mary Sullivan came in with Susan.

"Look who's here to see you," Mary said.

He rose, hitching up his pajama pants, and Susan came and hugged him as he kissed her cheek. "The doctor wants you to sleep," she said, "but he said I could sit with you for a few minutes." Susan and Mary sat in the chairs while Castleton sat on the bed.

Susan felt appalled as she silently faced her father. She had never been inside a mental hospital before, and she had never expected to see her father in one, most certainly not in such an impersonal situation, and in a hospital for the care of ordinary defeated men! She had never expected to sit with him in a locked two-room concrete stall which smelled of sweat and disinfectant. In such an impersonal prison, she asked herself, how can he live, much less recover? Don't they understand that my father is a private man accustomed to a unique private home . . . a home surrounded by wild flowering trees and shrubs, and filled with books, paintings, music, dignity, ceremony and celebration! Whatever we must do, Susan resolved, whatever it costs, we must get him out of this prison and take him home.

Castleton looked at his beautiful daughter and remembered moments in her creation: the morning in the mountains when he found the woman who was to be her mother; the evening when he learned that his wife had conceived; the family celebration of birth; the first step the child took toward his outstretched hands; the first night she slept in a sleeping bag alongside him and her mother in the mountains; her first party dress and high heels; and the evening she won the speech contest on the high school stage by reciting "The Highwayman" with such marvelous passion.

Gesturing toward the Yeats collection, which was lying near him on the bed, Castleton said, "I was reading 'A Prayer for My Daughter'. . . . 'How but in custom and ceremony are innocence and beauty born?' "

Susan nodded, smiling. She was relieved that he had begun the conversation. "I remember the first time you read that poem to me. I was twelve. You've given me so many good times, Daddy. Say, do you remember the day in 1936 when Norris Dam was dedicated? I was nine. I've told all my friends about that day. Would you like to hear just how I tell them about it?"

Castleton nodded, and Susan straightened up in her chair, glancing at Mary Sullivan. "Then you two imagine that you are two girls from Boston sitting in my room in Baltimore when I'm a freshman, and I'm telling this story. Well, then, it was a beautiful afternoon in 1936. The pink and white dogwoods were blooming, and the President and Senator Norris spoke at the dam to a huge crowd. But my family and I weren't there—we were waiting at home. Because when the dedication ceremony was over, the President was hurrying back to the Knoxville airport, but he was to make one brief stop . . . at our house. We were all in the front yard—Daddy and Mother, Cord and I, and Grandmother and Grandfather and Great-grandfather and about a hundred of our uncles, aunts and cousins. We were going to give the President a cup of the strawberry wine that Mother is famous for and that Senator Norris liked so much when he spent nights with us. And we waited and waited . . . and Daddy told us that there might be so many delays at the dam that the President wouldn't have time to stop, that we might only get to wave at him as he passed. Mother had the wine bottles and Grandmother had the cups, and we were all so afraid the President wouldn't have time to stop. Then at last we heard people cheering, and the caravan was coming and, lo and behold, there, coming up our driveway through the dogwoods, in that big open car, was the President! With that great smile . . . waving to us while we cheered . . . his great head thrown back . . . and the car stopped. He couldn't come inside the house, because he was crippled and in a hurry to move on, but he sat there in the car, and laughed so heartily, and was so happy while we gathered around him.

26

Daddy had Cord in his arms . . . Cord was only two years old . . . and the President reached over and took Cord and held him in his lap and kissed him. Mother and Grandmother and some of our aunts began to serve the wine . . . they were all so nervous, I was afraid they'd spill it . . . and the President loved it."

Susan looked ecstatic telling the story to her father. And he, in turn, was thrilled to hear her version of an encounter which had been so important to him and the rest of the family. He saw so much of his own enthusiasm in her. Susan continued. "Senator Norris demanded a second cup, and so did the President, and then the Governor of Tennessee came and demanded his cup . . . and we poured wine for everybody, even the Secret Service men, except most of the wine was blackberry or blueberry, because Mother ran out of strawberry. Daddy took me to the President, and he kissed me. Then we all had to stand back while Daddy led Great-grandfather up to meet the President. We all got quiet, and cried a little, because Great-grandfather was ninety-four and nearly blind. But he walked up just as straight, saluted the President and said, 'God bless you, sir! The people you see here are all descendants of my great-grandfather, a Yorkshireman who was privileged to fight at King's Mountain for the cause of America. I was privileged to fight in six major battles, including Chickamauga, for a cause we loved and lost. I thank God for allowing me to live to see this day. You are a great man, sir, and you have done us great honor by stopping at this house.' Then the President drove off, waving and smiling, while we waved and cheered. And when the caravan was gone Daddy said a few words to everybody. He still had Cord in his arms, and Mother and I stood with him, and he said, 'This is a memorable day for America, for Tennessee, for all the Castletons, and for Diane, our children and me. History will call Franklin Roosevelt and George Norris the greatest Americans of the twentieth century. None of us must ever forget this day. I'm glad that our daughter is old enough to remember it, and I hope that by some miracle our little son can remember it.' "

Susan leaned back in her chair and waited for her father to speak. For a while he said nothing. Tears came into his eyes, and his hands and chin began to tremble. Finally he said, "There will be no more such occasions to pour wine."

"You're going to feel better," Susan said. "Soon you'll be back home, dear. The dogwoods and azaleas are blooming, Daddy. Think how beautiful it is on the mountain at Sewanee. In a month you'll be there for Commencement."

He said nothing further. His respite was over, and again he was adrift in space, without position or direction, terror tearing at his heart. Susan and Mary Sullivan went out, and the nurse locked the door behind them. In the corridor Susan leaned against the wall and burst into tears. "Stop it, Susan." Mary shook the girl's shoulder. "You've got to help him now." They walked together down the corridor, rode down the elevator and rejoined Joe Bramwell in the doctor's reception room. Joe and Susan then walked out of the hospital and into the parking lot to Joe's car. For a moment Susan stood beside the car and looked up at the hospital tower. It was dark now, so lights burned in every room and the red beacon on the roof was blazing. Susan located what she believed to be her father's two windows. They looked high and far away. Then Joe opened the car door for her, and they drove in silence to his home in Virginia.

In his Georgetown home, Keith McDowell had begun writing the column which would shock the President and all of official Washington, along with much of the nation, at breakfast next morning. And later that evening Diane Castleton and her son, Cordell, walked through the Southern Railway station at Knoxville. The couple attracted attention, because Diane at forty-four was still an attractive brunette, and because Cord, taller than his mother, showed by his carriage that even though he was only fourteen he already had served many hours under the voice of a drill sergeant, and because two reporters tried to question them. Diane and Cord walked to the train and found their Pullman car, and a porter showed them to their accommodations.

At the door of their adjoining compartments, Diane kissed her son good night, then entered her room, locked the door and sank down on the bed and sobbed. She hadn't slept for forty-eight hours; she was exhausted and terribly afraid. On this same train, in 1925, in a Pullman compartment, she and Frank Castleton had spent their wedding night. They had been traveling to New York on their honeymoon, to stay at the Astor and see a musical, *No, No, Nanette,* and a disturbing play called *The Hairy Ape.* After she felt the train move she forced herself to get up and undress. Then, in her nightgown, she kneeled beside the Pullman bed and prayed.

THE Republican Party's campaign book of 1894 stated: "In this country an income tax of any sort is odious. Prepare for the funeral of any political party which imposes such a burden." In the Tennessee legislature that year was a twenty-three-year-old mountaineer—tall, slender and fair-haired, wearing a long Prince Albert coat and a wide-brimmed high-crowned white hat—who would make it his business to impose such an odious burden on the American people.

His name was Cordell Hull. He was born six years after the end of the Civil War, October 2, 1871, in a log cabin on a ridge between the Wolf and Obed Rivers, among the foothills of the Cumberlands. At thirteen, wearing homespun, he began rafting logs down the Obed and Cumberland Rivers to Nashville. He educated himself by reading, by briefly attending two normal schools and by spending nine months at Cumberland Law School, Lebanon, Tennessee. Before he was twenty he had been admitted to the bar, and as a self-proclaimed "Gladstone liberal" he had joined what he called "the long struggle for Anglo-Saxon liberty." He had found his political creed in Jefferson's Inaugural Address: equal and exact justice to all men; peace, commerce and honest friendship with all nations; the arraignment of all abuses at the bar of public reason; freedom of person; and trial by juries impartially selected. To achieve these goals, he had dedicated his life to the imposition of an income tax; to the repeal of all taxes on imports, in other countries as well as in the United States; and to the building of "world democracy."

After practicing law until 1898, then going to Cuba with a company he raised during the Spanish-American War, then serving as a circuit judge for ten Tennessee counties, Cordell Hull went to Congress in 1907. On the first day of his first session he introduced an income-tax bill despite the Supreme Court's having held an income tax unconstitutional in its five-to-four decision of 1895. In his first speech in Congress Hull said: "I have no disposition to tax wealth unjustly, but I believe the wealth of the country should bear its just share of the burden of taxation. The cost of the government too long has been paid by those least able to pay, while accumulated wealth has enjoyed the blessings of the government without paying for it."

The fight for an income tax, then for an inheritance tax, lasted from 1893 to 1916. It began as part of the great agrarian revolt of the 1890s: the Greenback Movement, the National Grange, Populism, Bryanism—all expressions of the resentment of farmers against years of declining farm prices, against the protective tariffs which compelled farmers to pay fixed high prices for manufactured goods and against the Panic of 1893. From 1907 to 1913 Cordell Hull introduced an income-tax bill in each Congress, until his bill was passed in 1913 and signed by President Wilson. In 1916 Congress passed his bill levying the first inheritance tax, and Wilson signed it, after which Hull wrote to Frank Castleton's father: "Gladstone called the income tax *an engine of gigantic power,* and it will be such an engine for our country. With it we can vastly improve our social conditions."

Cordell Hull served thirty-seven years in Washington, twenty of them as a member of the House, then as a Senator and finally as a cabinet member. No public servant ever worked harder or spent more hours study- ing. He didn't marry until late in life, and he avoided social functions, so he spent his evenings and Sundays studying and working. Other members of Congress, especially his fellow members of the House Ways and Means Committee, depended on his scholarship. He was a Jeffersonian, a Glad- stonian, a Wilsonian. During the years of Republican Reaction, 1921–33,

30

he felt deeply frustrated, and often considered quitting public service. But he took hope from Franklin Roosevelt, and served as Roosevelt's Secretary of State from 1933 to 1944, thereby holding that office longer than anyone else had held it. After he retired in poor health in November, 1944, he was called "the Father of the United Nations" and was awarded the Nobel Peace Prize.

Cordell Hull never looked or acted like a demagogue. He was a consummate statesman: tall, thin, white-haired, elegant, correct. His language tended to be verbose and high-flown, but when he was angry it could be as lean and low-down as Harry Truman's. He worked equally hard at supporting his friends and confounding his enemies. The people he liked he sincerely liked; the people he disliked he despised. He was never trusted by the more ardent New Dealers, because while he had fathered the income tax he didn't want it used to create a permanent welfare state. Part of his education had come from listening to Confederate veterans, who, to a man, distrusted federal government and hated paternalism. Like Jefferson, he was an agrarian, so he believed that to be free a citizen must rely on himself, on his family and on his land. He died at a good time, because he would have despaired of the United States when more than half of its citizens had become congregated in cities, without land or a strong family structure, wholly dependent on uncertain employment, unable to feed, clothe or house themselves in times of adversity.

F<small>ROM</small> 1898 until his death, Cordell Hull knew, liked and associated with members of the Castleton family. He initially knew Frank Castleton's grandfather, the old man Frank led up to shake hands with Roosevelt on the day Norris Dam was dedicated, who was named William Coppers "Cop" Castleton. Born in 1842, he lived until 1937, so his adult life spanned the years from the Civil War to the TVA. He was a thrifty farmer in Clinch County, active in the organization of Confederate veterans and a supporter of the agrarian revolt of the 1890s. By 1896 he was able to send his youngest son, Lambert, to the University of the South at Sewanee. In 1898, when Cordell Hull began raising his company to fight Spain, Hull sought volunteers not only from his own county but also from nearby counties, one of which was Clinch. Lambert "Bert" Castleton left Sewanee and joined Hull's company: Company H, Fourth Regiment, Tennessee Volunteer Infantry. The members of the company elected the twenty-seven-year-old Hull as their captain and the twenty-year-old Bert Castleton as their first lieutenant.

The Fourth Regiment never fought any Spaniards. Through the summer of '98 the men drilled and waited to be called, but the call didn't come until fall, and by the time the regiment reached Cuba the war was over. After a week in Cuba the Tennesseans were ready to go home. They had volunteered to fight for Cubans but not to police them. The War Department nevertheless "sentenced" the regiment to five months of garrison duty in Santa Clara. Captain Hull and Lieutenant Castleton had to endure five months of fighting to control a disappointed idle disgusted homesick rebellious company. Several of the men deserted and somehow got back to Tennessee. The others fought among themselves, drank, wenched, played poker and thanked God when they reached home in May, 1899.

After sharing such tribulations Hull and Castleton were lifelong friends. Even after Hull became Secretary of State, Bert Castleton addressed him by letter and in person as "Captain," and Hull called Bert Castleton "Lieutenant." When Captain Hull ran for circuit judge in 1900 he counted on Spanish War veterans, scattered through the ten counties of the circuit, to support him. He also hoped that these veterans would get their fathers to support him, and most of the fathers belonged to the Confederate Veterans of America, an organization which was politically powerful as late as 1912. When Hull ran for Congress in 1906, most of the counties he had served as a judge were in his Congressional district, and again he depended on Spanish War and Confederate veterans. Clinch County was in both his judicial circuit and his Congressional district, and in fifteen contested elections from 1900 to 1930 Captain Hull never failed to receive a heavy majority in Clinch County, delivered to him by Bert and Cop Castleton and their numerous relatives, friends and fellow war veterans.

Travel in Tennessee in 1900 was difficult. Candidates for public office went by train, boat and horse-and-buggy, so they reached many voters only by mail. But at least twice each year from 1900 to 1932 Captain Hull visited Clinch County, and he always spent the night in a Castleton home. From 1900 to 1906 he stayed in Cop's home. By 1907 Bert had a home with a guest room, so from then to 1930 the Captain stayed with the Lieutenant. In 1931 and '32 the Captain, as a United States Senator, stayed in Frank's new guest house.

For Whitsunday (the seventh Sunday after Easter), 1902, Captain Hull, then only a young judge, made a special trip to Clinch County, to appear in church as the godfather at the baptism of Thomas Francis Castleton, infant son of Bert and Lila Castleton and grandson of Cop and

32

Lucinda Castleton. On that first Sunday in June, 1902, the weather was bright and warm, not yet hot in East Tennessee. The air was fresh, the trees green; Nature's accent was on growth. The Epistle tells of that Pentecost when the Apostles received the Holy Spirit and *they were all of one accord in one place*. The Gospel is the fourteenth chapter of St. John, where Christ appears as the Comforter and speaks of Love and Assurance. *Peace I leave with you . . . Let not your heart be troubled, neither let it be afraid . . . I will not leave you comfortless: I will come to you.*

In the small white Protestant Episcopal Church of Clinch City, two hundred farmers and small-town residents were gathered—the men in their Sunday suits with starched white collars and black ties; the ladies in their prints; the children trimmed, soap-scrubbed, disciplined. After the Second Lesson at Morning Prayer, the minister, the godfather, the father and mother and the grandfather and grandmother gathered at the font. Bert Castleton held his infant son in his arms. The godfather was Judge Hull.

So Cordell Hull held Frank Castleton in his arms while Frank was signed with the Cross, and he never dreamed at that moment that years later he would introduce Frank to Woodrow Wilson, Franklin Roosevelt, Winston Churchill, Charles de Gaulle, Josef Stalin and Harry Truman. In fact, on Whitsunday, 1902, Circuit Judge Cordell Hull had never heard of any of those men.

In 1948 the Southern Railroad's night train from Knoxville to Washington reached Charlottesville, Virginia, about breakfasttime, and the Washington morning papers were brought aboard. When Diane Castleton, on Wednesday, April 28, 1948, went into the diner and sat down for breakfast, the waiter placed before her, along with the menu, a front page black with world conflict and the Castleton case. The eight-column headline was HOLY LAND FACES ARAB INVASION. The British Mandate in Palestine was ending on May 15, so there were reports on how the Irgun, the Haganah and the Stern Gang were fighting the battle to establish Israel. On the left side of the page, under a three-column head, was the Castleton case; the other two prominent stories were about more victories for the Chinese Communists over Chiang Kai-shek, and more hardships for blockaded Berlin.

Diane ordered her meal, ignoring the paper. She had slept well and now felt poised and refreshed. She had dressed in a stylish red gabardine suit, which was narrow-waisted with a flared skirt which reached below her knees. She had the same blue eyes and black hair, which she wore loose around her shoulders, that her daughter had, and she was pleased that she was not graying. Her perfume was Bellodgia. On her ring finger were a wedding ring and a matching engagement ring which had cost twenty-four hundred dollars in 1925. She was still a perfect size eight, and she weighed the same hundred and six pounds she had in 1925, when she was twenty-one and married Frank Castleton. She looked seductive, proud, capable, disciplined, cared-for and well-off. Her troubles obviously hadn't disappeared during the night, but now she felt equal to them. Whatever happened, she intended to retain her poise, protect her children and herself and do the best she could for her husband. But it is sad, she thought, that in response to all my efforts to help him, he has been drawing away from me for two years.

Turning to the newspaper, she began reading Keith McDowell's column, which normally ran on the editorial page but which today was on the front page. The three-column head was on McDowell's SENSATIONAL CHARGE that the Administration intended to hold Frank Castleton in the Service Hospital until after the election in November. "They'll claim they must do it to keep him from telling Russians how to make the bomb," McDowell wrote, "but their real purpose is to keep him from telling Americans how Truman has lied about the bomb and failed with it."

Diane smiled and shook her head. Thirty-six men had graduated with Frank Castleton in the Sewanee Class of 1922. At subsequent reunions, homecomings and commencements Diane had met them all, and Keith "Stumpy" McDowell was the most interesting one. He had been a fullback-linebacker for the Purple Tigers—a blond good-looking super-aggressive battering ram. He liked to knock men down, pick them up and knock them down again. Only five eight, he weighed one ninety, and the weight was in his forearms, chest and thighs. He was also the class's exuberant practical joker, and in the years after graduation he became the class's self-styled son of a bitch—the hated irreverent combative satyr who worked his way up through Washington journalism to become the syndicated columnist who exposed the sins of public officials. Much too selfish to allow any woman a claim on him, he maintained a luxurious bachelor's home in Georgetown, gave Sunday brunches for people who interested or assisted him, had his clothes made in London and proclaimed that while other men wasted themselves on sports like swimming, bowling, hiking, jogging, tennis, handball and golf, his only sport was luring wives of public officials into his adulterous grasp. "Cuckolding pretentious public servants," he liked to grin and say, "is the true sport of kings." Diane remembered once when he had grabbed her and kissed her more ardently than an Arcadian is supposed to kiss a classmate's wife. Dropping her eyes, she continued reading the column:

> A few hours after the bomb fell on Hiroshima, President Truman said, "I shall make recommendations to the Congress as to how atomic weapons can be used to maintain world peace."
>
> That was two years, eight months and twenty-two days ago! Truman has made no such recommendations; he has revealed no details of the policy planning done under Roosevelt; he has had no bomb policy except to wait for the ruinous atomic-arms race with the Russians to begin.
>
> Time is running out. The Russians will soon have the bomb, and the race will have begun. The Joint Congressional Committee on Atomic Energy should now question Frank Castleton in executive session, and make public whatever he can report relative to bomb policy. Perhaps a way can yet be found to avoid an arms race which we can't win.

Diane then read about the press conference at the hospital. There was a picture of Paul Blanton and Dr. Palkin talking with reporters. The picture of Frank was one taken at home by the Knoxville *News-Sentinel* in 1940 when he was appointed to the Advisory Council. Frank had never before been newsworthy in Washington, so no Washington paper had had a picture of him in its morgue. When her son came in for breakfast and the waiter handed him a paper, Diane said to him, "Don't let any of it upset you, Cord. Your father will be back home in a week or so."

Cord read what was said about his father, then turned to the sports section. His having to come to Washington with his mother had cost him a planned trip to Louisville to see the Kentucky Derby on Saturday, May 1. Shirley Povich, the sports writer, told Cord what he was going to miss: the Race of the Century, between Citation and Coaltown. Sighing, Cord said, "If only Dad hadn't become hysterical, tomorrow morning Granddad and I would be leaving for the Derby."

Diane frowned and put down her coffee cup. "Your father can't help the condition he's in."

"I know he can't," said Cord. "But it seems to me that a man like Dad ought to be able to put out of his mind thoughts that are worrying him. He's always been pretty strong."

Cordell Hull Castleton had inherited more of his mother's features than his father's. He'd never be as tall as his father was. His hair was not sandy like his father's, but a darker brown, and it wasn't crew-cut. It was short, but it was long enough to be parted on the left side. He appeared less wiry than his father, and his face didn't look so lean or bony or rugged. He appeared softer, friendlier, for he did have his father's smile and white teeth. He said, "Of course I want to help Dad. But I honestly don't see how I can."

"The doctor will talk with you," said Diane. "He thinks you can help, and he'll tell you how."

After eating some breakfast, reading more sports news and noting film listings, Cord said, "Well, since Dad isn't dangerously ill, when the doctor isn't talking with me it'll be all right for me to go to ball games and take in a couple of shows, won't it, Mother? The Yankees are playing in Griffith Stadium tonight and tomorrow night, and the Red Sox are coming in on Friday. I can see both Joe Dimaggio and Ted Williams. And Rita Hayworth is on in *Lady from Shanghai*. It'll be all right for me to go, won't it?"

Having paid her check, Diane collected her change from the tray, leaving a little more than a 10-percent tip. "Yes, you can go," she said. "I'll try to persuade Dicky Bramwell to take you, and the two of you can play tennis and swim at the hotel, and you can go to the zoo. On Saturday you can listen to the Derby on the radio, and fly back to Chattanooga on Sunday to get the bus to Sewanee."

At Union Station in Washington Diane and Cord were met by Susan and Joe Bramwell, and Joe drove the three of them to the Shoreham in his Buick and left them. They checked into a three-room suite, and Susan began telephoning her friends. Having spent four years in a college only fifty miles away, she was virtually at home. In Washington and its suburbs she had sorority sisters and several suitors, and on Friday afternoon a group of her Baltimore sorority sisters, with their dates, would arrive at the Shoreham for the weekend, for Tommy Dorsey and his band would be playing at the Washington Arena both Friday and Saturday evenings. Her favorite suitor, a midshipman at the Naval Academy, would arrive from Annapolis to escort her to the dances.

Susan hoped that when she wasn't at the hospital trying to help her father, or with her friends, she could do some shopping with her mother. No sooner had Diane sat down than Susan showed her Garfinckel's ad, which insisted that "on the first warm day you'll take gratefully to our Maurice Rentner cool casual confident rayon sheers, only $139.95." Other

ads featured the new shoes with round toes, broad high heels and p
soles.

Only when both Susan and Cord were telephoning did Diane fin
to think of what she might do when she wasn't at the hospital. She
in the papers that Sloan's Auctioneers were selling items from the former
German Embassy; that the National Gallery was showing some of the
canvases which Hermann Goering had stolen and collected during the
Hitler reign; that the Bach B-Minor Mass was to be sung on Thursday by
the Cathedral Choral Society at Washington Cathedral; that Lawrence
Tibbett would sing at Constitution Hall on Friday evening; that Jane Cowl
was at the National Theater in *The First Mrs. Fraser;* that at a new film
theater, the Playhouse, an important film was opening . . . *The Search*
. . . which Richard Coe said would win Academy Awards; and that on the
coming Sunday and Monday, in two sessions, Mr. and Mrs. Joseph E.
Davies would hold their annual garden party at their magnificent estate,
Tregaron. Diane had been handed messages at the desk, and she returned
calls for several engagements. The wives of Joe Bramwell and Paul Blanton
wanted her for dinner, as did Stumpy McDowell, and Dr. Palkin was
expecting her at the hospital at 2:30 P.M.

While Diane, Susan and Cord were lunching in the Shoreham's Blue
Room, Diane was handed another message: Developments would prevent
Dr. Palkin from seeing her at 2:30, and would she please come instead at
3:30 P.M.?

DR. Arthur Leo Palkin had postponed
Diane's appointment because Vice-Admiral Clarence Evans Potter had
telephoned him at noon, asking to see him at the hospital. In the United
States Navy, three-star admirals visit captains only to inspect their work,
so Captain Palkin waited apprehensively for the man with whom he had
ridden down in the limousine, who, as director of Combined Intelligence
for the United States, was the second most powerful man in Washington,
and one of the most powerful men on earth.

No reporter had ever questioned or even met Admiral Potter, and few
had ever seen him. No newspaper photographer had ever photographed
him. All the public knew about him was what the record showed. He was
born in Missouri in 1894, son of a small-town druggist. He finished third
in the Naval Academy Class of 1916, and by 1942 was commanding
destroyers in the North Atlantic, protecting convoys from German planes

and submarines. President Roosevelt assigned him to help build a world-wide undercover security organization, and in 1947 President Truman made him director of that organization. Outside his organization, only the President and a few others knew where his office was, and his home was in the guarded Flag Rank Section at the Naval Air Station across the Potomac from the Pentagon. Because he was so seldom seen, and because his spare figure, lean face and crew-cut salt-and-pepper hair gave him the look of an ascetic, reporters always described him as shadowy bleak hard-fibered or beady-eyed. His hobby was studying security systems of great nations through the ages, particularly British Intelligence in the eighteenth and nineteenth centuries. He was a man rigorously devoted to the duty of secretly protecting the United States.

Admiral Potter arrived at the hospital in an unmarked Chevrolet. Two men in civilian clothes were in the front seat, and the admiral, also in a civilian suit, was in the back seat. He got out at the main entrance, was passed instantly by the guard and walked alone down the corridor to the doctor's outer office, where he was promptly shown into the inner office. The doctor greeted him, gesturing toward the sofa, but the admiral chose a chair in which he could sit erectly. The doctor sat facing him in a similar chair.

The admiral leaned forward. "Captain, I'm here at the direction of Secretary Blanton and the President. When do you expect to begin the psychiatric examination and treatment of Castleton?"

"Tomorrow morning, sir. Today we are examining him for possible physical symptoms. If we find none, we'd like to begin psychiatric examination tomorrow."

"Then we must agree on all ground rules today," said the admiral. "First, all parties, including Castleton and his wife, must agree that Castleton has no legal right to psychiatric treatment."

Dr. Palkin raised his brows and rubbed his face with his left hand. He understood now why the admiral was calling him "Captain" instead of "Doctor." "Admiral," he said slowly, "I hate to begin trying to treat a demoralized man by first asking him to concede that he has no right to treatment."

"But he knows that he has no right to treatment, don't you see. He will concede it readily." The admiral relaxed slightly in his chair. "Three years ago, shortly after Roosevelt died, Castleton began to fear that he might crack under the strain of what he knew. He wanted psychiatric treatment, but he didn't ask for it then, and he hasn't sought it since, because he knows he has no right to it. He reported to Roosevelt from October, 1942, until April, 1945, on the most secret activity of the government. He talked at length with Roosevelt when no one else was present and when the conversations were not monitored. He talked with Roosevelt on occasions when the President was sick and may have been out of his mind. So those conversations were strictly privileged. Which means that Castleton is forbidden by law to repeat any portion of them to any person or authority . . . not even to the Congress or the Supreme Court, and certainly not to a doctor while he's drugged or shocked or in a hypnotic trance."

"When Truman became President," Dr. Palkin asked, "did Castleton tell him what Roosevelt had told Castleton?"

The admiral nodded. "Yes. The right of Executive Privilege belongs to the Presidency, you know, not to just one President. That's the right which allows a President to keep his decision processes secret. He can seek and receive information, weigh conflicting advice, consider alternatives and options, without any public disclosure. A new President has the right to be informed of the decision processes of his predecessor. Not until he became President did Truman learn that the atomic bomb existed. To learn what Roosevelt had said, thought or considered during the three years the bomb was being made, Truman had to depend on Castleton. Virtually nothing was on the record. Castleton told Truman everything, and in so doing he and Truman engaged in conversations in which Truman expressed himself freely and weighed his options."

"And you want those conversations with two Presidents to remain locked in Castleton's memory forever?"

"That's how our Constitution says it should be," said the admiral firmly. "If we were in Russia, we could make sure of it. We would have arranged for Castleton to stumble off a cliff somewhere. Or I'd order you to obliterate his memory." The man sounded logical and practical rather than heartless.

"But we aren't in Russia, are we?"

"No, Captain, we aren't. So we must risk being humane. Castleton needs his memory examined, so the President is going to permit you and Nurse Sullivan to examine it. You can drug him, hypnotize him, shock him and examine his conscious, subconscious and unconscious mind. You can treat him, and we hope you can help him. But you can't make any records, nor can you allow him to write anything. Only you or the nurse can question him or be alone with him. No visitor, not even his wife or his lawyer, can see him except in your presence or the nurse's. You and she can't allow anybody else to learn what Castleton knows and feels. If you do, you'll face secret court-martial under the National Security Act of 1947."

Admiral Potter took three documents from his coat pocket and handed them to Dr. Palkin. "Two of these documents, Captain," he said, "make you and Mary Sullivan special assistants to the President so that you will come under the strict regulations of Executive Privilege. They also give each of you a Q-clearance for atomic weapons. The third document gives Castleton the President's permission to be treated by you and the nurse, and to tell you whatever is bothering him."

Dr. Palkin read the documents, then got up and laid them on his desk. The admiral went on. "This case is an unusual opportunity for you, Captain. You must handle it so that it causes no further harm to the nation."

Dr. Palkin remained standing. "Are you saying that it has already caused some harm?"

"Frank Castleton has done harm—of course he has," said the admiral. "For a man with knowledge of the bomb to become hysterical makes people uneasy. For him to say 'If only Roosevelt had lived' makes people distrust Truman. In today's world, to sow distrust of an American President is harmful and may be criminal. What would happen to a Russian who moaned in public, 'If only Lenin had lived'?"

Dr. Palkin sat down. "Under your proposed ground rules, sir," he asked, "am I expected to report to the President all that I may learn from Castleton?"

"Yes. Castleton may have committed crimes we don't know about. Or he may have information he has withheld from the President."

The doctor dropped his eyes, rubbed his chin, then said, "I'll accept your ground rules if you'll allow me some discretion. As I said to you and Blanton yesterday, if I'm to have any chance to help Castleton I must not only win his confidence but also deserve it. So I'll report to the President only on what I learn from Castleton that directly involves national security."

"You think you are qualified to decide what does and what doesn't involve national security?"

"Yes, sir, I think I'm qualified to do that."

The two men looked at each other for a moment. Then Admiral Potter nodded and said, "I too think you are qualified, Captain. You may proceed. Now let me offer you a little advice before I leave. Be careful with Diane Castleton. Warn Mary Sullivan against her. She has told us that she mistrusts the government, and she's close to Keith McDowell, a moral leper who wants Congress to investigate this case. Let Blanton handle her. After all, he's supposed to be an expert at handling Castletons. And don't be upset by Blanton's false public statements about this case. His job is to handle Congress and the press while he raises ten million dollars to try to reelect Truman. Also, remember that Nurse Sullivan should be exceedingly careful about her conduct outside the hospital. All sorts of people will be trying to obtain information from her as well as from you."

The admiral got up. He appeared to be satisfied. He shook hands with the doctor, then took another paper from his pocket and gave it to him. "This is a further report on Castleton," he said. "Jack Hardwick will furnish us further reports from his raw files and from his continuing investigation."

After the admiral had gone, Dr. Palkin sat at his desk and read:

Frank Castleton got rich off the government's efforts to relieve poverty and to oppose aggression. In 1933, in Clinch County, Tennessee, he and his calculating old daddy, Bert, owned large tracts of "poor, eroded, worthless" land. They also owned the county's only bank, an insurance agency, the Ford agency and the Standard Oil and Coca-Cola franchises. Since their county was "backwoods" and had very little money in it, the Castletons were relatively "poor" in 1933. But during the next fifteen years they got rich off the government.

First came the TVA. Frank Castleton wants to believe that he was being altruistic during the years of his young manhood when he was dreaming, weeping and working in support of the TVA idea. His daughter has told her classmates in Baltimore about how her father, when he was seventeen, sat with Wilson and Hull in the White House and dreamed of making the Tennessee Valley into a hydroelectric Paradise that would be the pattern from which to remake all such eroded hungry regions of the world. Susan Castleton has said that her father, while paddling his canoe down the Tennessee River in the Summer of 1920, felt that he was kin to every poor creature who lived along its banks.

Frank Castleton doesn't want to face the truth that when the government built the TVA dams, the "poor" creatures who profited most were Castletons! The first dam TVA built was in Clinch County. Norris Dam. The government bought 60,000 of those "poor, eroded" acres, covered most of them with water and boosted the value of the remaining acres in the county. When he was fifteen Frank Castleton learned from the Army Engineers where all the other dams were likely to be built. That was in 1917. Twenty years later, when the government began completing the dams, who do you suppose had long held options to purchase the best sites for factories near the dams and lakes? Bert and Frank Castleton!

But TVA only made the Castletons Little Rich. It was the bomb that made them Big Rich. In 1942 the government bought 60,000 more of those "poor, eroded" acres in Clinch County and built Oak Ridge Atomic Laboratory. Seventy-five thousand workers built Oak Ridge, and today it's an ultra-modern city with a highly paid, permanent population of 30,000, standing on land that buzzards wouldn't fly over in 1933. That adds up to a lot of Ford cars and gasoline and Coca-Cola and insurance and bank services, as well as inflated value of land the government didn't buy.

Our first investigation of Frank Castleton in 1940 showed he had an estimated net worth of $400,000. A hurried check today indicates that he and his wife and children are worth in excess of two million dollars. This doesn't include an equal amount they stand to inherit from Bert when he dies.

During the war Frank Castleton avoided combat, lived luxuriously, traveled extensively and luxuriously at government expense and served his country "unselfishly" for a dollar a year.

WHEN Diane Castleton was shown into Dr. Palkin's inner office, she was dressed as she had been at breakfast, although she had added a hat. She wasn't the upset often-tearful wife of a demoralized serviceman or veteran that the doctor was accustomed to seeing. She sat down on the sofa, crossed her legs and took a package of Lucky Strikes from her bag. She pressed out a cigarette, and the doctor lighted it for her. Then he sat down and told her that her husband was bearing up well under a physical examination, and that his psychiatric examination would begin tomorrow.

"As I indicated to you yesterday in Tennessee," he said, "during the next few days, while I'm questioning and trying to help your husband, I shall need to talk to you frequently. My time is severely limited—I can't spend more than half an hour with you each time we meet—so I'll ask you prepared questions and expect concise answers." When she nodded agreement he said, "My first question is, how do you feel about Frank Castleton as of this moment?"

"I'm . . . it's a love-hate feeling." Her voice was low and controlled. "As of this moment I'm afraid I hate him more than I love him."

"Why?"

"Because of . . . for what he has done to himself and to me. Life has been good to him. He is an only son, you know, with two sisters who adore him. His parents and grandparents gave him self-respect, freedom from fear, respect for others, the desire for knowledge and the means to go to college. For twenty years he and I had a perfect marriage. Our honeymoon began the day we met in 1925 and lasted to the end of the war. He loved our children and stayed close to them. He was a gentle loving fortunate man who could make music and enjoy life."

"What changed him?"

Diane inhaled smoke, then slowly exhaled it. "An unrestrained desire to improve the world, Doctor. When the war ended he couldn't celebrate the victory and come home and resume his life like normal men did. No, he felt he had to help save the world from future war. Gradually but surely, he has allowed his disappointments to cripple him. He has lost his ability to reason, to work at his painting or his business, to make music and dance, to give or receive love. He's lost contact with me and his children. Now, because he has been close to two Presidents, the whole world knows the condition he's in."

"Have you considered divorcing him?"

"Oh, God, of course I have!" She uncrossed her legs and sat up straighter. "Listen, I've got to tell you—he has been impotent with me for a year. He hasn't slept in the same room with me for four months. There have been painful scenes between us as I tried to help him be a normal man again. I mean, I really tried. But I'm still capable of loving him, I'm sure of that. I want to protect him and help him in any way I can. I'm willing to hope that he can be brought to his senses. Well, I can hope, of course, we all can, but in reality I believe he is lost, and I can't understand why he allowed it to happen."

"From his early experience," asked the doctor, "can you suggest a clue as to why it happened?"

She put out her cigarette and sighed. "Certainly Mr. Hull had something to do with it. When Frank was growing up, he was the only boy in Clinch County with the active assistance of a Congressman."

"Mr. Hull took a continuing interest in him?"

"Oh, yes. Mr. Hull had no children of his own. He saw Frank twice a year and watched him grow. Mr. Hull had considered himself a man at sixteen and was practicing law at nineteen. So when Frank was fourteen he was writing letters to Mr. Hull and receiving long patient replies. You know, it was really an extraordinary relationship. Other boys may have read *The Federalist* and *Democracy in America* and *The American Common-wealth* at fourteen, but they read them as required reading. Frank delved

43

into them on the advice of a friend, a Congressman who discussed them with him. Mr. Hull's secretaries mailed books to Frank from the Library of Congress, and Mr. Hull gave Frank subscriptions to *Harper's Weekly* and *North American Review*. One of the prizes in our library now is a first edition of *The Education of Henry Adams*, given to Frank by Mr. Hull when it was published in 1918. And part of Frank's idealism came straight from Mr. Hull—it was he who first interested Frank in improving the world, and who introduced him to Wilson, Norris and Roosevelt . . . men who thought they could improve it."

Diane reached into her bag and pulled out a packet of old letters. "I thought this might help you. It's correspondence between Frank and Mr. Hull, going back to 1916. Mr. Hull's secretary gave it to me several years ago."

Dr. Palkin took the packet and laid it on his desk. "Thanks, yes, it could be very helpful," he said. "I'll read the letters first chance I get. Now, go back a bit, if you will—what else in his early life contributed to his present demoralization? Just think about all the details."

Diane folded her hands and answered slowly. "I think, well, definitely Sewanee made its contribution. It's isolated, high up on a mountain: a ten-thousand-acre domain owned by the Episcopal dioceses of the old Confederate states. The men who go there call it Arcady—they call themselves Arcadians—and it's unreal. In 1922 you could get there only by train, and it was a dinky called *The Mountain Goat* which chugged up a spur line once a day from Cowan. Sewanee is three schools, you know: the military academy, the university and the theology school. They're separate but sit together on the Domain. In 1922 there were about a hundred and fifty boys in the military school, about a hundred and eighty in the university and about fifty in the graduate school of theology, all ranging in age from fourteen to twenty-five. There was, and is now, as a matter of fact, a faculty member for every nine boys. The only women living with the boys are those legendary little old ladies who live in the dormitories and take their meals in the dining rooms to help the boys become educated Christian gentlemen. It's just such a rarefied atmosphere! The only other females who live there are the wives and young daughters of the faculty. And only three times during the term do all these isolated young males have girl visitors. That's for the fall, winter and spring dance sets. Then everything is beautiful and romantic, like Camelot. In the fall the leaves are turning, in the winter there is snow and in the spring the mountain is ablaze with flowers. For each set—there are three dances each time—the girls arrive on the train and stay in the homes of faculty members, and for three days and nights boys and girls picnic together, stroll down lovers' lanes, caress each other while they sit at magnificent overlooks and dance the nights away in the decorated gym with a famous band playing. I recall Frank telling me they listened to all the old songs—'The Sweetheart of Sigma Chi,' 'Girl of My Dreams,' 'Kiss Me Again,' and 'A Pretty Girl Is Like a Melody.' "

"But many private colleges are like that, aren't they?" asked the doctor. "Isolated, romantic, unreal?"

"Sewanee is more so," insisted Diane. "Every young man who goes there comes away with a proprietary attitude toward the United States. The nation belongs to him; he inherited it, so damn it, he's responsible for it. During his lifetime, in addition to developing his talents, he realizes he's got to make a voluntary contribution toward improving the United States, and of course *that* means he must improve the world, because the cause of America is the cause of mankind. Sewanee graduates only activists. It was founded by Episcopal bishops who were also graduates of West Point and generals in the Confederate Army. And it's simply a known fact, Doctor, that the Episcopal Church glorifies war. The chapel at Sewanee, with its vaulted ceiling, is hung with battle flags and battle streamers. Well, it's almost spooky—the heavy atmosphere of patriotism, duty, faith and proud heritage that pervades Sewanee Mountain."

"So Frank Castleton breathed that atmosphere for six years?"

"Certainly did—from 1916 to 1922. From the time he was fourteen until he was twenty. His first disappointment was that he was too young to join the band of Arcadians who rushed to Europe to fight."

"With the A.E.F.?"

"Oh, no," said Diane. "The Arcadians went before the United States entered the war. They went to fight for Britain. You've got to understand —an Arcadian is as ready to fight for Britain as for the United States. Church of England money helped found Sewanee. Oxford University has donated books to the Sewanee library, many of the Sewanee faculty have studied at Oxford and elite upperclassmen at Sewanee wear gowns to class, just as they do at Oxford. Frank was too young to fight, but he stood in formation to listen to Wilson's amplified voice, coming over a telephone line, calling on Congress to declare war, and later, pleading with the Senate for support of the League of Nations. I know that while he was at Sewanee Frank met both Wilson and Norris. Moreover, Frank was a campus leader. He was valedictorian and cadet major of the military academy's Class of '18, then valedictorian of the university's Class of '22. You could never have found a more model Arcadian—a painter, a musician and a soldier, sworn to help preserve and extend what Cordell Hull called 'world democracy.' "

Dr. Palkin got up, poured a glass of water and handed it to Diane. It was a maneuver he employed during all his interviews and counseling sessions to compel a pause. Diane drank the water, then selected another cigarette, which the doctor lighted. "Since you didn't meet Frank until 1925," he said, "you never visited Sewanee while he was an undergraduate?"

"No, true, I didn't," she said. "But he told me all the stories, and of course he had other girls then—one in particular. He told me about her the day we met. Her name was Carole Curtis—a beautiful blonde from Chattanooga. She came to all the dance sets during his junior and senior years at the university as his guest. They were going to be married after his graduation. A week before the scheduled marriage, she died in an auto accident on Lookout Mountain. A lumber truck's brakes failed, and it crashed into her family's car. It was very tragic—he can tell you about it, I don't really think it's my place to. He also knew a young mountain woman who lived a few miles from Sewanee. I think her name was Bess Foshee. He's never mentioned her to me, but one of his classmates, Stumpy McDowell—that's Keith McDowell—once joked after a few drinks at a reunion that I should ask him about her. She was the first for Frank—apparently she taught him sex when he was seventeen, and continued teaching him for quite a while. After he graduated, and after Carole's death, he went around with several women, but I guess he wasn't ready for a real commitment, since one or two of them had husbands. When I met him he was twenty-three, and all those women had taught him well. I mean, you know, he was an experienced lovemaker."

The doctor sat down on the sofa with Diane, and she turned toward him and crossed her legs. "Here's my last question for this session," he said. "You say your honeymoon began the day you met Frank Castleton. Tell me about that meeting."

For the first time, the doctor saw her smile. "I met him about ten A.M. on the second Friday in June, 1925." Her dark eyes sparkled, and she began talking rapidly. "I had just graduated from UT. Three of my sorority sisters and I went up to Camp Perry in the Smokies on Thursday evening. Four young men, including one I was thinking of marrying, were to arrive on Friday evening for the weekend. On Friday morning the other three girls slept in. But I just felt so good, and it was such a glorious morning, that I got up early and went for a walk in the woods. I had walked about, oh, I guess two miles into the forest when I saw this young man sitting high

46

up above me on a big rock, sketching. I climbed on up and sort of walked around the rock until he spoke to me, and I sat down with him and we began talking. He fascinated me from the start. He looked like Nature Boy, you know. He had this warm relaxed smile, like he was every man's friend. He saw beauty everywhere. I had always been told I was pretty. Well, actually, I was one of the 'Ten Beauties' in the UT yearbook, so I had a good opinion of myself. But as he sketched my face and commented on my features, he made me feel like I was Helen of Troy."

Diane's face bloomed, and she suddenly seemed eight or ten years younger than she was. "Well, we talked for two hours, telling each other about ourselves. He told me about the hillside home he had started building over in Clinch County. He said it was to be his Monticello, and he expected to work on it all his life. He told me about Sewanee, and about his painting. And he told me about meeting Wilson and Norris, and about how the Tennessee Valley region would be transformed into a paradise. When noon came we walked back down to Camp Perry and had lunch with the three other girls. None of them had met Frank Castleton before, but, coincidentally, one of them had a brother who had been his fraternity brother at Sewanee, and another one had a cousin who had been Carole Curtis's sorority sister at Agnes Scott. So by two P.M. Frank wasn't a stranger to me; I knew all about him. But still, I'll tell you, when he asked me to go with him up to his camp, which was about half a mile from the rock where we had met, I had to hesitate."

"It was like being asked to go up to a man's apartment to see his etchings?"

Diane gave a short laugh. "Well, I guess a little like that," she said. "If I went with him, it meant, of course, that I agreed to a certain amount of love-play. I was a preacher's daughter, you know, my father was pastor of one of Knoxville's more prosperous Baptist churches. And I was a virgin— because I had been taught to be—and because I had never really been in love. So I had to hesitate about going with him, but, honestly, I didn't hesitate long. We went up to this beautiful spot where he had his tent. He had been there two days. He had ridden in on a horse, and brought another horse to carry equipment and supplies. We drank a little strawberry wine. Then he invited me inside his tent. Well, since tents are only for sleeping, it was sort of obvious that if I went in with him I'd be agreeing to do the love-playing while lying down. I hesitated, but I went in, and we talked a little and got really close. I told him to call me Jemmy, from my surname, Jemison. That's what really good friends have called me since I was a child.

And after that, the love-play began. I didn't expect him to expect—well, penetration—especially after I told him I was a virgin. He knew the rules as well as I did, and I thought he was supposed to leave me at least technically a virgin. But he rather firmly insisted on going all the way, and he assured me that he knew how to protect me. So I was confronted with the age-old problem. By then I knew how I felt about him. I was absolutely sure. I intended to marry him if I could. But I wasn't clear how he felt about me. He didn't tell me he loved me or wanted to marry me; he only told me how pretty I was, and how much he wanted me—meaning having intercourse with me."

Dr. Palkin smiled. "So you had to decide whether to gamble or not?"

Diane returned his smile and nodded. "There's something, Doctor, you may not have heard yet about East Tennessee women. In the mountains we have folk songs warning young maidens against the danger of 'courtin' too slow.' A maiden can lose her true lover that way, you see. The songs say she should court slow while she's looking around—naturally, you have to beware of false lovers. But when she thinks she has found her true lover —bingo! She must quit procrastinating and play trumps, or she may lose him."

"So you played trumps?"

"For three hours in that tent. It was after dark when we got back to Camp Perry. My other young man was there waiting for me, but he took one look at me and saw that he had arrived too late. I won. Frank and I were married four weeks later in my father's church. And our lovemaking was mutually and deeply satisfying for twenty years."

Dr. Palkin moved to his desk and told Diane wryly, "You know, you were really fortunate. Not every maiden who plays trumps so quickly is a winner. Do you have any questions before you go?"

"Only one. May I see Frank now?"

"I suggest that you wait until tomorrow afternoon. By then I will have had my first conversation with him, and we'll have been able to talk again. I'll call you before noon tomorrow and suggest a time for you to come. And I'd really like you to bring your son. Is that all right?"

"Yes." Diane got up to leave. "I'm going to Paul Blanton's home tomorrow evening for dinner. I want to tell him about two or three errors I have noticed in the papers. They're just atrocious—he must have been misquoted."

"I understand," said the doctor. "Oh, I knew there was something else. The Secretary wanted me to ask you to spend a few minutes talking with radio and newspaper reporters who are waiting, on your way out of the hospital."

"Must I?"

"Well, the Secretary feels that if you avoid the reporters their speculations will be more damaging than if you confront them. It can be very brief."

"All right, if I must."

"I'll go with you and see that they don't hold you more than a few minutes."

Six reporters and two photographers were in the improvised press room when Diane and Dr. Palkin entered. After the doctor seated Diane, the reporters all took chairs. Dr. Palkin said, "Ladies and gentlemen, this is Mrs. Diane Castleton, of Norris, Tennessee, wife of my patient, Thomas Francis Castleton. She has consented to answer a few of your questions." The doctor sat down, and the questioning began. The photographers focused their cameras on Diane, then waited for candid shots as she talked.

"Mrs. Castleton, have you seen your husband today?"

"No. He's undergoing a physical examination. No man wants a visitor while he is being dosed with barium and then being probed and X-rayed. I'll see him tomorrow."

"How long do you expect to be in Washington?"

"Perhaps a week. Until Dr. Palkin completes his examination and his diagnosis. Then we'll go home. If my husband needs continuing treatment by a psychiatrist, we can obtain outpatient care in Knoxville."

"You don't regard your husband as a threat to Free World security?"

"No."

"Is there any dispute between you and representatives of the White House over his having been brought here?"

"No. It was I who notified the White House of his illness."

"That isn't quite what I'm asking. I'm trying to clarify when, where and by whom the decision was made to bring Mr. Castleton here. When Secretary Blanton, Admiral Potter and Jack Hardwick came to your home yesterday as representatives of the President, did you ask them to take your husband into custody and bring him to this government hospital?"

Diane hesitated, then answered, "I don't recall just who said what to

49

whom. I was worried. We discussed what to do, and I agreed for them to bring my husband here for examination."

"Suppose they inform you next week that they must keep him here indefinitely? How will you react?"

"I don't anticipate any such development. No psychiatrist wants to hospitalize a patient if he can be cared for at home, and if there is a reasonable chance that he won't harm himself or someone else."

"Has your husband ever discussed the atomic bomb with you?"

"Yes—after Hiroshima. He hasn't told me how it's made, though."

"Has he recently been worried about breaches in our security through which the Russians may have learned our bomb secrets?"

"Well, no, that isn't what worries him. Once the uranium atom was split in Berlin in 1938, scientists of all nations knew that the bomb was a probability. Both Hitler and Stalin were told this by 1940; of course you're aware that *The Saturday Evening Post* published an article on it. My husband told me that Stalin knew by 1943 that the United States was trying to make the bomb. So he has assumed that the Russians would have the bomb soon after we got it."

"So he thinks the Russians will have the bomb in five years? Ten years?"

"He thinks they will have it next month—next year at the latest," said Diane. "You see, he has never believed that the construction and components of the bomb could be kept secret from Russian scientists very long. He felt that what they didn't learn by espionage they'd learn by research, just as our scientists learned. And that's why he has opposed our government's policy of secrecy."

"Has he wanted our government to reveal everything?"

"No, not every process," said Diane. "But as early as 1943 he wanted President Roosevelt to reveal to the world that we were making the bomb. And also, in the almost three years since Hiroshima he has felt that by pretending we own secrets, and by pretending that we can monopolize the bomb indefinitely, our government has given our people and the Free World a false sense of security."

There was a buzz throughout the room. The reporters were excited by this and asked Diane to repeat what she had said. The photographers kept clicking their cameras, and two wire-service reporters hurried from the room. Then another hand shot up, and Diane acknowledged the speaker.

"Mrs. Castleton, since your husband has not believed that our atomic secrets could be kept, isn't it possible that he may have carelessly revealed secret information to Russian sympathizers?"

"No, he hasn't done that."

"Is *he* a Russian sympathizer?"

"Well, it all depends on how you mean that. In a sense he is," said Diane. "He's deeply sympathetic with the Russian people. He reads Russian literature, plays Russian music. However, let me stress that he has no sympathy for the Soviet government."

"Is he sympathetic with domestic Communists?"

"No, not with Americans who have been Communists since 1940. And he has never been sympathetic with Communism; he hates what it does to people. But understand this—he is a Christian, he believes in redemption, so he has not regarded as irredeemable those Americans who turned to Communism during the despair of the Depression. During the Depression he helped several of them get conservation jobs with the TVA. Mr. Hull knew he did this; President Roosevelt knew it; and President Truman knows it."

"Are you saying, Mrs. Castleton, that your husband once helped known Communists obtain employment in a government agency? That President Roosevelt knew this, and that the President nevertheless obtained for your husband a Q-clearance in atomic energy in 1942? And are you saying that President Truman, apprised of this same derogatory information, renewed your husband's Q-clearance for the years 1946, 1947 and 1948?"

"Your phrasing of my answers will be correct after you add this: My husband helped several known *former* Communists obtain employment, not in the State Department or in any other agency dealing with national security, but as conservationists with TVA—as men and women who helped teach poor despairing Americans how to terrace eroded land, how to fertilize it, how to plant trees the government provided and how to grow grain, vegetables and poultry to feed their hungry children. My husband did that, he has never denied doing it, and Mr. Hull and Presidents Roosevelt and Truman have ruled that he was nonetheless trustworthy for having done it."

"Mrs. Castleton, your husband is an artist, isn't he? He can draw accurate sketches rapidly and from memory? Have you ever seen drawings around your home of curious apparatus such as might have been used in producing or exploding the atomic bomb?"

"No. I've seen no such drawings. My husband is an expressionist painter, and I must say some of our visitors find many of his paintings puzzling, even frightening. In one painting, for example, he tried to express what he felt at Hiroshima. But I doubt that any of his drawings or paintings reveal clues to bomb secrets."

"Mrs. Castleton, according to a report from Tennessee, one of the two

51

men who accompanied your husband on the hiking trip says that twice during the two days Mr. Castleton left his companions and was gone into the forest alone for as long as three hours. It was after he returned from one of these lonely hikes that he became hysterical. Have you any reason to suspect that he met someone during those hours—someone who could have been a Russian agent or sympathizer?"

"No. There is nothing unusual about his being in the mountains alone. Not only is he a painter but he's also a charter member of the Appalachian Trail Conference. And he's a cross-country runner—he often runs as much as ten miles, and he runs the twenty-six-mile marathon yearly. He just likes to be alone in the forest, that's all. He's a reflective introspective man."

Diane rose and ended the interview with "Thank you for your interest in my husband."

AT 9:00 that evening Frank Castleton was asleep, after an injection of Demerol given to him by his nurse. And Dr. Palkin and Mary Sullivan were in the doctor's office, talking. He had shown Mary the documents Admiral Potter had given him.

"You see, Mary," the doctor explained, "when you gather secret information for the President, report directly to him and discuss problems with him, you mustn't get drunk or take drugs or behave recklessly or allow yourself to panic. For you must never risk revealing what you said to the President, or what he said to you, or what you heard him say to someone else."

"When Castleton panicked he violated the rules?"

"That's it—specific 'rule' being the National Security Act. He exposed the President and the country to risk. In a police state, of course, he'd be shot, or his memory would be obliterated by psychosurgery. Here he could be court-martialed secretly and imprisoned. Instead, the President wants him to be repaired to a point where he won't panic any more. You and I are the repairmen, so we are now subject to the same laws that apply to Castleton. We can learn what Roosevelt or Truman said to him, and how the bomb is made, but if we allow anyone else to learn it, the best we can hope for is secret court-martial under the National Security Act."

"We'll be watched?"

"Constantly. We mustn't drink much, or take drugs, or engage in sexual intercourse with any partner who, by threat or entreaty, might be able to obtain information from us. It's going to be very tough, Mary—the telephones in my home and in your apartment will be tapped. Of course, the security people won't try to record our conversations with Castleton, or with each other, for no records are to be made. But the security people will want to know what we say to outsiders."

Mary Sullivan felt tired. She leaned far back in her chair, stretched her legs out and sighed. "It's a frightening way to have to live and work, isn't it?"

"You're not kidding," said the doctor. "To protect itself at home and extend its power abroad, the police state can do anything—it can use murder, torture, psychosurgery, bribery, forgery, wiretapping, mail interception, kidnapping, extortion, breaking and entering and the contrived lie. Our government, per Truman's National Security Act of 1947, has decided it's got to fight fire with fire and employ some of the same measures."

Mary Sullivan reflected a moment. "What if we fail with Castleton? What if we can't repair him as required?" she asked.

The doctor grimaced and shook his head. "That's a question for which you can find several different answers in the newspapers. For our own sakes, you and I had better not fail." He paused, then said, "As of now, of course, you are relieved of all other duties. Castleton is your only responsibility. You are his private nurse, guardian and companion."

Mary was silent again; then she took a deep breath. "I hope we can help him. Oh, God, I hope so. When I look into his eyes I want to cry. All day I have been asking myself: How can a man who is so talented, gentle and physically healthy and attractive—how can he be so sad and demoralized? We've simply got to find the answer."

When Mary got up to go, Dr. Palkin handed her an envelope. "Here are three letters of his," he said. "Take them and read them before we start treating Castleton tomorrow."

Mary went out the back entrance of the building and walked along a well-lighted path, under spreading oaks and tall pines, to her apartment, on the hospital grounds. After she had bathed and put on her gown, she got into bed and took out the letters. The first one, dated April 25, 1917, was from Congressman Cordell Hull in Washington to Frank Castleton at the Sewanee Military Academy.

> Dear Frank:
>   As you know, the government has begun building a giant dam at Muscle Shoals, Alabama, on the Tennessee River to generate electricity which will be used in extracting nitrogen from the air. The

nitrogen will then be transformed into nitrate compounds from which explosives will be made. The government is building a nitrate plant at the damsite—the war has made this move urgent since we must become independent of the Chilean sources of nitrates on which we have heretofore relied.

This activity, so important to the nation, has focused interest on the potential power resources of the entire Tennessee River basin, including the five mountain tributary rivers: the Clinch, the Holston, the Little Tennessee, the French Broad, and the Hiwassee. Pursuant to this interest the Army Engineers this summer will make a survey of the tributary rivers. They will be looking for sites where storage dams could be built which would assure a controlled and steady streamflow on the Tennessee at Muscle Shoals.

If you haven't made your plans for the summer, it occurs to me that it would be advantageous for you to accompany and assist this survey party. As a military student this assignment would give you valuable experience in the field. Many thousands of other young Americans, three or four years older than you, are now rushing to camps to train to fight in Europe. If the war lasts long enough, you will go to Europe, and experience with the Army Engineers will be helpful.

I also see a peacetime advantage for you. Both your father and I have long belonged to the Tennessee River Improvement Association, and I am also a member of the larger Mississippi River Improvement Association. The time will come when the entire resources of the Tennessee and Mississippi must be developed, to reduce flood damage, to assure year-round navigability, and to generate electricity. The more information you can acquire now, the more effective you can be in making this dream come true.

By going with this party you could also be of service to me. In due time I will be furnished the official reports of this survey, but it would be helpful if I also had a personal representative on this trip: a young man whom I trust and whose judgment I respect. You could give me an eye-witness report which would make me see more clearly, and therefore enable me to more clearly present to my colleagues in the Congress, the great promise of our mountains and rivers.

When I suggested to the appropriate Army authorities that I might want you to go on this expedition, I was told that the Army can't take fifteen-year-old boys on such missions, that it would be illegal for the Army to employ a boy of your age, and that the Army on such a trip can't be responsible for anyone who is not on the muster roll. But a colonel has now come to see me, and I have convinced him that you would be an asset to the expedition, that you would expect no pay, and that I would expect nothing more from the Army than adequate food, transportation, shelter, and any necessary medical attention. I assured him that your parents would waive any further responsibility on the part of the Army for your safety and well-being.

I have sent Bert a copy of this letter, and I suggest that you show it to your headmaster at SMA and ask his advice as to whether you should go. If the decision is that you should go, I will so inform the Army, and you will be made a member of the party and assigned duties just like every other good soldier on the expedition. It won't be easy; the work will be hard; and you will be sleeping under canvas, eating field rations, and moving equipment with mules through some of the roughest and most magnificent terrain on earth. I wish I could go with you.

I congratulate you again on the excellent record you are making at SMA, and I await the decision.

As ever your friend,

Cordell Hull

The second letter, dated August 31, 1917, was from Frank Castleton to Mr. Hull, whom he too always addressed as "Captain."

Dear Captain:

Thanks to you, sir, I have just completed the most exciting summer of my life. The survey trip lasted nine weeks, and we studied sites in North Carolina, Virginia and Tennessee. I am now preparing my detailed report to you which you will receive in about a week. It will include my sketches which show you how the sites look now and how they will look after the dams are built. Meanwhile, here is a brief report.

The Engineers told me a lot about Muscle Shoals. They say it may be the greatest power site on earth, because the river runs sharply downhill for thirty-two miles. Therefore this stretch has never been navigable, because the river flows through it so rapidly that it is nothing but rapids and shoals. Not even the Indians could navigate it in canoes, and for many years the government has tried to maintain a crude canal around it for rafts and flatboats.

The Wilson Dam is now being built at the western end of these shoals, but the Engineers say that four high dams should be built in a stretch of a hundred miles, and that these dams would maintain a year-round, nine-foot minimum channel even in the shallowest spots. The Engineers also say that these four dams could generate enormous quantities of hydro-electric power which would be invaluable in wartime. What is more important: in peacetime this electric power could be used to manufacture nitrogenous fertilizers which could be sold dirt-cheap to farmers and which could completely revitalize the land throughout the region!

We found a dozen great damsites on the tributaries. And note this, sir! The Engineers say that on these sites dams can be built which not only would store water and prevent floods and regulate flow for maximum generating power at Muscle Shoals, but that these dams, too, could be power dams, generating electricity as the water is released from them! This means, Captain, that the Tennessee River basin is potentially the finest place for human beings to live on earth! Rich land, temperate climate, majestic mountains, unlimited quantities of pure water, pure air, cheap electricity for home and industry, and vast forest and mineral resources!

Can you guess where the finest damsite in the tributary system is located? Right in my own back yard! Cove Creek runs into the Clinch within a few miles of our home. Also, you know that the Powell River runs into the Clinch in the same area. For most of its length, the Powell runs roughly parallel to the Clinch, about ten to twenty miles west of it, and it runs between high ridges like the Clinch does. Then the Powell turns sharply eastward and runs into the Clinch in the Cove Creek area. This means that a high dam built on the Cove Creek site would back up millions of acre-feet of water not only in the Clinch but also in the Powell! As the crow flies, the Cove Creek site is only 220 miles from Muscle Shoals. The Engineers say that this short distance is a great advantage because it means that all the power lines can be tied together and the whole river system, with all its many dams, can be operated as a single vast power generating system!

What this means, Captain, is that you must work harder than ever before, and I see a future for myself here. I must devote much of my life to helping you. *We must persuade the government to build these dams and nitrate plants!* Then in this whole vast region we will have no more panics, no more poor land, no more poverty, and this region can then help the rest of the country and the rest of the world. The Engineers say that this area can become "the Ruhr of America." I say it can become a much better place than the Ruhr for healthy, happy, prosperous, peace-loving people to live.

On the personal side, well, as you predicted it was a lot of hard work, and field rations are not what Mother cooks. The Engineers hazed me a lot during the first week. I got all the unpopular assignments. Then they saw my drawings and paintings. Every one of the men (thirty in all) wanted me to draw him riding a mule so he could mail it home. That gave me something to trade, and the hazing stopped. Also, one man had brought along a guitar, and I played better than he did. So I became the camp artist and the camp guitarist, and I was promoted to Muleskinner First Class.

Since the survey ended at Cove Creek where we were close to home, Dad and Mother gave the entire company a barbecue, with whiskey to wash it down with. We had a fine time and all the fellows were kind in what they said about me to Dad and Mother and Granddad. Major Lumpkin, who commanded the company, says that when he retires he wants to come to SMA and teach mathematics. I told him that you'd help him get the job.

You will have my complete report in a few days. I just hope that I can help get done what so obviously must be done. When the great war is over in Europe, our men who have made the world safe for democracy will deserve to come home to a big, hopeful development. Here in the Tennessee basin we can give them such a development. Surely there is no American who will oppose building these dams once they understand how much good they can do!

Be assured, Captain, that I shall always be grateful to you for this experience.

Respectfully,

Frank

Mr. Hull replied to Frank's letter on September 5, 1917:

Dear Frank:

I read your preliminary report with great interest and satisfaction. Now I must perform that doleful task which comes to men my age when dealing with men your age. I must speak of *political realities!* If you will keep remembering that I am thirty-one years older than you are, perhaps it will help you forgive me for what I must say.

Be patient. Persist, but for your sanity's sake, be patient. Free government is a blessing, but it moves so slowly that it can break the hearts of the impatient young. Twenty-three years passed between the time when, as a young legislator I perceived that the income tax was a necessity for this nation, and the time when I saw such a tax imposed. And I suspect that quite a few years will now pass before you see a dam built at Cove Creek.

That the government should build navigation dams at Muscle Shoals was first advocated in Congress eighty years ago. The hydroelectric power potential there has been known for twenty years. Only under the pressure of a national emergency did the government finally move to build Wilson Dam. And then only as a means to obtain nitric acid to make gunpowder, bombs and torpedoes!

I must tell you in confidence that I doubt that Wilson Dam will be completed any time soon. The war will end before it can be completed, reaction will set in, and how do we get appropriations from a Republican Party which regards the existence of such a dam as a threat to private enterprise?

I weep for you, my son, when you say that "surely there is no American who will oppose building these dams once they understand how much good they can do." It is my duty to inform you that there are legions of powerful Americans who will allow construction of those dams only over their figuratively dead carcasses.

Reluctantly, the government is building Wilson Dam to generate electricity. But in peacetime how is this electricity to be distributed and sold? The generation, distribution and sale of electricity is a job for private enterprise. And there is a giant power lobby to see that this remains so.

Reluctantly, the government is building Wilson Dam to make nitrates. But in peacetime, nitrates are for fertilizer; and the manufacture, distribution and sale of fertilizer is a job for private enterprise. And there is a giant fertilizer trust to see that this remains so.

Private enterprise is a tenet of our national religion. Our creed says that it built America. Its initiative, its energy, its genius, its vision made our people strong, sturdy and rich. Congress chants this creed. From every city street to our most remote rural regions, our people believe it. Governmental operation and ownership is looked upon with suspicion, distaste, even open resentment.

Wilson Dam is an accident of war. Once the war is over I wouldn't be surprised to see patriots tearing it down with their bare hands in the sacred name of private enterprise. At best, the patriots will insist on giving it to private enterprise.

Don't let this discourage you, Frank. I welcome you to the fray. I believe that much of what you envision will become reality. But don't expect it to come in five years or even in ten. It can come only after bitter, expensive, protracted struggle—perhaps only after another national emergency. Meanwhile, work hard, keep the faith, and be of good cheer.

I'm proud of the way you conducted yourself with the surveying party, and I look forward to seeing you on my next trip to Tennessee.

As ever your friend,

Cordell Hull

Feeling vaguely disturbed and lonely, Mary Sullivan laid the letters on her night table, switched off the light and began trying to fall asleep.

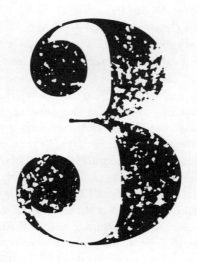

3

AFTER Gary Cooper began appearing in films like *Farewell to Arms, The Virginian* and *Sergeant York,* people who knew Frank Castleton began saying that he looked like Gary Cooper. Both men were tall lean and wiry; they were about the same age (Cooper was born in 1901); and there certainly was a resemblance in their faces. But Castleton's thick sandy hair was lighter than Cooper's, and his crew cut made his face seem leaner and bonier. As a former Cadet Major he walked more erectly, and as a folk dancer he seemed lighter on his feet. He spoke more distinctly than Cooper, in a deeper voice, and he was more articulate than the actor was allowed to be on the screen. He smiled more readily, and showed more teeth when he smiled.

As Castleton walked down the hospital corridor with Mary Sullivan, his face still seemed anguished, but he was not crying or trembling. He was well groomed, and the nurse had given him back the drawstring for his pajamas, so he no longer had to hold up his pants. He walked briskly with the white-clad nurse, whose head came to his shoulder. She noticed several nurses staring at them and told him, "Some of the patients who saw you yesterday told me you look like Gary Cooper."

"I hear that wherever I go," he said. "It pleases my son and daughter, but I doubt that it would please Mr. Cooper if he heard it."

"Oh, I think it would," she said, and smiled. She personally found Frank Castleton extremely attractive.

They entered the elevator and went down to the first floor. There they walked along another corridor to Dr. Palkin's office. "You look much better this morning," the doctor said, turning to them from X-ray film he was examining. "How do you feel?"

"Shaken, uneasy, embarrassed," said Castleton. "But I guess I'm better —my eyes aren't watering as much as they were yesterday."

"You're regaining control, and that's certainly a positive sign." The doctor pointed to the chair beside his desk. "Please sit down."

Castleton sat down and crossed his long legs. Mary Sullivan took another chair, and the doctor sat behind the desk, reports spread before him. "I have good news for you," he began. "The tests made yesterday show that you're in perfect health. Your heart is beating too fast, and you're breathing too fast, but those conditions will return to normal as your morale improves. Today we'd just like to begin helping you feel better. But—and now this is important—first we need your permission and your promise to cooperate. Would you take a look at these? They're some documents delivered to me by Admiral Potter which you'll find self-explanatory, I think."

He handed the documents to Castleton, who read them carefully. He sat there, looking at the papers, frowning, but he made no comment. The doctor looked at Mary and went on. "The President wants you to feel good as quickly as possible. He values your support. So he has ordered Miss Sullivan and me to help you, and he is permitting you to accept our help."

Castleton dropped his eyes, then looked up and asked, "What procedure do you have in mind?"

"Complete relaxation for you, in the first place," said Dr. Palkin. "Here we have two hundred beautiful acres. There's a nine-hole golf course, tennis courts, and flower-lined paths for walking, jogging or cycling through the woods. Indoors we have a gym, a pool, sun decks, handball, squash, saunas and masseurs. We want you to enjoy them. And something else you'll enjoy —in our canteen there's music and dancing each evening. We want you to dance and really hope you'll play the piano and the cello for our patients and staff. You like to read; we have a good library. You are a painter; you can paint and help others here who are trying to paint. Mary and I will be your companions. Each day you and I will spend an hour together, and then you and Mary will spend several hours together. We don't have to stay closeted here—we can sit or walk around, as you'd like, wherever. And we want to hear everything about your goals, your accomplishments, your disappointments. We'll respond with, well, with friendly counsel."

"What about medication?" asked Castleton.

"You don't need much," said the doctor. "A relaxant like Ritalin. Subshock doses of insulin. A narcotic at night for a while to help you sleep. Your only real need is to live for a while in an environment that helps you to relax, work, play and hope."

"And how long will you want me to stay here?"

"Only as long as you want to stay."

Castleton's eyes had begun watering again. His chin trembled, and his knuckles whitened as he gripped the arms of his chair. He muttered angrily, "Quit lying to me! The fact that you and this nurse were chosen to treat me, and that you were given these clearances, means that you are regarded as reliable by Truman, Blanton, Leahy, Potter and Hardwick. You're going to do with me whatever you are ordered to do!"

Dr. Palkin spoke slowly and quietly. "All right. There's some truth in what you've said. Unless we were regarded as reliable by the men you mention, Lieutenant Sullivan and I would not be officers in the United States Navy. But—now listen to me—I am also bound by the Hippocratic Oath. So whose orders we will follow in your case remains to be seen. We've never treated a man who's had a confidential relationship with two Presidents and who's been trusted with the nation's most closely guarded secrets. We didn't volunteer for the job of treating you, we were drafted. And since you can be treated only with Presidential permission, you must be treated by persons regarded by the President as reliable. So I suggest that we proceed on a day-to-day basis. Mary and I will work to win your trust. Because we are two people who very much want to help you get well, regardless of who employs us. If you can't begin to trust us, we can't help you."

Castleton put both his feet on the floor, relaxed his grip on the chair arms and wiped his eyes. "You can't help me," he said. "There is no cure for what I'm suffering from."

"What are you suffering from?" asked the doctor. "Tell us."

Gripping his hands together, Castleton pulled his forearms tight against

61

his chest. Looking down at his gripped hands, he said, "In 1915, when he was about as old as I am now, Winston Churchill suffered intense emotional distress after being dismissed from the Admiralty. He later wrote something I memorized a while back. He wrote, 'I had great anxiety and no means of relieving it. I had vehement convictions and small power to give effect to them. At the moment when every fiber of my being was inflamed to action, I was forced to remain a spectator of the tragedy, placed cruelly in a front seat.' Well, I'm not a Churchill but my predicament is like that. During the war a man of great vision, Niels Bohr, showed me how war could be ended among nations. I brought Professor Bohr to Roosevelt, and after procrastinating for eight months Roosevelt decided to activate his plan. Then Roosevelt died and Truman became President. From then until now, handicapped by secrecy, I have worked to persuade Truman to do what Roosevelt intended to do. I failed."

Gasping for breath, tears streaming down his cheeks, his entire body trembling, Castleton said, "We had the opportunity of the ages, don't you see, the opportunity to relieve mankind of international war. We've lost that chance, and it may never come again. Oh, dear God, we have failed our war dead, and the suffering people of the Soviet Union. We have failed the victims of Hiroshima. And our fathers who built America and our sons who could have inherited peace. All of them, oh my God. Our failure has doomed America to become another Rome—to spread armies around the world and suffer decay and defeat."

Lowering his face into his hands, Castleton wept uncontrollably. Dr. Palkin remained seated at his desk, but Mary Sullivan went to Castleton, knelt beside him, put her hands on his shoulders and helped him dry his face when his sobbing ended. They were all silent for five minutes. Then the doctor said quietly, "We can help you if you'll let us."

"All right," said Castleton, heaving deeply. "Oh God, we've got to try it. Let's try it."

"Good," said the doctor. "Now I suggest that you go with Mary. She'll get you settled into a routine. After lunch you and she can go for a walk on the grounds. And your wife is coming here at four P.M. Do you want to see her?"

Castleton shook his head. "I'd like her to wait two or three more days. I don't want her to see me inside this building, as Susan did. Maybe by the weekend she and I can meet on the grounds and sit or walk together."

In 1941 the most impressive room in Washington to Frank Castleton was not the Oval Office of the President in the White House or the Senate Chamber in the Capitol. It was the rectangular office of the Secretary of State on the second floor of the old-fashioned State, War and Navy Building which stands just west of the White House. It was not a corner office, because it was designed to have connecting rooms and entrances on three sides of it. It was about thirty feet wide by forty-two feet long, with a fourteen-foot ceiling, and its three windows looked south across the Mall to the Washington Monument.

At 8:15 A.M. on Sunday, December 14, 1941, Secretary of State Cordell Hull was at work in this room. Since 1908 he had been in his office in Washington nearly every Sunday morning. Usually he had found himself in a building empty except for guards. But on this Sunday the State, War and Navy Building was filled with people working to ready the nation for war. By 9:30 the Secretary had handled the more pressing matters, so he rang for Frank Castleton, who had asked to see him. He came in promptly and sat down in the visitor's chair. A telephone call occupied the Secretary for several minutes, so Castleton had time to look around the room he liked so much.

At the center stood the richly polished mahogany desk, first used by John Quincy Adams when he was Secretary of State. Its top was six feet by twelve feet—half the size of a bedroom in some modern homes. Behind the desk was the massive high-backed black leather chair in which the Secretary sat, sunlight pouring in over his shoulders from the windows at his back. Beyond those windows was the inspiring view of the Mall and the Monument. Farther to the Secretary's left was a large marble-faced fireplace, and near it was the elegant Treaty Table on which the Secretary signed treaties with other countries and above which hung a portrait of Andrew Jackson.

The faces of Lincoln, Grant and William Henry Harrison looked down from the north wall. Below these portraits were cases of maps on rollers, and below the map cases was a bookcase which filled the entire wall between the heavy doors at each end. Through the right door ambassadors and ministers could enter from the diplomatic waiting room. To the Secretary's left, over the fireplace, was a large mirror framed in redwood and crowned by the coat of arms of the United States. On the mantel there was a bronze statue of Andrew Jackson tipping a cocked hat from the back of a rearing horse. To the right of the fireplace was a heavy door which admitted general visitors.

At the Secretary's right, between him and the wall, was a black leather divan and two chairs. Above them, on the right wall, were portraits of Monroe, Washington, Jefferson and John Quincy Adams. The ornamentation on the south wall, in back of the Secretary, was fitted in between windows. One spot was occupied by what Castleton considered the most beautiful art object owned by the State Department: a marble bas-relief of Madison, done in 1792. Behind the Secretary was a floor standard which held two flags: the Stars-and-Stripes and the flag of the Secretary of State, which is white with a gold star in each corner, and the Seal of the United States in gold in the center. (The Secretary of State is Keeper of the Seal.) To the right of the flags was a rubber plant, personally attended by Secretary Hull, which grew from three feet tall to twelve feet tall during his long tenure.

As Castleton's eyes wandered back to the face of the frail but still fierce old man talking on the telephone, he made a mental list of some of the great men who had preceded him as Secretary of State: Jefferson, Madison, Monroe, John Quincy Adams, Henry Clay, Daniel Webster, John Milton Hay, Elihu Root and Charles Evans Hughes. And Castleton took pride in the thought that history might call Cordell Hull, born in a log cabin in the Tennessee mountains, the greatest Secretary of them all.

Secretary Hull ended his conversation and put down the telephone. He turned to Frank with a brusque hello. "Frank, I know what you came here to tell me. You want to join the Army. Now, wait a minute. After I've had my say, I'll let you argue with me. But first; before I forget, the President has invited Mrs. Hull and me to a religious service at the White House at eleven A.M. She doesn't feel like going, so I want you to go with me." Castleton nodded, and the Secretary shifted to a more comfortable position in his big chair.

"It is uncertain how long this war will last," he said. "But its outcome is evident—Hitler will lose. He is now extended from the Channel to the Volga, and he will become weaker each year while the mighty engine of the United States, free from attack, grows more powerful. And Japan will lose as well. Last Sunday she destroyed much of our old fleet, so now we will build a new fleet, stronger than any the world has ever imagined, and Japan, utterly dependent on the seas around her, will be at our mercy. Do you realize that on the day the war ends the United States will be at the absolute zenith of her power—morally, industrially, militarily? That's a certainty, Frank!"

The Secretary reached for a glass of water. He'd begun drinking a lot of it after giving up the twelve long Havana cigars a day he had smoked for forty years. He was seventy years old and in poor health, but Pearl Harbor had rekindled the fire in him.

"Now, how shall we use that power?" he asked. "To become another military empire? Or to free the world of international war so that we and all nations can disarm and devote ourselves to raising living standards? The cost of this war—in human life, in misery, in natural resources—will have been incalculable. Our victory will be wasted unless we have created during the war an international agency which can—*by force if necessary*—keep the peace among nations in the future." He tapped on the desk with a long finger. "Now note, Frank, I say that this agency must be created *during* the war! If the effort is postponed it will fail, and the war will be followed by arms races and more wars."

Castleton tried to speak, but the Secretary raised a hand. "Now Franklin is going to run the war and win the victory." Only three people in Washington called the President "Franklin": his mother, his wife and Cordell Hull. "He's like a child with a new toy. He wanted this war; now he intends to enjoy it. Yesterday he pulled me aside and asked me not to refer to him any more as the President but as the Commander-in-Chief. He said that the President had gone to war so he should now be called the Commander-in-Chief." The Secretary chuckled contemptuously. "During the First World War Franklin was thirty-six and wasn't yet crippled—a big strapping mama's boy, you know. Since he was kin to the old Rough Rider, he pretended he wanted to join the cavalry. But he grabbed a cushy job as Assistant Secretary of the Navy. Then for the next twenty years he lied about all the dangers he faced during his war service. To hear him tell it, he spent most of the war aboard warships, and every time he boarded a ship German submarines converged on it. His whole war experience was a series of hair-raising escapes from danger. Of course, the only danger he ever faced was overeating with admirals and war profiteers."

The old Secretary's shoulders shook as he laughed, and Castleton laughed with him.

"Franklin is such a liar." The Secretary seemed to be enjoying sharing this with Castleton. "He's not going to let me play any part in this war, but he wants me to stay on. And I'm going to stay, and with the help of God I'm going to render my greatest public service. I'm going to win the peace, damn it. Oh, Franklin is going to make the same mistake Wilson made. He's going to become so absorbed in his war that he'll neglect Congress. And hell hath no fury like a neglected Congressman. Well, you see, Frank, I know how to treat Congressmen; I was one for twenty years. So what I'm going to do is to make every Congressman and Senator feel like he's personally winning the war. Then he'll go down the line with me on the peace. And I'm counting on Frank Castleton to continue helping me keep the support of Congress."

"Well, Cap'n," said Castleton, "I don't have any unusual talent for influencing Congressmen. You know I don't even like to stay in Washington or to wear a business suit more than once a week. There are a hundred men in the State Department who can do what I'm doing."

"No, but that's where you're wrong," argued the Secretary. "You're my most effective lobbyist. You've been the most effective lobbyist TVA has had—George Norris says that. You actually like Congressmen and Senators, and they feel that you do, so they like you back. When I send you to see a Congressman, you don't talk much, and you listen. You surprise him by making him realize that you didn't come to tell him how to vote; you came to learn his views so that the Secretary of State can be guided by them in drafting foreign policy. You make him feel appreciated, so he tells his wife about you and he calls me on the phone and says he enjoyed your visit and he'll be glad to see you any time he can help us."

Castleton smiled at the old man's tenacity. "It's kind of you to say that, sir. But I advocated this war, so I should help fight it. When my son goes to Sewanee in a few years I don't want him told that during the Great War his father risked no more than overeating with diplomats and war profiteers. After all, you rushed off to war in 1898, didn't you?"

"That was different," contended the Secretary. "I was twenty-seven, single and in politics. You're thirty-nine and have a family. And look what going to war got me. Garrison duty in a jungle! And God knows what would happen to you. This war will be so immense that any one man will be a cipher in it. Even if you get a field command, Frank, you'll be lost on some jungle island. Winning this war can be taken for granted, and there is no shortage of men to fight it. What's in doubt is the peace, and that's what you must fight for."

Castleton got up and walked to a window and stood looking across the Mall toward the Monument. It was a chilly overcast day, and the trees were already bare. Winter was coming early. The Secretary drew him back to the conversation. "It's Diane, isn't it?"

"She doesn't make my decisions," said Castleton. "But I must consider her. She thinks I'd be happier in the Army."

"She's wrong. Now don't worry, Frank. I'll call her and explain everything to her."

Castleton continued looking out the window. He thought of the lonely nights he already had spent in Washington, and of the many more lonely nights he'd spend if he continued to try to help the Secretary. How easy it would be in the Army—leading men into battle for Great Cause—how simple and exciting!

The old Secretary went on. "You must also consider me, Frank. There is no guarantee that I'll be here four or five years from now. I need a man to whom I can pass the torch, and you're the nearest thing I've ever had to a son. I've been proud of you all your life, so your position is right behind me in the line of march in this war."

Castleton wished that the old man hadn't gone so far to have his way. "I'd rather you didn't call Diane," Frank told him. "Tonight I'll talk with her and with my father. I'll give you my decision tomorrow morning."

CASTLETON and the Secretary of State went out the south entrance of the State, War and Navy Building and walked toward the south or Mall entrance of the White House to attend the religious service. At the White House the two tall slender men were directed into the East Room. The service primarily was for the President and his family. Two of the President's sons already were in uniform. The President didn't walk into the room, since he hadn't bothered to put on the metal supports which enabled him to stand and to walk while holding on to someone's arm. He rolled in in his wheelchair, smiling and nodding to his guests. He positioned himself in front row center, with his wife on his right, his mother on his left, and the other members of the family sat down around them. Then the invited guests took chairs behind the family. Today, there were about thirty men invited, some with their wives or aides. In addition to the Secretary of State, they included Vice-President Wallace, Secretary of War Stimson, Secretary of the Navy Knox, Senators Connally and Russell, Speaker of the House Rayburn, Governor of New York Dewey, Admirals Leahy, Stark and King, General Marshall, John Edgar Hoover, Justice Black and British Ambassador Lord Halifax, with Lady Halifax and a British admiral and a British general. Behind these guests sat members of the President's office and household staffs. There was an Army sergeant at the piano, and standing up to conduct the service, wearing a dark business suit and a clerical collar, was the minister, the Reverend Joseph Bramwell. Castleton, seated two rows behind the President, between Mr. Hull and Mrs. Wallace, smiled and felt proud that Mrs.

Roosevelt had chosen his roommate at Sewanee to conduct the first service after the declaration of war.

When the minister stood up, everyone opened *The Book of Common Prayer*, which, along with the hymnal, had been placed in every chair before the service. In his beautifully inspirational voice, trained during many hours of speaking into the wind on a mountain in Tennessee, Joe Bramwell said, "The Lord by wisdom hath founded the earth; by understanding hath he established the heavens. By his knowledge the depths are broken up, and the clouds drop down the dew."

As the service proceeded with the Responses, the Versicles, the Canticle, the Lord's Prayer and the Creed, Castleton examined the faces around him. He felt at home here. These were his kind of folks, just like the folks in Clinch County and at Sewanee—no Negroes, no Jews, no Catholics. The responsible heirs of the Founding Fathers were praying before battle. Washington, Jefferson, Adams, Madison and Monroe would have felt at home with them. So would have all the signers of the Declaration. So would have Lincoln, Jackson, Webster, Clay and Wilson. Two inspirational voices led all the rest: the voice of the minister and the voice of the great man in the wheelchair, the Commander-in-Chief. "I believe in God the Father Almighty, Maker of heaven and earth: And in Jesus Christ his only Son our Lord."

They all said they believed it, the Commander-in-Chief most fervently of all. Most of them didn't need to follow the prayer book: they knew the service by heart. Mr. Hoover knew the Creed; so did Governor Dewey; so did the generals and admirals; and so did Lord Halifax. Joe Bramwell led them into the "Prayer for Our Country," and the President selected the first hymn, "Onward, Christian Soldiers."

During the singing Castleton could hear four voices over all the rest: Joe Bramwell's tenor, Governor Dewey's deep baritone, the President's not-so-deep baritone and the majestic bass of the British admiral. What was missing was soprano. The Roosevelt women, Mrs. Wallace, Mrs. Dewey, Mrs. Marshall and Lady Halifax were all singing lustily, but their voices were not strong enough to match those of the fervent males. After the hymn came the "Prayer for the Army," and then the "Prayer for the Navy."

Joe Bramwell used the text requested by the President for his brief sermon: the old bearded prophet Elijah, standing on Mount Carmel, mocking the four hundred priests of Baal, and shouting down through the ages: "Choose ye this day whom ye may serve! How long halt ye between two opinions? If the Lord be God, follow him; but if Baal, then follow him!" The service ended with the most spirited of the Christian battle songs and the President's favorite, "Stand Up for Jesus!"

An effusion of good will followed the service. The guests greeted each other as they waited their turn to greet the President and his family. Castleton and Mr. Hull shook hands with nearly everyone, then had their moment with the President. "You look hale and hearty, sir," said Castleton.

"I'm in top shape, Frank," the President said. "I'm glad to see you here."

Mr. Hull tapped the President on the shoulder. "I've spent all morning trying to talk him out of joining the Army."

The President chuckled as he held Mr. Hull with one hand and Castleton with the other. "I know just how you feel, Frank," he said. "In 1917 I had my heart set on joining the cavalry, but older heads wouldn't let me. You stay right here with me and Cordell. And that's an order from the Commander-in-Chief."

The President kept the three cabinet members for lunch in his office, so Castleton left the White House with Joe Bramwell. They walked through the rose garden, then to where Joe's car was parked, as Castleton brooded over his dilemma. "Are you going in the Army, Joe?" Castleton asked.

"No," said Bramwell. "There's no place in the Army for a forty-year-old chaplain. See, if you're twenty-five you can serve with troops in the field. If you're fifty-five you can be a colonel and say prayers for generals. But if you're forty the bishop keeps you on the home front. I believe I overheard the President ordering you to stay here, yes?"

"I may or may not stay," said Castleton deliberately. "Mr. Hull wants me around because I'm the only one to whom he feels free to ridicule the President and call the Under Secretary of State a shitass."

Joe Bramwell smiled. "Well," he said, "Hull's a tough old campaigner. He ought to retire, sure. But as long as he stays in harness, trying to build a new League of Nations, he deserves you to listen to him. Come on, you'll have to stay with him, Frank."

"But I feel ineffective in Washington, don't you understand?" said Castleton. "Promoting TVA, talking with businessmen, farmers and Congressmen—that's my place—I felt effective there because I was at home. We all had time to talk. Here everybody is in a hurry. I have to talk to Congressmen in their offices with the goddamn phones ringing and petitioners waiting to see them."

69

"I think you should move your family here. Rent a place in Virginia close to me. Then you'd be less lonely and more effective."

"We've considered that," said Castleton. "But Cordell is seven, Susan is fourteen, and they're in school and have friends. The place for children of that age during a war is at home."

"Not necessarily," said Bramwell. "Children who feel secure are adaptable. They can move with their parents when necessary."

"Well, we aren't going to move ours, Joe. There's no telling whether I'll be here in a month or three years. The Captain's health is uncertain, and he's always feuding with somebody—the President could decide to ease him out tomorrow. Look, next Sunday I'm going to go home for Christmas and stay a week. If I decide to remain in Washington, after New Year's I'll go home once a month—say, for three or four days. Diane will come here once a month, as she has been doing, so we won't be apart more than two weeks at a time."

They had reached Joe's car. The minister shook Frank's hand. "Then you must make my home your home. Don't wait for an invitation—you're expected any time you can come, all right? Bring Diane when she's here. You have a car?"

"Not yet," said Castleton. "I generally walk or use buses and cabs. If I decide to stay here, I'll bring a car back when I go home Christmas."

Joe Bramwell got into his car. Before he stepped on the starter he rolled down the window and said, "Frank, speaking as your minister, avoid the sin of vanity. Work hard for peace but don't expect it. Man has an infinite capacity for pulling the roof down on his head. Nations rise and fall; wars beget war. Where freedom is, slavery soon will be."

Castleton grinned and said, "That doesn't sound like the young preacher who roamed the ten thousand acres at Arcady. What about John Stuart Mill and meliorative democratic change? There's still hope in enlightenment, isn't there, Joe?"

"I'm not so sure any more," said Bramwell. "The Japanese are the most literate people on earth; the Germans are the best educated. Enlightenment, it seems, has its limitations." He rolled up the window, started his engine and drove away.

After he finished work that afternoon Castleton walked the three miles from his office to the Shoreham. He telephoned Diane, and they talked for a long time about whether he should go into the Army or stay with Mr. Hull. She argued strongly for the Army. But when she saw that he couldn't go against both Mr. Hull and the President, she yielded gracefully and said,

"Well, there's one good thing about you staying in Washington. We won't have to be apart for more than two weeks at a time." He then talked with his children and his parents. The following Sunday he went home for Christmas. He and Diane had planned a gala event, and had seventy-two members of his family for Christmas dinner. He told them, over a toast of fine wine, that with God's help this war would be the last great war on earth. Most of them believed what he said.

CASTLETON and Mary Sullivan returned to his room and discovered that some of the clothing he had brought from home had been delivered to him. There were no closets, hangers or drawers, but tissue paper had been spread on a portion of the floor, and slacks, shirts, underwear, socks and shoes had been neatly laid out. The only belt was of blue cloth no stronger than a pajama drawstring.

"Now you can begin living like a guest instead of a patient," Mary told him as he sat down on the bed. "I'll go get your lunch, your Ritalin, and your insulin. Then I'll leave you while you eat. After that, a nap—all right? I'll come back about two, and we'll go for a walk. You like the program?"

Castleton nodded without enthusiasm. But Mary was accustomed to dealing with apathetic men. Her job was to lend them a hand, pull and coax them through routines and try to get them functioning well enough to be restored to duty. After delivering Castleton's lunch and giving him his medication, she ate her own lunch in the cafeteria, smoked a cigarette and went to her apartment to change out of her nurse's uniform. She decided on a pale green skirt and a yellow blouse, and she fastened a wide red belt around her narrow waist. She pulled back her brown hair, which had dark red highlights, and fastened it with a barrette. Then she put on a cap the same color as her skirt. If possible, she wanted to make Castleton notice her, and start thinking about her instead of himself, and thinking of her as a companion instead of a therapist, and a female companion at that.

When she went back to his room and unlocked the door, she found him dressed in gray slacks and a blue sport shirt. She smiled and said he was looking like a man again, but he said nothing about how she looked. They walked out of his room, and Castleton jumped at the sound of the door closing behind them. Mary led him down the corridor and began showing him the hospital. They visited several wards where young men with hollow eyes and vacuous faces, all of them in slacks and sport shirts, sat looking out windows, or playing solitaire or gin rummy, or trying to work puzzles.

"Normally we have about a thousand patients lodged in the various buildings of the hospital," Mary explained. "They aren't psychos—we don't treat psychos here, we send them on to the various VA hospitals. Here we treat only the in-and-outers—what we call the Three F's—the frail, the faltering and the failing."

For the first time Castleton responded. "Is that what you call them?"

"Well, you know government labels. It's initials all the way. They all fall into what we call the Second or Third Orders of Dysfunction. On the outside they can function fairly well for a few weeks, maybe months. Then they foul up—get drunk, fail to report for work, forge checks, do a little stealing, maybe hold up a filling station. Their military service entitles them to be brought here instead of being put in jail."

Mary showed him the gym, where other men were swimming in the pool or jogging on the treadmills or punching bags. She took him to the library. "While I'm here I'll get a book for you," she said. "The doctor wants you to start studying it tonight so he can discuss it with you."

"What is it?"

"Freud's *Civilization and Its Discontents*," she said. "It's too deep for me. But the doctor is prescribing bibliotherapy for you. That means books. He thinks it can't help but help you. Ever read it?"

Castleton stood by while she checked out the book and gave it to him to carry. Then they went outside into the bright daylight. She showed him the tennis courts and asked if he played. "I haven't played much in the last few years," he said. "But I played on the team when I was in school."

"Well, I love to play," she said. "And I'm pretty good. We'll play some tomorrow. How about golf?"

"I learned to play while I was in school," he said. "Oh, I've played a little over the years. But not enough to play well."

Mary smiled and said, "You can play some with Dr. Palkin. Of course, you've got to be careful. He's a real menace on the course. He doesn't get to play much, so he tries to hit the ball a mile. But he loves it." She laughed, but Castleton did not respond.

As they walked along the paths, under the trees, Mary was silent for a while. She was trying to force him to ask a question, but he said nothing. He seemed tense and walked almost rigidly erect. His breath was short, and from time to time he wiped his eyes. Finally he spoke. "These men here . . . were they in combat during the war?"

"Actually, very few of them were," she answered. "Unless they've been publicized as heroes, men capable of combat in wartime can usually make it in peacetime. Our patients are males who functioned only fairly well even before they entered military service. Then, when they joined up, they were generally all right in non-combat roles, because they were relieved of responsibility. But naturally the war ended, and they were told they had to accept responsibility for themselves and others. That they can't do . . . not for long, anyway."

They walked on, until at Mary's suggestion they stopped and rested on a bench. A few other people walked past them: a man walking alone, then one with a woman who came in to work as a volunteer therapist. Castleton looked at Mary searchingly. "Do these men come here willingly?"

"Most of them do, yes," she said. "The first-timers are often brought by relatives; the repeaters are brought by police. The men are really glad to get here, where they can get away from both their relatives and the authorities."

"And they're held here as prisoners?"

"You don't have to put it that way. But, yes, about half of them are on closed wards because they've been transferred here from jails and are under court order to be held in confinement while being treated. The other half are on open wards and can leave when they choose. Of course, they aren't supposed to leave until they are officially discharged, but if they run off, I'm sad to report, nobody cares enough to look for them."

Castleton looked resentful. "Don't their relatives care?"

Mary snorted disdainfully. "Lord, no! The relatives of most of these men hope they never see or hear of them again. Relatives believe that their husband, son or brother could have exerted some willpower, see, and that would have kept him from faltering and failing. They tried over and over to help him and persuade him to be a man. Then they gave up and dumped him here."

As Mary had known he would, Castleton became anguished. She had wanted to bring the problem home to him—to make him face it. "Can't the relatives realize that a man may not be to blame for the anxieties which cause him to foul up?"

Mary replied relentlessly. "Well, the relatives have their problems too. I mean, imagine what the wife of one of these men has endured. First, because of his selfishness, he became unable to feel any affection for her or for their children. Then he became impotent with her, blamed her for it and began fighting with her. She suffered until she found the strength to dump him here and divorce him."

Castleton's chin was trembling again. His hands were gripped together tightly. Mary continued. "After being divorced, one of our typical patients will find another lonely woman and treat her just as he treated his former wife. Although, it's interesting, he generally won't be impotent with his new woman—not for a while. He can mount her, penetrate, thrust, ejaculate and impregnate, but he can't feel any tenderness for her. He'll fuck her and steal her money until she runs him off."

Castleton turned his eyes away from Mary and seemed unable or unwilling to converse with her. She decided to go on with her insistent psychological pummeling. She felt she was somehow getting through. "Does my using the word 'fuck' offend you?" When he didn't respond, she said, " 'Fuck' is a necessary word here. It's not an obscenity—it's a precise definition. 'Fucking' means sexual intercourse without affection. Polite terms like 'lovemaking' and 'going to bed with' and 'sleeping with' are inaccurate here, understand? They imply affection, or at least a little concern or compassion. But a faltering failing man is too self-involved to make love. He's impotent with the woman he once loved, and he seeks other women to fuck. So here we deal with fuckers, not lovers."

Castleton turned on her bitterly. "What sort of goddamn woman are you? A nurse who despises her patients and calls them frail faltering failing fuckers!"

Mary said nothing, and they sat silently for a while. Then she got up. "It's time for us to go back." As they walked toward the building, she said quietly, "When you know me better, you'll know that I don't despise these men. I try to help them. I call them frail faltering failing fuckers because I'm honest—that's what they are. If I didn't know and admit what they are, if I pretended they have strengths they don't have, how could I hope to help them?"

At his room she gave him another pill and said, "Now you rest and read some Freud for a while. I'll be back at six to make you a cranberry-juice cocktail—my special for patients on relaxants. And then a marvelous cafeteria dinner. After that, I propose a visit to the canteen, and we'll sing and dance and have fun. Sound good?" She got no reply.

DIANE had brought Cordell to the hospital for an interview with Dr. Palkin. As she waited in the outer office, the doctor tried to make the boy feel comfortable. After some easy small talk, he started in.

"Cordell, a man's relationship with his only son is very important to his emotional health. So I need to know how you feel about your father. I'll begin by asking you: Are you proud of him?"

Cord looked down at the floor, then back up at the doctor. "I don't know whether I am or not. I used to be very proud of him. Gee, I wanted to be just like him. He taught me to swim, to paddle a canoe, to run a motor boat, to fish, to ride horses, to handle a campfire. It was fantastic then. And he loved to take me with him—fishing or camping or to see the TVA dams or just when he went somewhere in the car on business. But when I was about seven he became involved in Washington and began staying away from home, so since then I've had to depend on my grandfather. I'm very proud of Granddad."

"Well, back when you were close with your dad," said the doctor, "do you remember anything he did that made you feel particularly proud of him?"

Cord reflected, then grinned. "It may sound funny to you, but I felt very proud of Dad when I learned that two Indians liked him."

"Indians. Who are they? Have you met them?"

"Yes, sir. They're Cherokees. They admire men who can run long distances through the forests, and Dad's a runner, you know. Long John Cotton and Billy Birdsong are two of Dad's best friends, and he's run with them most of his life. It's a fact that Indians won't run with a white man unless they feel close to him. And Dad not only runs with the Cherokees, he also dances with them. And it's a really important kind of dancing. You see, when Cherokees do it seriously it's part of their religion, and white people are almost never present. The Indians think that men should dance together when they pray or when they're afraid, or when they're very sad, or before they go to war. In 1941 when the Indian boys began going to the Army there was a lot of dancing, I can tell you. Each family, when one of its sons got ready to go, would invite, oh, maybe forty other men of the tribe, old men and young men, and they'd all sit out in the woods and talk and pray together. When Billy Birdsong's son had to go, Billy invited Dad, and Dad took me and I sat with some Indian boys about my age and watched the men. They talked and prayed, then four old men began beating drums and all the other men began dancing and chanting with Billy's son, giving him courage and asking God to protect him. And Dad —wearing work pants and shirt, just like the Indians wore—was dancing and chanting with them. It was all very solemn."

"And you felt proud of your father?"

"Yes, sir, I did," said Cordell. "I guess most people would have thought

Dad was crazy. But he thought it was good, you see? And that was enough for me. He told me that white men used to dance when they chanted in the Christian church, and that we'd be better off if we went back to dancing when we were in trouble."

"Those two Indian men—Long John Cotton and Billy Birdsong—they were with your father when he panicked the other night?"

"Uh huh. Yes, sir. They brought him home. They had gone up to run along the Appalachian Trail. And I guess you understand, Doctor, that running like they do, it's not a race but sort of, well, sort of a religious exercise, just like dancing. It eases a man's mind."

"Have you ever felt ashamed of your father?"

Cord looked up abruptly, then looked down at his hands.

"Well," he said hesitantly, "when he didn't go to the Army he put me in an embarrassing position. See, other boys told me he was using his friendship with the President and Mr. Hull to get a cushy job and make money out of the war."

"Don't those boys know now that your father worked hard during the war and had a part in producing the atomic bomb and in creating the United Nations?"

Cord's young face clouded. "People down home don't know much about that, Doctor. All they know is that Dad made a lot of money out of Oak Ridge and the bomb."

"And that bothers you?"

"I've had a couple of fights about it."

"Has your dad ever whipped you or slapped you?"

"No, sir. Oh, he's spoken to me a few times about my manners. But never raised his voice to me."

"Has he discussed sex with you?"

"Oh, well, sure—many times. So has my grandfather, and my sister and mother and grandmother. We've always talked about it—it's not a hush-hush subject in our family."

"Is there any conflict between you and your father over plans for your future? Over what you want to do in life?"

"Not yet, no. But I suppose I'll disappoint him. I mean, I know what he wants, and it's not what I want. Dad thinks that when a boy finishes college he should start building his home close to his folks and then live right there and help look after the family the rest of his life. But I won't do that. After I finish college I'm not going back to Clinch County except to visit."

"I have only one more question, Cord, and then we'll call it a day," Dr. Palkin said. "What do you think made your father sick?"

Cord Castleton hesitated, then said, "In the last nine months I've been alone with Dad only once. Last fall when I left home to enroll at SMA, he went with me. He left Mother at home so he and I would have the two hours while we were driving to talk. Some of the talk was good—and he sounded almost like his old self. Then he just quit talking and stared at the road while he drove. He seemed embarrassed and miserable . . . like he didn't want to look at me. I think what made him sick was his failure to go to the Army. Instead he got all wrapped up in things he couldn't do anything about . . . and his feeling of helplessness has been more than he can bear."

Cord swallowed hard and added, "Please help him, Doctor. I can't help him . . . Mother can't . . . none of us can."

CORD Castleton took a taxi back to the hotel, and his mother went in to see Dr. Palkin. Diane didn't object when she was told that her husband preferred not to see her until the weekend. "By Saturday afternoon he should be feeling much better," the doctor said, "and he can go walking with you.

"Now, for today," he went on, "I'd like to confine our discussion to one important question." He paused, looked directly at Diane, then slowly phrased his question. "How soon after you married Frank Castleton did his desire to improve the world begin to annoy you?"

The question surprised Diane. Her first thought was that it was unfair. Her first impulse was to resent it. "I'm not sure I understand."

"Well, look. Sooner or later everybody near him becomes annoyed by a man who wants to improve the world. Wives and children of fanatics always feel embarrassed. You met Frank Castleton in the woods one morning. That afternoon you crawled inside his tent, and you married him four weeks later. And you say that twenty years of perfect marriage ensued. Now I ask you if, in addition to loving him, you didn't also quickly become annoyed at his irrational behavior?"

Diane suddenly felt uncomfortable. She hadn't expected to have to defend herself. Straightening up in her chair, she said, "Let's go back a bit before I answer, all right? Day before yesterday you drove to a beautiful twenty-acre hillside, in the fashionable suburb of Norris, Tennessee, up the driveway through flowering trees and shrubs, to the showplace home of

Frank and Diane Castleton. While you were there you were served by two of the four Negro servants who live on the place and tend to all the gardening and do the cooking, cleaning and serving. Well, Doctor, do you think that's how it was in 1925?"

"No, certainly not," he answered. "I know approximately how it was then. There was no Norris, Tennessee, no Norris Dam, no TVA, no Oak Ridge, and the road was tiresome and rough—Clinch County was backwoods. The Castletons were land-poor, and they and their wives worked like niggers. Frank Castleton had built no more than the foundation of one portion of his dream house, and you had to work damn hard for the next five years helping him build it."

"That's exactly right," said Diane. "I married Frank before I had time to see the one big disadvantage in being his wife. Oh, and was it ever a disadvantage! *There were no Negroes in Clinch County!* Now, Doctor, you must understand that I'd been reared in a home where Negroes did all the cleaning and most of the cooking, but when I went to Clinch County I had to do all of it. When the weather was good, Frank and I lived in a tent at the construction site. When it was bad, we stayed at his parents' home. Like his idol, Mr. Jefferson, Frank was building a Monticello. But Frank had overlooked one point. Mr. Jefferson owned a hundred slaves, while Frank owned only one slave—*me!*"

Dr. Palkin's smile became a broad grin. "Did it occur to you that you might have played trumps too quickly?"

Diane shook her head. "No. Definitely not. I never once regretted the marriage. And I never complained. I couldn't afford to, because Frank's mother was one of those enormously capable women who had done most of her housework and in addition had been a bank director and a member of the school board. Well, you met her, you could see, yes? She has never been unkind to me, but she watched me like a hawk after I married Frank, expecting me to gripe or fail. So I had to match her stride for stride, which, by God, I did. I expected both me and Frank to work hard for several years, and save our money, so that we'd have enough to persuade two good Negroes to come from Knoxville and live and work on our place. And I knew this would be expensive, because of course we'd have to give our servants money to make frequent trips back to Knoxville to go to their own church and attend funerals and weddings and suchlike. But whatever the expense, to live graciously we had to have Negroes, and Frank promised to save our money and get them."

"But he didn't save much money?"

"Of course he didn't. He had to finance the dream of TVA. He had to run back and forth to Washington to see Senator Norris. In 1927 Congress passed the Norris Act creating TVA, but President Coolidge vetoed it. So for the next six years Senator Norris and the supporters of TVA worked and spent money until they finally established it in 1933 with Roosevelt's help. Oh, I was so exasperated—Frank spent money like we were millionaires when we didn't have money to spend, and when nobody in Clinch County believed that there'd ever be a TVA—nobody, of course, but Frank, his father and his grandfather."

"What about his mother? Did she believe it?"

"No, I don't think . . . she didn't really believe it," said Diane. "But because Frank did, she pretended, and gave him money to help Senator Norris get reelected in Nebraska."

"You mean Frank helped finance the Senator's campaign?"

"Of course. The utility companies which felt threatened by the TVA idea put up money to defeat Norris in Nebraska. So Frank did little else for weeks but travel around badgering people in East Tennessee for money. He went to Sewanee alumni, and bankers who did business with the Castleton bank, and other Ford dealers, and other people who were distributing Standard Oil, even the Coca-Cola company. And when he had raised all he could, he contributed three thousand dollars of our money— our own, that we'd worked so goddamn hard for. It made me sick! Believe me, Doctor, that was an enormous sum for us in 1930, and Frank spent it in Nebraska while I still didn't have *one* Negro to help me! Now, that wasn't fair to me, was it?"

Diane wanted support, and Dr. Palkin gave it to her. "No, it wasn't. But you have to realize that fanatics are never fair to their wives. Eventually, though, you got what you wanted, didn't you?"

"In time I got *part* of what I wanted," said Diane. "Six months after we married we moved out of the tent and into two rooms of our home. By 1931 the place had begun to look a little like it looks today."

"And you got your Negro servants?"

"We didn't get the first two *good* Negroes until 1931. And we didn't get two more good ones until 1935."

"Well, all right, let's go on. TVA came, and land values went up, as did the demand for Fords, gasoline and Coke. So your husband made you rich, didn't he? Did you ever tell him that you'd been wrong and he had been right?"

Diane was shocked. She considered walking out of the room. Angrily she said, "You are being unfair to me, Doctor. I wasn't a spoiled selfish woman demanding riches. My objection was to Frank's wasting his life on TVA, do you understand? For eight years he worked to help get the legislation passed. Then after 1933 he worked seven more years to help sell TVA to the people of the Tennessee Valley. He spent money on demonstration farms to teach poor farmers how to terrace their land and plant trees and rotate their crops and use fertilizers, all of that. Country people had to be organized into co-ops to build power lines into rural areas. Farm women had to be taught how to prepare fruits and vegetables for storage in community freezers. Since I had been a Home Ec. major at UT, Frank had me working like a Negro, showing farm women methods. Now, I never complained; I was glad to help. But, remember, that wasn't all—I had also had to convert my home into a hotel for a parade of guests, both domestic and foreign. Congressmen had to be entertained and persuaded to continue supporting TVA, and foreign officials, from Nehru on down, came to our guest house, and Frank sat up all night with them talking about how to raise living standards in Asia, Africa and South America."

"But surely, Mrs. Castleton," said the doctor, "a little of your husband's enthusiasm for improving the world must have rubbed off on you. Didn't you feel a little pride in what he was trying to do?"

Diane's shoulders drooped, and she sighed deeply. "Doctor, you still don't understand. I don't know why I'm not getting through to you. I'm saying he was wasting the best of himself. Frank Castleton was the most talented man to ever go to Sewanee. By mail, by telephone and at every Commencement, the professors who had taught him urged me to plead with him to cut down on his humanitarian activities and devote himself to his painting or his music. His teachers thought that Frank could have become a great painter, and I feel, as they did, that one great painting is worth more to the world than all the dams ever built on all the rivers."

"Did you let him know how you felt? Did you remind him that he was wasting his time, and should work more at painting or music?"

Diane replied wearily. "Well, I never nagged or made scenes. Frank knew my feelings and, oh, all right—sometimes I reminded him. But I was *not* bitter, and we never went to sleep angry at each other. He is an intense, emotional man who just needs sexual comfort before he can simmer down enough to sleep. Truthfully, Doctor, I comforted him and loved him, but I told him he wasn't put on this earth to build TVA, that TVA wouldn't amount to all he hoped it would and that his duty was to work at business only enough to support his family. Then he had a responsibility to work at developing his God-given talents."

"And when the war came, and he got involved in another world-improving effort, you felt even more annoyed, didn't you?"

"Indeed I did," said Diane firmly. "I wanted him to join the Army and help win the war. He would have felt like a winner then, you see. And, God willing, if he survived, he'd come home and work at his painting. If he stayed with Mr. Hull and the President, I felt that he would be a loser. And, yes, I thought about it even then—I feared that he might wind up in an insane asylum with a shattered spirit and a broken heart."

Dr. Palkin made a note and consulted his calendar. "All right, we'll talk more about that when I see you again. I suggest that you don't come here tomorrow but wait until the next day—Saturday, May first. You can also see Frank then. Tomorrow I'm seeing the Reverend Bramwell. Oh, and when you come on Saturday, could you bring Susan? I'd like to talk with her again."

"Yes, certainly," Diane said, "but I do want you to know both Susan and Cord will be leaving to return to school on Sunday."

THE taxicab carrying Diane from the hospital drove along East-West Highway from Bethesda to Chevy Chase, passed the Columbia Country Club, then turned onto Connecticut Avenue for the four-mile drive to the Shoreham. It was the late-afternoon rush hour, and traffic was heavy, so as Diane sat in the back seat, staring blindly at the passing streets, she tried to relieve her despair by remembering happy previous trips to Washington. She had first come with her parents in 1921. They stayed at a hotel near Union Station and took trolleys around the city. She remembered how excited she was when she first saw the Capitol, the Monument, Ford's Theater, the Smithsonian, the White House; then there was the boat trip down the Potomac to Mount Vernon. The most emotional moment was at Lee's home at Arlington, because her grandfather had been the chaplain who rode with General Lee and prayed with him before the great battles. In the living room of the Lee home, although other tourists were milling about, her preacher father had asked her and her mother to kneel with him while he thanked God for "the inspirational life of Robert E. Lee."

But the trip to remember was the one she had made with Frank in 1935. They left the children with his parents and stayed four days at the Willard. They lunched at the Capitol with Senator Norris, and to Frank that was like lunching with Saint John. They dined at the Carlton as guests of Secretary of State and Mrs. Hull with two Tennessee Congressmen and their wives, and to Frank that was like dining with Saint Peter. Then, late on the third afternoon, the telephone in the hotel room rang, and they dashed the three blocks to the White House. There, behind his cluttered desk, sat the Good Lord Himself: the great smiling President, reaching his long arms toward them, saying, "Frank, how *ahr* yah! And Diane! I'm so glad to *see* yah! Sit down and tell me what ay can *do* fahr yah!"

In ten minutes they were out of his office, but that was long enough for them to be made to feel that, just as God Almighty follows the flight of every sparrow, so the President of the United States had known of their arrival at Union Station, had followed their every movement and had devoted himself and his staff to arranging time for him to greet them. Diane told Roosevelt that Susan was now eight, and that Cord Castleton had passed his first birthday and could walk. The President smiled. "Frank," he said, "you remember that day in 1931 when Cordell brought you to see me in Warm Springs? We've come a long way since then, haven't we, boy!"

"We sure have, Mr. President," said Frank. "Thanks to you, sir, and to George Norris."

"Well, next year *I'm* coming to see *you,*" said the President. "I'm coming down there with George and dedicate that big dam. And I'm coming to your house and drink some of that strawberry wine that Diane is so famous for."

When Frank and Diane left the White House Frank felt so exhilarated that, walking back to the Willard, he stopped twice and startled other people on the street by hugging Diane joyously. "It's happening, Jemmy," he said, "and we're part of it." Diane, too, felt buoyant, but for very different reasons. She was happy because at thirty-one she was a proud confident beautiful woman who had borne two lovely children, who had acquired the graceful way of life she valued and who had an exhilarated husband who showed every day that he loved her and who still excited her when he hugged her.

Three minutes after they got back to the hotel suite, Jemmy was ready for her husband's passion. She was descended from sensuous gentlewomen who had left England before Victoria was born and who, in the mountains of East Tennessee, had learned not only the mistake of courting too slow but also that of courting without skill. She had taught herself early on at college how to perfect control of her "love muscles." This was one reason why Frank Castleton, when he took her for the first time in the mountains in 1925, held her for three more hours in his tent, and partly why he decided to marry her. Now, in their hotel bed years later, he got on top of her and experienced an hour of extraordinary delights. After twenty minutes of rest, her lips were again on his chest, her hand in his crotch, and when he was ready and begging, she mounted him and gave him twenty more minutes of ecstasy before they came together and she leaned forward, panting, on top of him. After a while they dressed, had dinner and went to the theater, where they saw a delightful play, *The Road to Rome.*

Yes, she thought, as she rode along Connecticut Avenue, that was the best trip. She recalled the wartime trips when she took the train from Knoxville to Washington to spend weekends with Frank. They had vowed that never in their lives would they stay apart more than two weeks, so after one weekend away she always went to him for the next weekend if he couldn't come to her. He stayed at the Shoreham so that he could walk and run in Rock Creek Park. On her trips she left home on Friday evening and he met her at Union Station the next morning and they spent their thirty hours together until she left like most wartime lovers. Except they were not twenty but about forty, parents of a sixteen-year-old daughter and a nine-year-old son. Sometimes they went to the theater, or movies, or to dinner at Paul Blanton's or Joe Bramwell's home, or to the Sunday brunch at Keith McDowell's. As they walked with the uniformed men and their girls, Diane felt young and alive, especially when Frank kissed her, not caring who was around, just like the young soldiers kissing their girls. Always on Sunday night, riding home in the dark Pullman room, she relived their most recent hours together and rejoiced at Frank's continuing ability to hope and believe and to celebrate life when they made love together. And always, before she said her prayers and went to sleep, she wished again that he had gone into the Army and helped win great battles in far-off places instead of allowing himself to be assigned unsatisfying duties in Washington and Oak Ridge and in some place near Santa Fe, New Mexico. God knows what use he is here, she thought then.

Her last trip to Washington was in January, 1945, a few days before Frank left for Yalta with the President. Both of them were pensive, for they sensed a fateful year ahead. Riding home in the Pullman room, she felt afraid for the first time in her life. Three times during 1945 they were apart for as long as two months, and when, near the end of the year, Frank came home from Hiroshima, he was distracted. It seemed he had lost his ability to hope and to make love. On his numerous trips to Washington during 1946 and '47 he never stayed longer than two weeks at a time, and he never invited her to go with him. He was a man who wanted his wife with him when he felt he was winning, not when he felt he was losing.

When her cab pulled up at the hotel, Diane went immediately to her suite. It seemed hideously impersonal and empty. She ordered a double whiskey sour, and when it came she sat down and drank it slowly while she smoked a cigarette. The doctor's words kept running through her mind: *Everybody becomes annoyed by a man who wants to improve the world. Wives of fanatics always feel embarrassed.* Well, she was tired of feeling annoyed and embarrassed. She was tired of being denied enjoyment. She wanted to be with people who found her exciting and delightful. When she finished her drink she marched into her bathroom, dried her tears, undressed and began getting ready for dinner at Paul Blanton's home.

W HEN Mary Sullivan unlocked Castleton's door at 6 P.M., she looked as little like a nurse as she possibly could. She had let down her hair and fluffed it out, and she wore white earrings and a necklace of glass balls the size and color of ripe cherries. She carried a tray on which were two tall frosty glasses filled with cranberry juice, topped with a piece of lime. "This is de luxe service," she said. "Only our VIP guests get cocktails." Castleton neither thanked her nor made any comment on how she looked. He laid down the book he had been reading and joined her at the table, on which she put the glasses.

"Feel better?"

He sipped, then drank deeply from the glass. "Perhaps I am. I've been reading Freud, as instructed. How a civilized man must struggle to keep misery at a distance. Perhaps I haven't struggled hard enough."

They sipped in silence while Mary again tried to force him to speak. Finally, as if reading her thoughts, he looked directly at her and asked, "Why do you work in a hospital like this? Why don't you work in a regular military hospital where your patients would be men who became ill or wounded through no fault of their own? What attracts you to this type, anyway—to frail faltering failing fuckers?"

"That's two questions. You get two answers," she said. "During the war, I was a regular nurse and had a few NP patients. After it ended, the Navy wanted some of us to train to become psychiatric nurses, and I decided to try it. I haven't been sorry at all. A regular nurse, well, she does her job. It's routine. She enters on the chart what the gauges show, and the laboratory reports. A psychiatric nurse, though, enters on the chart her observations and judgment. She must supervise therapy, watch for changes in the patient's attitude and behavior and evaluate the changes precisely. She spends hours with the patient, the doctor spends minutes. So the psychiatrist is dependent on what the psychiatric nurse can tell him." She drank from her glass, then continued. "As to the sort of men who attract me . . . professionally I try to help frail men. But privately I'm always searching for a strong man who can stand up to life . . . who can help me sustain the illusions which make life bearable . . . and, well, one who can love me at least a little, and not just fuck me."

"Your search hasn't been successful?"

"Hmm. Partially. I've found two or three men capable of enough affection for me to give me some comfort. And, naturally, I've also made a few mistakes and gotten fucked." She smiled at Castleton. "But I haven't given up. I'm still searching. Whenever you start telling me about your successes and disappointments, I'll tell you about mine."

Mary and Frank went to the cafeteria, where they stood in line for their food, then found a table. The room was crowded with perhaps twenty women and two hundred men. None wore any sort of uniform, so there was a kind of college-dining-hall atmosphere to the room. Castleton attracted glances from those who had seen his picture in the paper or who now noted his resemblance to Gary Cooper. As they sat down, Castleton asked, "These women here, are they nurses or relatives?"

"A few of them are paid professional nurses," Mary replied. "The rest are unpaid volunteers. We have only about fifty professional psychiatric nurses for the entire hospital. Each nurse, with a male assistant, supervises treatment of the forty men on her ward. That doesn't give her much time for each patient, so a number of outside women come here one or two days or evenings a week and try to give each one a little individual attention."

"You mean you normally work with forty men at a time?"

"Uh huh. And Dr. Palkin normally sees each of his patients five or ten minutes a week. See how special you are? Now he devotes two or three hours a day to your case, and I devote myself completely. You're an enormously important and fortunate man."

"Level with me. That isn't why you do it," said Castleton, shaking his head. "I'm neither important nor fortunate. Only irritating."

He seemed suddenly angry and upset. He kept his head down as he picked at his food, and said nothing. Then he looked up and asked her, "Why aren't the professional and volunteer women wearing uniforms like in regular hospitals?"

"We try very hard to avoid the institutional look," Mary said. "There's a saying here that the only way can you tell the difference between the patients and the men on the staff is that the patients don't carry keys."

"Yes, I've noticed that," said Castleton. "With all the distinctive treatment you say I'm being given, why don't I get a key?"

"Wait a few days. You'll have one."

After they finished eating, they sat drinking coffee, and Mary took out a cigarette. As Castleton made no move to light it for her, she did it herself. Castleton asked, "You say you watch for changes in a patient's behavior? What sort of changes?"

Mary exhaled slowly, then replied, "Every morning we go through the chart. Did the patient dress himself carefully this morning? Did he greet me cheerfully or at all? When I took him walking did he converse or was he silent? Does his face seem more relaxed and less vacuous? Is there stiffness in his posture? Does he smile? Does he pay attention to other patients and ask them questions? Does he express any wish to do something or go somewhere? Is he showing any desire to express his energy in ways approved by his peers: to paint something or grow something or make something or learn something?"

"To improve his condition he must pay attention and show desire?"

"Yes, that's about it," said Mary. "And the two last and most important questions on the chart are: Does the patient show any indication of optimistic expectation? If my answer to that has to be no, then I hope I can answer yes to the final question: Is the patient bravely trying to make the most of a bad situation? If I can't give that one a yes after two or three weeks of trying, I mark 'CCO' on his chart, and he's shipped off to where he receives custodial care only."

"That's pretty quick. Why do you give up so quickly?"

"There are too many other men waiting who still show a spark of hope or courage. When you pull a drowning man out of the river, you work frantically trying to revive him. But the moment you know he's dead you abandon him and look for someone else to help. Am I right?"

Mary led him from the dining room into the half-lighted canteen. Many men were sitting at tables sipping Cokes, coffee or juice, and the few women were trying to coax some of the men to join in folk dancing to records. Mary and Castleton sat down at a table and watched a group form for a square dance. "Do you like to dance?" Mary asked.

"I always have," he said. "Clinch County is the folk-dancing capital of East Tennessee, you know. I come from generations of fiddlers, banjo and guitar pickers, piano players and dancers. The TVA got interested in promoting folk dancing for its revival program, so my wife and I spent many hours doing the polka and varsoviana with our neighbors at the Community House in Norris. And of course we do regular dancing, like I did in college."

"Will you dance with me?"

"I'm not up to it now," he said quickly. It was as if he was talking about another person, she thought—about Frank Castleton, the dancer that was.

"I don't mean now. How about tomorrow evening . . . when you'll be feeling better?"

"I'll try." He sounded as if he'd said it only to please her.

When the music changed to waltzes, more men ventured onto the floor to dance. The third waltz was "The Sweetheart of Sigma Chi," and Mary noticed tears welling up in Castleton's eyes. She moved closer to him, took his hand and held it in her lap. She said softly, "I believe one dance would make us both feel better." Still holding his hand, she got up, and he didn't resist. They moved onto the floor and into the waltz.

"It's obvious you've danced all your life," she said. "You move beautifully."

"I had graceful partners and teachers like you," he said.

"La Golondrina" played next, and as Castleton felt Mary's body against his, and looked down at her head on his shoulder, he shuddered. "My God," he said to her, "it's astounding how much you remind me of another woman."

"Was she nice?"

"She was a brave and good person—Bess Foshee. A long-haired mountain woman, barely literate. When I was seventeen she taught me how to fuck, then how to make love."

"You must tell me about her . . . tomorrow."

When the music ended, a song fest began. One of the women played the piano, and the other women coaxed the men to request songs and then join in the singing. Mary, still holding Castleton's hand, sang along, but he didn't open his mouth. So again she got up and pulled him with her. "Please. You must play just one request for me," she said. The pianist gave up her seat, and Mary sat down on the bench with him. " 'The Last Time I Saw Paris.' You play and I'll sing."

They began the first phrase, and several others in the room joined in on the next. Then there were shouted requests, most of them from the women but two or three from the men, and Castleton played "I'll Get By," "Harbor Lights," "Red Sails in the Sunset," and "The White Cliffs of Dover." He played well but without spirit, for he knew that he was not playing for a celebration but for a therapy session. The women were volunteers—brave, helpful, adequate, competent. The men, himself included, were patients—frail faltering failing fuckers.

Then Mary stood up, and in a loud voice she said, "The gentleman playing for us now is Frank Castleton of Norris, Tennessee. For the next few evenings he'll be playing the piano and the cello for us. Let's quit singing now and just listen to him perform his last number." She turned to Castleton and, lowering her voice, said, "Quit being a frail fucker and play like the man you are. 'Stardust.' "

She sat down with him, and he played. It wasn't his best, but it was good. When he finished and walked out with Mary, all the women and most of the men applauded.

When he and Mary were back in his room, she felt a sense of elation about the evening. "We've had a good day, and we're going to have better ones," she told him. "Now get undressed and put on your pajamas. I'll be back soon with your medication." When she returned he was sitting on the bed, and she noted that he looked toward the door as she came in. Previously she had had to attract his attention by speaking before he acknowledged her presence. Quickly and skillfully she injected the Demerol into his arm. "Now you'll sleep," she said, "and I'll see you in the morning. Good night." She went out, and he heard the door lock behind her.

In the few minutes before he lost consciousness, Castleton went back to an afternoon in 1922, during Commencement Week at Sewanee. A twenty-year-old member of the graduating class was playing Chopin to a cultivated and knowledgeable audience. *Nocturne No. 17 in B, Op. 62, No. 1, Fantaisie in F Minor, Op. 49, Etude No. 23 in A Minor, Op. 25, No. 11, Ballade No. 3 in A-Flat, Op. 47, Waltz No. 7 in C-Sharp Minor, Op. 64, No. 2.* When the recital ended, everyone applauded, shook his hand, drank coffee, and there were predictions of a career in music for the young man. Then the old man, his teacher, passed a judgment. And now, to Castleton, the old man seemed to be standing tall as a mountain, glaring at him, pointing a long accusing finger and shouting down through the years: "Francis, as a musician you can be whatever you want to be. You have all the requirements except one: the terrible yearning to be great."

In the last seconds before the drug conquered his consciousness, Castleton screamed in anguish, "My God! My God! What right did I have not to yearn! What right did I have to neglect my talent, to fail myself and my family and wind up in a madhouse thumping out 'Harbor Lights' for faltering failures!"

In the backwoods counties of East Tennessee during the Civil War the able-bodied men between fifteen and fifty went from their cabins to join the armies, leaving their women and children to defend their food supplies against thieves. The cruelest battles, therefore, were not those fought between soldiers under Grant and Lee, but those fought by women and children against poachers. In the spring of 1865 the dearest living thing in the backwoods was a horse, a cow, a pig, or a chicken which had been hidden in a cave by a boy or his mother.

Cordell Hull's father nearly lost his life defending a mother and her children against thieves. Billy Hull was shot and left for dead. The bullet had entered his right eye and gone out the back of his head, miraculously missing his brain and spinal cord. For a year his recovery was in doubt, but he recovered, nursed by the woman he had defended, and lost only the eye. By the end of the war he had learned the name of the thief who shot him, so Billy Hull went to Kentucky to find him. The search took six weeks, and it was hard for a frail one-eyed young man, weighing a hundred and forty pounds, begging food and lodging as he traveled afoot. Billy found his man, faced him and shot him dead. Then he walked back to Tennessee, rented a ridge farm, built a log lean-to on it, went to work and eventually married. He had no money; Confederate money was used to start fires in cookstoves. He had only his body and the ability to work every day from 4 A.M. to 9 P.M. He bought a horse on credit; he fed and clothed his family by subsistence farming. He grew vegetables, fruits, grain and sorghum; corn and hay to feed cattle; hogs and chickens to feed his wife and children. He grew cotton and sheep for fiber, and he traded his excess to his neighbors for the goods he was short of. His wife spun thread from cotton and wool and made clothes, and he made shoes from cowhide, caps from coonskin. He distilled whiskey and bartered it for salt, tobacco, seed and coffee. He got U.S. dollars from the timber around him. He cut oak, walnut and cedar logs and used the creek-and-river system to raft them to Nashville. He worked and encouraged his five sons, and when he died in 1923 he left to his son Cordell, for his own use and for division among his brothers, money and property worth three hundred thousand dollars. None of that profit came by striking oil, or by stealing from Indians, or by profiteering from wars, or by ravaging the forests, or by depleting mineral resources, or by exploiting any other man's labor. He accumulated it from his own labor, and from improving land.

In order to understand the size of Billy Hull's accomplishment, one has to remember the size of the dollar between 1880 and 1920. A subsistence farmer in East Tennessee in 1880 saw $50 a year in cash. In 1910 a man swung a maul in a railroad section gang six days a week, ten hours a day, for $3.80 a week, and he raised a family on it. In 1920 the day when Henry Ford would pioneer the payment of $5 a day to a worker was still in the future. Yet Billy Hull was not a frontiersman—he lived only five hundred miles from Washington, D.C., and he was the father of the Father of the United Nations.

Billy Hull's story, with amendments, was Cop Castleton's story. When Cop returned to Clinch County after Appomattox he was riding a mule. Before he could go to work, he too had to kill a thief, who had held a gun on his mother and stolen her last milk cow. Cop did his duty, then married Lucy Polk, moved into a log cabin and went to work. He worked the same hours Billy Hull worked, subsisted in the same way. He didn't have to rent land, though, because his father had given him two hundred acres of ridge and bottom land worth a dollar an acre. Fifty U.S. dollars would buy one horse or fifty acres of good land. To get dollars for his tools, implements, salt, tobacco, seed and coffee, Cop distilled whiskey and sold it to Federal occupation troops in Knoxville.

Cop had another advantage over Billy Hull: A railroad ran through Clinch County. So Cop could load logs onto flatcars and ship them twenty miles to Knoxville. Moreover, railroads needed crossties, and Cop hewed them. These ties, hewed out of oak logs, had to be eight and a half feet long, seven inches thick and nine inches wide. A man skilled with a broadax could hew five ties a day, and the railroad paid thirty cents a tie.

Cop also arranged it with the railroad so that he would become the tie buyer in Clinch County. Every Saturday farmers hauled their ties to Clinch City and stacked them in the tie yard along a railroad siding. Cop measured them, counted them, branded them and paid for them with money advanced to him by the railroad. Every four months a work gang loaded the ties onto cars, and the railroad paid Cop a profit of 3 cents a tie. This meant that when he hewed 100 ties a year and the county's total production was 10,000 ties a year, Cop paid other farmers $2,970 and he received $330.

From 1870 until 1935, when the railroads quit buying the ties, Cop, Bert and Frank Castleton ran the business in Clinch County. Their annual profit grew from $300 in the early years to $2,000 in the middle years, then to $4,000 as the number of ties increased along with the price and profit per tie. By 1920 the railroads paid a dollar for a tie, and by then most of them were sawed from the logs at sawmills. Thus, over a period of sixty-five years the Castleton family collected about $130,000 for handling the county's production of railroad ties, and they paid the county's farmers about $1,300,000.

By 1912, when he was ten years old, Frank Castleton's Saturday job was to meet the farmers at the tie yard, inspect the ties and help stack them and give the farmers receipts which they cashed at the Clinch County National Bank, of which his father and grandfather were directors.

In addition to being a farmer and a tie hewer and buyer, Cop Castleton bought and shipped logs, particularly walnut and cedar. With the cooperation of the railroad he helped bring the first sawmills to the county; then the stave mill to make barrel staves, and the handle mill to make hammer, ax and hoe handles out of hickory. He bought excess cattle and hogs, shipped them and sold them. By 1880 he had gone in with a merchant, Phil Scott, to organize the bank which was located in Scott's store near the courthouse. This was how Cop, by 1896, when he was fifty-four years old, was able to spend the $400 a year to send his youngest son, Bert, to

Sewanee. But he could barely afford it, because for all his activities he had an annual cash income of less than $3,000. Everything he was involved in was small: The capital stock of the bank was $10,000; the mills were small; the population of the county was small; there had never been much money in the county, because there was no big money crop. The most expensive building in the county, the courthouse, had cost $9,000. The most expensive home, Phil Scott's, had cost $2,000.

By 1896 some of the subsistence farms were changing. In 1866 the farms had provided shelter, food and clothing. But by 1896 Cop Castleton's farm provided only shelter and food. He no longer grew and processed his fiber. He had moved the spinning wheel and the hand loom into the barn loft, and he and Lucy bought cloth at Phil Scott's store. Homespun and the coonskin cap were disappearing. Now hats, and even a man's Sunday suit of clothes, were bought at the store. But nobody in Clinch County wanted to get any further away from the subsistence farm. Even Phil Scott grew most of what his family ate. Obviously, the land was everything—it was a man's security against panics. And when the panics came and money disappeared, a man with land could still shelter and feed his folks, and even clothe them by raising a patch of cotton and a few sheep and bringing the spinning wheel and hand loom down from the loft. Only land and his ability to work it makes a man free.

When Bert Castleton returned from war in May, 1899, he didn't have the problems his father had faced. Thieves hadn't pillaged his home, money was sound, food and draft animals were plentiful and Bert had had two years at Sewanee and five months in Cuba. Otherwise he wasn't much different from his father in 1866. He was a farmer, so he knew how to run a plow and castrate a pig and breed his mares, cows and sows. He married Phil Scott's daughter Lila, who was a high-school graduate, and they moved into a frame house seven miles from the courthouse and went to work. Lila Scott Castleton didn't know how to spin and weave, but she knew how to cook and sew, how to milk a cow and care for the milk, and how to grow pigs and calves and chickens and vegetables. Not until 1907 did Bert and Lila and their three children move into a new nine-room house only two miles from the courthouse. That house too was a farmhouse, and they still grew most of what they ate. But Bert spent less time farming, because his father needed him more to look after their interests in the bank, the mills and the log, cattle and crosstie buying and selling. The county's total population had grown to twelve thousand. The bank had its own building near the courthouse, its capital stock had grown to $25,000, and the three controlling stockholders were Cop Castleton, Bert Castleton and Lila Scott Castleton.

In 1922, when Frank Castleton returned home from Sewanee, he wasn't much different from his grandfather in 1866 or his father in 1899. He had a college education, but he wasn't a professional man—he was still a farmer, although he read books and magazines and was a musician (he could play the church organ), and he drew and painted pictures. And he did his own work. He didn't hire and oversee labor. He knew how to plow and cultivate, how to plant and harvest, how to milk a cow, how to castrate a pig and how to breed cows, mares and sows. He also knew how to cut timber, how to scale logs, how to buy crossties, and how to approve or disapprove bank loans. In 1925, when he married Diane Jemison, they moved into a farmhouse he had begun building. The house was unusual and expensive, but it was a farmhouse. Diane Jemison didn't know how to spin or weave, or how to milk a cow, or how to grow chickens or vegetables, but she had a college degree in Home Economics and she knew how to cook and sew and launder and make a farm home. Three additional responsibilities had recently been assumed by Cop and Bert Castleton. They controlled the sale of Standard Oil products, of Ford cars and trucks and of Coca-Cola in Clinch County. But their return was still small from each of their activities, because they had associates and there still wasn't much money in a backwoods county.

By 1932 Frank Castleton was thirty, Bert Castleton was fifty-four and Cop Castleton was ninety. No man was their enemy, and in all of Clinch County there wasn't a man that one of them couldn't call by name. Cop's father had had three brothers and a sister born in the county, Cop had had six brothers and two sisters, Cop had three sons and two daughters other than Bert, and Frank had two sisters. When all the Castleton children and grandchildren and great-grandchildren were counted (not even including the ones who had gone to Texas), along with all the families like the Polks and Scotts which were connected by marriage, a fourth of the people in Clinch County in 1932 claimed kin with the Castletons. They were all doing fine, even though the rest of the United States was suffering a depression. Everybody in Clinch County had quit spending money, gone without new clothes, and grown more food; every able man was sheltering and feeding his family. In cities from New York to San Francisco, unemployed men stood in bread lines. Banks everywhere else were failing, but the Clinch County National Bank was sound. Its capital stock had grown to $100,000 and its controlling stockholders were Bert Castleton, Lila Scott Castleton, Frank Castleton and Diane Jemison Castleton.

T HE morning of Friday, April 30, 1948, Castleton was beginning his third day in the hospital. He looked and felt better. He had shaved carefully with a locked razor, and had actually thought about what he was going to wear before dressing in a long-sleeved Burgundy sport shirt and blue slacks. He greeted Mary cheerfully and conversed with her as they walked along corridors and rode down the elevator to Dr. Palkin's office. The psychiatrist had decided to do some probing about Castleton's family, and was pleased to see that he talked easily of his grandparents and parents and their way of life in Clinch County.

"Tell me about Cop Castleton's other three sons," said the doctor. "They don't appear to have been given their father's affection to the extent that your father was."

"Actually, I think the point was that my father's brothers were born too early," replied Castleton. "They were born, let me see, in 1866, 1868 and the third one came along in 1869, so they were born dirt poor. The Federal military occupation of the South didn't end until 1876, and even then it wasn't until 1884 that my grandparents pushed above the poverty level. By then my uncles were well into their teens, and, of course, they were poorly educated. Of necessity my grandfather had been hard on them, so they got away from him as soon as they could. One of them went to Texas; the other two moved onto their own land in Clinch County. My father wasn't born until 1878, two years after the occupation ended. By 1884 there was opportunity for him to go to elementary, then to high school, and luckily by 1896 there was money for him to go to Sewanee. By 1899 he was in a position to marry Phil Scott's daughter, the best-situated young woman in the county. So you see, he was fortunate in being born late. The way I look at it, *when* a man is born determines the course of his life as much as *where* he's born. My father became his father's business partner, and my grandfather lived his last years in my father's house."

"It seems you had everything going for you. You were the only son of your grandfather's favorite son. That made you your grandfather's favorite grandson, as well as the godson of Cordell Hull."

"I was fortunate in many ways," said Castleton. "My other grandfather, Phil Scott—he was a good man. And my mother, Lila. Before I was three

94

years old she was teaching me to read, sing, dance, love and play the piano. She drilled into me that my life was important and must not be wasted . . . that I had been brought into this world for the sublime purpose of *being*, not of *having* . . . that I must educate and cultivate myself so I could be an effective helper of my family, my community, my nation . . . an effective helper of all mankind. She became the first woman member of the Clinch County School Board. She did most of our cooking, sewing and cleaning, but she found time to enjoy life to its fullest. Well, you met her at my home—you could see. She's sixty-seven now, and you know, she still rides and dances and plays the piano and works for better lives for all children."

Dr. Palkin poured a glass of water and brought it to Castleton. "Now let's start examining what caused you anxiety in that simple way of life. What was the worm in your apple? What threatened the self-esteem that your mother tried to give you?"

Castleton replied promptly. "Being considered white trash and a redneck when I went to Sewanee."

"That was when you were fourteen?"

"Yes. It hurt my father when he went to Sewanee even more than it did me. He got into many fist fights over it. My fights may have been fewer, but they were bitter ones. You've got to understand the conflict between the Appalachian South and the Cotton South—between white men and women who worked their own fields and cooked their own food and washed their own clothing, and white men and women who used Negroes to do it for them. As in many Tennessee counties, there were no Negroes in Clinch County. Cordell Hull never saw one until he was thirteen and rode a log raft into Nashville. Neither my father nor I had ever seen one except in Knoxville, nor ever eaten a meal cooked by a Negro or worn a shirt washed by a Negro woman, when we first entered Sewanee Military Academy."

Castleton had become tense. His shoulders were tight, and his hands gripped the arms of his chair. "Try to relax," said the doctor. "Rest until you feel like going on."

Castleton breathed deeply and flexed his fingers several times before moistening his lips. He spoke now in a more subdued voice. "In 1860 Episcopal ministers in the Cotton South preached that slavery was divinely ordained. But damn it if Episcopal ministers in the Appalachian South didn't preach just the opposite—that slavery was evil and must be abolished. White men who worked in the fields in the Cotton South in 1860 were called rednecks and white trash by the slave owners, and, of course, that's why the South lost the Civil War. Most of the officers in the Confederate Army were slaveholders, but in the ranks nine out of ten men came from redneck and white-trash families. The same army, same cause, and these men didn't speak the same language. That's why so many Southern white men joined the Union Army, and why the Confederate Army had the highest desertion rate of any Anglo-Saxon army that ever took the field. Slavery divided the Confederate Army, not only the nation."

"Cop Castleton was a loyal Confederate, wasn't he?"

"He was a more loyal Confederate veteran than Confederate soldier. Two of his brothers joined the Union Army, and he thought about going with them, because, after all, he hated slaveholders. But, still and all, he joined the Confederates. He never deserted, but he sympathized with deserters, because he hated his officers. Oh, but in later life he became a rebel-yelling Confederate veteran. Do you know, in 1936 that old man told President Roosevelt how he had fought at Chickamauga for a *cause we loved.* At ninety-four he too had become a romantic."

"Sewanee was the Cotton South?"

"Largely, yes," said Castleton. "In 1896 and in 1916 all but a few of the students were sons of families which were served by Negroes. Now, I don't mean that all these boys were from wealthy families; many of their families were not as well off as the Castletons. But they came from areas of the South where a Negro cook cost three dollars a week and a Negro handyman was paid a quarter and his lunch for a day's work. At Sewanee there was a colony of such Negroes who served the Domain—that's the whole Episcopal establishment, the faculty, the retired bishops, the military school, the university and the theology school. The students who took Negro servants for granted regarded my father as inferior. They didn't invite him to join a fraternity, because naturally they didn't think he represented 'the best of the Old South.' And this was at a time when he already felt inferior over not being promptly admitted to the university because Clinch County High School hadn't adequately prepared him. He had to attend the military school for a year before he could become a college freshman, and the man just never did very well. The Spanish-American War was his out—it let him leave college honorably when he was failing his courses. Oh, he knew he would have had to leave college anyway at the end of his freshman year, because he just didn't have the background, he couldn't have made it. I learned all this when I got to Sewanee, and he knows that I know it, but we've never mentioned it to each other."

"Then your father sent you to Sewanee to do what he couldn't do when he was there? He wanted you to prove that the rednecked Castletons were as good as any cotton-country family with Negro servants? That's an anxiety-producing situation, isn't it?"

"Yes, it is."

"Did you succeed in doing what he wanted you to do?"

"I'd say . . . I'd say only partially," said Castleton. "I succeeded as a student because of what my mother had taught me. I was valedictorian and cadet major of the military school's Class of 1918. That earned me a fraternity bid when I entered the university that fall. But my refusing to play football hurt me, since football for the Class of '22 was a religion at the university. For a student with athletic ability to refuse to play was cowardice. I had athletic ability, but I wanted to turn it to something else —to run in the Boston marathon, not to score touchdowns for the Purple Tigers. So I was called a yellow redneck at more than one drinking party, and I had to fight. Since I was also valedictorian of my college class, I suppose I proved that the Castletons are as intelligent as 'the best of the Old South.' But the girl I was going to marry didn't want to live in Clinch County because we had no Negro servants."

"You mean Carole Curtis? Oh, I know about her because your wife mentioned her to me. Did you and Carole quarrel?"

"We never really quarreled," said Castleton. "Not bitterly. We loved each other, but we had differences. What couple doesn't? I visited her home in Chattanooga, and she came to Clinch County several times. We compared our parents and our homes—well, that's natural, I guess. I mean, you *do* that. My parents had more money and property than her parents. We drove Fords and they drove Chevrolets. Our homes were about equal. We both had electricity and indoor plumbing. But our home was a farmhouse, and their home was on a city street near a country club. And in their back yard was a shack housing a Negro woman who did their cooking and cleaning, and a Negro man who was their handyman."

"And those Negroes made all the difference in the world?"

"They made a very big difference," conceded Castleton sadly. "Since she loved me, Carole was willing to live in the backwoods without servants. Had she lived, we would have been married." Tears began rolling down his cheeks, and his lips began to quiver. "Her death all but crushed the life out of me. After her funeral I spent a week in the mountains alone, weeping, often crying out bitterly, doubting that I could go on without her. But over the years I've sometimes wondered how we would have got along had she lived. She was ambitious for me; she wanted me to strive for distinction as a painter or as a musician. She would have kept trying to persuade me to leave Clinch County for Paris or New York. She would have hated having to work like a Negro, and she would have resented every hour and every dollar I spent working for the dream of TVA."

"That in fact was your experience with Diane Jemison, wasn't it?"

"Yes. And for Diane I did what I shouldn't have done: I brought the first Negroes into the county. That was a mistake. Damn it, that hurt the Castletons. It angered many of our depositors and customers. And the Negroes were lonely."

"Was white domestic help available in the county?"

"Yes," said Castleton, "and I wanted Diane to hire some of those people. But it's hard to explain—whites in the county who are reduced to working in other people's homes have lost their pride, so, it's true, they're just *not* as efficient or as dependable as good Negroes. Diane tried out and rejected a dozen white workers, insisted on Negroes, and in time I gave in. She got them."

"The Tennessee River doesn't flow through the Cotton South, does it? Not past any plantations like the Mississippi, or the Savannah?"

"No," said Castleton. "The Tennessee serves the Appalachian South. I see what you're getting at. TVA was an effort to revive the land as a rewarding way of life for small farmers who did their own work. That's why I worked so hard for TVA, and why I admired Senator Norris so much for his long effort to create it. When the big utilities tried to defeat him for reelection, I would have spent the Castletons' last dollar to help him. By God, that was crucial to me—to the whole country, too. And because President Roosevelt supported TVA, I did whatever he asked me to do as long as he lived."

"Our time is up for today," said the doctor. "From now on we'll devote most of our time together to your problems with the two Presidents, all right, so we can begin to work on that tomorrow." He nodded to Mary, who had come in when she saw the buzzer light on her telephone extension, indicating the end of a session.

"There are several more books I want you to study," the doctor continued. "Mary will get them for you. How about a game of golf on Sunday afternoon? I plan to play golf with two other doctors. Would you care to join us?"

"Yes, I'd like to, that's fine," said Castleton. "Could I . . . I'd like one more minute to tell you about a new problem I have. Until I panicked and was brought here this week, all my despair stemmed from my failure with Truman. We were talking about my creative side before, and of course I regretted not giving more time to painting and music, but that didn't really upset me, because I rationalized that my work for TVA and world peace had been more important than developing my individual talents. But last night while I was trying to fall asleep, I began thinking about what had been expected of me, and what I might have done in music, and I began suffering intensely. Only the narcotic saved me from hysteria."

"That's natural. You'll have to expect that for a while," said the doctor. "Your suffering is worst because it stems from not just one fear but an accumulation of fears—that's what anxiety is all about. Once a man's ego is overwhelmed by anxiety, and equilibrium is lost, and he succumbs to hysteria, all his mechanisms of ego defense begin to fail. He loses all ability to rationalize and avoid feelings of guilt, so he lies helpless and often hysterical under the punishing blows of his superego. I know all this jargon isn't much comfort personally, but you're an intelligent, rational man, so I want to share the professional explanation with you. You'll feel much better as we discuss your disappointments and help you come to terms with them. As you regain your equilibrium, you won't need the narcotics any more. Now, you and Mary have a good day. I'll see you tomorrow morning."

THAT morning, Diane Castleton was having breakfast alone in her suite at the Shoreham, glancing over a pile of newspaper clippings on the table as she picked at her meal and smoked a cigarette. Since her arrival on Wednesday, the hotel had been delivering to her not only the morning and afternoon Washington papers but also the papers from Chicago, Cleveland, Detroit, Baltimore, Philadelphia, New York and Boston. She had cut from these papers all the reports on the Castleton case, although until this morning she hadn't been able to bring herself to read them through.

Not until this week had Frank Castleton ever been a newsworthy person. Until the day when he was seized by the government, his name had never appeared in a newspaper outside of Tennessee. The sole exception was in the spring of 1925, when he ran in the Boston marathon. The Boston papers listed him among the ninety-four starters in the race and among the forty-seven finishers. He finished twenty-fourth, and he had achieved his goal: He had run the twenty-six miles from Hopkinton, Massachusetts, to the finish line in Boston in two hours, fifty-eight minutes, and thirty-two seconds. Not one in a hundred marathon runners trains in the hope of ever winning a race. The running is ritualistic. The typical runner endures all the lonely training hoping only that he can finish the race in less than three hours and not have to drop out. The completion of the run will be victory to him, but most everyone else will consider it defeat. Now, when Frank was forty-six, and headline material because he was a threat to national security, a reporter had retold the story of his Boston marathon, and had published the photograph of him crossing the finish line.

Diane adjusted her glasses and examined the photo again: young Frank at the finish line in downtown Boston, in his track suit, tall, lithe, long-striding, exultant. That was Frank only five weeks before she met him in the mountains on the magic June day, and memories of that day flashed across her mind. What spoiled the newspaper story for her was that it went on to point out the "strange" fact that, twenty-three years after his Boston marathon, Castleton had succumbed to hysteria in the company of two Indians while preparing to run the marathon distance in the Great Smoky Mountains. The effect of the story was to make Castleton look like a "strange" man who had been allowed privileged knowledge of the bomb secrets only because the sick and senile President Roosevelt had made another serious mistake.

Much of the reporting was in this vein, and Stumpy McDowell had telephoned Diane to say that Jack Hardwick was feeding columnists and reporters material to make Frank look "queer." Stumpy cited columns by Westbrook Pegler, Hedda Hopper and George Sokolsky as cases in point. Pegler had ridiculed Frank as "a star-gazing consulter of gurus who had gone batty while sitting on a mountaintop with two Indian medicine men." Miss Hopper had revealed the "long close friendship between Castleton and Henry Wallace, who consults gurus and watches the skies for omens." Sokolsky called Frank "an obviously unstable man who should never have been placed in a position where he could endanger the nation."

From FBI files another reporter had learned of Frank's "bizarre behavior" on the night in 1942 when he was "halted and questioned by police when he was seen running and crying along Connecticut Avenue." The implication of the story was that police regarded the assistant to the Secretary of State as *queer*—meaning that they thought he was a sexual deviate of some sort, probably homosexual.

In the Marquis Childs's column, however, Frank was described as "a sensitive man, a musician and a painter, who had watched the development of the bomb and inspected the wasteland at Hiroshima, and who then developed a *guilt complex* which overthrew his mind." Fellow members of the Evaluation Team which had been sent to Hiroshima had been found, and they remembered that he had "wept openly" at what he saw. Other reporters supported the theory of the guilt complex, and Frank's parents seemed to support it. His mother had been photographed in her riding habit, standing beside her horse, in front of "Frank Castleton's palatial home." She was quoted as saying, "My son is a good man who worries about the condition of the earth and the suffering of people."

"But, Mrs. Castleton," she was asked, "if he was a good man who worried about suffering people, why did he favor dropping the bomb on Hiroshima for *maximum effect?*"

"He'll explain that to you after he leaves the hospital," she said.

Frank's "millionaire father" was photographed standing in front of the bank. "Frank's trouble is that he takes things too much to heart," he said. "But he'll recover and be all right again."

Diane smiled at the clipping about Secretary of Agriculture Henry Wallace, even though it, too, was damaging to Frank. She remembered when Wallace and his Iowa-born wife visited her home in the pre-war days when Tennessee Valley land was being restored and the Secretary, who was an agricultural scientist, was developing corn hybrids. He used to travel up and down the valley with Frank—both of them so loved the land! Now, in 1948, Wallace was running for President, and was blaming the United States for the Cold War with Russia. It was said that Communists were running his campaign. A reporter had asked him to comment on the Castleton case. "Frank Castleton is my friend," Wallace was quoted as saying. "I know him well; I've traveled with him. My wife and I have spent nights in his home and enjoyed evenings of conversation with him and his wife. He's a fine man, a patriot, and Truman ought to release him and leave him alone."

How kind of the former Vice-President to try to help Frank, thought Diane. And how damaging!

Another reporter had learned that the House Un-American Activities Committee had files on both Castleton and his college roommate, lifetime friend and spiritual counselor, the Reverend Joseph Bramwell, of Alexandria, Virginia. The files revealed that Castleton had helped known Communists obtain government employment, and that Bramwell, who had conducted religious services in the White House, had raised money for the Scottsboro Defense Fund and for a pro-Red school in the Tennessee mountains.

The worst revelation was that Castleton had been at Yalta. By 1948 Yalta, in the public mind, had come to mean "sellout." Yalta was the shameful place where a senile Roosevelt had been induced by his pro-Communist advisers to sell out to Stalin, to sell out Poland and China, to sell out the Atlantic Charter, to sell out all the aims for which so many gallant Americans had fought and died. And now the world would know that one of those pinko advisers responsible for the sellout was a Tennessean named Frank Castleton.

One reporter called Diane "an attractive and spirited defender of her husband." A wire service story said she was "a former Miss Tennessee in the Miss America contest," but this was an exaggeration—she had entered the Tennessee competition, but was not the winner. There was a layout of four candid photos of her face, taken as she replied to questions at the hospital. Luckily, she looked attractive in all of them. But the quotes which ran under the photos had been taken out of context and were harmful to Frank: "my husband is deeply sympathetic with the Russian people," "he is an expressionist painter, and our visitors find his paintings puzzling, even frightening," "he thinks the Russians already have the bomb secrets," "he often roams in the mountains alone."

Susan and Cord were reported to have come to Washington "to pull for their dad to recover," but photos showed them to be enjoying a holiday, untouched by their father's tragedy. Susan was giggling over a champagne glass at the Colony Restaurant, and Cord was grinning as he received an autographed baseball from Joe DiMaggio.

Frank's only defenders among the reporters were Stumpy McDowell and Tris Coffin. Each day in his column McDowell explained and denounced the "smear campaign" against Castleton, and insisted that "he must be freed from prison and from the straitjacket of Executive Privilege so he can tell a Congressional committee and the people of the United States how Truman has mishandled the bomb and bomb policy." Coffin daily reported statements of Senators and Congressmen who said that Castleton was not a pinko or a kook or a security risk, and that he had not been a party to the sellout at Yalta. "I've known him and respected him for fifteen years," said Senator Arthur Vandenburg, of Michigan. "I don't share all his views, but he has been a capable and conscientious servant of Norris, Hull, Roosevelt and Truman."

Taken as a whole, the press reports seemed to be a horrifying indictment. They implied that life as Frank had lived it for forty-six years was at an end. How could he ever again find privacy and peace, or even freedom?

At Paul Blanton's home the previous evening, Diane had noticed that each of the other nine guests, as well as Paul and his wife, assumed that she was looking for a new husband. At the table, while the diners listened to Paul, or to Monsignor Fulton J. Sheen, or to Senator Lynnwood Costigan, the men as well as the women glanced at her frequently, appraising her chances of finding a new mate. Her dinner partner, Senator Costigan, fifty-five, whose wife had died in 1947, had been invited, apparently, as a "possible."

Blanton admitted this to her when they had a moment together in the patio. "Everybody in Washington reads the papers, Diane," he said. "Everybody knows that Frank is no longer a satisfactory husband for a woman with your looks and money. Everybody assumes that you'll make a change pretty soon. You and Lynn Costigan would be good for each other."

"This isn't the time for that," she said. "I'm interested only in trying to help Frank. Next week, after the doctor gives us the diagnosis and prognosis, I'll expect your help in doing whatever should be done. I can't think about other men now, Paul. It's kind of you, but no thanks."

"You know you can depend on me," he said.

Several statements at the party bothered Diane. Monsignor Sheen was Blanton's political instructor. He selected books on Marxism-Leninism for Paul's edification. When the subject at the table was the Cold War, the monsignor nodded when Paul said, "The cornerstone of any plan which undertakes to rid the world of the curse of war must be the armed might of the United States." And when the subject was Palestine, everyone nodded when Paul said, "In an election year the President must extend prompt recognition to Israel . . . but the armed might of the United States must have oil which Arabs control . . . so we must never allow the Jews to poison our relations with Arabs."

Diane knew that had Frank been sitting at that table he wouldn't have nodded to those remarks. He would have challenged Blanton and Sheen with statements like "Converting America into another Rome will be digging America's grave," and "We must support Israel as a matter of principle, and let the Arabs drink their oil if they don't want to sell it to us."

Diane walked to a window in her hotel bedroom and stood looking out over the green magnificence of Rock Creek Park. For two years she had found some comfort in believing that even though Frank was becoming a fanatic, at least he was a fanatic who was right in what he believed. Now she had to rethink that. Surely a man who was as good and as intelligent as Fulton J. Sheen was not entirely wrong. Why shouldn't the United

States maintain the mightiest military machine on earth? And why should a little state like Israel ever be allowed to become a millstone around the neck of a mighty nation like the United States? Diane sighed and became aware that a telephone in the next room had been ringing for some time. As she picked up the receiver, she had a sinking feeling that everyone else had been right—that Frank was now that most ridiculous of human beings, a fanatic who is wrong.

The call was from an editor of *Time*, asking if and when she would show him Frank's paintings, particularly his *Hiroshima*. This call was followed by one from an art dealer in New York who wanted to examine the paintings for a possible public showing. Diane told both the editor and the dealer that she would discuss their requests with her husband over the weekend, and give them an answer on Monday.

A few minutes later the telephone rang again, and Stumpy McDowell said, "Hi, sweetie. I see you broke bread with the Papists last evening. God, you must have been bored!"

"Not really," said Diane. "It was a nice party."

"I'll bet! Well, tonight you can let your hair down with the heretics at my place. We'll chew tobacco, spit on the floor and make irreverent remarks about popes, bishops, monsignors, and that peerless Knight Templar, Paul Blanton."

"I'm looking forward to it." She smiled to herself. Talking to Stumpy was like doing a few rounds with a prizefighter.

"Good," Stumpy said. "Now hear this! Mrs. Davies quit counting her Post Toastie millions this morning long enough to call me and insist that I bring you to the garden party at Tregaron on Sunday. You'll receive her telegram shortly. Doesn't that tickle your ribs?"

"I'm giggling already," said Diane.

"Then you run out and squander a wad of Castleton war profits on new duds. I want you to outshine the local wenches and frumps."

"For you, Stumpy, I'll try," she said.

"You try hard. See you tonight, Sweetie."

Diane began dressing to go shopping. She felt much better.

JOE Bramwell was a troubled man as he faced Dr. Palkin in his office. "The past two days have been a nightmare for me," he said. "Public disclosure that I once contributed to what are now considered Communist causes may cost me my parish. And I have been horrified by the cruel attack on Frank."

"I'm upset by all that too," said the doctor. "Last Tuesday evening when I raised the security question with you, and specified Scottsboro and the mountain school, I was trying to warn you that the FBI had information on you, and that you should anticipate seeing it in print."

"How did you know that the FBI knew?"

"Psychological profiles on his close associates, including you, are in Castleton's security file. On the airplane last Tuesday I was shown your profile, since you were expected to be waiting at the hospital to see Castleton. Those contributions, of course, are noted in the papers on you."

Bramwell dropped his shoulders and sighed. "God, this nightmare gets blacker by the moment! The government profiles *me* because Frank has a security clearance! Then, when the government feels threatened by Frank, derogatory information on me is published to degrade him!"

"It's the nature of our present environment, I'm afraid."

"It's madness," said Bramwell. "Malicious madness! I suppose there is no way now for me to help Frank? You can't even allow me to talk with him?"

"Your situation may not be as bad as it looks today," said the doctor. "I don't believe you'll lose your parish. And as long as I'm present during the conversation, I can allow anyone I choose to talk with Castleton. So here and now I'm inviting you to assist me in treating him."

"You mean . . . you and I together?"

"Why not? You know Frank better than I can ever know him. You know as well as I do that much of his trouble comes from his unrestrained belief in the capacities of man. And on one point a Christian minister and a Jewish Freudian psychiatrist are in complete agreement—on the limitations of man and his institutions."

Joe Bramwell felt easier; he sensed the warmth in the man opposite him. "I see what you mean. Ever since he was fourteen I've tried to get Frank to tone down his expectations."

"Well, that's all we can do for Frank now," said the doctor. "I'll listen to his account of his disappointments, and you and I will try to help him come to terms with them. I've assigned him three textbooks, and we can discuss them with him: *Civilization and Its Discontents, Moral Man and Immoral Society* and *The Holy Bible.*"

"That's a good treatment plan," said Bramwell, smiling. "I'll come here as often as you and Frank want me."

"Fine. Now that we're partners, give me a few answers that may help me, all right? Is Frank Castleton a religious man?"

Joe Bramwell replied promptly. "Only in the sense that he respects life's mysteries. He is a professing Christian and a practicing Christian, but he is not a believing Christian."

"If he doesn't believe, why does he profess and practice?"

"Because he considers life barren without ritual. He values religious ceremony as a sustainer of individual life."

"Has he ever told you that he only professes, that he doesn't believe?"

"He'd never tell anyone that," said Bramwell. "He wouldn't risk disturbing his family. He credits Christianity with contributing to the United States the essential idea of individual worth. Of the men he most admires . . . Wilson, Roosevelt, Hull, Norris . . . all were Christians. Roosevelt and Hull were Episcopalians; Wilson was a Presbyterian; Norris was reared in one of the strict old German sects."

"Were those men believers? Or only professors?"

Bramwell reflected, then answered, "I never knew President Wilson or Senator Norris. Wilson's biographers say he was a believer; he read his Bible every day and prayed on his knees. I knew Secretary Hull. He was a believer. I knew President Roosevelt. During the war years I conducted a number of White House services. I noted how fervently the President sang the hymns and recited the Creed. He was always proud of being a Senior Warden of the church. He was a believer."

Dr. Palkin then asked, "If Wilson, Hull, Norris and Roosevelt could believe and Castleton cannot, why does Castleton admire them so much? A man usually admires men with whom he shares belief."

"Oh, but there *was* a shared belief," said Bramwell. "A passionately shared belief. Those four men shared Frank's belief in man. They believed that men can rationally remake the world. It was in that belief that Frank was their disciple. Roosevelt's proudest accomplishment was TVA, which successfully remade part of the world. During the war Frank believed that Hull and Roosevelt were taking steps which would lead to the successful remaking of all the world."

With his right hand Dr. Palkin rubbed his neck. "You say that since he was fourteen you've urged Frank to restrain his expectations. What was there in his experience which made him expect so much?"

"Simplicity and success," said Bramwell. "Life in Clinch County was simple. Everybody was the same kind of folks, and most everybody could subsist on the land. The society was successful, and in it the Castletons were a successful family."

"And his experience at Sewanee was simple and successful?"

"Yes. We call Sewanee 'Arcadia,' and as freshmen we must learn to recite the dictionary definition of 'Arcadia': 'A mountainous and picturesque district of Greece, celebrated as the abode of a simple, pastoral people, dwelling in rural happiness. Hence, figuratively, any region or scene of simple pleasure, rustic innocence, and untroubled quiet.' Students come to Sewanee from the owning dioceses, and there are no Negroes, no Jews, no Catholics. The student body is governed by the Order of the Gownsmen, the upperclassmen with the highest grades and the best manners. It's a simple isolated community of scholars, and Frank was successful there."

"But not without a struggle?"

"That's right," said Bramwell. "The few little churches in Appalachia are the poor relations in the Episcopal Church. They can't send many boys to Sewanee. The few boys who do come are Spartans among Athenians, rustics among better-prepared boys from the plantations and cities of the Cotton South. Frank was an exception. He was a graceful Spartan, a rustic who was a painter and a musician instead of a football player. He had to fight, sure, but he succeeded by being talented and friendly."

"And TVA? Was it simple too?"

"Relatively," said Bramwell. "It helped homogenous people in a relatively small and rural area. Frank fought for that idea for ten years, sacrificed for it, then saw it succeed. So when he was forty years old, in 1942, he'd known only success, and he thought the world was simpler than it is. He had had no personal experience with conflicting religions, races and ideologies. He thought that Roosevelt could do for the world what he'd done for the Tennessee Valley, you see."

"An interesting analysis," said the doctor. "One more question. You knew Carole Curtis before her death in 1922, and you've known Diane since 1925. How do the two women compare?"

Joe Bramwell hesitated, then said, "Diane compares favorably with Carole. They were both pretty . . . Diane still is, of course. Carole was taller than Diane, more willowy, more reserved, perhaps more demanding, and she had golden hair. I remember how gracefully she and Frank danced together at Sewanee. I always thought, 'What a handsome couple.' Well, now, Diane is earthier, more sensuous, better educated than Carole was, I'd say. And I'd guess that Diane has made Frank a better wife than Carole would have. Diane complained, but she stuck with him during the tough early years—Carole would have complained more, and she might not have stuck."

The two men stood up. "You've been helpful, thanks," said Dr. Palkin. "Give me a few days to hear Frank's story, then I'll arrange some three-cornered discussions for us. Meanwhile, don't worry about your Un-American activities."

"Thank you, Doctor," said Bramwell. "I'll wait for your call."

T HAT afternoon after they had played tennis, Frank Castleton and Mary Sullivan sat on a bench under big trees, drinking Cokes from paper cups. There was a light, comfortable breeze in the air. "Tell me about Bess Foshee," Mary said. Frank looked up into the trees, then down at the ground, as he focused on a bright memory. When he turned to Mary and began talking, he was on Sewanee Mountain on an April afternoon in 1919.

A cove is a deep recess or small valley in the side of a mountain. There are many of them in the mountains north of Sewanee Mountain, and the people who live in the inhabited ones are ignorant and deprived, the descendants of English and Scotch-Irish settlers who mated with Indians. The privileged young Episcopalians who attend school at Sewanee and call themselves "Arcadians" look down on these people and call them Cove-ites. The only contact between the Cove-ites and the Arcadians is commercial: The Cove-ites have sold moonshine whiskey, in gallon jugs and quart-size Mason fruit jars, to generations of Arcadians. But not sex, as a rule. That's a commodity they don't peddle. The Cove-ite girls marry at fourteen or fifteen, and after they bear four or five children they are faded and worn. Most of them had pellagra in 1919 from undernourishment, and the lesions from the disease are really awful to look at or feel. And these people are proud: A Cove-ite woman won't lie with any man who she thinks looks down on her.

There's nothing unusual about groups of Arcadians or even a lone Arcadian walking or running through a cove. Lots of boys at Sewanee go hiking around there. But unless they want to buy whiskey, they never call at a Cove-ite shack. On the April afternoon in 1919, Frank Castleton was running alone. He was wearing a sweat suit, and the weather was warmer than he had anticipated. After he had run five miles he felt thirsty and began looking for a spring. Pure chance led him to the spring near Bess Foshee's shack, which was far back in the cove against the mountain. Frank called out, "Is anybody home?", wanting to ask permission to drink from the spring. Two children, a boy about four and a girl about three, came to the door, followed by their mother.

IN THE HOURS OF NIGHT

Bess Foshee had several distinctions among Cove-ite women. At nineteen, she had had only two children instead of the usual four or five, and she was better-nourished, because the United States of America had been sending her forty dollars a month for two years. Her husband had fought in France, and been gassed, and was in an Army hospital in Kentucky. Forty dollars was a considerable amount of cash in the Tennessee coves in 1919: A mother could save herself and two children from pellagra with it. So Bess didn't look worn and faded. She still had good teeth, and her long hair was healthy and shining. She was one of the black-haired and black-eyed Scotch-Irish, and perhaps one-fourth Cherokee. Instead of being shrunken and bony, with her breasts beginning to sag, as so many of her contemporaries were, she was full-bosomed and full-bodied. In a red gingham dress, her hair in braids, her legs bare, and in moccasins that were almost new, she didn't look like any ordinary Cove-ite. She nodded at Frank's request for water, and he said, "Thank you, ma'am." He went to the spring, stretched full length on the ground and drank.

When Frank stood up, he was surprised to see the children and the woman standing near him. "That's fine water," he said, smiling, "and this must be the hottest day we've had this year." The woman and children said nothing, which didn't surprise him, because the Cove-ites were usually sullen and silent in the presence of the Sewanee students. In his friendliest manner he said, "That's a mighty pretty little girl and a fine boy. I wish I had something to give them." He was about to thank the woman again and leave when she said, "Yuh wanna set? Yuh want coffee'n'shine?" This puzzled him, because no Cove-ite ever offered hospitality to an Arcadian. He was curious and answered, "Yes, thank you, ma'am, if it's not too much trouble."

She told the children to go to "mam-maw's"—Frank assumed this was to their grandmother's—then led Frank into the two-room shack, where he sat at the table in a cane-bottomed chair. She threw some bark into the cookstove, put the coffee on, then came and stood near him but did not sit down. He was wondering why she had sent the children away and what she wanted from him. At last she said, "Ah wanna larn muh little younguns some'pin." Frank nodded, and after another interval she asked, "Is there readin' books fer little younguns at Swawny?"

Now Frank understood the hospitality: She wanted books to help her children learn to read, and she wanted him to help get them. "Yes, we have them," he said. "There's a nursery school at Sewanee for the children of faculty members . . . the teachers. And there are books at the supply store."

Again there was silence as she considered what to say next. Then she said, "Yuh come this way reg'lar? Ah could give yuh money and yuh could fetch me some'pin?"

"Sure I could," he said. "I run twice a week, and I often come in this direction. I could bring you, well, whatever you like."

The coffee was boiling, and she brought him a mug of it along with a half-filled quart jar of moonshine. He poured a little whiskey into the coffee and tasted it. "That's good," he said. "Thank you, ma'am." Again she stood near him but didn't sit. It was evident that she was trying hard to express herself, and that this was difficult for her.

"Ah ain't got much larnin'," she said. "Ah can read a little 'n' write muh name. Bess . . . Bess Foshee."

"My name's Frank," he said. "Frank Castleton. I'll be glad to pick out the two or three best books and bring them to you."

"Ah'll be obliged," she said. "How much money?"

"Oh, nothing now," he said. "Wait till I bring them. In fact, I'd like to give the books to your children."

She reacted as though she had been struck. "Naw!" she snapped. Her black eyes flashed angrily. "Naw! Yuh give muh little younguns nothin'! *Ah* give to 'em, not *yuh!* Yuh fetch books 'n' Ah pay yuh 'n' *Ah* give to muh little younguns!"

"All right," said Frank. "I'm sorry. I didn't mean to offend you. But, please, I offered only because there's no reason to pay for the books. You see, every Saturday evening the students at Sewanee visit the homes of the teachers. We call it 'open house.' I have teachers whose children are now in elementary school. They've outgrown their nursery and kindergarten books, and their parents are glad to give the books to any mother who needs them for her children. You can buy new books if you insist, but, honestly, we're all just glad to give you the books and anything else you need to help teach your children."

Bess Foshee wasn't prepared for such friendliness. While she was thinking of something to say, Frank stood up. "Just wait till I come back again, then we'll talk. I'll bring the books next Sunday about mid-afternoon, if that's all right, since I usually run on Sunday afternoon. And thank you again for the water, the coffee and the whiskey."

During the following week Frank gave little thought to Bess Foshee. But by the next Sunday, which happened to be Easter, he had assembled a variety of teaching aids for three- and four-year-olds: alphabet blocks, numbered blocks, coloring pencils and books, sticks of modeling clay, tablets and lead pencils, and several books, ranging from one-syllable-word books like *See Jack Run* to three books for the mother to read to the children: *Chicken Little, Goldilocks,* and *The Three Billy Goats Gruff.* Most everything had been given to him, and he had bought the rest for ninety-five cents. He didn't wear his sweat suit, and he didn't run. He wore his hiking boots, khaki cotton pants, a cotton pullover, and he hiked the five miles to the cove, enjoying all the color and new life in the woods. He guessed that Bess's husband probably worked in a coal mine up toward Tracy City and that he'd be with her and the children for Easter Sunday. Frank planned to deliver the materials, perhaps instruct the children briefly in how to begin using them, and accept ninety-five cents from Bess if she insisted on paying him.

But he found Bess alone in the thoroughly scrubbed shack. She was prettily dressed. Her hair, unbraided, hung down her back and was held in place at her neck by a red ribbon. She wore a yellow blouse and blue skirt and black silk stockings and black slippers. She had the coffee'n'shine ready, along with a pan of hot chestnuts. But she was tense and unsmiling. She felt certain that Frank looked down on her, so having to reveal her ignorance and poverty to him was painful. She nodded awkwardly as he entered the shack and watched him set the box on the table and open it. "If you'll call the children," he said, "I'll explain to them how to begin using the colors and the clay."

She shook her head. "Yuh show me," she said. "Ah'll show muh little younguns."

Now Frank understood why, at their first meeting, she had sent the children away before she asked him about the books, and why she had sent them away today before he arrived. She didn't want her children to think of him as a provider or teacher. She wanted him to equip her to teach them so they'd be able to look up to her. "All right," he said, "sit down here beside me."

Uneasily she sat at the table beside him. He opened a tablet and picked up the colored pencils. "Man is the only one of God's creatures who can draw pictures. For a child to be educated, he must be invited to imagine and then to express his imagination by drawing pictures. So you must encourage your children to draw. Don't ever tell them what to draw—just give them these colors and sheets of white paper and encourage them to go ahead. They'll draw pictures of anything and everything—of you and their father and themselves and each other and your house and animals and trees and the sun and moon and sky. Don't ever laugh at what they draw. Ask them to explain their drawings to you, and you tell them how interesting they are. If they draw a cow and color her green, don't tell them that there are no green cows, because there *are* green cows in imagination. Encourage them every day to face the blank sheet of paper and create. Now you and I'll make two drawings. First I'll draw you, then you'll draw me."

He began drawing rapidly, and she leaned over to watch. "When I draw a young woman," he said, "I observe her carefully to see how she looks, while I try to guess how she thinks and feels. And I try to show her character as well as her looks." He talked as he worked, his eyes darting from the paper to her, then back to the paper. "Now, this young woman is Bess Foshee. No other person in the whole world is exactly like her. Bess is unique and individual. She has an oval face with long black hair that she parts in the middle. Her eyes are large and black . . . a slightly turned-up nose . . . full red lips . . . a rounded chin. She has a red ribbon in her hair, her blouse is yellow and high-necked, and . . . let's see . . . how old is Bess?"

"Ah'm nineteen," she said.

"Bess is nineteen years old," said Frank. "She lives in a house against a mountain with her two children and her husband . . ."

"Muh man's in the hawspital in Kaintucky," she said. "He got gassed across the wah-ter. Ma 'n' Pa 'n' muh other kin . . . they live down the cove aways."

"So there we have Bess Foshee!" said Frank. He tore the sheet from the tablet and presented it to her. She stared at it in wonder and delight. For the first time she smiled. She let him hold it while she got up and walked away from it, viewing it from different distances and angles. "Am Ah that purty?" she asked.

"You sure are," said Frank. "Now you draw me."

She didn't believe she could, but she wanted to try. "Look closely at my face," he said. "I'm easier to draw than you are. I had to use curves to draw you, but you can draw me with straight lines. See? My face isn't oval, so you can start by drawing two up-and-down lines slanting in. Then a little curve for my head and a straight horizontal line for my crew cut. My hair is short and sandy and stands up and isn't parted. My eyes are smaller than yours, and they're blue. My nose is straight and doesn't turn up. My lips are a little thinner than yours. My chin is sharper, so you can draw it with almost straight lines."

"How old are yuh?" she asked.

"I'm seventeen," he said, "and I'm a runner and a farmer and a student, and I live in the mountains just like you do. So I'm tall and wiry and masculine, and you're middle-sized and full-bodied and feminine."

When she finished her drawing she was more pleased with it than with his drawing of her. Her black eyes sparkled as she compared the two drawings. She brought the coffee and moonshine and hot chestnuts, and this time she brought a mug for herself and sat close to him while he showed her how to use the clay. "The human hand is a miracle," he said. "It can grow food and build shelter and fight battles and soothe and comfort and create great beauty. You must encourage your children to mold little animals."

As they examined the books he told her that she must be very dramatic when she read and told the stories, that she must act out the stories with the children, and that she must teach them to sing songs. They got down on the hooked rug on the floor to build an alphabet pyramid with the blocks. By then she had decided that he didn't look down on her and that she wanted more help from him in teaching her children. She wanted him to come back, and she knew only one way to keep him coming back. As they arranged the blocks into one-syllable words, they drank more coffee and moonshine and ate more hot chestnuts; and they moved closer and closer together, touching and rubbing until she was leaning against him and his arm was supporting her. Then, easily and naturally, she kissed him, first on the throat, then on the lips. "Yuh got a girl?" she asked.

"Well, uh . . . yes," he said, "but . . ."

"Yuh mean yuh ain't had none yit," Bess said, smiling.

"I shouldn't admit it," he said, "but it's true."

"Yuh're just about t'git some," she said. "Ah'm gonna give yuh yuh first."

Frank was never able to reconstruct in his mind exactly what happened during the next two or three minutes. His previous experience with erections and ejaculations had been confined to wet dreams, masturbation, and the times he dry-fucked girls who would allow their blouses to be opened, although he'd never met one who would take her pants off. Now as Bess opened his trousers he felt a wild desire he had never felt before; in a flash he had a vision of young bulls breaking down a fence to get to a heifer. Then somehow Bess's skirt was above her hips, and in a series of sinuous motions she was under him, he was inside her, and he ejaculated. He lay silent and still, holding her, feeling embarrassed about having lasted no longer. That the connection had been made so easily surprised him. He had seen young bulls mount heifers and thrust wildly, unable to make connection until helped by a human hand. He guessed that Bess had so helped him. Then she wriggled free of him, and he was lying on his back, and she was looking down on him, smiling warmly.

"Yuh ain't through yit," she said. "Yuh jist got started. Take yuh boots 'n' yuh pants off."

They had reversed roles: Now she was the teacher. He obeyed, and when he turned back to her she was naked except for her long hair and her black stockings, which were held above her knees by tight rolls. While he lay on his back she exposed his chest by pushing up his pullover, put her breasts against him, fastened her mouth to his and held his cock in her hand. When she slid slowly down his body and took his cock in her mouth, he felt the wild desire again and began thrusting. She looked up and said, "Jist lay still 'n' let me suck it slow 'n' easy." He thought she meant sucking with her mouth, but she mounted him, resting on her knees on either side of him, took his cock back into her cunt and slowly began to manipulate her muscles. She could suck even stronger with her cunt than she could with her mouth. When he couldn't help thrusting toward her she said, "Lay still 'n' yuh can hold it till ah git'ta Jesus. Jist look at me 'n' lemme milk yuh slow." He looked at her, and she was blooming. Her face glowed, then began to contort. She gasped, "Uh, uh," then "Je-sus, Je-*sus*," and when Frank began ejaculating in response to her orgasmic spasms, she wiggled and writhed and put her hands to her face to muffle her gasps of "Je-*sus*! Sweet Je-*sus*!"

They lay exhausted together for several minutes, then drank more hot coffee and moonshine. When they lay back down together on the rug, she gave him a third erection. And this time she put him on top, between her legs until the connection was made; then she showed him how to put his legs outside hers so that she could hold her thighs together. She smiled up at him, kissed him and said, "Now show me yuh're a man! Fuck me hard 'n' deep, like a good man fucks his woman!"

The action lasted much longer this time. The floor creaked, the cabin shook and the "Sweet Jesus" was even more ecstatic. When it was over and Frank was dressed, Bess said, "Now yuh're a man. Will yuh be comin' back?"

Frank grinned at her. "You know goddamn well I will! Next Sunday afternoon." When he left the shack the sun was coming down, and he had to walk faster than he felt like walking to keep darkness from catching him in the woods.

MARY Sullivan had listened to this story almost without interruption. Now she asked, "How long did you keep going . . . *running* . . . back?"

"I went back most every Sunday, except during vacations, for the next three years," said Castleton. "Her husband couldn't come home more than twice a year, and he couldn't stay more than a week at a time. He had to have oxygen and hospital care to stay alive. So for three years Bess Foshee was my woman."

"Did you fall in love with her?"

"No, it wasn't love," said Castleton. "Sometimes, at first, I'd get irritated with her, since she was so obviously using me and paying me with pussy. I'd walk or run out to the shack, thinking only of fucking, with my cock hard as a rock, and when I got there she was fully dressed, and she'd make me spend an hour or more helping her read new books, or sing or dance, or paint more pictures, before she'd undress and go to bed. Then, gradually, I came to enjoy teaching her, and dancing, singing with her. She became the best educated Cove-ite woman in Tennessee, and her children became the best-prepared Cove-ites ever to enter the first grade in that county. I became fond of her—she mattered to me, she had the power to affect me—but I wasn't in love with her, or she with me."

"Did you tell anybody about her?"

"Only my father. I had to tell him about her, because I wanted to give her money. That was one day when we were in a boat on the Clinch River, fishing."

"WELL, son," said Bert, "you've finished your freshman year at the university. So I suppose you've started frigging?"

"Yes, I have," said Frank.

"In Chattanooga on Saturday nights?"

"No. I stay away from those whores." Then Frank told his father about Bess, and concluded, "I was with her every Sunday afternoon from Easter until I came home. When school starts again I'm going to see her regularly. I may go to see her once or twice this summer. Dad, listen. I've given her thirty dollars, and I'd like you to let me give her twenty-five dollars a month from now on."

"Goddamn, son," said Bert, "that's a dangerous situation. If her husband comes home unexpectedly from that hospital and finds you on his nest, Tennessee law gives him the right to shoot you dead. Him being a war veteran makes it look worse, and him being a disabled veteran . . . goddamn, that makes it look awful!"

"I know it does," said Frank. "But I've done it, and I don't intend to stop."

"Look at the position it puts me in," Bert said. "I go up with a delegation and welcome Sergeant York home, and us Rotarians give him a farm for killing Germans, while at the same time my boy runs into the wife of another hero who's killed Germans and he starts frigging her. That looks awful!"

"I don't think I'm doing anything wrong," said Frank. "And you don't either."

"Well," said Bert, "let's see. There may be other ways to look at it. After all, I guess it's pretty unlikely for her husband to catch you with her. Nobody can ever get within a mile of a cove without every Cove-ite knowing he's coming. And her folks got to know what she's doing. When she sends her kids down to their shack on Sunday afternoon, they know she's rustling the bed sheets. You're not fooling anybody in that cove. Where pussy and whiskey are concerned, Cove-ites are smart. Every time her husband approaches that cove, she'll get plenty of warning. But, Frank, what about babies? If you want to give her twenty-five a month now, how much'll you think you ought to give her after she's had a baby by you? I don't suppose you're using anything to keep from knocking her up?"

"She says I don't need to use anything . . . that I'm not doing it often enough to knock her up."

Bert Castleton's laughter rolled up and down the Clinch River. "Bullshit!" he roared. "You know better'n that. You know that one good pop by the bull is enough to put a calf in most heifers. It can be the same with a woman. But now, you say, her youngest child is three years old?"

"Yes, sir."

"Well," said Bert, "if she's gone that long without getting pregnant again, maybe she can't. Maybe something happened—like the clap—that fouled her up. Maybe she caught a dose and got over it but it left her where she can't conceive. She'd never admit that to you, but maybe that's why she tells you not to worry. And, I suppose, well, even if you knock her up, well, we can help her with it. As for her husband—I guess that poor bastard lying up there in the hospital figures that *some* neighbor is tending his garden for him. If it wasn't you it'd be somebody else. In fact, she may have a couple of other good men helping you look after her. Sunday's not the only day in the week, you know."

"No," said Frank, "I'm the only one. She's ambitious for herself and her children. This woman wouldn't give it to just any man. She's giving it to me because I can help her better herself."

116

"Can't you go see her some other afternoon besides Sunday?" asked Bert. "Somehow that makes it worse—you rushing out of Chapel and running through the woods to hop on a poor disabled veteran's wife. Can't you make it on a weekday?"

"No, Dad, I can't," said Frank. "Sunday is the only day I can go regularly."

Bert Castleton didn't like the situation, but he could see some advantages in it. Frank wasn't chasing whores in the city, and he'd be less likely to knock up some girl in Clinch County or one who came to the dances at Sewanee. Twenty-five dollars a month was a lot of money, but . . . well, all pussy has a price tag on it, and some other situation might be even more expensive.

Mary Sullivan asked, "Why were you so confident that your father would give you the twenty-five dollars a month for Bess?"

"Because he knew I knew about his woman," said Castleton, smiling. "Sometime I'll tell you about Miss Edna."

"Yes, of course. I want to hear about her," said Mary. "But go back a bit. Did you give money to Bess as long as you saw her?"

"Yes, I did," said Castleton. "And three months after I met her, the government raised her allowance to sixty dollars a month. Her total of eighty-five dollars was a lot of money in a Tennessee cove in those days. In June, 1922, when I told Bess good-bye, I gave her two thousand dollars in cash. A year later her husband died and the government paid her ten thousand and gave her a pension. She moved to Tracy City and married a coal miner, and she's living comfortably there today. My father must have guessed right: She never got pregnant again. Every Christmas, by registered mail, she receives a plain envelope with five one-hundred-dollar bills in it. She knows where it comes from, and she writes to me now and then."

"Bess and your relationship is a very significant part of your case history, Frank," said Mary. "Dr. Palkin will be very interested in it. Oh, by the way, he told me about Carole Curtis. When you began courting Carole, preparing to marry her, weren't you still seeing Bess?"

"Sure I was," said Castleton. "Carole would come to the dances on Thursday, and for three days and evenings I'd dance with her, picnic with her, stroll with her, and pet her and dry-fuck her until my nuts ached. After she left on Sunday, I ran to see Bess."

117

"All those Sunday-afternoon jaunts of yours—weren't your fraternity brothers curious as to where you went?"

Castleton grinned. "That's when I began building my reputation as a mystic. I told them I had to be alone in the woods to reflect. Oh, they didn't all think I was a saint. During my senior year Stumpy McDowell tried to follow me several times, but I threw him off. He did guess the right cove, though, and he went there and asked around. He even found out Bess's name and went over to get the truth out of her. Neither Bess nor anyone else ever confirmed anything to him. But he spread the word that I wasn't really communing with God and Nature . . . only getting Cove-ite tail. Stumpy hasn't changed any in twenty-five years." Castleton shook his head. "He's spent his life disproving claims of innocence."

"Well, to come back to Carole," said Mary. "After you became engaged to her, did you and she start . . . frigging?"

"Yes, but not often," said Castleton. "She was in school at Decatur, Georgia, and I was at Sewanee. But I went to see her a few times in Decatur, and in Chattanooga, and she came to Clinch County. There were no motels then, of course, so we had only back seats and blankets in the woods."

"And she was only the second woman you had had?"

"That's right," said Castleton. "I know what you are getting at. All I'll say is that I loved Carole and would have married her. She was a wonderful girl, so my giving her her first sexual experience, was a moving experience. But . . ."

"But you weren't as hot for her as you were for Bess. She lacked Bess's talents to arouse and satisfy you. Well, all right—go on—after you finished college, and Carole was killed, and you paid off Bess and went back to Clinch County, what did you do?"

"Oh, hell, you know what I did," said Castleton. "I tried out one woman after another, trying to find another Bess Foshee."

"And you couldn't find one?"

"Not for more than two years," said Castleton. "Then I got lucky. On a June day in 1925, in the Smoky Mountains, the Good Lord delivered to me a radiant young woman who was a preacher's daughter and had a college degree, and who could do everything for me that Bess could. I fucked her, but I learned I could love her as well, and I married her. And I've never regretted it."

118

W<small>HEN</small> Mary Sullivan went to her apartment to bathe and dress for dinner, she found that another report from Castleton's security file had been received by Dr. Palkin, who had sent a copy over to her. As she soaked in the bathtub, she read:

Frank Castleton, like his lecherous old daddy before him, is a moral degenerate.

Since he holds a Q-clearance in atomic energy, the security agencies have been obliged to observe his sexual conduct since 1942. Because his children were in school in Norris, Tennessee, he never moved his family to Washington. During the weeks he spent at Oak Ridge Laboratory he of course stayed at home. His wife sometimes came to Washington for weekends with him. But he spent many weeks alone, both in Washington and New Mexico. During his weeks in Washington he sometimes attended social functions as Hull's representative; but the place he most often visited, for long lunches or long convivial evenings, was the Georgetown home of Keith McDowell, the news columnist, who is a moral leper. McDowell is also a Southerner, and he is a bachelor, a cynic, a satyr and an old Sewanee classmate of Castleton's. McDowell's home is where a restless wife may go on the afternoon she doesn't play bridge or consult her psychiatrist, or on the evening her husband is out of town. Castleton partook of such bounty, and some of the sex acts were both unnatural and illegal.

Castleton also played David to a Bathsheba in New Mexico. On one of his visits to the weapons laboratory at Los Alamos he met a woman whose husband was an Army officer in the ETO. Thereafter she spent nights with him in the La Fonda Hotel in Santa Fe; and on the night her husband gave his life at St. Lo she was cuddled in a sleeping bag with Castleton in the Jemez Mountains!

His profile shows that Castleton began his sexual career at Sewanee when he was seventeen. He avoided the football, basketball and baseball weekends in Chattanooga and Nashville hotels where his college mates learned the facts of life. Instead he had a mountain woman who lived in the woods about five miles from the campus, and he visited her on Sunday afternoons. And here's what makes that arrangement so despicable. That poor woman was the wife of a World War I veteran who, having been gassed in the Argonne, had to spend the rest of his life in Army hospitals.

So, even to those of us who are not psychiatrists, Castleton's despair at age forty-six becomes understandable. He carries an uncommonly heavy load of guilt. He wants to think of himself as an idealist who believed in both World Wars. Yet he avoided battles and enriched himself while lifting the skirts of the wives of heroes who gave their lungs and lives.

That evening in the cafeteria, then in the canteen, Mary noted with professional satisfaction that Castleton was beginning to show more interest in things that were happening around him, and in her as well. This meant he was regaining equilibrium. Unbalanced men, of course, are completely absorbed in themselves and their own problems.

But now Castleton wanted to know about her and her background. In answer to his question she said, "I came out of a bad situation. A small town in Georgia. A father who was a barber who couldn't put bread on the table for his wife and three daughters, so he often had to go out and get drunk. Four females against one weak man—some life." She gave a short laugh. "I had to be careful to avoid being raped by some Negro, and to avoid being knocked up by some white boy before I could finish high school. Well, it wasn't easy. In that situation life can be hard for a fifteen-year-old girl, you can imagine. How does she persuade a boy to take her to the high-school banquet without having to give him a chance to knock her up? Nursing was my only hope to better myself. So I worked like a dog, studied, prayed, starved and kept my legs crossed, determined not to make the mistake my mother had made, and get entangled with a man who'd pull me down."

"Didn't you ever fall in love?"

"I couldn't afford to."

"Then I suppose most of your sexual partners have been married men?"

"They *are* kinder . . . especially the older ones. A younger unmarried man may feel that he's doing you a favor. That hurts."

During the dancing Castleton danced a polka, then a waltz with Mary, and at her insistence he danced foxtrots with two of the volunteer women. When the dancing ended he was asked to play a cello which had been brought by one of the volunteers. She also offered to accompany him on the piano.

"Do you really want cello music here?" he asked. "As a solo instrument the cello makes many people feel sad, you know. Here the need is for gaiety, isn't it?"

"Not entirely," said the pianist. "The need here is for affective music. Why don't you try?"

Unconvinced, doubting that he could affect this audience, Castleton began playing "The Old Refrain." As he played he searched the vacuous faces of the other patients. The attention was good; the applause was fair.

So he played "Deep River," "Shenandoah," and "The World Is Waiting for the Sunrise." He began to see tears welling up in the eyes of several of the men; the attention was perfect; the applause was vigorous.

"You're affecting them," the pianist said to him. "So give them something great. The 'Intermezzo.'" So Castleton, doing his best, played the "Intermezzo" from *Cavalleria Rusticana*. As he played he looked into Mary Sullivan's eyes, and they were shining with tears. When he finished, the crowd came to its feet, shouting as well as applauding. He stood up with the pianist, a gray-haired soft-featured woman well past forty. He bowed to her, then hugged her, and she kissed him on the cheek, saying, "You have heart. It's a privilege to play with you."

He went upstairs with Mary, where, as usual, she told him to undress while she went for his medication. When she returned he was in his pajamas, lying on his back on the bed, and she sat down by him and injected the Demerol into the vein of his right arm. As she pulled out the needle and rubbed the puncture with alcohol, they both noted a substantial erection beneath his pajamas.

"This new symptom," said Castleton gravely, "how will you report it on the chart?"

Sternly professional, Mary replied, "As compelling evidence that the patient is showing a desire to express his energy in a way generally approved by his peers."

"Can you suggest a therapy?"

"I'll discuss it with the doctor," she said. "If the symptom persists, we'll try to relieve it."

With a flirtatious smile she walked out, and the door locked behind her.

May Day, 1948, was on Saturday. The front page of the *Washington Post* reported: ARAB, JEWISH FORCES BATTLE FOR HOLY CITY; RUSSIANS WILL BRANDISH NEW ARMS IN MAY DAY PARADE; "Air Force Secretary Stuart Symington warns that time is running short if we are to have a 70-group Air Force by the time the Russians have the A-bomb"; "Justice David Pine criticizes the defense for wasting time in the Dalton Trumbo trial"; "Citation and Coaltown will today run for the roses before 100,000 racing fans"; and "At a meeting of the Federation of American Scientists, Clifford Durr, member of the Federal Communications Commission, warned that scientists in government employment are functioning in an atmosphere of corrosive fear." Smaller stories near the bottom of the page reported that "100,000 people will today come out in the sunshine to attend the 21st annual Shenandoah Apple Blossom Festival in northwest Virginia," and that Castleton's condition was said to be improving.

122

IN THE HOURS OF NIGHT

At the hospital, Dr. Palkin and his patient, both of them born in 1902, began discussing Castleton's reactions to the major political events in his life; and they began with the Russian Revolution.

The fourteen days of February 27 to March 12, 1917, were regarded by Woodrow Wilson, Cordell Hull, George Norris, Franklin Roosevelt and cadet Frank Castleton as days of hope for the human race. For during those days the Russian people, while resisting a German invasion, discarded their absolutist government. The old pre-revolutionary Duma carried on, rapidly expelling the rightist members, until only socialists and other leftists remained. Meanwhile, a new group arose—the Soviets—which shared power with the Duma (renamed Provisional Government), and the latter was gradually taken over by Communists. Said *The Times* of London, "This is now Europe's springtime: Russia is free!"

On March 22, 1917, the United States recognized the new government, and began rushing food and arms to it. President Wilson told Congress, "The great generous Russian people have been added in all their majesty to the forces fighting for freedom, justice and peace in the world."

"Wilson made that speech a few days before my fifteenth birthday," Castleton said to the doctor. "There had been a heavy snow at Sewanee. But the battalion was turned out, and we stood at Parade Rest in the snow, flags flying, while the Cadet Major read us portions of the President's speech. We heard how Russian soldiers, starving and without ammunition, when informed of Russia's freedom had attacked the German lines with stones and rifle butts. The battalion cheered."

But the Russian republic had two enemies—Communists inside and Germans outside—and these enemies supported each other. The Communist leader, Vladimir Ilyich Lenin, was in Switzerland, directing Communist propaganda against the Allied war effort. The Germans returned him to Russia so he could organize a revolt against the Russian republic. One of his first actions in Petrograd was to send a "people's" demonstration against the American and all other bourgeois embassies. Seven months later the Communists captured Petrograd and proclaimed a dictatorship. They burned the old Czarist constitution and murdered members of Kerensky's Provisional Government. Then, with their secret German financiers, they signed the Brest-Litovsk peace treaty, withdrawing Russia from the war and releasing German armies to fight France, Britain and the United States.

123

Thus the Communist regime came to power in Russia hating the United States and being hated in return by our government and most of the American people. During the 1920s the regime continued to murder its opponents and suppress their rights. Trying to eradicate religion, the Communists converted churches into warehouses. That the United States should recognize such a regime and thereby assist its enslavement of the Russian people was out of the question.

But after the Depression began, a movement toward recognition gained support. The Communist Party of America claimed one hundred thousand Americans, although they did exaggerate. Other Americans who would not actually join the Party still sympathized with Communism. Some conceded that only by murder and confiscation could Russia be developed into a modern nation. Others said that recognition would help relieve the Depression by opening "a vast new market on the steppes" for American manufacturers. Still others hoped that recognition might influence Stalin and push him toward becoming a counterweight to Hitler. Then the argument was advanced that recognition need not imply approval. The Communist regime was loathsome but it was a fact, so why not give it de facto recognition, exchange ambassadors with it, try to trade with it, in the hope that in time it would begin granting measures of freedom to its subjects?

Franklin Roosevelt was elected President in 1932 on a platform containing a promise to recognize the Soviet Union. And on November 17, 1933, President Roosevelt announced the recognition agreement.

"I was disappointed," said Castleton. "Mr. Hull wrote me that he had supported recognition because he felt that if he could continue to talk with Litvinov and Stalin he could do some good. I replied that I was sorry he and the President hadn't been able to get something for the Russian people in the deal. I remember how I ended that letter—it was something like: 'What depresses me most about our recognizing Stalin, Captain, is that from this day forward we Americans will be assisting a Communist regime in Russia while our Russian heroes will be the liberty-seeking men and women who defy that regime and who either are crushed by it or manage to escape from it. This, I believe you must agree, is a melancholy prospect.'"

"Then Hull had nothing but disappointments with Stalin until 1941," said the doctor. "But here's what we want to get at, Frank. We're not looking for Hull's disappointments, but for yours. During a man's life he collects disappointments, you might say, and he can feel good only by coming to terms with them. A disappointment can become a fear, and a learned fear is a phobia. In the years from 1933 to 1941, did you begin to fear Communist Russia, and, if so, do you think that fear became a phobia?"

"No, I'm sure," said Castleton. "I didn't think about Communist Russia very often. Those were happy years for me. And I'd say I despised Communist Russia rather than feared it. I despised it as an injustice to the Russian people, but I didn't consider it a threat to the United States."

"You discussed Communism frequently?"

"Domestic Communism, yes. Well, of course, people who opposed TVA called it Communism, and I defended TVA against those charges. How absurd! In every county where we organized a co-op to purchase power distribution lines from a privately owned utility, I maintained before the Rotary Club that the process was not Communism or even creeping social- ism. I insisted that TVA, instead of threatening private enterprise, was safeguarding it. I said that we who supported TVA were the effective anti-Communists because we were relieving depression, on which Commu- nism thrives."

"But there *were* Communists in TVA?"

"A few, yes."

"And you didn't despise them?"

"No. I was sympathetic with Americans who had turned to Commu- nism during the Depression. Those who were in TVA made the task of defending TVA more difficult, certainly. But I didn't think they endan- gered the United States."

"Are you a Rotarian?"

"Yes. My father's a charter member of Rotary in Clinch County, as a matter of fact."

"Then there must have been times when you wondered if you might be wrong in supporting TVA, yes? When you feared that your opponents might be right, and that in supporting a collectivist enterprise you might be contributing to the loss of freedom in America?"

"That's interesting—I asked Senator Norris those questions," said Cas- tleton. "He said that in the United States what we must safeguard is political and intellectual freedom, not economic freedom. That's what I believe. To preserve political and intellectual freedom, I'm willing to re- strict the power trust, the fertilizer trust—all the other trusts."

"So let's go back a minute. You were a Rotarian and a New Dealer; a despiser of Communists in Russia and a sympathizer with Communists in the United States?"

"Yes—that's approximately correct."

Dr. Palkin got up and poured two glasses of water. "Pause whenever you feel tired or agitated," he said, handing one of the glasses to Castleton. "All right, let's move to June, 1941. That was when you began staying in Washington, working at the State Department. On June 22, 1941, Hitler invaded Russia. How did you react? Did you hope Hitler would destroy the Communist regime you had despised since 1917? Or did you want Stalin to win? Senator Truman reacted by saying, 'Now that the two scorpions are in the same bottle, let's help them sting one another to death,' if I remember correctly. Was that your reaction?"

"No—no, I didn't feel the same way," said Castleton. "Hitler's war machine had to be destroyed, but Britain couldn't do it. And the United States was determined not to try to. You know, our college youth had massed at the White House and ridiculed the President's appeal that they join in opposing Hitler. So the Red Army was the only hope to destroy Hitler."

"You wanted us to help Stalin?"

"By all means," said Castleton. "Congress had passed the Lend-Lease Act, empowering the President to send war materiel to any nation fighting Hitler. So I wanted us to start a flood of tanks, planes, trucks and guns flowing to Russia."

"You thought the Russians could win?"

"Mr. Hull thought they could. General Marshall advised him that the Red Army would collapse in eight weeks, but Mr. Hull didn't believe it. He thought the Russians might retreat a thousand miles but they'd hold. And that's what I thought. That evening I telephoned my family in Tennessee, and we were all elated. Then I went over to Stumpy McDowell's home. What a night that was—a party of men and women drinking toasts to the great generous Russian people and celebrating until two A.M."

"And five months later," asked the doctor, "on Pearl Harbor day, did you celebrate again?"

"Yes, I did," said Castleton, and as he talked, the day came back to him in vivid detail. On Sunday, December 7, 1941, he was enjoying brunch at Stumpy's house with fifty other guests.

STUMPY McDowell's house was 20 percent a home and 80 percent a place of business, as his tax returns showed. The Filipino couple, who were his permanent domestics, like his three secretaries and three leg men, were employees of the syndicate which distributed his column. His Sunday brunches, as well as his two or three dinner parties and his lunches during the week, were business occasions, so the huge annual cost of the food, the drink and the platoons of extra servants was paid by the syndicate. Tax auditors granted the legitimacy of this business expense, for the purpose of the entertaining was to produce material for the column and for Stumpy's Sunday-evening radio broadcast.

Each of Stumpy's columns or broadcasts was constructed according to his successful formula: one part attack, one part revelation, one part exposure, one part commendation. The attack was usually on an organization, a company or a movement. The revelations were exclusive news items and predictions of future developments. Then came Stumpy's specialty: the exposure of one individual's cupidity, stupidity, venality or immorality. This was the process which Stumpy enjoyed describing as "turning some bastard's ass up to the stars" or "giving some son of a bitch a barbed-wire enema." Most of Stumpy's targets were elected or appointed public officials or officers in the military, and the information for giving it to them was leaked to Stumpy by their bureaucratic underlings. In his commendations Stumpy plugged the books, films, radio programs or other endeavors of publicized people who assisted him by coming to his parties and making them colorful newsworthy entertaining and impressive.

The fifty guests at a typical Sunday brunch fell roughly into three categories: 1) thirty-five unknown bureaucrats, some with spouses, who were being rewarded for leaking or set up to leak, 2) five lone attractive women, usually separated or divorced, who kept their ears open for Stumpy at other people's parties, and 3) ten publicized people who had something to promote and who were willing to entertain and impress Stumpy's leakers in return for his plugs.

"I was in the first category—no special privileges accorded old friends or classmates," said Castleton ruefully. "I was another bureaucratic underling expected, sooner or later, to leak. I listened to the celebrities, and sometimes, when Diane wasn't with me, I

127

played Chopin waltzes in the music room for the women who had tired of all the pontificating in the salon."

On Pearl Harbor day the guests in the third category were Wendell Willkie, who after being defeated for President in 1940 had turned one-worlder, and who was leaving on a trip around the world to preach one-worldism and write a book; Gloria Swanson; Adolphe Menjou and Gabriel Heatter; Major Alexander P. De Seversky, a Russian-born airplane designer whose book *Victory Through Air Power* was a bestseller; a burly defector from the Russian spy system, Victor Kravchenko, whose book *I Chose Freedom* was selling well; Raymond Clapper, a columnist; a shy reporter named Ernie Pyle, who drifted around the country writing about local characters and who was now turning to the New Army; and Lawrence E. Spivak, who owned *The American Mercury*, published Ellery Queen mystery books and would soon own a radio show called *Meet the Press*.

Presiding over the salon with zest, wit and calculation was Stumpy. Since two of his guests were Russian-born, he rose to the occasion, wearing black Russian boots, baggy beige pants with matching tunic and a red sash. As he circulated, urging more consumption of Bloody Marys, vodka and aquavit, with smoked fish, corned-beef hash and eggs benedict, his bull neck, bear hugs and belly laughs made him seem all the more Russian. Kravchenko grinned and called him "Marshal Stumpy Zhukov."

The talk was about the war in Washington; the bitter conflict between the Interventionists and the Isolationists; the Americans, led by the sick and crippled President, who were determined to take the country into war by lies, by covert maneuver, and by ignoring Congress and the Constitution; and the America Firsters, led by the Hearst-McCormick press and Senator Wheeler, who were determined to keep America out of war. The gossip was about the Princess Martha, the handsome woman Hitler had run out of Norway, who was now in favor at the White House, and Harry Hopkins, the frail widely-hated former social worker whose halitosis apparently didn't bother the President, for Hopkins lived in the White House and he and the President made decisions together in their bathrobes.

Willkie was explaining how he would convert Stalin to one-worldism when he met him, and Seversky was showing how, even if the Red Army folded, Hitler could be defeated by American bombers. Kravchenko was revealing new terrors of the Lubianka. The door to the kitchen swung open, and Tomas, the Filipino butler, rushed in and whispered to Stumpy what was coming over the radio. Stumpy made immediately for the large radio in the salon and switched it on, and its volume halted all conversation.

". . . Japanese planes are bombing Pearl Harbor!"

The party was dumbfounded: "Can't be true" . . . "Orson Welles again" . . . "The Japs couldn't be that stupid" . . . "We couldn't be that lucky." The three telephone lines into the house were commandeered by Stumpy, Ray Clapper and Gabriel Heatter, but all they could get were busy signals. So some of the men began leaving for offices, but none of the women wanted to go. They were afraid of being left alone—they wanted to stay together and try to feel that they were part of the apocalyptic drama.

"WHAT did *you* do?" asked Dr. Palkin.

"I did what I was supposed to do," said Castleton. "I ran out of Stumpy's house and persuaded a passing motorist to take me to my office. Congressmen were being called by constituents for information about their kin at Pearl Harbor or Hickam Field. But all lines were jammed to the War or Navy Departments or the White House. Of course, Congressmen lose votes when they can't get information for constituents. The State Department lines were jammed too, but I got the telephone company to fix four of them so they could be used only for outgoing calls. With three women helping me, I began calling Congressmen and giving them the information we had. At seven P.M. I went with Mr. Hull to the White House, where we were briefed on damage and casualties. This was secret information, but back at my office I worked out something for a release which would convey most of it to a Congressman, and during the next four hours we informed the entire House and Senate. So for nine frantic hours after the attack began, the State Department was the only one in organized shape sufficient to serve the interests of Congress."

"And I suspect Mr. Hull was pleased about that, yes?"

"Of course," said Castleton. "Particularly since I had made a special effort to help the Isolationist Senators and Congressmen. He was determined to avoid Wilson's error of not cultivating Congress in 1917–18 so that at the end of this war he and the President could take the United States into a world organization powerful enough to end international war and arms races. At midnight I rode with Mr. Hull to his home. I remember he was very tired and still angry at the Japanese diplomats who had been in his office when the attack began. I was tired too, but I was too excited

129

to sleep, so I had the government car drop me off at Stumpy's house."

"Was the party still going?" asked the doctor.

"Well, it was mostly a new gang," said Castleton, "though several of the brunch guests were still there. Most of the guests were Interventionist newspaper or radio folks, and they were celebrating the victory of the Interventionists over the Isolationists. Everybody knew by then that war would be declared next day—that Japanese stupidity had won the war for American Interventionists. Stumpy was telephoning some of the better-known Isolationists, taunting them and letting them listen to the noisy celebration at his home. The Isolationists were replying bitterly, and Stumpy, that perverse guy, had set up an amplifier on his telephone so that the whole party could enjoy these bitter replies. I remember how Cissy Patterson, publisher of The Washington *Times-Herald*, railed at the celebrants: 'You shameless war lovers! You gravediggers of America! You heartless ghouls, celebrating while good Americans lie dead at Pearl Harbor! Why don't you telephone the mothers of those dead men and let them hear your drunken laughter! You baited the Japs until they had to attack! Now the blood is on your heads!' "

"Did you laugh or cry?"

"I certainly didn't laugh." Castleton shook his head and sighed. "I felt ashamed at having welcomed the news that Pearl Harbor was being attacked, at having felt joyful over an event which was tragic for two thousand families. I wanted the United States in the war, but I didn't enjoy taunting Isolationists. So I decided to leave the party."

Castleton lowered his eyes as he returned to his memory of that midnight at Stumpy's.

ALICIA Mayfield, a slim hazel-eyed blonde in her late thirties, stopped him at the door. "I'm leaving, too, Frank. I can drop you at the Shoreham."

He nodded briefly, and they walked together along the street to her car. He scarcely knew her. He had been sitting by her, listening to Kravchenko, when the flash came. After she started the car he asked, "Have you been at Stumpy's since noon?"

"Yes," she said. "For the last twelve hours I've done nothing but drink and eat and listen and feel scared. I have an eighteen-year-old son at Princeton."

"You've got to try not to worry."

"Oh, Jesus, I should have gone home long ago." She looked at him despairingly. "My mother is alone there. But—you know how in London in times of danger people huddle at Number Ten Downing Street and just stand there together? I felt like going and just standing outside the White House."

"Several hundred people have been doing that all evening," he said.

"I should have been with them," she said. "Instead I stayed with the rest of the people glued to Stumpy's radio." Stopping for a traffic light, she turned to Castleton and, with some difficulty, asked, "Do you want to . . . to take the short way home or the long way?"

He met her gaze, and suddenly he liked her for having propositioned him so directly and without smiling. She was tense, tired and afraid, didn't want to be alone and needed sexual release. "The long way," he said.

She lived in one of the luxury apartment buildings along Connecticut Avenue. She was one of those women in Washington who were waiting for a divorce from their second husbands while looking for their third.

She left him in her living room while she went to her mother's room, reported in and said good night. When she came back and led him into her bedroom, she was trembling as he embraced her. "Hurry!" she begged, pulling him to a couch, kicking off her shoes and jerking up her dress. Since the only underclothing below her waist was a garter belt, their contact was immediate and desperate. The action was intense for several minutes; then it subsided. "God!" she sighed. "I've never been as hot in my life! I haven't masturbated for twenty years, but I would have tonight if you hadn't been here." They undressed, moved into her bed and lay together for a while, talking.

"War makes people want to fuck," he said. "A State Department man just back from China says that the bombing by the Japanese in 1938 raised the birth rate in Shanghai. Every time the bombers approached, men and women by the thousands ran to each other and started fucking, even in alleys and streets."

"Mother Nature compensating," Alicia said.

After a while, they turned to each other again, and they came together in another frenzy of desperation. Then he showered, dressed, and she pulled on a house coat and went to the door with him. "It's a short walk from here to the Shoreham," she said.

"And the walk from the Shoreham to here?"

"Even shorter for you. With bombs falling all over the world, you can run."

131

As he walked along Connecticut Avenue in the moonlight, he thought of Bess Foshee saying to him, "Will yuh be comin' back?" Halfway across the bridge over Rock Creek Park, he stopped and stood at the rail, looking out over the park. He decided he had to join the Army—a decision which Mr. Hull and the President reversed for him a week later.

"ALL right," said Dr. Palkin, "you went home for Christmas and you drove back to Washington on New Year's Day, 1942. Now let me just get your activities down. Thereafter, you flew home one weekend a month, and your wife came to Washington by rail another weekend during the month. Much of your social life was at Stumpy McDowell's place, where you played the piano, and your extramarital sex was stress-free with undemanding women like Alicia Mayfield. You ran each morning in Rock Creek Park. Now tell me what else you did and what you thought during '42."

"The major activity. What I knew I *had* to do—I simply had to. I worked at planning a world organization to end arms races and war among nations," said Castleton. "At selling such an organization to Congress and to pressure groups like the American Legion, the labor unions, the council of churches and the National Education Association. I wrote the first drafts of Mr. Hull's speeches. On the evening of July 23, 1942, over the combined radio networks, he made his first report to the nation on the progress of our effort to end war. He said then, and, by God, I can hear him saying the same words today—he said, 'The people of no nation can progress toward order, freedom and abundance while they live in fear of external attack and must be burdened with armament. Therefore, our national purpose is to create an agency which, by force if necessary, can relieve all nations of the fear of external attack, so that the people of all nations, relieved of the burden of armament, can then progress toward order, freedom and abundance.' "

Castleton had become agitated. He jumped up and banged his fist on the doctor's desk. "Goddamn it, Doctor," he shouted, "you can't help me unless you feel what I'm saying. You've got to remember and understand that the purpose of this nation is to *lift the burden of arms from the shoulders of mankind.* Those are Lincoln's words, and Wilson, Roosevelt and Hull repeated them. An America trying to become another Rome is a monstrous denial of national purpose! Do you understand that, sir?"

"Sit down and compose yourself," ordered the doctor. "Certainly I understand that ending war among nations is our national purpose."

Castleton drank more water, inhaled deeply several times, rubbed his face and neck and sat down. He was calmer, but his voice was intense. "Then we had to persuade the Russians to accept our national purpose as their national purpose. We began this effort when Molotov came to Washington that summer. We had several meetings with him in the conference room at the State Department."

"Was he agreeable?"

"Oh, well, he tried to appear to be, although it was damned hard for him," said Castleton. "He's a stone-faced man who has hated the United States all his life. The Russians hadn't yet halted the German Army—the battle for Stalingrad didn't end until January '43. So Stalin had sent Molotov here for only one purpose: to get more warplanes, tanks, trucks and guns. To get what Stalin needed in '42 Molotov tried to appear to accept our postwar purpose. He said that Russia would need to disarm in order to rebuild, so Russia wanted friendly neighbors."

"You believed him?"

"Partially," said Castleton. "But there were difficulties. Now, take that word 'friendly.' In our conferences Litvinov interpreted for Molotov. Litvinov said in English that Molotov had said in Russian that after the war Russia wanted *friendly* neighbors, and would not tolerate unfriendly ones. That seemed reasonable to Mr. Hull, so he nodded agreement to Molotov. Then the State Department interpreter upset everything. He told Litvinov that the Russian adjective Molotov had used did not translate as 'friendly' but as 'agreeable' or 'submissive.' Mr. Hull frowned. He didn't think the Russians should demand submissive neighbors, or even agreeable ones. They should be satisfied with friendly unarmed neighbors, was his thought. Litvinov explained the problem to Molotov, who then suggested several other Russian words which might translate into English acceptable to Mr. Hull. How about 'neighbors who would listen to Russia'? Or 'cooperate with Russia'? After everyone's patience was exhausted, the matter was dropped, and we just hoped like hell there had been agreement."

"But there hadn't been one," said Dr. Palkin. "The English concept of being friendly while remaining independent and sometimes disagreeable can't be understood by the Russian mind. To the Soviet regime an unfriendly citizen is a criminal to be imprisoned, and a disagreeable neighboring state is an enemy to be crushed."

"Well, you're right—that has proved to be true," said Castleton. "But despite such difficulties, Mr. Hull believed that by the time the war ended he could persuade Russia to join the United States in demobilizing, limiting arms and depending on a collective security organization for protection, so that both great nations could work toward helping their people to achieve order, freedom and abundance."

"That brings us through August, 1942," said the doctor. "On October 20, 1942, the President summoned you to the White House. Tell me everything about that meeting."

Castleton cleared his throat, and his thoughts went back to that afternoon when Secretary Hull called him to his office.

"THE President wants to see you, Frank. You are to be at the White House this evening at nine."

"Just me . . . alone?"

"Yes."

"What's it about?"

"I don't know," said the Secretary. "The President told me he wants you to do something for him. He thinks it might take half your time, and you're to do it in connection with what you're doing for me. He asked if I objected to sharing you with him, and I said certainly not, so he said to send you to him. That's all I know."

At 8:55 Castleton left his office and walked past the guard to the south entrance of the White House, where he was met by an usher who led him upstairs to the Oval Study. He noted that the house was as quiet as his own home. No sound indicated a war was on. The President was alone, working on his stamp collection. His collar was open, and he wore a maroon smoking jacket. He greeted Castleton with the usual wave and handclasp and inquiries about his family. As Castleton sat down he said, "You know, Frank, I was just thinking about sailing at Campobello when I was twelve. Sailing's something you missed in your backwoods. Take a twelve-year-old boy alone in a ten-foot sailboat in choppy blue water with a fifteen-mile breeze. Let him sail a three-mile triangular course skillfully, and *there* you have a confident boy. I'm sorry you missed that, Frank."

Castleton grinned and accepted the challenge. "You're forgetting, sir, that what every boy wants most is to paddle his own canoe. I was doing that when I was twelve—and let me tell you, a fourteen-foot cowhide canoe is more challenging than a ten-foot sailboat. To take that canoe through a mile of white water on a wild river during the spring flood—that can give a boy more confidence than sailing a triangular course on blue water at Campobello. I'm sorry *you* missed canoeing."

The President chuckled, his broad shoulders shaking. After a day of directing war from a wheelchair, his favorite recreation was reliving his untroubled boyhood. Reluctantly he came back to the present. "Down there on Sewanee Mountain, how much physics did they teach you?"

"Not much," said Castleton. "I remember a little about atoms and molecules."

"That's the way with me at Harvard." The President's mood had changed abruptly; he was no longer smiling. "For a very grave reason, Frank, you will now have to concern yourself with atoms. You've read about how one day we'll split the atom and use its energy?"

"Yes, sir. TVA engineers believe atomic power will one day generate electricity."

"Well, actually, that day is nearer than they think. The atom has *been* split. In December, 1938, at the Kaiser Wilhelm Institute in Berlin, a German physicist split the uranium atom. Every physicist in the world is excited about it, and fortunately most of the world's nuclear physicists are now in the United States. A dozen of them came here from Europe to escape Hitler, and they've joined our own Nobel Prize—winners. They believe that Hitler's physicists may be close to producing an atomic bomb which could flatten New York."

The President suddenly became grim, and Castleton became apprehensive at his change of mood. "Now, Frank, you will understand how this unexpected peril has affected me. It has compelled me to assume power that no president has ever dreamed of using. With an atomic bomb, Hitler would be master of the world. So without informing Congress, I have been compelled to order a gigantic secret effort to produce an atomic bomb. At whatever cost in money, materials or freedom, we *must* beat Hitler to this weapon!"

Castleton was now thoroughly alarmed, and he began using a challenging tone of voice he had never expected to use with the President. "To do this without telling Congress . . . haven't you become a usurper?"

"No. When the nation is in peril, the inherent power of the President is unlimited."

"Have you told Mr. Hull?"

"No. No member of the Cabinet will know about it except Henry Stimson."

"Then why are you telling me?"

"Because as of now you are my eyes, ears and legs on this project. The bomb will be made in your back yard—in Clinch County, Tennessee."

Castleton caught his breath. "You'll build a laboratory in Clinch County?"

"Not just a laboratory. Less than one percent of uranium atoms are the kind that can be split, you see. Those few must be separated from the many others. Laboratories can separate only microscopic quantities, but we must have pounds . . . tons. We're devising industrial processes to obtain such quantities, and we're proceeding to build a giant complex of laboratory-factories in Clinch County."

"But our county is backwoods!"

"That's why we chose it," said the President. "We need a sparsely settled county in the TVA area where land is cheap and broken by high ridges. This complex will use an enormous amount of electricity, which only TVA can supply. Of course, if we hadn't built TVA we couldn't make this bomb. Your father must have told you that the government is acquiring more land in Clinch County?"

"Well, yes, but he thinks a thousand acres are being acquired for a research laboratory!"

"We will acquire sixty thousand acres." The President's voice was calm but very firm. "The site is perfect. A rectangle six miles wide and sixteen miles long. A railroad runs along one side of it, the Clinch River along another side. It's broken by five long parallel wooded ridges. Each of the laboratory-factories is going to be located in a narrow valley between ridges and will be several miles from the others, you understand. This way, if one laboratory-factory is destroyed by enemy bombing or cataclysmic accident, the others won't be damaged."

Castleton jumped up and stood glowering down at the President. Enraged and terrified, he lost all thought of the fact that he was addressing the President. "Goddamn you, I'll fight you! I'll fly to Tennessee, warn my neighbors, and we'll defend our homes against a usurper named Roosevelt!"

"You try that," said the President, "you even make that threat again, and I'll have you seized, taken out to sea and shot!"

Castleton began walking about the room. He was utterly stunned. The President watched him, and then said, "I made that counter-threat, Frank, to try to make you accept the realities of our situation. Now sit down and listen to your President, who's your old and proven friend."

Castleton struck the desk with his fist. "First, goddamn it, you listen to me!" He was so excited that he ran his words together. "Clinch County's my home. Its people are my relatives and friends. Damn it, we've worked to keep our county agrarian. With the help of TVA—with *your* help—

136

we've replanted our forests and halted the erosion of our hillsides. We've obtained electricity for farms and for small industries to process the produce of the land. Now you tell me that in the national interest we must destroy Clinch County—drive hundreds of settled families from the land. We must tear down their newly electrified homes and churches and tear up their old cemeteries. We have to expose the county to bombing or to cataclysmic accident, and if it escapes those perils it will certainly be destroyed by an invading army of strangers to whom it can never be home." He had begun crying. "If I allow that to happen without fighting, goddamn it, I'll never be able to respect myself again."

He stood there, tears streaming down his cheeks, looking angrily at the President. After a moment the President said, "Now that you've made your speech, dry your face and sit down here and listen to me."

Castleton took a deep breath and sat down, wiping his eyes. The President turned to him sympathetically. "You're exaggerating what's going to happen to your county. Less than a thousand families live on those sixty thousand acres, you know that. That isn't many people to be resettled. Where else east of the Mississippi could we find such a site with so few people to move? Your home will not be endangered. Six weeks ago when I learned that this site was being considered I examined the map and noted that the perimeter of the site comes no nearer than twelve miles to Norris Dam and no nearer than ten miles to your home. The atom project will occupy only a sixth of Clinch County, so the Castletons won't be crowded out. And remember this! When we built Norris Dam we displaced many families and tore down old churches and tore up old cemeteries. You favored that, remember?"

"But that was entirely different," said Castleton. "I told the people being displaced then that they had to move so that we could conserve the land and the water. What shall I tell people who have to move so that we can make a more destructive bomb? What am I going to tell George Norris? He's old now, and sick and being defeated for reelection. Am I going to tell him that the electricity from Norris Dam is to be used to make bombs which can incinerate the earth?"

The President was becoming impatient. "Listen to me, Frank! Like it or not, you will study this project. Its code name is the 'Manhattan Project.' There is going to be another laboratory-factory complex in the state of Washington, using power from the Columbia River dams. The weapon will be designed at a site near Santa Fe, New Mexico. You will visit the three sites often. You'll examine files, read reports, witness tests, ask questions.

137

Whenever I summon you, you'll come and tell me what you know. This will be the only war industry I can never visit—I can't risk calling attention to it. So you'll ask the questions I'd ask, and bring me the answers. You'll have one contact in the War Department: Paul Blanton, an assistant to Henry Stimson."

"I've met him."

"He's expecting your call. He'll give you travel priorities and reimburse you for your expenses. He'll prepare the War Department's weekly progress report to me on this project—of course, he'll show that to you and tell you everything the War Department knows. You, however, must tell him nothing."

The President picked up an envelope on his desk. "Here is the broadest security clearance this government can grant. A Q-clearance for the Manhattan Project. It's yours. You've noticed that I didn't *offer* you this assignment. The situation doesn't allow that. I couldn't reveal the existence of this project to you without first clearing you for it and assigning you to it. If you now refused the assignment, I'd have no choice but to kill you or confine you. You understand?"

"In time I suppose I shall." Except for his rapid breathing, Castleton was now calm.

"But why should knowledge that we are making the bomb be confined to you and me and the physicists and the Joint Chiefs and a few other men in the War Department? Why shouldn't Mr. Hull know of it? And key members of Congress?"

"In time we'll tell them," said the President. "Now I must warn you about Executive Privilege. Do you know what it means?"

"That I'm your slave."

"If you choose to look at it that way—but only in regard to this bomb. The knowledge you acquire will belong to me, not to you. You can impart it to no one but me. Never in your life, not even to Congress or the Supreme Court, will you have the right to divulge anything you said to me, or that I said to you, or that you heard me say to someone else. Do you understand that . . . *very clearly?*"

"Yes, I understand. I don't like it, but I understand."

"Then here's my final word." The President leaned back in his chair and began to talk more easily. "The security agencies have spent six weeks examining your life. There is little about you, or about your close associates, that is not now documented. And I must tell you that the experts regard you as a questionable risk. You're emotional. A musician . . . a painter

138

. . . you read poetry . . . you run alone, or in the mountains with Indians. You're soft on domestic Communism. You regularly visit the pleasure dome of your classmate Stumpy McDowell, who's a cynic and a satyr. Worst of all, you sometimes fuck women to whom you're not married. Such as Mrs. Alicia Mayfield. Extramarital fucking, Frank, is a red flag in the security file of any man holding a Q-clearance. So the security experts urged me not to give you this assignment and to give it to a disciplined man dependent on government employment."

"Then why in God's name didn't you?" asked Castleton. "You knew I wouldn't want it. Why have you forced it on me?"

The President took off his glasses and rubbed his eyes. "Oh, my God, I'm surrounded by disciplined men. Disciplined physicists will report to me on this bomb in language I can't understand, and I'll get no end of reports from disciplined military men. But when I sit down somewhere to really think about this thing, I want to be with a man more like me. Essentially I'm a tree farmer, a country squire and a senior warden in the Episcopal Church, and if the government was threatening to make this bomb near Hyde Park, New York, I'd be shouting and banging on desks and shedding tears just like you were doing a few minutes ago. As to fucking—I've never thought it was subversive. I know Mrs. Alicia Mayfield, and I wouldn't mind fucking her myself." The President grinned. "So, old top, that's why I insisted on you for this job. You're stuck with it, so you may as well grin and enjoy it."

Castleton could only shake his head in amazement. "Goddamn, Mr. President, you take the cake! I'll do the best I can."

"I know you will. Just remember that you're a watched man. The Manhattan Project will have hundreds of its own security and counteres-pionage experts. They'll suspect everybody, especially each other. They'll read your mail, tap your telephone and try to hide under any bed you're in. So be prudent. Get to work, and I'll summon you whenever I can talk. Most likely I'll want to speak with you at Shangri-la or Hyde Park or Warm Springs or aboard ship." He held out his hand, and Castleton got up and took it. "Good night, old top."

"Good night, Mr. President."

D<small>R</small>. Palkin asked, "How did you feel as you left the President? Were you frightened?"

"Yes," said Castleton. "I certainly was. The President had shown me

139

what the war would cost me. Clinch County would be overrun. The character and purpose of TVA would be changed. To supply enough electricity to separate fissionable atoms from non-fissionable ones, TVA would become the world's largest burner of soft coal, and its strip mines in 1944 would denude the hillsides we reforested in 1934. At the end of the war I'd be homeless and rootless, existing at the mercy of bombs."

"Well," said the doctor, "how did you rationalize and come to terms? What hope did you catch sight of to enable you to carry on?"

"The hope that by collective effort, we could disarm all nations. I believed in that, and I had to help make it happen, you see—now more than ever."

"We'll come back to this," said the doctor. "Now tell me, are you sure . . . did the President make you understand clearly the meaning of Executive Privilege?"

"Yes."

"And did he make you understand clearly the penalties you'd suffer if you ever revealed, or appeared likely to reveal, any secrets of the Manhattan Project?"

"He made me understand very clearly."

"Then you're under no illusions as to your present situation?"

"None whatsoever."

The doctor looked at the clock on the wall. "All right. Good. Now, your file shows that after you left the White House that evening you were halted by police. Tell me about that."

Castleton recalled the incident.

Stunned and wounded by what the President had told him, he began walking toward the Shoreham. When he reached the Mayflower he thought of stopping for a drink, but he continued walking. By the time he reached Dupont Circle he had begun to run. The sidewalks were deserted. He was bare-headed, and he carried an attaché case in his right hand. In his left hand he carried a handkerchief —he was crying again. He ran for almost two miles, and had crossed the Rock Creek Park bridge and was turning into the Shoreham grounds when a police car came alongside and a policeman told him to stop. He stopped, wiped his eyes. Two policemen got out of the car.

"What's the trouble?" one policeman asked.

"No trouble," said Castleton.

"What you running for?"

"I live here at the Shoreham. I was coming here from my office and felt like getting some exercise."

"You been drinking?"

"No."

"Doping?"

"No."

"Then what you been crying for?"

"I wasn't really crying," said Castleton. "I was feeling low and my eyes watered."

The policemen looked at each other. They were thinking of taking him to St. Elizabeth's. "Can you show us some identification?" one of them asked. He handed them his State Department identification card, which bore his photograph, office number and title. They looked at it, and one of them scratched his head. "You an Assistant Secretary of State?"

"I'm an assistant to the Secretary of State," he replied.

They asked him to wait while they moved away several paces and conferred in low voices as one of them copied his name and title into a notebook. Then they returned his card. "You can go."

"Thank you," said Castleton. As he walked toward the hotel the policemen stood watching him. "Goddamn!" one of them said. "The Assistant Secretary of State running and crying on Connecticut Avenue! That's one for the books."

"The State Department's full'a queers," the other said.

"That went into your file as bizarre behavior," said Dr. Palkin. He leaned back in his chair and smiled. "You know, I wouldn't say you were bizarre, to my way of thinking. You're doing well, Frank. This afternoon you can stay out on the grounds and talk with your children and wife. This evening you and Mary can dance and play some music; then tomorrow morning you'll be left alone to read and study. And, let's see, what else—oh, in the afternoon we're on for some golf, and in the evening Mary is making dinner for you at her place. Sounds like a good weekend to me."

Castleton replied without smiling, "Whether it's good or not depends on my performance, doesn't it?"

The doctor nodded. "Performance is everything. Performance and manner. What you do and how you do it."

THAT afternoon Castleton and Mary Sullivan selected a shady spot on the grounds where they could sit and receive his visitors. The temperature was comfortable and the breeze was gentle. Castleton seemed edgy, and asked nervously, "What can I say to them that will make them feel less embarrassed by having to visit me here?"

"Don't say anything about yourself," Mary answered. "Talk about what they're doing—activities they're busy with right now. Cord will get here first so he can be back to the Shoreham in time to hear the broadcast of the Kentucky Derby."

"Oh yes, that's today. I'd forgotten."

"Don't tell Cord that. It's the race of the century—Citation and Coaltown. That's a good subject for a conversation opener. And try playing devil's advocate, all right? He thinks Citation will win, so you pick Coaltown. And say something to Cord about next year—you and he won't make the mistake of missing the Derby next year."

Mary took a newspaper cutting from between the leaves of her book. "Here's another subject for you." She showed him the photo of Cord and Joe Dimaggio. "On Wednesday, Thursday and Friday evenings Cord saw the Yankees and the Red Sox play the Senators at Griffith Stadium. And because you're in the news, the Shoreham's press agent arranged with the Yankees' press agent for Dimaggio to give Cord an autographed ball. You should tell Cord that you cut this out of the paper and let him tell you about it."

Castleton looked at Mary in wonder. "How do you know all this?"

"Aha. Research. That's my business," she said. "I'm trying to help you regain your balance, right? For eight years you've neglected your son, and you're not going to do that any more. These are all vital parts of a father-son relationship: Citation and Coaltown, and Ted Williams and Joe Dimaggio and the American League pennant race."

Castleton swallowed hard and rubbed his face. "Cord was born at the wrong time. During the thirties Susan was old enough for us to take to Europe twice, to Hawaii, Mexico and Canada, and to the World Fairs at Chicago, New York and San Francisco, since she was born in 1927. She was old enough to be thrilled by the TVA drama. But Cord wasn't born until 1934. By the time he was six I was tied up in the war!"

"And you've been tied up ever since," said Mary. "That's how you lost your balance. You can start regaining it by restoring contact with your son."

Cord was coming across the grounds, guided by a tall Negro hospital attendant. Castleton and Mary watched him approach, and Mary looked at the boy with interest. "He walks like you do—light on his feet. He won't be as tall and wiry as you are, but he's fine-looking." When he saw his father Cord seemed to hesitate and feel uncertain, but Castleton stood up and called, "Come on over, Cord. I'm mighty glad to see you."

Cord slipped one arm around his father's waist and kissed him on the cheek, and then Castleton put an arm around his son's shoulders and hugged him. He turned to Mary. "Mary, this is my son, Cord, and Cord, this is Miss Mary Sullivan."

Mary smiled. "I'll move over to another bench and read while you two talk. I don't want to disturb you." She moved to about thirty feet away, not out of earshot. Then Castleton and Cord sat down together.

"Is she your nurse, Dad?" Cord asked.

"No, not exactly—I don't need a nurse," said Castleton. "She's what they call a therapist. My trouble, as you know, is that I've worried too much about some things, so she tries to get my mind on more important matters, such as music and dancing and painting . . . and which horse will win the race this afternoon. I figure it'll be Coaltown."

Cord turned eagerly toward his father. "I believe you're wrong, Dad. I'm picking Citation."

"Really? Why?"

Cord, warming to the subject, began to gesture excitedly with his hands. "Dad, you've just got to remember that this is a mile-and-a-quarter race. Ten furlongs. Now, Coaltown holds the world record for six furlongs. But Citation was bred for both speed and distance. I figure Coaltown'll be leading coming into the stretch. Then Citation'll begin to get to him. And in that last furlong . . . Citation'll kill him!"

"That's going to be some race! I'm sure sorry we're not there."

"Oh, that's all right, Dad," Cord said. "You couldn't help getting sick. I don't mind. I'll be at the hotel, listening, anyway, and that's always great. Clem McCarthy'll call the race, and he can make it almost as exciting as being there."

"We'll be there next year all right."

"Sure we will. You and I and Granddad."

Castleton unfolded the newspaper cutting. "I cut this out of the paper." When Cord saw what it was, he smiled proudly and said, "That's something, isn't it! Me with Dimaggio!"

"Yeah, that's really something," said Castleton. "Good picture of you.

But don't you think Ted Williams is a greater hitter than Dimaggio? He may be the greatest natural hitter of all time."

Cord shook his head very slowly and pursed his lips. "I don't know, Dad. Ted's great, all right. He really strides into that ball! But he has a sour disposition. Now, Dimaggio . . . he's just one great guy! He talked to me as one man to another. Asked me about things at Sewanee. And he can hit that ball a mile. He's just one great guy!"

After a pause Castleton said, "Son, in the two summers since the war ended, we haven't traveled as a family like we used to do before the war. I've been too tied up in Washington. But this summer I want us to take a long drive out through the Rocky Mountains and the West."

Cord couldn't believe his ears. "Oh, gosh, Dad! Can we really go?"

"Sure we can. We'll leave a week or so after Commencement and be gone five or six weeks."

Cord was happy, excited—he jumped up and stood looking down at his father. "Can we ride horseback in Yellowstone and Yosemite and in Colorado? And can we ride those donkeys down into the Grand Canyon?"

"Sure."

"Just you and me and Mother . . . and maybe Susan?"

"Susan'll probably have other things planned with her friends," said Castleton. "But you and I and your mother can go. Would you like to take along one of your classmates at Sewanee?"

"Oh, no, Dad. Just you and me and Mother."

For ten more minutes they talked about exciting things they were going to do together. Then Mary decided it was time to end the interview. She closed her book, got up and said that Cord should be starting back to the hotel. She took the boy down the tree-lined path, and when they were out of Castleton's hearing Cord said, "Gee, Miss Sullivan, you and Dr. Palkin have sure helped Dad a lot."

"You've helped him a lot, too," she said. "Most of all by the way you treated him today."

"Did I do all right? I tried to do just what you told me to."

"You did fine. You showed your father you love him."

"I do love him," Cord insisted. "And I want to keep on helping him."

When they were about a hundred yards from Castleton, Mary said, "Let's stop here." She stood close to Cord, facing him. "Let me help you understand your father better. You told Dr. Palkin that he embarrassed you by not joining the Army in 1941 and by making money out of the war. Well, for your sake, he wanted to join the Army. He stayed out only when asked to do so by President Roosevelt and Mr. Hull. And he never wanted to make money out of the war. If he could have prevented it, Oak Ridge would not have been located in Clinch County or anywhere else in the Tennessee Valley. And regardless of how you see it now, believe me, he hasn't neglected you for seven years. Instead he has done you the greatest service a father can do a son, by trying to help build a world in which you wouldn't have to kill or be killed. He's here now because that effort has been defeated. And your father is not a weak and foolish man, as you have read this week in the papers. He's a strong and wise man who believes that men must strive to improve the world, even if they seem certain to fail."

Gently she put her hand on Cord's cheek. "Do you understand?"

He put his hand on hers. "I'm beginning to . . . thanks to you."

The tall attendant arrived to escort Cord to the taxi stand, and Mary bid him good-bye before returning to Castleton. She found him worried. "I shouldn't have told Cord we'll take a trip," he said. "Truman won't let me go."

"Yes, he will," said Mary, sitting down with him. "The President became afraid of you only after you lost your balance. When you regain your balance, he won't be afraid of you and you'll be free."

Castleton looked anxious. "Who's coming next, Susan or Diane?"

"Susan."

"What am I supposed to say to her?"

"Very little. Unlike Cord, she doesn't feel that you've neglected her. Her only complaint against you is that you've neglected her mother. Today she wants you to be happy with her. She's coming here to tell you that she has decided to get married."

Castleton sighed. "To Curt Jackson?"

"Yes. She decided last night at the Arena, where Tommy Dorsey's playing."

"I thought she was going to delay that decision for a while."

"Well, she might have, but there's really no reason for her to delay it," said Mary. "Naval Academy men traditionally marry during the week they are commissioned. And Susan thinks you approve of Curt Jackson. Don't you?"

"I scarcely know him. I took a boat ride with him during one of his visits down home. He told me he hoped to marry Susan. I wished him luck, but I hoped she'd choose someone else. He struck me as a cold fish—a Maine Yankee with more brains than heart."

"He's finishing first in his class," said Mary. "He's going into rocketry,

145

so the Navy will send him to MIT for two years. I understand he wants to be the first man on the moon. He's like you in at least one respect: He believes more knowledge can save the world."

"Then God help him," said Castleton.

"You don't think he's marrying her for her money, do you?"

"I hope not. But her money should prove helpful to a Navy ensign bent on rocketing to the moon."

Castleton looked pensive and cynical. After inhaling deeply several times, he turned to Mary. "Do you tell every visitor to this hospital what to say to the patient, and the patient what to say to the visitor?"

"I wish we had time to do that," said Mary. "We could prevent a lot of unnecessary suffering. A family visit here usually hurts both the patient and the visitor. In your case, we're trying to prevent that."

"Then you *have* told my family what to say to me, just as you're telling me what to say to them?"

Mary nodded. "It's part of our effort to help you. All that Dr. Palkin learns about you, he tells me. All that I learn about you, I tell him. When I'm not with you I'm often on the telephone talking to a member of your family or with someone else who's been important to you. I'm trying to gather information from them and tell them what they can do or say to help you."

"Is all that necessary?"

"The doctor thinks it is. Understand, Frank, we're trying to help you readjust to your environment, and that's a particular space and time and circle of people."

They both saw Susan coming when she was across the lawn. Her mass of curled hair bounced on her shoulders as she walked rapidly beside the tall attendant. Her desert-tan wool-gabardine dress looked stylish and comfortable. She rushed to Castleton, put her arm around his waist and presented her cheek for him to kiss. "You look so much better today, Daddy!" She and Mary exchanged nods, and Mary moved to the other bench with her book. The tall attendant moved away while Castleton and Susan sat down together.

"I can't wait any longer to tell you, Daddy! Curt and I are going to be married next month!"

"That's wonderful," said Castleton. "Have you begun planning the wedding?"

"There won't be much planning to do," said Susan. "We're going to be married simply in the chapel at Annapolis."

"No!" Castleton spoke abruptly. "You are *not!* You'll be married at home . . . in the rose garden."

"But, Daddy—" She tried to interrupt him, but he held up his hand and continued.

"You aren't alone in this world, Susan. You are a member of a family —an extensive family. They gathered and celebrated your birth, so they will gather and celebrate your wedding. Now, just because you think I may not be able to perform my duties as a father, you're talking about a wedding away from home. I appreciate your consideration . . . but I'll be there . . . and I'll perform. And if I'm not able to, your grandfather will do everything in my place. So start planning your wedding *at home!*"

Susan smiled as tears came into her eyes, and she leaned over and kissed her father on the cheek. "Of course, Daddy, it's what I've dreamed of having, but . . ."

"I know," he said. "But just because I'm in a nut house this week doesn't mean I'm going to stay here or that my children must be neglected. Have you forgotten Yeats's line, 'How but in custom and ceremony are innocence and beauty born?' You are a member of a family which values custom and ceremony, so your wedding will take place in the presence of, well, at least four hundred of your relatives, including the Jemisons and the Scotts. Your Grandfather Jemison will perform the ceremony, assisted by the Episcopal Bishop of Tennessee. And Curt's relatives will be there. Since his father's a rear admiral, there will be guests from the Navy. And we have to invite members of the community, so there will be guests from the TVA, the Atomic Energy Commission and the State Department. The Governor of Tennessee will be there, of course, and Senator Kefauver, members of Congress, judges and legislators. And Rotarians. And major depositors of the Clinch National Bank. And friends from Sewanee. And since both you and your mother are Kappa Kappa Gammas, there'll be representatives of both generations of the sorority." His voice sounded full and excited as he spoke.

"Lord, Daddy," said Susan, laughing, "the guest list will run to eight hundred, maybe a thousand."

"Let it run," he said. "We'll serve food and drink in tents, and have a dance band from Nashville. I'll paint your portrait in your wedding dress, and you'll honeymoon in our cottage in the Smokies where your mother and I met twenty-three years ago. And soon your mother must go with you to Boston to help you select a house. So you get busy and plan it all carefully, young lady."

Again Mary closed her book and stood up, and a visit was over. Susan hugged her father, kissed him and thanked him again. Then she and Mary walked away. When they were out of Castleton's hearing, Susan said, "Now *that's* the father we knew up to about three years ago! So full of life . . . enthusiastic . . . able to celebrate—to make music, dance, laugh and sing and enjoy living. How has he managed to recover so rapidly?"

"To come to terms with his big disappointments—those in the nation —he knows he just has to find new satisfactions in his family and community and in himself."

"But he still has doubts," said Susan. "You noticed how he said that if he weren't able to be at the wedding, then Grandfather Castleton would take his place?"

"I think he'll preside at the wedding," said Mary.

"I do too," said Susan.

The attendant took Susan away, and Mary returned to Castleton. "Will I be able to do all I've promised Susan I'll do?" he asked as she sat down with him.

"Easily," said Mary. "You can easily entertain a few hundred guests, most of them for only an hour or so. You can paint her portrait in her wedding gown. And you can certainly hike and ride around in the Rockies with Cord and Diane. You can function as a father again."

"And as a husband?"

"No, not quite so easily," she said. "You slighted your wife when you wasted yourself on the idea of TVA, then on the idea of ending war among nations."

Castleton turned angrily to her. "How can you say that I wasted myself on those ideas? They were and are great ideas. How could I have been wrong in supporting them?"

"Wait a minute. Don't fly off the handle. You were wrong in the way you supported them," said Mary. "A man should support ideas reasonably, not emotionally. And at the same time he should invest his emotions in the individuals he loves. There are millions of people to support ideas for public action, but your wife has only one husband, your parents have only one son, and your children only one father. Neither Roosevelt nor Truman became emotional over Hiroshima, but you did. You wasted so much emotion that finally you had none left for your wife. Now you can no longer convince her that you love her, since you can no longer desire her."

"God knows I've tried to desire her," said Castleton.

"Sure you did. And the harder you tried, the more certain you were to

148

fail. No man can force himself to want a woman. He can't will himself an erection."

"After twenty-three years of marriage, can't there be love without erections?"

Mary shook her head. "Not between you and Diane Jemison. She's a proud woman who's worked hard at keeping herself seductive. At forty-four she can't be happy with you unless she can excite you. You've got to acknowledge that—you know that woman. She won't continue living with you unless you can desire her again."

"Then how can I become able to?"

"If I could tell men that," said Mary, with a deep sigh, "I'd resign from the Navy and make a million dollars a year. I can only tell you how to begin to try."

"Then go on, say it!" Castleton looked nervous, anxious.

Mary took his hand and held it in her lap. "Breathe deeply and remember I'm on your side," she said. "You begin trying to regain desire, first by understanding. On the day you met Diane she was so attractive to you that you insisted on fucking her. Okay, we've talked about this before. Fucking requires no emotional investment. But love does! When you began investing emotion in her, you began loving her, so you married her. Then, she ceased being attractive to you when you became neurotic and your emotional well went dry. It's classic, you see, not that this makes it any less upsetting, but a husband's impotency with his wife is the commonest symptom of neuroticism. For a neurotic husband to revive a marriage, he's got to regain his ability to love tenderly and with normal potency restored. So, for you to revive your marriage to Diane Jemison you must begin reinvesting emotion in her so that she will again become attractive to you. Otherwise you must find another woman who attracts you, makes you feel potent, and hope that you can begin investing emotion in her. That's how you'll relearn love, and you know you must be able to love again if life is to be tolerable for you."

"I don't want to love another woman," said Castleton. "I want to love the wife I have. Please give me a clue, Mary. How do I begin reinvesting emotion in her?"

"By being interested in her—in the little daily routine things," said Mary. "You must convince her that you are more interested in her today than you have ever been. You must be particularly interested in what she has been doing in Washington this week."

"Well, tell me—what?"

"She's been visiting with your friends, all of whom are concerned about you."

Castleton dropped his shoulders and sighed. "God, it must be embarrassing for a proud woman like Jemmy . . . to have her husband in a concentration camp for frail faltering failing fuckers!" He stood up and began sighing deeply and rubbing his neck.

"Sit down," said Mary, "and hold my hand." In a moment he did as she had asked. She said, "Diane's been going to dinner parties. She went to the Bramwells', then to the Blantons', and last night to Stumpy's. At the Blantons' she met Monsignor Sheen, and at Stumpy's she met Rita Hayworth and Dr. Kinsey, author of the new report on sexual behavior. And Mrs. Joseph E. Davies has invited her to the garden party at Tregaron tomorrow. She's going with Stumpy. As you well know, she isn't the sort of woman who is much impressed by such affairs, but she likes to look nice so she got herself some new clothes. Ask her to tell you about it, and appear interested in all her activities."

"Well, I *am* interested," said Castleton.

"Then show her you are, damn it. And bear this in mind. At these parties the other guests are assuming that a woman with Diane's money and looks is not going to remain married to you. So she'll be receiving invitations from men."

"I hadn't thought of that," said Castleton. "Oh, Jesus, don't tell me that. I can't believe that she will divorce me."

"You must start believing it," said Mary. "Unless you can regain your ability to work, love her and be happy, she will certainly divorce you and marry another man. If you want to keep her, you must convince her that when you leave here you are going to make her proud of you."

That statement hurt Castleton. His eyes began to water. "Has she had no pride in me before?"

"How could she have had?" asked Mary. "What have you done? You became rich as a matter of course. Otherwise you've done little more than run errands for politicians and drive yourself crazy. Diane knows that you are a talented painter. Dr. Palkin says that your paintings reveal a deeply emotional man trying to express a personal view of his world. Diane and Dr. Palkin and I know that had you worked hard at your painting instead of wasting yourself on ideas to improve the world, you would now be recognized as an important painter. So tell Diane that now you are going to become the important painter you were expected to become."

"Isn't it too late?"

"Certainly not. You're only forty-six. Many painters have done their best work in their sixties, even seventies. So tell Diane that you are ready to concentrate on painting, and that after Susan's wedding you and she and Cord are going out West on a trip that will be a second honeymoon for you and her."

Diane was approaching with the attendant. Bare-headed, in a red-and-white-checked shirtdress, she looked stylishly casual. She smiled as she came closer, and reminded herself that she must not show the embarrassment she felt; she must try to treat her husband just as though he were in a regular hospital suffering from a physical disorder. As Castleton was a foot taller than she, he had to bend down to kiss her on the cheek while she hugged him affectionately. "You look so much better, Frank," she exclaimed.

Diane and Mary exchanged nods, and Mary took her book and moved to the nearby bench. Castleton and Diane sat down together. "I'm going to be all right, Jemmy," he said. "I'm worried about you."

"I'm fine," she said. "All I need is for you to get well."

"Susan told me about the wedding. Are you pleased that it's Curt?"

"Yes, he's a bright ambitious young man. We'll be proud of him."

"Then we must give them a wedding they'll remember with pride."

"But nothing big," she said. "A simple ceremony in the chapel at Annapolis. Didn't Susan tell you?"

"Yes, certainly," said Castleton. "But that wouldn't be right for your and my daughter, so I changed the plan. She'll be married at home, in the presence of family and community. You get busy with her and plan it like it should be."

Diane smiled, then turned and hugged him and kissed his cheek. "Are you sure you'll be up to it?"

"Of course I've got to be, Jemmy. And you go to Boston with her and help her buy or rent a suitable house."

"It's wonderful to hear you talk so hopefully again, Frank."

"Now tell me what you've been doing," he said.

"I've been dining with our friends," she said. "Much of the talk has been about you. Everybody wants to help us."

"Well, it's good to know I've got friends," said Castleton. "What do they want to do?"

Diane delayed her answer. She had been asked by both Dr. Palkin and Mary Sullivan not to discuss "problems" with Castleton. She had agreed to confine her conversation to a pleasant report on her social activities and on Susan's wedding plans, to a positive reaction to Castleton's proposal that he take a trip with Cord and to expressions of hopeful expectation. But now her husband was looking into her eyes and repeating, "Tell me, Jemmy, how do our friends propose to help us?"

She decided to say what she felt was true. "Well, Frank, I think we must admit that we've misjudged the President. He seems to be bending over backward trying to help you. You've felt for three years, ever since Roosevelt died, that psychiatric treatment might be beneficial. Now the President is allowing you to have it. And you're being given good and effective treatment which obviously is doing something for you. That's true, isn't it? We have no reason to complain of your treatment?"

Castleton sighed and began rubbing his hands together. "Dr. Palkin and Mary seem to be doing their best to help me," he said. "At times I feel better than I have for a year. The hell of it, Jemmy, is having to sleep behind a locked door which I can't unlock." His eyes began to water, and his chin trembled as a wave of fear hit him. "It's a terrifying and demeaning experience. I don't think anyone who experiences it ever completely recovers from it. Without narcotics I couldn't survive a night of it. I'd choke, smother, become hysterical, go mad. Diane, it's horrible."

Mary Sullivan considered stopping the conversation, but she decided to let it continue. Diane's impulse was to put her arms around her husband and try to comfort him. But she had done that so many times before she had been compelled to admit that she had lost the ability to comfort him, or that he had lost the ability to take comfort from her. Now she only reached over and put her hand on his tightly clasped hands. "You won't have to endure that much longer," she said. "Paul says that in another week, after the doctor completes his examination, you can live with me at the Shoreham for a while, and we'll go to the hospital twice a week for counseling. As soon as they're sure you're really improving, we can go home, and perhaps fly back here once a month to see the doctor."

This news seemed to calm Castleton. He put his arms around his wife, drew her close to him and said, "Don't give up on me, Jemmy. Not yet. The best of me is invested in you, and I want to increase that investment, not write it off as another loss."

"I only want more of what we've had, Frank," she responded. "I want you to be what you were and what you should be—a happy man who loves his wife and family, making music and painting pictures."

He held her for a moment, then released her. "I'll be that way again, I promise you. Because I want to be. Now tell me more about what you've been doing."

"Well, let's see. I've met several interesting people," she said. "Monsignor Fulton Sheen was at the Blantons'. There's music in his voice, and goodness in his eyes, if you'll pardon my sounding corny. He talked about the worldwide conflict between Communism and Christianity, and agreed with Paul that American strength is the only hope for peace. Stumpy put on a wicked one-man show at his own den of iniquity last night to make fun of Monsignor Sheen. He recreated what he said was the scene in which Monsignor Sheen—the Monsignor of Menopause—converted Clare Boothe Luce to Catholicism. Hilariously imitating Monsignor Sheen, he explained the way of salvation to Mrs. Luce; then, whipping on a blonde woman's wig—I truly think he bought it for the occasion—he gave her responses leading to her surrender to Christ. We all laughed until we cried! It was sacrilegious but it was so funny! Then, since the featured guests were Rita Hayworth and Dr. Kinsey, we talked about sex. Dr. Kinsey discussed the effect of the war on sex habits, and Stumpy said that the art of the war was typified by two photographs: the rear-end photo of Betty Grable and the photo of Rita in a black negligee lying across a golden bed waiting for a lover. You know, men took those photos into battle instead of crucifixes. Stumpy said that Rita received the most significant honor of the war when her golden-bed photo was pasted onto the Hiroshima bomb. I simply had to tell the story about how you actually saw the ground crew paste the photo on the bomb. Rita said she didn't know whether to feel honored or shamed by it. She's a nice person—doesn't demand or seem to expect attention—and she is prettier in person than on the screen."

Diane paused for Castleton to comment, but he was silent—paying attention to her but apparently content to listen. So she told him about receiving the invitation to the Davieses' home, about the new outfit she would wear and about how Susan and Cord would return to school tomorrow, leaving her alone at the hotel until he could join her. "Oh, and before I forget," she said. "An editor of *Time* magazine and an art dealer in New York, they both want to go down home and look at your paintings. Shall I let them?"

Castleton replied quickly, "No."

"But why not?" asked Diane. She began speaking insistently, in a firmer voice. "You've been urged for years to show your paintings in New York. Secretary Wallace began begging you in 1935 to exhibit your landscapes —he said they were hymns to the earth. You know he's always loved your portraits and pen drawings of the earth-loving people of the valley. Why not show those paintings now? Let it be the start of a new life for you as a painter."

She clutched his arm with her hand and pleaded, "Please, Frank, your decision on this can be enormously important to you . . . to us. I want to show your paintings."

He frowned and rubbed his face and neck. "I hate to oppose you, Jemmy. But those paintings will be called naive now. Because Clinch County is no longer that way. TVA is no longer the servant of the earth as a way of life. It's the servant of bombs and bombers. It no longer uses clean falling water to generate electricity to grind corn and light milksheds and preserve the produce of the land. Now there's sulfur-bearing coal generating power to separate explosive atoms from non-explosive ones, and to smelt aluminum for bombers and automobile engines. The fumes are choking the people and killing the earth. The people are no longer earth-loving Arcadians but dispossessed servants of war industry. The paintings I completed before 1940 are now falsehoods, don't you see that—how could you want to show them?"

"They are not falsehoods," said Diane. "They *are* the earth and the people you loved, and they're beautiful. And what about the few paintings you've completed since the war ended? God knows those are ugly, but they're impressive. The men from New York want to see them. Particularly *Hiroshima.* I want to show them."

Castleton got up and walked away a short distance, continuing to rub his neck before coming back. "All right. I'll compromise with you, Jemmy. You invite the men in New York to visit our home next Wednesday. Then on Tuesday you fly home and gather up everything I've drawn or painted since 1945 and burn it. Including *Hiroshima.* On Wednesday you can show the men everything I completed up to 1941 . . . sketches, genres, pen drawings, water colors, scale oil portraits, landscapes . . . everything. Will that satisfy you?"

She was puzzled. "Why do you want me to destroy all your work since 1945?"

"I'll explain that in a week or so," he said. "But it's got to do with . . . you see, I'm beginning to believe that I can imagine another goal worth seeking . . . that it's possible I can work again . . . and love . . . even aspire. But now I want your promise that you'll destroy everything since 1945. Then you can show all my earlier work."

Diane wondered what she should say. She looked at Mary Sullivan, but Mary didn't look up from her book. Her husband, more resolute than he had been in two years, was demanding an answer. "All right, Frank," she said. "I'll do what you want done, and tell you all about it next Friday afternoon. Then you'll leave the hospital with me, and we'll stay at the

Shoreham for two or three weeks. And then home."

Mary and Diane walked away together, leaving Castleton on the bench. When they were out of his hearing Diane asked, "How was I? Did I say anything I shouldn't have said?"

"No," said Mary, "you did fine. You were direct and definite. That's what works best with him."

"He responded more to me today than he has in months," said Diane.

"Yes, he's getting better," said Mary. "Today has been an uncomfortable day for him—you know, both you and I told him that he's got to fish or cut bait."

"Are we pushing him too hard?"

"I don't think so," said Mary. "You heard what he said about confinement. He feels that it degrades him. We're got to cure him in a hurry or we will have crushed him. And maybe that's how it must be. You see, it may sound heartless, but the purpose of Navy medicine is to restore men to duty. The job assigned to Dr. Palkin and me is to restore Frank to duty as a father, a husband, an artist and a trusted supporter of the Commander-in-Chief. All patients here say that they have good days and bad days, and that's an accurate estimation. Their good days are when we commiserate with them; their bad days are when we remind them that they must shape up and return to duty."

They stopped, for the attendant was approaching to escort Diane to the taxi stand. Diane asked, "Do you believe he'll ever be a man again?"

"Yes," said Mary. "Do you?"

"I don't know," said Diane. "I hope and pray for him, but somehow it's hard for me to believe at this point that he'll ever feel sure of himself again."

On Sunday morning Frank Castleton was sitting on the side of his bed, yawning, stretching, waking up from narcotized sleep, when a key rattled in the door. The Negro attendant came in, said, "good morning," laid the safety razor on the table, and went out, locking the door behind him. Castleton stood up, shed his pajamas, went into the bathroom and urinated into the bowl, then went to the window, which faced southeast toward Washington. The sun was an hour high, and he did some bending and breathing exercises. His muscles responded to the fresh oxygen pumped into them, and he felt a new sureness, a physical strength, course down the length of his body. Then, picking up the razor, he went back into the bathroom, lathered his face and began shaving. The razor was unwieldy, because a lock was built into the handle to keep the blade from being removed without a key.

I never before realized that keys are so important, he thought. Or that the title Keeper of the Keys is so prestigious. Possession of the keys—that's the difference between the trusted and the distrusted, the balanced and the unbalanced. The thought made him feel ashamed. Goddammit, he vowed, today, after two years of being unable to do it, I'm going to muster the will to start being a man in possession of himself again. I'm going to start planning, working, completing, fucking, loving and celebrating life again. Mary Sullivan can begin reporting that *this* patient is showing optimistic expectation, that he is bravely trying to make the best of his situation, and that he won't have to be consigned to Custodial Care Only.

After shaving he showered, then stood toweling himself. His cock was hanging heavier than it had for months—longer and thicker—and this pleased him. He smiled as he recalled that Picasso had said that he painted with his prick. Some of Picasso's paintings, Castleton thought, look like he literally painted them with his prick. But Castleton understood what the artist meant. If a man feels that his cock is losing its ability to thrust, he has no confidence in himself. To be capable of action a man should wake up every morning with his cock looking him in the face, challenging him to act like a man.

When Castleton stepped out of the bathroom, stretched and tightened his gut, his cock had hardened to the horizontal position. It wasn't as hard as it could be when a desirable woman's hand was on it, guiding it into an orifice, but it was hard enough to make him delightfully conscious of its weight. He recalled an incident at Sewanee when he was sixteen. About twenty cadets were naked in the locker room, some of them in the communal shower, when Stumpy McDowell pounded his chest and boasted that he was "hung heavier" than any man at the academy. "Not as heavy as Frank," another cadet shouted, and in the ensuing referendum Castleton won by a two-thirds vote. Stumpy has never forgiven me for that, Castleton thought, grinning.

As he pulled on his slacks and sport shirt, his attendant came in again, set the breakfast tray on the table, retrieved the razor and went out. Castleton relished the oatmeal, eggs, bacon, toast and coffee, although he was very much aware of the paraffin-coated pasteboard bowl, plate, spoon, fork and cup. Tomorrow I'll have crockery and silver again, he said to himself. Today is my turnaround day. Each day hereafter I'll feel more confident—I'm determined that I will. I'll describe my experiences with Roosevelt and Truman to the doctor and Mary; they'll listen and question; then with will and effort I'll accept, adjust, regain balance and become a functioning man again. This morning I'll organize my thoughts and prepare for next week's therapy. This afternoon I'll play golf . . . and I'll win

... for golf, once you know how to swing, is a game of confidence. You can hit a good shot only if you can imagine it before you swing. You can sink a putt only if you can stroke it smoothly and not jab at it.

After breakfast Castleton went back into his bedroom, to the table on which lay the three books the doctor had asked him to study: Freud's *Civilization and Its Discontents*, Niebuhr's *Moral Man and Immoral Society*, and the Bible. He sat down, opened a tablet and picked up a blue wax crayon—the only writing implement he was permitted. He wasn't allowed anything as rigid as a pen or pencil. Across the top of the page he wrote: "The Case of the United States Against Frank Castleton." He drew a horizontal line and under it wrote: "The Charge: Extravagant Expectation leading to Unjustified Despair in which Castleton Imperiled the Nation, Embarrassed his Family and Made a Fool of Himself." He then drew a vertical line dividing the remainder of the page. On the left side he wrote: "The Plaintiffs," and quickly drew profiles of Truman, Leahy, Blanton, Potter, Hardwick, Diane, Susan and Cord. On the right side he wrote: "The Defendant," and drew a profile of himself.

That's my situation, he concluded. I'm on trial, with Dr. Palkin and Mary Sullivan as my appointed judges. He tore the page from the tablet and laid it on the table. On a fresh page he wrote: "Witnesses for the Plaintiffs against the Defendant":

SIGMUND FREUD, saying: A man who regards the reality of war as an unbearable source of human suffering may try to eliminate war. But whoever, in desperate defiance of reality, sets out upon this path to happiness attains nothing. Reality is too strong for him. He becomes a madman who finds no one to help him in carrying through his delusion.

REINHOLD NIEBUHR, saying: Yearners for permanent peace among nations cannot see that the limitations of the human imagination, the easy subservience of reason to prejudice and passion, and the consequent persistence of irrational egoism, particularly in group behavior, make conflict between nations an inevitability in human history, probably to its very end.

THE HOLY BIBLE, saying: From whence come wars and fighting among you? Come they not of your lusts? Ye lust and have not; ye kill, and desire to have, and cannot obtain. . . . Your life is but a vapour that appeareth for a little time, then vanisheth away.

JOE BRAMWELL, saying: Frank, avoid the sin of vanity. Work for peace but don't expect it. Man has an infinite capacity for pulling the roof down on his head. Wherever peace exists war impends.

He then wrote: "Witnesses for the Defendant":

ONLY HIMSELF, saying: Your Honors, to the charge of *extravagant* expectation and *unjustified* despair, I plead not guilty. I will convince you, beyond doubt, that had the American people known what I knew in 1943 and 1944 and 1945, the United States would have achieved its national purpose of ending war among nations and lifting the burden of armament from the shoulders of mankind.

In 1945, as Cordell Hull foresaw, the United States reached the zenith of its power. It then failed, irretrievably, and began its decline and fall. But that failure was not due to the limitations and perversities of man: It was due to the failure of Roosevelt and Truman to inform the American people.

By revealing to you what I knew during that pivotal period . . . what Roosevelt and Truman could have revealed to every man . . . I will convince you that my expectation was reasonable and my disappointment justified.

Castleton now read carefully what he had written, and he began to feel relaxed and comfortable. Jesus, I've found the way to my salvation, he thought. I must first justify my depression, fanaticism, neuroticism, hysteria and impotence. Only after justification can I accept national failure, adjust to it and find sustaining purpose in cultivating myself for myself—in being a painter and musician in pursuit of happiness.

Justification, he repeated to himself. I must first feel completely justified. And that depends on how clearly I can remember and describe my experience . . . what I knew on certain dates, what Roosevelt and then Truman knew, what I believed and they believed. Take January, 1943. The American people knew nothing about the bomb. Congress knew nothing. Cordell Hull and Truman knew nothing. But what did Roosevelt and I know? Castleton's memory fastened on the afternoon of January 3, 1943.

AT 1:20 P.M., at the New York Central station at Hyde Park, New York, three men stepped off the train from New York City: Frank Castleton accompanied by a security officer and a film technician from the Manhattan Project. All three carried luggage, and they wore heavy overcoats, for snow was on the ground and the temperature was below freezing. A car, which had been waiting for them, transported them to the President's home. There, while the President completed his customary after-lunch nap, they waited in a cottage with Secret Service men. At 2:35 Castleton was summoned to the President's study. The security officer and the film technician helped him carry the luggage; then they returned to the cottage, leaving Castleton alone with the President.

"It's good to see you, Frank," said the President, who sat at his desk with his shirt collar open. "I hope you and your family enjoyed the holidays."

"We had a good Christmas, sir," said Castleton. "I hope it was good for you."

"My only complaint is my usual dratted cold. Now . . . you've been working two months. Make me understand all you've learned."

Castleton took a bottle of gritty greenish earth from a bag and handed it to the President. "All right, that's uranium ore," he said. "The richest on earth. It's from the Shinkolobwe mine in the Belgian Congo. It's three hundred times as rich as any known North American ore. The reason we happen to have plenty of it today is because of one Belgian businessman's faith in Franklin Roosevelt."

"In me?"

"Yes, sir. His name is Edgar Sengier—president of the Union Minière du Haut-Katanga, the world's largest producer of uranium ore. In 1939 the French atomic scientist Frederic Joliot-Curie informed Sengier of uranium's potential military value. Early in 1940 Joliot-Curie approached Sengier with a plan to develop atomic weapons in the Congo. But Joliot-Curie is a Communist. Sengier rejected his offer and shipped twelve hundred tons of uranium ore to New York. He offered it to our War Department—they didn't want it—so he stored it in steel drums in a warehouse on Staten Island. He wanted any decisive new weapons to be in the hands of Roosevelt and the United States. Two years later he learned that we were ready to develop atomic weapons and were preparing to use the poor Canadian and American ores. He reminded the War Department of his treasure-trove and delivered it to us at the market price. From now on we'll get the entire production of the Shinkolobwe mine."

"That's great!" exclaimed the President. "I knew that we were getting ore from the Congo, but I hadn't heard this man's story. What's his name again?"

"Sengier—but, Mr. President, he's not alone in trying to give the United States the bomb," said Castleton. "In 1939, when Joliot-Curie was telling Sengier about uranium's military value, Niels Bohr, a Dane, brought the news that fission had been accomplished to the United States. It was Bohr who first suspected that the U-235 atom was the one that men could split, and it was he who explained this to American physicists, some of whom had studied under him in Copenhagen. Bohr was the man who initiated the series of conferences which led to your decision to make the bomb. He foresaw that, if all else failed, the atomic bomb could be used to free Europe from Hitler. Now we had the idea for the weapon, as well as the ore from which to make it."

The President fitted a cigarette into his long holder, lighted it, inhaled and leaned back in his chair. "Would you say that Bohr is the most brilliant of the atomic scientists?"

Castleton nodded. "Without question. He's been the towering genius since 1913. But Enrico Fermi and John von Neumann are also geniuses, you understand. The little nation of Hungary, considering its size, is making the greatest contribution to the bomb. In addition to Neumann, Hungary has sent us Eugene Wigner, Leo Szilard and Edward Teller—all giants. And remember this, sir! In 1940, when Joliot-Curie was urging Sengier to help make the bomb in the Congo, he was urging all these other men to go with him either to the Congo or to Moscow and help make the bomb. Joliot-Curie wanted Stalin to have the bomb, not Roosevelt. But the scientists chose Roosevelt and came here. So the atomic bomb will not belong to America but to mankind. America will be mankind's trustee, and the purpose of atomic energy will be to relieve some of the ills of mankind, beginning with that of international war."

Removing the cigarette holder from his mouth, the President grinned. "After hearing such talk, Frank," he said, "I can't help but remember your reaction a few weeks ago when I assigned you to this project. You went white with rage and fear, and threatened me with insurrection, public condemnation, even physical violence. Now you sound like a convert. Have you lost your fear?"

"No, sir," replied Castleton. "I'm still afraid, only now I've also developed a sense of awe about what we're doing. Atomic energy is the basic energy of the universe. If mankind can't use it to end war, then mankind will have lost its last chance to progress, perhaps even to survive. I'm awed by the responsibility on your shoulders."

The President ignored the statement. "What other *information* have you brought me?"

Castleton showed him a color photograph, saying, "This is what uranium metal looks like. The Congo ore is sixty-five percent uranium oxide, and the oxide reduces to a heavy hard nickel-white metal. It's radioactive like radium and can damage body tissue, so I couldn't bring you a sample."

From a bag Castleton now took a glass bottle filled with blue and yellow marbles. The bottle was flat-sided, about twelve inches high, six inches wide and two inches thick. "This represents the common uranium atom," he said. "It's the largest and heaviest atom in the universe. At the center of every atom there is a grouping of particles called protons and neutrons. Held together by the strongest force in nature, these protons and neutrons form the atom's nucleus. Each element has a distinctive number of protons in its atoms. The U atom has the most protons: 92. So, you see, this bottle contains 92 blue marbles representing protons. The common U atom also has the most neutrons: 146. So this bottle contains 146 yellow marbles, standing for neutrons. Ninety-two protons plus 146 neutrons makes 238 particles in the nucleus of the common uranium atom: U-238. There it is." He set the bottle on the desk before the President.

"This is the atom we can't split?" asked the President.

"That's correct," said Castleton. "Now, here's the one we *can* split." He took a second bottle from the bag and set it beside the first bottle. It looked exactly like the first bottle, and was also filled with blue and yellow marbles. "This is the rare U atom: U-235. It contains the same 92 blue marbles . . . protons . . . but it has only 143 yellow marbles . . . three less neutrons. So the U-235 atom is smaller and lighter than the U-238 atom."

While the President stared at the two models, Castleton continued. "Now you see what the physicists did at the Kaiser Wilhelm Institute in December, 1938? Because the uranium atoms are so heavy with that great number of protons and neutrons, the physicists suspected that if they bombarded uranium atoms with neutrons, some of the uranium atoms might break up and release their energy. So, using radium as a neutron source, they did just that. A neutron, unless you slow it down by compelling it to pass through a moderator, travels at ten thousand miles a second. The neutron bombardment failed to split the U-238 atom, but it did split the U-235 atom."

"How did the physicists know they had split an atom?"

"Because they suddenly noted the presence of barium," answered Castleton. "The barium could have come only from uranium. So, with the bombardment, the physicists were splitting one heavyweight uranium atom into two mediumweight barium atoms . . . converting one element into another."

"How did they know that it was only the U-235 that they had split?"

"Well, actually, they didn't know that at first. Bohr studied the experiment and, with calculations you and I could never understand, demonstrated why the U-235 is more vulnerable to bombardment than the U-238."

"How does energy result from such splitting?"

"Let's see—well, when you tear apart an atom, it's like squeezing a toy balloon until it bursts. You reverse the force that held the atom's protons and neutrons together, and you release atomic energy."

The President nodded. "And if the neutrons from one splitting atom," he said, "speed on and split other atoms, we get the chain reaction which will release a devastating quantity of energy?"

Castleton nodded. "Yes. Right, Mr. President. That's what heats the sun: the constant fissioning and fusioning of trillions of atoms. But to get the release which will be devastating, we first must separate the few U-235 atoms from the many U-238 atoms and create uranium metal composed almost entirely of U-235 atoms. Just a minute—I want to demonstrate the separation problem."

From another bag Castleton took a volley-ball-sized glass bowl and set it before the President. "As you can see," he said, "this bowl appears to be filled with white marbles . . . 1,390 white marbles. Now, take the bowl in your hands and shake up the white marbles and see if you can expose a bright red marble." The President shook the bowl and exposed first one, then a second red marble.

"There are ten red marbles in the bowl," said Castleton. "And there you have nature's uranium metal: 139 U-238 atoms to every one U-235 atom. And that's our separation problem."

"Looks impossible," said the President.

"It would be impossible under ordinary conditions," said Castleton. "But we've got everything in our favor—we have most of the atomic geniuses of the world being assisted by Franklin Roosevelt and the resources of Dupont, Eastman, General Electric, Allis-Chalmers, Westinghouse and all the other industrial might of America. With unlimited money and highest priorities. Here's how we'll do it."

Castleton handed the President a six-inch-long glass tube, fused at both ends, filled with a brownish gas. "Since you can't separate atoms in solid metal," he said, "the first step is to convert uranium metal into a gaseous compound. Uranium will convert into only one gaseous compound: uranium hexafluoride . . . UF_6 . . . what you see in that tube. The molecule is formed when one uranium atom combines with six fluorine atoms. In uranium hexafluoride, of course, there are 139 molecules containing the U-238 atom to every one molecule containing the U-235 atom. All right, our problem is to separate these molecules. We can do this because the UF_6 molecule containing the U-235 atom is 3 neutrons lighter than the molecule containing the U-238 atom. Once we have separated the molecules and have a quantity of UF6 with only U-235 atoms, we can then separate the uranium from the fluorine by chemical process and have what we seek: uranium metal with only U-235 atoms."

"And that's what we're building Oak Ridge for," said the President.

"That's right, sir," said Castleton. "Oak Ridge is to be a billion-dollar molecule-separation center. With your permission, I'll now call in the film technician, and we'll set up and show you what's happening at Oak Ridge as of three days ago."

For half an hour the President and Castleton sat in semidarkness and watched the clearing and construction activities at Oak Ridge: old forests and newly planted forests, old homesteads and old cemeteries being plowed under by bulldozers; roads and railroads being built; trainloads of lumber, cement and machinery arriving; the hiring, transporting, feeding and housing of forty-five thousand construction workers. Castleton explained as the silent film ran:

"Here are some of the thousand homesteads being destroyed . . . the process which saddens both you and me, sir. We are creating American refugees . . . people with no place to belong.

"We will use two processes to separate the molecules: the electromagnetic process and the gaseous-diffusion process . . . Here's where we have begun to build the vast plant for the electromagnetic process. We hope to have this plant in operation by the end of this year, 1943. When completed, it will require twenty-four thousand persons to operate it day and night. It will use more electricity than the city of Boston . . . By the spring of 1945 we will have spent four hundred million dollars on this process, and by then we expect it to have created ten pounds of U-235 metal.

"The electromagnetic process will use hundreds of the largest magnets ever built to attract the lighter molecules containing U-235 atoms and thereby separate them from the heavier molecules containing the U-238 atoms.

"The gaseous-diffusion process is a filtering process . . . the gas is forced into a perfect vacuum, then through thousands of filters and hundreds of miles of pipe, and after each filtering the gas will contain a few more of the lighter molecules and a few less of the heavier molecules.

"Here is where we have begun to build the gaseous-diffusion plant. We hope to have it in operation by June, 1944—next year, that is. It's located four miles from the electromagnetic plant as a protective measure against catastrophic accident . . . and, as you see, the two plants are separated by high ridges. The gaseous diffusion plant, too, will require twenty-four thousand people to operate it around the clock. By June, 1945, we will have spent four hundred million dollars on this process, and by then it will have created ten pounds of U-235 metal.

"The twenty pounds from these two processes will be enough for the first atomic bomb, which will have cost us one billion dollars. After July 1, 1945, these two processes will create U-235 metal at the rate of hundreds of pounds a year."

After the film was shown, the machinery cleared away and the lights turned on, servants brought tea and cakes, and the President and Castleton talked for another twenty minutes. The President looked intently at his visitor. "After working for ten weeks, Frank, are you convinced that this bomb will be a reality—an enormously devastating force?"

Castleton replied promptly, "I'm completely convinced. I was under the grandstand at Stagg Field with Fermi just a month ago. What Fermi did, in effect, was to build a crude atomic bomb and explode it, except that he slowed and controlled the explosion. He achieved a controlled, slow-neutron chain reaction in natural uranium in which only one atom out of every 140 is fissionable."

"And that *proves* that an atomic bomb will work?"

"Beyond reasonable doubt," said Castleton. "You see, Mr. President, a neutron may travel at ten thousand miles a second, but it's possible to slow it down. A bullet leaves a rifle barrel at high speed, but you can reduce the speed by firing the bullet through water or wood. Well, that's what Fermi did with his neutrons. He first considered using water, then decided to use graphite as the moderator to slow down his neutrons. He and his assistants assembled six tons of natural uranium metal, fifty tons of uranium oxide, and four hundred tons of graphite into a twenty-eight-foot-high pile —that's an atomic bomb. Each six-pound lump of uranium was separated from other uranium by eight inches of graphite. When the U-235 atoms began splitting and throwing off neutrons, setting off the chain reaction, there was no explosion because the graphite slowed the neutrons to where the atoms released only controllable amounts of heat and radiation. There are substances like cadmium which not only reduce the speed of neutrons but also absorb them. So Fermi could stop his chain reaction by inserting cadmium rods into the reactor—the *bomb* is the reactor, you see. Then he could start the reaction again by withdrawing the cadmium rods. But I can assure you, sir, that had Fermi used less graphite in his bomb, and no cadmium rods—had he let his chain reaction run out of control—his bomb would have devastated much of Chicago."

The President turned a grim face to Castleton. "You are telling me then that you have already witnessed what, in effect, was the explosion of an atomic bomb?"

"That's exactly right, sir," said Castleton. "All that we will be doing for the next two years is refining uranium and designing a container that will fit into the bomb bay of a B-29. When we explode the first atomic bomb we will use twenty pounds of almost pure U-235 metal, in which almost every atom will be fissionable. When we start the chain reaction, with neutrons from those splitting atoms traveling at ten thousand miles a second, the splitting of all the atoms in that twenty pounds will be virtually instantaneous, and all the fissionable material will be consumed. The result will be an explosive release of heat and radiation that will incinerate a city."

The President sipped his tea and reflected. "Why is it, Frank, that a good and capable expert like Bill Leahy—an acknowledged expert on explosives—regards the Manhattan Project as foolishness? He feels absolutely certain that atomic weapons will never be a factor in warfare."

Castleton breathed deeply, then answered, "Admiral Leahy was not at Stagg Field with Fermi. I was. I looked at that huge pile of uranium and graphite, and I had no conception of what might happen inside it. But I knew that something was going to happen that had never happened before. I knew it because Fermi knew it. That man is incredible, you know—a stocky bald-headed Italian, dirty from graphite, with a slide rule and a notebook in his hip pocket. Every now and then he'd jerk out his slide rule, consult it, then jot down rows of figures that only Bohr or Neumann could understand. And you know the most amazing thing, Mr. President? The achievement of the chain reaction was an anticlimax, because Fermi had so obviously known what was going to happen that the rest of us knew it too. Hours before it happened we had accepted it as an accomplished fact. So now, thirty months before we are likely to explode a U-235 bomb, I know it's a certainty. And I urge you, sir, to accept it as a certainty."

The President was silent for a moment. Then he smiled and said, "Well, old top, you've given me about all I can absorb in one afternoon. You're doing a grand job for me! You're helping me understand what I see in the War Department reports. Have you run into any problems in getting information?"

"No, sir."

"You and Paul Blanton get along all right?"

"Yes, sir. I've invited him to spend nights at my home whenever he visits Oak Ridge. He and I will travel together to Hanford this month. You know, construction is getting underway there."

"Good. Keep at it. I'll arrange to see you again in a few weeks."

Castleton knew he was being dismissed, but he stood where he was before the President. "Before I go, sir, may I say this. The scientists know the battle of Stalingrad is ending this week. They know the decisive battles have been fought in the Pacific. The Germans and Japanese have lost, and the scientists don't believe the bomb will be used in this war—it won't be ready in time. So their hope is that all atomic weapons will be monopolized by the new world organization and used only to end all international war and preparations for such war."

The President stirred impatiently. "I understand that, Frank," he said sharply. "Tell the scientists I want exactly what they want. You and I'll discuss it when we get further down the road."

Castleton persisted, knowing he was risking the President's anger. "Would you consider telling Mr. Hull this week about the imminence of atomic weapons?"

"No!" The President was visibly irritated. "Not yet! And you leave that *strictly* to me!"

Castleton got up quickly, fearing he had gone too far. "I understand, sir. I hope you can go to Warm Springs soon and get rid of that cold."

The President relaxed but didn't smile. He held out his hand for Castleton to shake, and wished him a pleasant journey back to Washington.

THE memory faded, but it had destroyed much of Castleton's new resolution. Again he felt weak, his chest felt constricted, his neck muscles rigid. He walked about the room, rubbing his neck, breathing deeply. "My God," he said aloud, "if only I could have made him feel a sense of urgency! That was where I failed first. I couldn't *move* him!"

This time, however, Castleton was determined not to surrender to depression. "I've got to fight it and beat it!" he muttered as he paced the room. "This is my turnaround day, damn it. By sheer willpower I'm going to regain confidence and start functioning as a man again!" He continued pacing, then suddenly stopped to stand at a window. He expanded his lungs, twisted his neck, flexed his fingers and tried to fight his rigidity and despair and the feeling of impotence. Gradually he began to feel a bit more relaxed. Then he began to look forward to the afternoon of golf with the doctors and the evening with Mary Sullivan. When the Negro attendant came to accompany him to the golf course, he was ready.

THE warm bright afternoon of Sunday, May 2, 1948, was a successful one for Castleton, for his wife and for Stumpy McDowell. Castleton proved adequate on the golf course, after a bad beginning as Dr. Palkin's partner against the other two doctors. On the first tee he was tense and nervous. He was wearing borrowed shoes that didn't quite fit, and using clubs that were an inch too short for him. He knew the doctors were all watching him closely, and the feeling of being scrutinized, even in a game, made him anxious and uneasy. He hit his first drive far over the fence enclosing the hospital grounds. On the second hole he shanked his approach shot. Continuing to miss shots, he parred only one hole of the first nine, and he and Dr. Palkin were two down in the match.

On the second nine Castleton began to relax and improve his concentration and timing. His caddy, the Negro attendant, began talking with him, calming him and advising him on distances and rolls. Castleton realized that he had not, up to this point, asked the Negro's name (it was Sam), and they soon became friendly. The result was that Castleton parred five holes and bogied the other four, and he and Dr. Palkin won the match when he parred the long eighteenth hole.

After the game Castleton was not invited into the doctors' lounge for a drink, but Dr. Palkin assured him, "You did fine, Frank. Now enjoy your evening with Mary. She's a good nurse, but she's also a marvelous cook. You and I'll talk tomorrow." The Negro attendant accompanied Castleton back to his room and locked him in. Over their drinks the other two physicians commented to Dr. Palkin:

"I believe he can stabilize himself with your help. He can still coordinate, concentrate and compete. So he isn't likely to become paranoid."

"Of course, he'll always be crippled to some extent by his obsession. But you can help him adjust to where he can live with it."

DIANE Castleton and Stumpy McDowell began noticing that they complemented each other at the garden party at Tregaron. In all his years in Washington, Stumpy had never before escorted a woman anywhere. He was not a man who went with women, preferring to enter and leave parties alone. He used women to gather information for him, to adorn his own gatherings and flatter his male guests. Other than that, they were to slip into his house twice a week, lunch with him, get fucked and get out. He never went after them; he never drove them home.

The party at Tregaron was the most important of the year. It was an occasion for everybody who was somebody in Washington to gather in sunlight, stroll in flower gardens, sip champagne, inhale fresh air and nod to one another. And this year Stumpy was attracting more attention than usual. He was *with* a woman! Everybody recognized her from her pictures in the paper, and everybody could see that she wasn't gorgeous, dazzling or youthful. She was, however, pretty, mature, self-assured, pleasant, sensuous and graceful. She was skilled only in the art of being with a man. But what did she have that Stumpy wanted so much? It couldn't be that he simply wanted to fuck her and cuckold another husband! He could do that, if he hadn't already done it, without bringing her to Tregaron. No, what he wanted wasn't sexual, so it had to be political. He expected to use her to learn what her husband knew, since Frank Castleton was said to have knowledge damaging to Truman.

"That son of a bitch!" Paul Blanton said to his wife as they nodded coolly to Stumpy and Diane. "He's after her, and I've got to keep him from getting what he wants."

Stumpy himself wasn't sure why he had arranged for Diane to be invited. He had asked himself the question while he waited at the Shoreham for her to come down. What the hell, he had hated Frank Castleton at Sewanee! Once he wanted to kill him. So why had he pretended to be friendly with Frank over the years at reunions? Why had he invited Frank to his home so often during the war? Why had he urged him to go back to Tennessee and forget his disappointments after the war? Why was he being nice to his wife now? Stumpy wasn't sure, although he supposed it had something to do with his ego. Frank had been first in the class at Sewanee. Stumpy had been last.

Stumpy didn't realize, though, that his wanting Diane with him was partly a result of his having begun to feel like a card-carrying member of society. During the Depression and war years he hadn't felt respectable because he hadn't been respected. At a time when people needed to believe in God, country and man, publishers were not proud of publishing daily reports on how government officials were lying, stealing, drinking and fucking. Publishers ran Stumpy's column on back pages and told their friends that they bought the column only because so many readers wanted the low-down. Both Roosevelt and Truman had denounced Stumpy publicly as a lying son of a bitch, and most members of the Washington press corps disliked him. But after the war, with Missouri *muzhiks* infesting the White House and disenchantment mounting, Stumpy's exposures came to be regarded as sound journalism. Publishers moved the column onto editorial pages, the radio network moved the broadcast to prime time and Stumpy became a fair-haired boy. So one reason he had Diane with him at the party was that, respecting himself, he had become capable of respecting her.

As he moved with her through the gardens, nodding or speaking to colleagues, he noticed that he was enjoying himself and that she was adding to his enjoyment. When they got into his car and drove away, he found himself saying, "Diane, I've got to run and get ready for the broadcast. I'd like you to watch it. So why don't I drop you at the hotel, then in about an hour one of my leg men will pick you up and bring you to the station. We'll get you a grandstand seat where you can watch and hear everything."

"I'd like that," said Diane.

"Then," said Stumpy, "after the broadcast you and I can drive out to Olney Inn for supper?"

"I'd like that too," she said.

The broadcast amazed Diane. She found it intensely dramatic. She had heard the program several times on the radio, but listening to Stumpy's voice was nothing like watching him perform. Waiting for the signal to begin speaking, he crouched at the desk like a linebacker anticipating the snap. The instant he began, he was the people's embattled watchdog on the Potomac: growling at rascals, tearing into thieves, ripping the pants off hypocrites, exposing their bare asses to the stars. Belligerent! Defiant! All in the cause of truth and justice! He rang bells, buzzed buzzers, sounded alarums. He became mischievous when he hinted at homosexuality. His was the Voice of Doom when he intoned, "In Truman's Lubianka Frank Castleton is still being held incommunicado! He must be freed before they destroy his mind!" Near the end he was every good man's friend as he plugged the books, films and magazine articles of people who did him favors; and when he closed every listener must have felt that he could sleep safely so long as Keith McDowell was at his post.

Diane was breathless herself when Stumpy rushed over to hear her opinion of his performance. "Good Lord! No wonder you have millions of listeners and earn a mint of money! Think what the stage missed when you became a reporter."

Diane, riding beside Stumpy in the Cadillac Coupe de Ville through the Maryland countryside, realized quietly how satisfying it felt to be with a man who was not disappointed . . . a successful man who relished his success . . . a hearty man who could grin impishly as he attacked other men. Strangely, however, the Stumpy who rode beside her now seemed pensive and subdued.

"Diane," he said finally, staring straight down the road into the dark, clear night, "I want you to know me better. Every time you've seen me up to now, I've been playing a role, see. At the class reunions I've been the bachelor boy telling dirty jokes and kissing all the wives, especially you. Here in Washington you've seen me as the roistering muckraker, and you've heard that I'm an after-lunch stud-horse for rutting wives. You've never met the real Clark Keith McDowell."

"I'd like to know the real Clark Keith," she said. "Let's start by you calling me Jemmy. Diane is a cold name."

"Okay, Jemmy." He kept his eyes focused ahead of him. "The real Clark Keith is a lonely troubled man who has had a hard time clawing his way to the top of the dungheap. Did Frank ever tell you about a fight he and I had at Sewanee?"

"No, not Frank," she said. "But I know—other classmates mentioned it. When I asked Frank about it he said it was nothing more than corn likker and Saturday night."

"It was more than that. I had hated him for five years. I wanted to kill him."

Diane turned to Stumpy. "That's pretty serious! What did he do to you?"

"It wasn't what he did but what he was. God, he was the most graceful man I'd ever met—I envied the way he ran, marched, danced. The way he played a piano or drew at picture."

"Of course."

"For twenty-six years I've been haunted by a song and a scene. The song is 'Till We Meet Again.' You remember it? 'Smile awhile . . . '" He hummed a few bars.

"Sure, I remember it," she said. "We've danced to it all our lives."

"You and Frank have danced to it. Not me. Well, I never could dance anyway. The scene that haunts me is the decorated softly lighted Sewanee gym on a moonlit night with snow on the ground. George Olson's band is playing 'Till We Meet Again,' and everybody but me is dancing. I'm standing in the corner watching—clumsy, bull-necked, barrel-chested, no sense of rhythm, hands like meat hooks. And I'm watching Frank Castleton and Carole Curtis. Poetry in motion! Frank in his tuxedo and Carole in a long blue gown, bare-backed, with that golden hair piled high on her head. I thought she was the most desirable girl in the world. When the music stopped she pulled Frank down and kissed him. God, did she love him! I watched them and ate my heart out."

"But you had no reason to!" exclaimed Diane. "You were a great football star. Everybody wanted to meet you."

"That wasn't enough," he said. "You see, I wanted what Frank had. Then I went to a lot of trouble to look up his other girl. For a couple of years several of us had guessed that he was meeting a girl somewhere on Sunday afternoons. He was never around the fraternity house then, and he never went with any of us to bang whores in hotels in Chattanooga or Nashville. So I figured it was some professor's daughter or wife . . . maybe he was meeting her in some cave or shack on the mountain. I had to find out, so I began trying to follow him. That wasn't easy—he never started in the same direction twice, and he'd circle around, backtrack and lose me. I began just going out into the woods and hiding, watching for him. I tried it week after week."

"And you caught him?"

"Never," said Stumpy. "But I saw him enter a cove. That surprised me, because I couldn't figure Frank in bed with a Cove-ite. He lost me there, so I didn't see what shack he entered. But during the week I went back into that cove and visited every shack. The Cove-ites wouldn't tell me anything, but they didn't need to. I knew I'd recognize the girl if I saw her."

"You found her?"

"I sure did. When I hollered at her shack she opened the door and stood there. She looked like no other Cove-ite ever looked. Proud . . . pretty . . . part Indian . . . neatly dressed . . . cared for . . . well-nourished and healthy. Looking at her, I thought of all the ugly whores I had been on while Frank was on her. It ground my guts!"

"Did she tell you anything?"

"She never opened her mouth. When I asked her if Frank had ever been there she shook her head and closed the door in my face. But she was the one. I found out her name. Bess Foshee."

Diane was beginning to feel irritated. It all seemed so petty to her. She said, "So because of Bess Foshee and Carole Curtis and 'Till We Meet Again,' you wanted to kill Frank?"

"Goddamn it, Jemmy," said Stumpy, "I didn't want to kill him. I felt that I *had* to kill him. Just like Cain had to kill Abel. I thought of waylaying him in the woods and smashing his head with a rock. But I was too civilized for that. Instead, on Saturday night at the fraternity house I began drinking and calling Frank names. I called him a rednecked Cove-ite fucker. He had to go into the back yard with me. Several brothers came with us, and the fight began. Well, Frank wouldn't hit me with his fists, afraid he'd hurt his hands. I'd charge at him, trying to smash him down so I could beat his head in, break his hands and bust . . . get my knee in his groin. He fought defensively, using his goddamn agility—all elbows and knees. Twice I got him down and hit him hard in the face, but then he got lucky. When I charged at him he caught me with a knee in the groin and doubled me up in agony. That ended the fight."

"But you didn't stop hating Frank?"

"No, I guess I didn't. But I got where it didn't bother me so much. By Commencement, when we were all leaving, I was able to shake hands with Frank, tell him I was sorry and wish him well."

"What about Carole Curtis?"

Stumpy hesitated, then replied, "God help me, I guess I was pleased when I heard she was dead."

They had arrived at the Olney Inn, a rambling country home in which expensive food was served in several attractive rooms. When Stumpy and Diane walked in and were shown to a table, they were recognized, and Stumpy became his public self again. He spoke to several diners who said they had heard his broadcast and liked it. After he and Diane were seated, from time to time a man or woman came over to say a few words. Diane looked rather distracted. But when they were eating, she asked him, "Stumpy, tell me, feeling toward Frank as you did at Sewanee—I mean that incredible jealousy—how have you been able to act friendly toward him in the years since then?"

"Because he's my brother," said Stumpy, "and the particular brother I've always measured myself against. Young people in college today can't conceive of what five or six years on Sewanee Mountain were like from 1917 to '22. We were so few and so isolated—only thirty-seven in our class. We didn't even have a radio. We sometimes hated one another, being envious, jealous and so forth, but we ate, slept, drank, played, fought, marched, masturbated and learned together. Against the rest of the world we're united, and over the years we forget how we hated each other and remember only how good it was."

Diane asked, "Do you remember the reunion of '32? That's when I first met you. I remember that. Do you?"

"You were the main reason I attended," he answered. "I had felt hurt when Frank didn't invite me to his wedding. I had heard that you were a beauty and that Frank had really flourished—he'd gone ahead and built his Monticello. I wanted to see how you compared with Bess Foshee and Carole Curtis."

"Well . . . how did I compare?"

Stumpy stopped eating and turned his gaze away from her. Then he replied deliberately, "At first sight I thought you weren't the beauty Carole was. She was a stunning blonde, and you were just a pretty brunette. Then 'Till We Meet Again' was played, and I watched you and Frank dance together. I saw that you were fuller-lipped, fuller-bodied, deeper-eyed than Carole—designed a little more perfectly for loving and lovemaking. I knew why Frank had married you so quickly after he found you."

"So you still envied Frank?"

"Yes. I envied him you. I envied his gentle way of life. I was clawing desperately at the base of the dungheap here in Washington. He had nothing to do in Clinch County but dream and love and paint and make music and dance and hike through mountains while I clawed. Sure, I envied him."

Driving back to Washington, Stumpy and Diane smoked cigarettes and didn't talk much. They were weighing what had been said. He held her left hand in his right one, and she noticed how broad and thick his hand was, and how thick and short his fingers were, compared to Frank's. "Stumpy," she said at last, breaking the silence, "during the war, here in Washington, why did you invite Frank to your home so often?"

"Hell, you know why," he said. "I wanted him to see how successful I was—to admire me. Since I had become successful, I could afford to like him—to enjoy having him play my piano and charm my other guests. After dancing with him and watching him play the 'Moonlight Sonata,' every unattached woman and some of the attached ones wanted to leave the party with him. Instead of resenting that, I liked it. You see, it complimented me. And because Frank was so vulnerable, I began to feel a brotherly desire to protect him and keep him from making a fool of himself, from getting hurt in this jungle."

"You knew he was going to be disappointed, disillusioned?"

"From the day he arrived here with old man Hull," said Stumpy. "You see, Jemmy, Frank had always looked toward Washington hopefully. That meant he could only become a casualty. I tried to get him not to take all the crap about Four Freedoms and ending war among nations seriously. I told him just to enjoy the fucking war and expect nothing more from it than excitement and enrichment. But he wouldn't listen. He allowed Hull and

174

FDR to use him as their hope-filled waterboy, and they reduced him to a hopeless cripple."

"Oh, you're right. God knows, I tried to save him too," said Diane. "I begged him to go into the Army after Pearl Harbor."

"Yes, that might have done the trick," said Stumpy. "Near the end I began feeling sorry for him. I couldn't feel contempt, because Frank is so close to me. I remember a night in March '45. Frank had just returned from Yalta, where FDR kicked him in the stomach. There had been a party at my house, and I was downstairs, seeing the last guest out. When I started back upstairs I heard the piano. It was Frank, playing like his heart was breaking. 'Till We Meet Again!' I went to the door and watched him, then I walked over and put my hand on his shoulder. He turned his face to me, and he was crying, but he kept on playing. I knew what he was feeling, and he knew I knew. Neither of us said a word. I just stayed there a minute, then I left and went to bed."

At the Shoreham Stumpy pulled into the half-circle driveway, but he didn't stop under the marquee. Instead he stopped several car lengths beyond it, so he could have another few minutes with Diane. They both seemed reluctant to end their day together. Pushing back his seat, Stumpy turned to her and said, "Jemmy, you and I both know what's wrong with Frank. We don't need psychiatrists to tell us. He's loaded down with feelings of guilt. He feels guilty for no longer loving you, guilty for something he did or didn't do to Carole Curtis, for the way he treated Bess Foshee, for neglecting his children, guilty for Hiroshima, for failing himself, you, the country and mankind. So he's a cripple who can never hold up his head again. You know all that as well as I do."

"I hope that isn't true," she said. "But in any case, I have to protect him, don't you see? I must get him out of the hospital and back home. He's got to have a chance to do the best he can."

"I'll help you. We'll get a lawyer and we'll get him out."

Holding her hand in both of his, Stumpy began fumbling for words. "Meanwhile, Jemmy, I want . . . I want . . ."

She moved closer to him to help him. "What do you want?"

"I want you to know me a little better . . . every day."

"You mean . . . intimately?"

"I mean as a prospective wife."

"Good Lord!" she exclaimed. "You! You want a wife!"

"Why not? I'm forty-seven years old and on top of the dungheap. Why shouldn't I have a wife?"

"No reason why not, I guess. But why me?"

"Because for months I've been considering you as a wife for me . . . ever since I saw the change in Frank."

She sighed deeply. "Well, I'm . . . I am absolutely astounded. I've always thought of you as the most devilishly interesting of Frank's classmates. But the idea of you ever wanting to marry me, or I you . . . it just never occurred to me. I've thought that you might try to maneuver me into a bed, but marriage? Never."

"Well, start thinking about it, okay? I want to get in bed with you, but only as a husband . . . or a prospective husband."

After a moment she asked, "If we should start . . . prospecting? How can I know whether you're considering me for myself, or whether you're only achieving final victory over Cadet Thomas Francis Castleton?"

"Oh, you'll know," he said. "You're the sort of woman who'll know. All I'm asking now is that you start thinking about it. Will you?"

She smiled. "I won't put it entirely out of my mind." She moved to get out, and he got out, came around and assisted her. He walked with her into the hotel, through the lobby, to the elevators.

"I'll call you tomorrow," he said softly.

She nodded as the door closed.

EARLIER that Sunday evening, while Stumpy was preparing his radio broadcast, the attendant, Sam, returned to Castleton's rooms and unlocked the door. "If you're ready, Mr. Castleton," he said, "I'll show you to Lieutenant Sullivan's quarters. She asked me to bring you over."

Castleton eagerly followed Sam to the door. After the golf game he had asked the attendant to bring back the razor. He had shaved again, showered and put on another version of the hospital's uniform for patients: pants without a leather belt, a sport shirt without a necktie and shoes without laces. The uniforms differed in texture, value and color; otherwise, they were all alike, and were worn at all times except when the patient was swimming, sunning or working out in the gym. The two men left the hospital corridors and walked along the paths outside to Mary's apartment.

Except for a persistent sense of unease and unreality, he felt good. The afternoon's sunshine, the fact that he had functioned with three other men

177

on a golf course, had relieved the rigidity in his neck, and he walked easily alongside the Negro man. They passed the tennis courts, then entered a three-story brick building. They climbed a flight of stairs, and Sam rang Mary's doorbell. She opened the door, thanked and dismissed Sam and invited Castleton in. "Welcome to my humble abode," she said. "Look it over while I get you a drink."

It was a compact apartment with a small living area, dining area, kitchen, bedroom and bath. Gray shag rugs, black-lacquered Chinese modern furniture, green-tinted plaster walls, a seascape, bamboo-framed collections of photographs that a Navy nurse might collect while fighting her war in Hawaii, Guam and aboard hospital ships, and the record player playing Guy Lombardo records: "Red Roses for a Blue Lady," "Alice Blue Gown," "Poor Butterfly." Mary was wearing a yellow and red Chinese silk dress, split to above her right knee, and since she was slender and moved gracefully, she looked good in it. Her eyes twinkled mischievously when she handed him a drink and said, "I don't have any moonshine or hot chestnuts, but here's a cranberry special from Washington and macadamia nuts from Hawaii."

Over their drinks he reported on the golf game, and she chatted about a lazy day in which she had taken a sun bath, washed her hair and cleaned the apartment. Then she said, "There's one other woman who helped form some of your attitudes that I haven't heard about—your father's woman, Miss Edna. Tell me about her, okay? I'll get the food on the table."

From all that he had ever suspected, or been told by his father in several conversations over the years, Castleton related this story.

A man who buys and improves land can profit from exclusive tips given to him from the probate office in the county courthouse. Deeds, mortgages and wills are recorded at that office, so a clerk who works there is the first to know when title to a piece of land is conveyed from an aging or dead parent to a son or daughter who may want to convert the inheritance into cash. Land can be bought at a bargain only from an owner who wants to sell, and then only before competition develops among buyers. From 1910 until 1947, Bert Castleton held an advantage over all other land buyers in Clinch County. He was promptly and exclusively tipped from the probate office by an unusual woman named Edna Stabler.

Miss Edna, as she was known to most everybody in Clinch County, was

178

the chief clerk in the probate office from 1910, when she was twenty, until 1947, when she retired and moved to Florida. She was friendly; she knew how to meet the public; and she had a memory for names that no politician could match. She not only knew most everybody in the county, but she also knew what land he owned, how much it was worth, whether it was mortgaged or not and who was likely to inherit it. Men liked to look at Miss Edna, and take in the aroma of her body and perfume and pass the time of day with her. She always looked nice and fresh, she always smelled of a musky scent and she always knew what to say to make a man feel good. Men with no business at the courthouse often went there just to tell Miss Edna a good clean joke or give her a piece of gossip or put her wise to something that might happen. And since she drank coffee with the tax collector and the sheriff, and with lawyers and judges, there wasn't much that went on in Clinch County that Miss Edna didn't know about either before or soon after it happened.

What made Miss Edna even more unusual was that she didn't want to be a wife or mother. She was a pretty woman who could have had her pick of many men. They all tried to spark her when she was in her twenties, but by the time she was thirty they all knew that while she liked the company of men and all the banter of courthouse life, she never wanted any man to put his hands on her. This helped her with other women. After they decided they had nothing to fear from her, they liked her too. She sang soprano in the Methodist choir and attended socials, dances and fish fries, but whenever she entered the door of her own tidy little house, no man ever entered with her unless he was accompanied by his wife.

Miss Edna had no folks in Clinch County. Her father was a railroad man in Knoxville who was killed when she was twelve. Her mother then married an older man, and Miss Edna finished high school and took a business course. She was brought to Clinch County in 1910 by an old probate judge who needed an expert typist and recordkeeper. For a while she lived in a rooming house; then she built her own house, which over the years she made into a comfortable home. She lived alone there with a German shepherd dog.

What no one ever knew for certain and what only a few ever suspected was that a sexual relationship existed between Miss Edna and Bert Castleton. It was a limited partnership, arranged by Miss Edna to provide the extra security and occasional excitement she felt she should have. During her first weeks in the probate office she had evaluated the substantial men of the county. Since she didn't want a husband, she wanted a man who was happily married and who therefore would be unlikely ever to want to marry her. She didn't want one too old or too young. She wanted a man who was going to have something, who was dependable, who was not unattractive, who could keep his mouth shut and who was unlikely to impose much on her privacy or to try to limit her freedom. Bert Castleton was her first choice. He was thirty-two, married to an attractive woman he loved, father of three children he also loved, a pillar of the Episcopal Church, a Sewanee alumnus, a Spanish War veteran, a tall sunburned man with strong features and a friendly smile who didn't talk much and was a shrewd handler of money. As a banker he often visited the probate office to examine records —the bank was the probate office's largest customer, with mortgages to record every week—and Miss Edna went to the bank often to make deposits in the probate office's account. She also opened a personal account. By the end of the first month she was calling him "Mister Bert" and he was calling her "Miss Edna."

She grabbed the first opportunity to do him a favor. A farmer who owned a hundred and sixty acres along the Clinch River in the north end of the county dropped dead one morning while he was plowing. The moment Miss Edna heard of it, she went to the bank to tell Bert. But, as he was out fishing, she telephoned his home and introduced herself to his wife. Then she said, "Mrs. Castleton, I thought Mister Bert might want to know this. A farmer named Elbert Shaw has just died of heart failure. He owns one hundred and sixty acres of land which is unencumbered and which will likely go to his daughter who's married and lives in Detroit. She's expected to come here for the funeral."

Lila Scott Castleton was also a woman with a nose for profit. She was her husband's business partner as well as his mate. So her first impression of Miss Edna was favorable. She thanked her and said she must come to the Castleton home for dinner some Sunday. Two days later, after the funeral, Bert bought the one hundred and sixty acres from the daughter for $1,600. He made a little money on it each year until 1934, when he sold it to the government for $11,500. It was to be covered by water rising behind Norris Dam.

Bert made frequent trips to Knoxville for his various business interests, usually taking the morning train and returning on the late-afternoon train. Several times a year he stayed overnight, usually at the hotel but sometimes at a friend's home. Miss Edna also made occasional trips to Knoxville, to visit her mother or her sister. Twice during the next year Bert and Miss Edna found themselves on the train together, and they sat and talked. The second time they traveled together, Miss Edna mentioned that it was a shame that since she lived in a boarding house no one in Clinch County believed she could cook. To prove otherwise, and to repay him for Sunday dinners she enjoyed at his home, she'd like to cook him a meal at her mother's home sometime when they were both going to be in Knoxville. Bert said he'd look forward to it.

When she had been in Clinch County almost two years, Miss Edna was suddenly stricken with appendicitis and taken to a Knoxville hospital. Before the operation she told the surgeon she never intended to marry, so while he was removing her appendix he also was to tie her Fallopian tubes. He was shocked—such a mutilating action to a Christian virgin was unheard of! He protested it would be wrong—that she was only twenty-two and that later she'd regret it and become despondent and might even go mad. She replied that her body was hers and she had a right to alter it. The surgeon then demanded a written authorization, signed by her and witnessed by her family doctor. Although both doctors protested vehemently, they signed the authorization. After the operation she got a signed statement from the surgeon that her tubes had been tied and she could never become pregnant.

By six months after the operation, Miss Edna had won Bert Castleton's warm friendship. She had given him a dozen profitable tips, for which he had given her nothing but thanks. She had also become a friend of Lila Scott Castleton's, and was often in the Castleton home. One day, when Bert was in her office examining a mortgage record, she casually told him, "By the way, Mister Bert, I'm taking two days off next week. I'm going to Knoxville Thursday afternoon, and I'll stay till Sunday. My mother and her husband are going to Washington, so I'll have their house. If you happen to be in Knoxville on Friday or Saturday, I could cook you that dinner I've been promising you for a year."

Bert wasn't sure what she meant. Though they were alone in the office, she had dropped her voice to what sounded like a conspiratorial level, and he thought he saw color rising on her throat. He wanted time to consider. He said, "I hadn't expected to be in Knoxville next week. But something may come up. I'll let you know in a day or two."

Walking back to the bank, he considered her invitation. He wasn't a skirt-chaser, but he was an heir to the double standard of sexual conduct: A husband can do what a wife can't, but only if he does it a safe distance away from home, and only after he makes certain there can be no unpleasant consequences. He had heard the local skirt-chasers' verdict on Miss

Edna: that she'd be a prime piece if a man could get it, but she'd allow no man the opportunity to try. So what was she suggesting to him now? Conventional wisdom held that all pussy has a price tag on it, and the better it is, the higher the price. Was Miss Edna offering herself to him, and, if so, at what price? He resolved to proceed warily, but his curiosity helped him find an excuse to go to Knoxville. Next day he told her, "I can't stay overnight. But if you'd like to fix us a lunch about noon on Friday, I can make it." They both knew that the afternoon train to Clinch City didn't leave Knoxville until five o'clock. She gave him the address and said she'd be expecting him.

To reach the white frame bungalow in Knoxville he had to ride the trolley, then walk two blocks. The sky was black with thunder and lightning; a downpour was imminent. He walked rapidly, then ran to beat the rain. But he kept reminding himself that he mustn't act hastily, that she must answer his questions before they went any further, that he was too responsible a man to allow a stiff cock to make his decisions. He was going to figure first, before he fucked. A director of the Clinch County National Bank, the husband of Lila Scott Castleton and a pillar of the Episcopal Church damn sure wasn't going to risk knocking up the chief clerk of the probate office!

As he ran up on the porch, escaping the first sheet of rain, she heard him and opened the door before he could knock. Her long dark-brown hair hung down her back, pulled together by a barrette at the back of her neck. She wore an ankle-length form-fitting yellow cotton house dress, starched and frilly, and black patent-leather slippers. Her oval face was flushed, and her brown eyes were luminous. She took his hat and coat, led him into the dining room and gave him a glass of huckleberry wine as she made small talk about the rain. Then she brought the lunch: golden fried chicken, green beans, white potatoes and gravy and spiced peaches.

"Now, while we're eating," he said, "suppose you tell me what I'm here for."

"Because I want a partner," she said. "A business partner. I'm becoming the most efficient probate-office clerk in Tennessee, you see. In another year I'll know all there is to know about every acre of the four hundred thousand acres of land in Clinch County. I want a partner I can help and who can help me acquire some land. I want you to be that partner."

"You could have told me that in the bank or the courthouse," he said. "Why'd you bring me here?"

"Because I also want us to be sexual partners."

"You'd be disappointed," he said, looking straight at her. "I'm a de-

182

voted family man—you know that. You could never have much time with me for sex. Once a month . . . maybe not that often. And then only for an hour or so, like today."

"That'll be enough," she said. "And I can arrange safe meeting times and places."

"What about pregnancy? Responsible partners have to think about that."

She handed him the surgeon's statement. As he read it he shook his head in disbelief. "Are you telling me that while you were dangerously sick with a high temperature you were able to persuade this doctor to perform this operation?"

"A woman must look after herself," she said.

He stopped eating, sipped his coffee and looked closely at her. For the first time he noticed how young she was, and how small. She was twelve years younger than he; five feet three and a hundred and eight pounds. He was six two and weighed a hundred and ninety. "What you want from me then," he said, "is land? Whenever you help me find a good land buy, you want me to buy most of it for my family and a little of it for you?"

"That's right," she said. "And I want you to be a loyal partner to me. I don't have a family to fall back on, understand, therefore I want to build up an estate over the years so when I get old I can retire and live comfortably."

Bert Castleton chuckled heartily. "Goddamn," he said, "how did you become so capable of looking after yourself?"

"Oh, I just had to, that's all. I was an unwanted child of an unhappy marriage," she said. "I made up my mind to be independent and never get trapped."

"And you're a virgin?"

"Certainly I am. I've never even kissed a man."

"Then how can you know that you'll like a sexual partnership? Or that I'll like it? Or that after we try it both of us will want to continue it?"

"That's the only risk we'll have to take," she said. "All I ask now is your word that you like the idea . . . and that on Monday you'll approve a loan of two thousand dollars to me to build a house."

Again he chuckled. He thought of when as a Sewanee freshman he bargained with Chattanooga whores for thirty seconds of in-and-out. Or when in Cuba he had bargained for a night of suck-and-fuck. He said, "So this meal and my first rainy afternoon with my partner will cost me two thousand dollars? Is that correct?"

"No, not at all," she said. "I'll never cost you anything . . . not this afternoon or ever. You and the bank will make money from me. You're going to lend me two thousand dollars which our partnership will repay from profits."

Bert threw back his head and laughed. "All right, partner. I like the idea. Now, if you'll lead me to the bedroom, we'll seal this bargain."

"Just try to remember," she said, rising, "that it's a new venture for me. Give me time to catch on."

"You'll catch on fast," he said, grinning. "You're already blooming from thinking about it."

As they entered the bedroom he picked her up and lifted her so that her face was level with his. "Put your arms around my neck and start learning to kiss me," he said. Hesitantly she began, her lips together. "Now open your mouth and put your tongue in my mouth." She had begun to catch on when he put her down and said, "Take off your clothes."

"All of them?"

"Down to the buff. You mustn't hide assets from your partner."

When they both stood naked she looked at his erect cock and shuddered. "I never realized one could get that big."

"It'll be even bigger when it's inside you. Put your hands on it and feel it. Then it won't scare you."

When they were on the bed he sucked her nipples, then fastened his mouth to hers as he ran his hands over her entire body and slapped her smartly on the tail. He pushed her legs apart and noted with a fingertip that she was responding. When he mounted her he told her to pull up her knees; then, with his hand directing his cock, he thrust quickly downward and inward and ended her maidenhood with a minimum of pain and shock. As he thrust steadily, a little deeper each time, he told her to raise her knees as high as she could get them so that he could hilt it. In that position, after several powerful deep thrusts, he came, sighing heavily. And after a while he pulled back from her, smiled and said, "Thank you, partner."

"You're welcome, partner," she said. "Now what do we do?"

"We rest," he said. "We lie naked together and rest. You hold my cock in your hand, I nuzzle your breasts and neck and we talk a little. Then I'll get back on you and stay for an hour. We can listen to the rain pouring down on the roof, and I'll teach you some of the moves a good partner makes. Then this partnership will really be sealed."

In the thirty-five years thereafter Miss Edna got everything she wanted. She built her home and paid for it. She bought an annuity. She owned one of the first Ford cars, and traded for the new model every year. She acquired

Coca-Cola stock. When TVA came and began to make Clinch County land valuable, she made thirty thousand dollars on land she sold to the government for Norris Dam. When the atom bomb came and turned Clinch County land into gold, she made fifty thousand dollars on land she sold to the government for Oak Ridge. She leased two filling station sites to the Standard Oil Company for seven hundred dollars a month for fifty years. Moreover, she lived a satisfying life. She became a pillar of the Methodist Church. She reigned as queen of the courthouse even after it expanded and she had four clerks working under her to record all the wills, mortgages and deeds. She toured Europe, Mexico, Canada and the American West, and she made several trips to Washington and New York. She had hundreds of friends, the closest of whom was Lila Scott Castleton. The young man she helped most, when he began helping his father, was Frank Castleton.

Everybody learned, of course, that Miss Edna prospered by serving as a lookout for Bert Castleton. But only a few people ever believed that she was "Bert's woman." What ended most speculation on the subject was the judgment: "Hell, if Miss Edna had ever wanted a man she'd have married one." Most people just couldn't believe that she was interested in sex. And, indeed, she wasn't much interested—she would have tired of frequent intercourse, she was not orgasmic and she couldn't have responded at all to a man who needed affection from her or who wanted to live with her. She was interested in sex only as a means toward independence, and she could become aroused only by plotting and anticipating infrequent and profitable assignations. Money and conspiracy were the only aphrodisiacs which worked on her. Bert was perfect for her—he found her amusing, grinned at her when he got her naked and liked to fuck her now and then because she was so fastidious, calculating and capable. It was convenient, of course, to fuck her in the afternoon so he could be home with his wife by dark. Edna liked it that way too, because she didn't want his companionship; she wanted only to be profitably connected with him. When she had all the security she wanted, she planned her retirement. Everybody hated to see her go, but as of January 1, 1948, when she was only fifty-seven and still attractive, she resigned as queen of the courthouse, sold her home, gathered up her wealth and went to Fort Lauderdale, Florida, to find new interests to keep her from growing old.

Only two people in Clinch County ever felt absolutely certain that Bert and Miss Edna were sexual partners. They were Lila Scott Castleton and her son. They never shared their knowledge, and Lila never mentioned it to Bert or to anyone else. She too was an heir to the double standard of sexual conduct, and since there had to be some woman, she preferred that it be Miss Edna, who knew how to hide it and who added to the Castleton fortune more than she subtracted from it. The only person who ever mentioned it to Bert was Frank.

That was the day they were in the fishing boat, and Frank had told his father about Bess Foshee. After he had told about his own woman, Frank said, "While we're on the subject, Dad, what about you and Miss Edna? Every time she takes a trip you're usually gone too, at least for a day. Does that mean what it looks like it does?"

Bert took off his cap, scratched his head, then replied, "Frank, you're the only person in the world who has ever asked me about that situation. And you're the only one I'll ever give an answer to. I'm forty-one years old, and no man is more devoted to his family than I am to your mother and your sisters and you. No man gets more pleasure and comfort from his wife. But I'm not a god, I'm only a man who moves around, and who has money, runs into women who are not whores, and who don't pretend to be in love with him, but who, if he can protect them and help them a little, just plain want to sneak off with him somewhere and fuck."

"The Bible says that's sin," said Frank.

"I know it does," said Bert. "But such fucking also gives a man more pure pleasure than anything else he can do. So when I'm alone, and far enough away from home, and when I feel certain that nobody is going to be hurt, I'm not above doing it. I'm not recommending it to you. Maybe it's best for a man, after he marries, never to touch another woman. Maybe you'll want to live that way. But I think a man, if he's careful, and if he can afford it, can have it both ways. He can love his wife, give her all the sexual attention she wants, and be loyal to her, and he can also do a little secret fucking."

Bert pulled up his fishing pole and let it back down in the water, then continued, "Now, as for me and Miss Edna, we have a business relationship that's mutually profitable. And whatever else we do together, that's her business and my business, just as long as it doesn't hurt her or me or my family."

"What if a man falls in love with a woman he's fucking?" Frank asked.

"He can't do that," said Bert, shaking his head. "A man has no right to love any woman but his wife. Any man who loses his head over another woman is a fool. He tears up his family, and that's the unforgiveable sin. The family must be protected at all costs."

"So it's only a matter of money, isn't it?" asked Frank. "If a man has enough money he can go to another city and fuck another woman because he can help protect her, as well as his wife and family?"

"That's about what it comes down to," said Bert. "Nothing protects like money. So only a fool ever low-rates money. A man shouldn't worship Mammon, but he's got to make enough to provide for his family and to enable him to be mobile so he can find all the extra pleasure he can. When you're dead you're dead a long time."

MARY Sullivan cut off the electric lights and lighted two tall red candles, and she and Castleton sat down at the drop-leaf table to eat. He complimented her on the food: a casserole of asparagus, nuts and cheese; a molded salad with cream cheese, coconut, pineapple and sections of mandarin oranges; Southern-fried chicken with hot biscuits and gravy; and a cherry tart for dessert.

"I enjoy cooking," Mary said. "But I'm like Miss Edna. I cook only when there's a man around and that isn't often."

Frank looked at her, and after a moment she said, "Frank, the psychic wounds which cripple a man at your age are usually inflicted during his childhood or his adolescence. Suppressed feelings of shame or guilt are the usual culprits. How old were you when you first suspected the sexual relationship between your father and Miss Edna?"

"Fourteen," he said. "I remember it distinctly. One afternoon I heard a boy say that some man must be getting Miss Edna's tail on the sly. The next time she came to our house for dinner I watched her, and I concluded that the man was Dad."

"Then three years passed, and you were seventeen when your father admitted it to you. That's quite a while to live with a secret. Now, think about it—during those three years did you feel shamed by what he was doing?"

"No . . . I'm sure I didn't."

"Well, did you feel that your father was mistreating your mother?"

"No, I didn't feel that way either," said Castleton. "Dad and Mother have always been devoted to one another. They've always slept in the same bed. They still do."

"When you were fourteen did you believe that your father and mother still had sexual intercourse?"

"Certainly!"

187

WILLIAM BRADFORD HUIE

"What about dreams or fantasies—did you ever imagine your father on your mother, like, say, like a bull on a cow, and did the thought make you feel resentful or ashamed?"

"Good God, no!" Castleton was becoming irritated. "Oh, Mary, come on. I've never had any Oedipal problems. My father and I have fished together since I was a boy, and two men don't share a fishing boat together unless they enjoy being with each other, sharing things with each other. The last time Dad and I fished together, about a year ago, I told him I had become sexually weak. He said not to worry, that I'd get strong again. He said that for a brief period he had once had the same trouble. But he's seventy now, and he and Mother still do it once a week. My parents have always been well-adjusted, so my trouble doesn't come from anything that happened in my childhood or adolescence. I'm sure of that. Honest. Look elsewhere, good healer, for the source of my pain." He sounded annoyed and impatient.

Mary got up and poured some coffee. Holding the electric percolator in her hand, she bent over and kissed Castleton on the cheek. "Don't get irritated," she teased. "We're friends who may become partners." Then she sat down, smiling, and said, "Let's look for that source later, then— during your years at Sewanee. Joe Bramwell says you had trouble because you were a Spartan among Athenians. You say you had trouble because your parents worked like niggers. Would you say you were the only member of your class who ever fucked a Cove-ite?"

"Yes, I guess I was. I was the only one lucky enough to find a Cove-ite who was clean and healthy."

"When Stumpy McDowell found out about you and Bess Foshee, and confronted you with it, how did you react?"

"We fought—it was a legendary fight," said Castleton. "My God, that was awful! He called me a rednecked Cove-ite fucker, and I had no choice but to dig in and make him feel it where it hurt."

"I suppose that was like being called a nigger-fucker?"

"Something like that. He meant it to be insulting, but I've never felt ashamed of Bess Foshee or of my conduct with her."

"Then what about guilt?" asked Mary. "It must have been a sad afternoon for Bess when you paid her off and left her, never to see her again. Didn't you feel a little guilty?"

Castleton stopped eating and sighed. "At forty-six, I suppose every man wishes he could have done more for every person whose life has touched his. But why should I have felt guilty? I mean, look at it now. Just as Miss

Edna did with my father, Bess initiated her sexual relationship with me. She wanted something from me, and I gave her more than she asked. On our last afternoon she was heavy-hearted but not tearful. Cove-ite women don't expect much of life, you have to understand. Bess knew from the start that the day I left Sewanee would be my last day with her. When I walked away from her shack and stopped and looked back and waved to Bess, I felt lonely, as if I had experienced a rite of passage, but I wasn't aware of feeling guilty."

"Aware or not—there may have been unconscious guilt, even so," said Mary. "All right, what about Carole Curtis? After her tragic death, did you feel guilty or ashamed of the premarital sex you had had with her?"

"I felt sorry it hadn't been more often, and in bed, where it could have been much more satisfying . . . like I'd had with Bess," said Castleton. "Carole's death was an overwhelming sorrow for me. I felt bitter about it for months, and what I felt bitterest about was that we had been lovers with no place to make love. Those goddamn Sewanee dance customs which allow everything to be arranged for love but not for lovemaking!"

Mary gave him an understanding smile. "I know what you mean," she said. "It's spring, and the young men are full of juice. Yet when the girls arrive, all they can do is hug and kiss them."

"Exactly," said Castleton. "For three days and nights we lived in a sexual pressure cooker at Sewanee. Since there were no cars, during the day we walked and picnicked in groups, and couples would sneak off behind bushes to kiss. At night we danced, and there were always two or three girls who knew how to position themselves to make the boys feel that their hard cocks were all but inside them as they danced. You had to stand in line to dance with one of them for twenty seconds. At intermission we strolled in Abbo's Alley, a wooded ravine, where we could stand behind bushes with our girls and clutch and kiss. My God, what frustration! Some couples would dry-fuck until the boy came in his pants. Other couples would masturbate each other. The boy would put on a rubber and his girl would hand-fuck him while he clutched her with one arm, kissed her and finger-fucked her with his other hand. Next morning the Negroes would pick up the used rubbers."

"But of course you were different. You could run to Bess as soon as Carole left?"

"Yes, I was lucky."

"And when you saw Carole in Chattanooga or when she came to Clinch County, you made love normally?"

"Yes . . . if it's normal to make love in a car without benefit of a wash basin. Carole and I lived in an era which didn't provide beds or baths for unmarried lovers."

They had finished eating, so they moved over to the sofa. Mary poured more coffee for them, and Castleton lighted her cigarette. "Now," she said, "after you left Bess and Sewanee, and Carole was killed, what about the girls you went with before you met Diane? Did you feel shameful or guilty about sex with any of them?"

"No," he said. "Well, actually, the problem didn't come up much. For four months after Carole's death I shunned girls. I was back home working with my father and grandfather, and I spent a lot of time in the mountains either alone or with the Indians. Indian men are perfect companions for a white man who feels depressed. They are quiet and reverent of the earth and all forms of life. In the mountains I hiked, ran, painted and reflected. Then I started feeling better, and I began going out with girls in Clinch and surrounding counties. It was 1923 and '24, and I had a T-model Ford. I was twenty-one and twenty-two then, and I had been fucking and loving since I was seventeen. I wasn't inexperienced. I played by the rules, so there was no shame and no guilt."

"That brings us to Diane," said Mary. "She told Dr. Palkin about your first day together, so I know what happened between you. Wasn't it unusual for a girl in her position to make love on a first date? What do you think? Did that ever influence your attitude toward her?"

"It made me love her more dearly," said Castleton firmly. "It was a perfect place for making love. She and I were adults: She was twenty-one and I was twenty-three. We had spent the morning together, talking. We had hiked two miles to lunch, then back to my camp. It was a fantastically beautiful day, and we felt we wanted each other. We were inside a tent, lying on sleeping bags. We even had wash basins. What were we supposed to do?"

"Her resistance faded rapidly?"

"No, only gradually. Then we fucked for hours. The result was a perfect marriage."

Mary raised her brows. "Perfect? How long was it after you married her before you found another woman?"

"This may surprise you," said Castleton. "It was sixteen and a half years. Not until the evening of December 7, 1941, here in Washington. There was no Miss Edna in my life. The years from 1925 to 1941 were perfect for me and Jemmy. We built our home and began raising our children. I was working contentedly for TVA, Hull, Norris and Roosevelt. I was in business with my father and grandfather, and I painted and made music and hiked and enjoyed living."

Mary inhaled smoke, exhaled, then said, "So you believe now that until 1941 you were unaware of any feeling of shame or guilt?"

"Yes, I believe that."

"And you believe now that it was your experience with Roosevelt and Truman—*solely*—that made you feel the shame and guilt which reduced you to impotence and hysteria?"

"Yes, that's one way to express it."

Mary put out her cigarette. "That's enough questions," she said. "You're here to enjoy the evening, after all. Roll back the rug. I'll put on some new records, and we'll dance."

She selected Wayne King waltzes: "Save the Last Dance for Me," "Mexicali Rose," "The Waltz You Saved for Me," "Till We Meet Again." Mary had never danced with a man who moved as smoothly and confidently as Castleton, or who was so easy to follow, so she floated and loved it. She loved the feeling that they were performing beautifully together, and she wished that they were on a crowded dance floor so they could be admired. During the silent intervals when the record changer was working, they kissed tenderly. When the music started again, they quit kissing and resumed dancing. Neither of them spoke. When Frank heard the first bars of "Till We Meet Again," she felt him falter for an instant, but he recovered and moved confidently again. When the waltz ended she guided him toward the inner door and said, "Let's go to bed and make love."

C astleton had already decided that this was his turnaround day—the day he would will himself into being a man again. After a shaky start, he had functioned on the golf course. He had kept his confidence during Mary's inquisition over dinner. He had triumphed with his graceful dancing. But could he function as a man in bed with an aroused thirty-year-old woman?

He fought doubt stubbornly as he undressed in half light and waited for her to come out of the bathroom. He battled for confidence as she came into his embrace and he held her as they stood together next to the bed. He noted that her skin was still youthfully rose-tinted and her breasts were full and firm. He resisted anxiety as they moved onto the bed and continued their foreplay. God give me strength! he prayed, and he was thankful that

191

his cock was hard. When she took it in her hand he mounted, her legs came up around him as she moaned with excitement, and he felt the moist heat of her vaginal lips.

Then came failure! Feeling his hardness begin to soften, he surged frantically inside her, praying that the connection would harden it again. But it collapsed, and he ejaculated in an agony of shame and self-loathing. "God . . . damn!" he muttered. "What a frail faltering failing fucker I am!"

Mary knew she had risked crushing his frail ego, and she feared he might collapse all the way into hysteria and she'd have to summon help and deliver him to his room in a straitjacket. "Hush! Hush!" she ordered, holding on to him as he tried to pull away from her. "I knew this would happen the first time. So did you. Now hold on to me and listen!"

She turned over so she could look down at him lovingly. "Don't you ever say again that you're a failure! If you were a failure, you wouldn't be here in my bed with me. You're here because you're a gentle good and important man . . . the only man I've ever wanted to love . . . the only man whose life I want to share."

That startled him. "You want to . . . share my life?"

"Of course I do," she said. "How many men do you think I've known who can play the 'Intermezzo' on a cello? And paint beautiful pictures? And create a home like yours? And who has helped to make a great dream like TVA come true? And who has broken his health in an effort to build a better world? I want to love you, and I want you to love me and need me as long as you live."

He sat up and looked at her, still puzzled. "Is this a new therapy?"

"It's the oldest of all therapies," she said. "With me in your life you can always feel proud of yourself. I'm proud of you, and proud to be near you. You don't have to be a Paderewski or a Michelangelo for me, Frank. Just be the gentle and good man, and the talented musician and painter you already are, and I'll thank God for every hour I'm with you."

This ancient therapy began working. For ten minutes he lay beside her and listened to her tell him how superior he was, how much he had achieved, how much she admired him and what she wanted from him. As she talked and caressed him, he could feel anxiety receding and confidence rising. "After you leave here, there are many beautiful places we can meet conveniently," she said. "Hot Springs, Virginia Beach, Sea Island, Ashville or Charleston. I'd love to travel and spend weekends with you, whenever and wherever you have time for me." When she kissed him tenderly he mounted her with no sign of doubt or weakness.

The intercourse was a long and ecstatic triumph. For the first time since Christmas, 1944, with his wife, Castleton felt in full possession of a woman. She favored him with her various skills, and they made him equally as happy as those of Bess Foshee and Jemmy Jemison. When he finally collapsed on her, he moaned, "Thank you, thank you, Mary . . . for saving my life!"

The bedroom clock said 9:10 P.M., so Mary resumed her role as nurse. "Give me a moment in the bath," she said. "Then you take a quick shower. You've got to be in your room by nine thirty. I regret it, my dear, but we still have to go by the rules."

She didn't send for his attendant. Instead, in gray slacks and a pink pullover sweater, she delivered him herself. While he put on his pajamas she went for his medication, and he was lying on the bed, relaxed and pensive, when she returned. She injected the Demerol, rubbed the needle mark and said, "You won't need many more of these. You're going to be a new man."

When she bent over and kissed his cheek he said, "Thank God for you, Mary." Then she went out, locking the door behind her.

O<small>N</small> Monday morning, May 3, 1948, Dr. Arthur Leo Palkin reached his office at the hospital half an hour earlier than usual. He had enjoyed Sunday's golf game, but he had not slept well that night. Then at breakfast he had read on page one of the *Washington Post* a disturbing statement by Bertrand Russell, the world-famous British logician:

> "The gravest threat to mankind in 1948," said Lord Russell, "is the nuclear arms race which has already begun between the United States and the Soviet Union. This arms race must be halted, even at the cost of a nuclear attack by the United States on the Soviet Union's developing nuclear capability. Rival nuclear arsenals must not be tolerated; and all nuclear weapons and means to deliver them must, as soon as possible, be monopolized by the United Nations. Thomas Francis Castleton obviously is a man with information the world should have on this grave matter; and just as obviously Truman

is trying to suppress this information by confining Castleton in a psychiatric hospital. This means that Castleton must be protected and freed, so he can tell the world what he knows. I will leave at once for Washington to aid the effort to protect and free Castleton."

Dr. Palkin knew that this meant trouble for him. Admiral Potter would be calling on Admiral Leahy at the White House. Secretary Blanton would be summoned and given new instructions. Admiral Potter would pay another visit to Captain Palkin. Jack Hardwick would plant more derogatory information on Castleton in the press. And before the end of the week Secretary Blanton and Dr. Palkin would have to meet the press again, and Dr. Palkin would have to refute the charge that Castleton was being confined for political reasons, and that he had information which would be damaging to the Truman administration.

Sitting at his desk, the doctor began rubbing his reading glasses. He had been in the Navy only six years and three months, since February '42. He had come in as an obscure lieutenant-commander assigned to the NP (neuro-psychiatric) problem among the fighting men. He had quickly been promoted to commander, then to captain. Now he was all but certain to become the first Jewish admiral: Rear Admiral Arthur Leo Palkin, then Vice-Admiral Arthur Leo Palkin. How had he been so successful in the Navy bureaucracy? How could a Jewish psychiatrist hope to attain such exalted rank in the Defense Establishment?

Dr. Palkin knew that Admiral Potter was aware of the reason—as aware as he was himself. During his first thirty days in uniform he became a recognized Motivational Expert—a practical realistic hard-nosed military psychiatrist who knew how to help win wars. The process by which he became a recognized expert began in a seminar conducted by an admiral and a Marine general. Thirty officers were present, including Commander Charles Evans Potter, USN, and the problem under consideration was stated by a Marine colonel.

"Gentlemen," he said, "our gravest shortage in this war will be in teen-aged men—seventeen, eighteen, nineteen—who really *want* to slay the enemy. In time we shall have overwhelming superiority in machines and technicians, but we can't capture Tokyo and Berlin unless we also have half a million youngsters with a burning desire to spill the blood and guts of their individual adversaries. In the Pacific we face the most fiercely motivated foot soldier on earth. The young Jap wants to kill Americans because we're white and bigger than he is, and he's willing to die for his

Emperor. The young American has no burning desire to eviscerate Japs, and he wants to live to get back to his girl, malted milk and Mom's apple pie. So our problem in the Marines is: How do we teach three hundred thousand teen-agers to want to spill Jap blood so that they will attack recklessly, kill without hesitation, survive and win?"

The presiding admiral asked for discussion, but no one seemed ready to speak. Whereupon Lieutenant-Commander Palkin rose, identified himself, and said, "We must teach our assault troops that Japs are noisome animals. The average young American hesitates to bayonet a human being. He may hesitate to club to death an animal he doesn't loathe. But suppose the animal is a rat. An American boy enjoys pouring boiling oil down rat holes into their stinking nests. So we must portray Japs as rats and Jap bunkers as rat nests. Our dummies for bayonet practice should look like rats. Barracks walls should be covered with pictures of rat-faced Japs. Troops carrying napalm flame-throwers should feel that when they incinerate a Jap bunker they are incinerating a stinking rat nest."

Every officer present was impressed by the fact that these words were spoken not by a combat officer but by a psychiatrist. Dr. Palkin continued, "We can also make our assault troops more contemptuous of the Jap-rats by emphasizing their repulsive toilet habits. Americans are trained to defecate in a sitting position. But Japs defecate while squatting. Jap latrines are holes in the ground, and their ships have only holes in the deck. When a Jap uses an American toilet he stands on the seat and squats. So the walls of every American latrine should be covered with pictures of rat-faced Japs in their defecating position."

From that point on Dr. Palkin dominated the seminar. All questions and comments were directed at him. He was asked, "If it becomes known that we are teaching troops to regard Japs as subhuman, won't we be accused of teaching racism?"

"So what!" replied the doctor. "Let people who are safe preach brotherhood. The relatively few young men who must kill or be killed have the right to be taught to hate. Only by learning to hate can they hope to avoid the fatal mistake of hesitating to stab, slash, club or shoot."

A Marine major stood and said, "But, Doctor, all Oriental people resemble Japs, they all urinate in the streets, and they all squat to defecate. So if we teach our troops to hate Japs and to despise their toilet habits, won't we be planting a seed that may grow into a general American tendency to regard all Orientals as subhuman?"

"It's a risk we must take," replied the doctor. "Our combat troops have

196

the right to regard the Jap fanatics whom they must slaughter as subhuman."

What the doctor said to that group of officers was printed and distributed as a secret document titled "The Palkin Doctrine for Motivating American Troops Against the Japanese." Thereafter referred to as "PD," the doctrine was adopted and used, first by the Marine Corps, then by the Army, Navy and Air Force. PD saved American lives and helped win the war, for it made the evisceration of a Japanese infantryman or the incineration of a Japanese city psychologically easier. PD made Lieutenant-Commander Palkin Captain Palkin and was about to make him Admiral Palkin. The President and Admiral Potter wanted the author of PD to be powerful enough to dictate doctrine when the time came to motivate American troops against Communists. It was Admiral Potter who had selected the author of PD to handle the Castleton case.

Captain Palkin put on his reading glasses and looked again at page one of the *Washington Post*. Yes, he would obviously have to defeat Bertrand Russell's effort to use Castleton to discredit Truman. He would be *required* to oppose Lord Russell. But how strange it was: the Free World's leading pacifist advocating war—even nuclear war—to prevent nuclear-arms rivalry, and to preserve a monopoly of nuclear weapons! And shouldn't the author of a realistic doctrine like PD be supporting, rather than opposing, a realistic move to prevent nuclear rivalry among nations? And how could Dr. Palkin forget that under his Hippocratic Oath his first duty was to help relieve Frank Castleton? As the doctor had foreseen, he was in a complex situation.

Mary Sullivan came in, looking efficient and unperturbed. "Good morning, Doctor," she said. "I see you've read *The Post.*"

"It means," said the doctor, "that in examining and treating Castleton we must move faster than we would ordinarily. Sit down and tell me about his sexual activity with you last night."

"I know I must tell you," she said as she sat down. "But sexual activity with a patient is a new experience for me. And I now have an emotional interest in Castleton as well as a professional interest. So let's keep the report brief and professional."

"All right. How well did he function?"

"He was in possession of himself before and during the meal, and later while we were dancing. But when we went to the bedroom he began losing confidence. Anxiety seized him. He was trembling as he mounted, so he lost possession completely on vaginal contact, collapsed and ejaculated on

197

intromission and very nearly went into hysteria from shame and disgust."

"How did you react?"

"With a massive dose of reinforcement. He was then able to function normally and achieve an ego-lifting triumph."

"With profound penile penetration?"

"Very profound."

"Euphoria after the triumph?"

"If not euphoria, at least elation and gratitude. While we were walking to his room elation began to fade, and by the time he was in bed and I had given him his medication he was experiencing post-coital melancholy."

"Well," said the doctor, "even so, he ought to be feeling much better today. He knows he's not impotent. I must spend at least two hours with him. I'll very soon be ordered to make more public statements about this case, and before I say anything, I want to know all that Castleton knows and all that's bothering him. Go bring him here, then leave me alone with him and see that I'm not disturbed."

WHEN Castleton and the doctor were alone, the session began. Palkin sat down behind his desk. "Frank, now that you're feeling better, let's begin concentrating on your reports to Roosevelt and Truman. Today I'll set no limit on our time together. Don't feel you have to rush at all. I want you to lie on the couch, face me and fasten your mind on the events you are recalling."

"All right," said Castleton. "If I could just make a suggestion. At this session I'll try to inform you of everything that happened down to the end of 1943. Then, afterward, I want you to answer what to me are two very important questions."

"Okay," said the doctor.

Castleton lay on the leather couch and began. He told of his visit to Hyde Park in January '43, when he discussed the separation problem with the President and reported on progress at Oak Ridge. Then he told of a visit to the President's cottage at Warm Springs in March '43. He drove there from Oak Ridge, again accompanied by a security agent and a film technician. Again he arrived at 2:30 P.M., after the President's nap. For the first hour he and the President sat on the porch talking, and Castleton, as he lay on the couch, saw the scene clearly in his mind.

"TODAY, sir," he said, "I'll report on Hanford, Washington, where construction work is getting under way. Since the processes at Hanford are to be more dangerous than the processes at Oak Ridge, we've purchased eight times as much land for this part of the project. The Hanford site covers six hundred square miles in a bend in the Columbia River."

Castleton reached into a bag and set another glass bottle filled with blue and yellow marbles before the President. "Is that U-238 or U-235?" asked the President.

"It contains one more marble—one more neutron—than U-238," said Castleton. "So it's the atom of a new element not found in nature— plutonium—P-239. We can make it from U-238. You see, when a chain reaction is under way in a pile like Fermi's, and the few U-235 atoms are splitting and releasing heat and radiation, a small percentage of all those useless U-238 atoms will admit another neutron into their nuclei and be transmuted into P-239 atoms. And the miracle is that these new P-239 atoms are as readily fissionable as U-235 atoms. So we'll be making two kinds of atomic bombs: U-235 bombs of uranium and P-239 bombs of plutonium."

"We'll make U-235 at Oak Ridge and P-239 at Hanford?"

"Yes, sir," said Castleton. "But at Hanford too it's the mountain and the mouse. We must put tons of uranium metal into a reactor; we must fission pounds of U-235 atoms and generate unbelievable amounts of heat and radiation; then we will find *milligrams* of P-239 on the uranium slugs which have been subjected to three months of heat and radiation. To separate the P-239 from the remaining U-238, we must remove the radioactive uranium slugs from the reactor by remote control and drop them into a deep-water vat with concrete walls seven feet thick. Then, again by remote control, we have to take the slugs out of the water, put them in heavily shielded casks, load the casks onto special railroad cars and transport them five miles to a separation plant. There, by chemical process, the P-239 is separated from the remaining U-238 and other fission fragments. So while Oak Ridge is a billion-dollar *separation* center, Hanford is a billion-dollar *transmutation plus separation* center."

"Even so," said the President, "Hanford should give us enough for a bomb sooner than Oak Ridge. Maybe by the middle of next year?"

"No, sir," said Castleton. "It can't be done. Work is just beginning. A nationwide effort is underway to recruit fifty thousand construction workers. There will be six reactors, each of them three miles from any of the others to guard against cataclysmic accident. Each reactor will be a windowless concrete monolith rising one hundred twenty feet above the sagebrush. Those six reactors will be cooled with water, so they'll use more water and electricity than the city of Detroit. The three separation plants will be five miles apart and five miles from any reactor. Radiation means remote control. Machines must be designed to perform every task at the reactors and separation plants. Men watching dials and motion pictures and operating machines must be protected by lead, concrete or water walls. If the wall is lead it must be a foot thick; if concrete, seven feet thick; if water, fifteen feet thick. The water used in the reactors can't be returned to the river, because, once used, the water will contain irradiated fission fragments and must be stored in underground concrete lakes for a hundred years. So Hanford can't possibly give us twenty pounds of plutonium for at least two years—until the spring of '45."

CASTLETON sat up on the side of the couch, put his feet on the floor, and said, "Now, Doctor, I have come to the time when I believe I first began to feel guilt. July 1943. Until then I had only felt afraid, but while I was reporting to the President at Hyde Park in July '43 I began to feel something more crippling than fear. It's important to me that I make you understand why."

"Then go ahead," said the doctor. "But speak slowly. Don't get excited. Keep your voice down."

Castleton nodded. "In the summer of '43 the men who were to make the bomb from the fissionable material produced at Oak Ridge and Hanford began gathering at the Los Alamos Bomb Laboratory, thirty-five miles northwest of Santa Fe. I began talking with them. Over a period of six months the ones I came to know best were the four geniuses—Bohr, Fermi, von Neumann and Teller—and Hans Bethe, German-born; Victor F. Weisskopf, Austrian-born; George B. Kistiakowsky, Russian-born, German-educated; and Robert Oppenheimer, head of the laboratory, the only one who was American-born, a man who could understand and direct the others."

"What a group!" exclaimed Dr. Palkin. "What a privilege for you to know them!"

"Yes, certainly," said Castleton. "But I didn't want to just know them,

I wanted to help them achieve what they yearned for. They were not just brilliant men, they were good men—free of jealousy and hate. What they wanted was what every great scientist has wanted: to use technology to help cure the social ills of mankind."

"So they wanted to help Roosevelt achieve the American purpose of ending war among nations?"

"Exactly," said Castleton. "They knew it was Roosevelt who had given them the opportunity to create the bomb. Their hopes were invested in him. But note this! None of them had met the President. They had no way to communicate with him except by sending a letter through War Department channels. The only scientists he talked with were Dr. James Conant and Dr. Vannevar Bush, who gave him infrequent general reports. The War Department sent a weekly progress report to the White House, which was read first by Admiral Leahy, who thought the bomb project was foolishness and advised the President to ignore reports. The members of the Joint Chiefs of Staff received the War Department reports, but they ignored them and never discussed them with the President, since they were winning the war with the weapons they had and the atomic bomb was not in their plans. The only other way the President could receive atomic information was from me. Secrecy made it impossible for the press, Congress or anyone else to inform, advise or criticize him."

"So when the scientists at Los Alamos learned that you reported directly to the President, they began to use you?"

"Yes, but you've got to understand, I was glad to be used by them," said Castleton. "They sought the same goal the President sought. By serving them I thought I was serving the best interests of the United States and of mankind."

"Then what happened in July '43 to make you feel so upset?"

"First," said Castleton, "I have to tell you that by the summer of '43 the scientists knew that Nazi Germany was not trying to make the atomic bomb. They had learned that in 1939 Hitler had rejected the recommendation that the bomb be made, and had bet on rockets to be armed only with TNT. The ablest atomic scientists remaining in Germany had been sent to Peenemunde to work on rocketry. The Los Alamos scientists also knew that the bomb they were making would not be used against Germany, and some of them were disappointed about this. Bohr's trip to America in 1939 was made in the hope that the bomb in British and American hands could free Europe from the Nazis. But by the summer of '43 Bohr and the others knew that Germany would be defeated by British pluck, Russian blood and

201

American industry before the bomb could be ready."

"What about Japan?"

"Oh, the scientists knew that Japan couldn't make the bomb. Japan had no uranium, and very few atomic scientists. Since Japan must import all its oil, it was evident that when the United States destroyed the Japanese battle and merchant fleets, Japan would lie harmless and helpless. Japanese cities were pitifully vulnerable to firebombing. So the scientists knew that as soon as the United States established bases within bombing range of Japan, the Japanese cities would be incinerated with napalm. The thought of using the atomic bomb against the Japanese in 1945 didn't occur to anyone in '43 or even in '44. The men making the bomb believed that it would not be used during the Second World War and hopefully would never be used against human beings."

"Then why *did* those scientists want to make the bomb?" asked the doctor. "They were all volunteers. They were living uncomfortably in isolation, harassed by security agents, their mail was being intercepted and censored, their telephone conversations monitored. Why didn't they quit?"

"Because they knew that there was more at stake. Oh, Jesus, so much could have been possible! An arsenal of atomic weapons, monopolized by collective authority, could end international war. It could compel all nations to demobilize and disarm. It could guarantee all nations against armed attack. It could prevent any nation from maintaining an offensive force or an offensive-arms industry. It could therefore achieve the American purpose of lifting the burden of armament from the shoulders of mankind."

"And they believed that Roosevelt could do this?"

"Yes, they did," said Castleton. "That he could persuade Congress and the people of the United States to give our atomic arsenal to a collective authority which could then base unchallengeable air-atomic power on one or more of the strategic areas of the world, like, for instance, Alaska, Greenland or Kamchatka. This authority would have power, you see—it could then order the scrapping of all offensive arms; it could forbid the manufacture of atomic weapons, rockets, military aircraft and submarines except for its own use; and it could order all nations to consent to continuous inspection."

At this point in the conversation noticeable changes had occurred in both Castleton and Dr. Palkin. Castleton was calmer than he had been in two years, but Dr. Palkin was excited, sitting on the edge of his chair, his voice rising. "Wait a minute, Castleton. Are you saying that in July 1943 the scientists were not working on a bomb to be used in the Second World War?"

"That's exactly what I'm saying," said Castleton. "They were working on a bomb to make the war we were waging the last one between nations. And they were not working for the United States, they were working for mankind. That's why they cheered at Stagg Field when Fermi achieved the chain reaction, and that's why they endured the discomforts and the indignities at Los Alamos."

"Okay, okay," said the doctor nervously. "Now go on—tell me about your report to Roosevelt when you began to feel guilty and ashamed."

Castleton held up his hand. "I'm coming to that. But you must have one more bit of knowledge. In the summer of '43, atomic energy was already a reality, and they were working only on problems of adaptation. Suppose that you had been the first man on earth to note that water runs downhill and falls. You wouldn't have had to wait until you built a water wheel to know that falling water would turn it. The scientists at Los Alamos knew that not only the fission bomb but also the fusion bomb would be made. Because they knew this, I thought I knew."

"All right," said the doctor. "What about Roosevelt? I suppose he didn't know?"

"I think he did," said Castleton. "But it didn't seem to make any difference. In response to his order, I went back to Hyde Park with a security officer and a film technician. I showed him films of Los Alamos and explained the discomforts and the irritating security measures. I showed him progress films of Oak Ridge and Hanford. Then I told him that the scientists expected to use me to convey their thoughts to him. He said he approved of that—that one reason he had given me this assignment was to provide those men a way to communicate with him without having to go through the War Department. Then I said,

" 'Mr. President, we now have more proof that the Germans are not trying to make the bomb. If they were, they'd be operating the uranium mines at Joachimsthal, Czechoslovakia. Those mines are the only uranium source in Central Europe. Our agents have watched those mines. Here are photos taken over a recent three-month period. As you can see, the mines are not being operated.' "

"Did he concede," asked Dr. Palkin, "that neither Germany nor Japan was trying to make the bomb?"

"Yes," said Castleton, "he did. Then I told him everything I've told you about what the scientists' expectations were: how, after the surrender of Germany and Japan, they hoped the arsenal of atomic weapons would be controlled exclusively by the United Nations and used solely to end the large-scale manufacture of arms, to end international war."

"What did the President say?"

"He said for me to tell the scientists that he agreed with them a hundred percent. That they should make the bomb as fast as they could and count on him to use it to end war."

"But that's very positive. Why did you begin feeling so upset?"

"Wait a minute," replied Castleton. "I told the President I was worried about the fact that so significant a national enterprise with such portentous meaning for mankind was being kept secret. I pointed out that the longer he kept it under wraps, the more vulnerable he became to the charge of usurpation. I reminded him that persuading Congress to give our atomic weapons to the UN after the war was not going to be easy, and shouldn't we begin work on it at once? Shouldn't we now enlist the press, radio and motion pictures in the task of informing the people of the world?"

" 'Mr. President,' I said, 'now that we know that our enemies are not making the bomb, what excuse do we have to keep secret the fact that the atomic age has arrived, that the chain reaction has been achieved, that we already are utilizing atomic energy and that we are making atomic weapons for the sole purpose of delivering them to the UN? The sole purpose of all of this being to end war among nations?' "

"What did he say to that?" asked the doctor.

"Well, he agreed with me, but he also reminded me that production of the bomb was a joint British-American undertaking; that he couldn't change the secrecy order without first consulting Churchill; that Churchill in July '41 had signed a mutual-assistance treaty with Stalin promising to inform Stalin of any new weapons developed during the war. Since Churchill couldn't tell Stalin that we were making the bomb without also telling him how to make it, he preferred to say nothing to Stalin about it.

" 'Churchill is being ridiculous as well as dishonorable,' I said. 'Stalin knows that we are making the bomb, so he knows that Churchill is keeping things from him. There are only a few atomic scientists in the world, and each one is acquainted with some of the others. Many of them have been students of Professor Bohr in Copenhagen, where Bohr has lived for the last three years under Nazi occupation. He's been in regular contact with British Intelligence, and next month he'll be flown to England and on to Los Alamos. Six months ago Bohr was approached in Copenhagen by Russian agents and urged to come to Moscow to work on what the scientists call "the military potential of uranium." Joliot-Curie, the Communist atomic scientist now in Paris, urged some of the men now at Los Alamos to go to Moscow in 1940. Joliot knows that these men are now at Los

Alamos. So to tell Josef Stalin that we are his allies, then to pretend to him that we're not making the bomb, is self-defeating. Now or later we must persuade or compel Stalin to join the collective-security organization, to demobilize and disarm, to open the Soviet Union to international inspection and not to make the bomb. So to play false with him now is madness.'

"The President asked, 'Do the scientists think we should tell Stalin now how to make the bomb?'

" 'What can we lose?' I replied. 'If we tell him all we now know, he still can't make the bomb during the war. He lacks the industrial capacity. After the war the collective-security agency will have our bombs and can use them, if necessary, to compel Stalin not to make the bomb and to accept international inspection. If we don't tell Stalin now, we put him in an adversary position and make the task of persuading him to accept collective security more difficult. Not to bring him into the collective agency would be catastrophic. After the war he could make the bomb in no more than the three years we have needed to make it. Actually, he might shorten the time, for his scientists would have the advantage of knowing that the bomb can be made, and of knowing at least something about how we made it. Then we'd have to live in a perpetual nightmare under the threat of Soviet atomic power. Only by sternly and fairly facing Stalin with the realities of the atomic age and by bringing the Soviet Union under collective authority can we achieve our purpose of ending war and preparations for war.' "

Dr. Palkin got up and said, "Let's slow down a minute while I digest some of this. You say that in July '43 we knew the Germans were *not* making the bomb, and we knew the Russians knew we *were* making it?"

"That's correct."

"And the scientists wanted the President to tell Congress and the people that atomic energy was a reality and that we were adapting it to military use?"

"That's right," said Castleton. "Unless Congress and the people knew about it, how could we develop popular and Congressional support for a United Nations powerful enough to monopolize the bomb and to compel all nations to scrap offensive arms?"

"But the President insisted on continuing the secrecy?"

Castleton sighed. "The President continued it, yes, but he was always promising to end it within a few weeks. The President's practice was always to agree with me and the scientists a hundred percent. Then he procrastinated—turned his attention away from the bomb and did nothing."

205

"And you were ashamed of the fact that the bomb was being kept secret from Congress and the people? And your being part of this secrecy made you feel guilty?"

"Yes. I felt that for the President to keep knowledge of the bomb secret after July '43 was unwise, un-Constitutional and un-American, and might result in a catastrophe for America and for mankind. So each week thereafter I felt worse about it."

"All right," said the doctor. "What happened next in '43?"

"About the middle of September, the President ordered me to come to Shangri-la. A security agent and I rode together in a White House limousine through the sixty miles of Maryland countryside. This time, we carried only photos and a tape recorder. After the President got up from his nap, he and I sat together on a screened-in porch overlooking the Catoctin Valley. I gave him a progress report on Oak Ridge, Hanford and Los Alamos. Then I said, 'Mr. President, the Russians have already begun an effort to make the bomb. I have evidence to show you that they know about Oak Ridge, Hanford and Los Alamos, and they are being informed as to our separation and transmutation processes.'

"I handed him several photographs. The first photo was a daylight shot of a house at 3120 Grove Street, Oakland, California. It was the home of Steve Nelson, an American-born Russian agent. The second photo was made with a telescopic lens and infrared film at 1 A.M. It showed a man who was a scientist employed on the Manhattan Project approaching Nelson's home. Nelson's wife let him in, and he waited for Nelson to return. The third photo showed Nelson entering his own home about 1:30 A.M. Then I played a recording for the President of the conversation inside Nelson's home between the scientist and Nelson."

"What did the scientist tell him?"

"That work was proceeding on schedule at the three atomic centers. Then the scientist told Nelson to get his pencil and write down a formula. Nelson repeated each portion of this as he wrote it down, as well as the scientist's instructions to him about a sheet of paper he was giving him which explained information about nickel-plating and about using nickel for barrier. I then showed Roosevelt a photograph of the scientist leaving Nelson's home, and let him listen to a recording of a telephone conversation between Nelson and the Soviet Consulate in San Francisco in which Nelson made a date to meet the vice-consul, Peter Ivanov, at 'the usual place.' This was a spot on the grounds of the St. Francis Hospital in San Francisco. I then showed the President a photo of Nelson meeting Ivanov at that spot and delivering an envelope to him."

"What was the information given to Nelson and Ivanov?"

"It was enormously important," said Castleton. "The formula was a new one we were using at Oak Ridge in the electromagnetic process for separating U-235 atoms from U-238 atoms. Nickel-plating was one of our most important achievements. Uranium hexafluoride is extremely corrosive, and several companies worked for months trying to find a way to prevent this gas from corroding the miles of pipes through which it must be pumped in both the electromagnetic and gaseous-diffusion processes. Finally one company did it—they found a way to electroplate the interior of the pipes with nickel, which resists corrosion. In the gaseous-diffusion process the principal problem, not then solved, was what metal or alloy to use for the acres of barrier or filter in the thousands of filtering operations. Each hole in the filters is one thirty-thousandth of an inch in diameter—these submicroscopic holes must resist corrosion—and there must be billions of such holes through which the smaller molecules containing the U-235 atoms pass more readily than the larger molecules containing U-238 atoms. Very thin nickel appeared to be the best bet for barrier. So when Nelson gave the Russians that formula, along with information about nickel-plating and nickel barrier, he saved them months of time."

"Good God!" said Dr. Palkin. "What did the President say?"

"Well, at last he began to feel uncomfortable," said Castleton. "I was forcing him to defend himself, and no President likes to do that. 'I was told something about this,' he said. 'The War Department wanted to arrest Nelson before he could reach Ivanov, or to arrest Nelson and Ivanov when they met and then arrest the scientist. I ordered them not to do that because it would cause all sorts of trouble. We'd risk exposing the bomb project; we'd jeopardize our developing relations with the Soviet Union. We have to worry about Stalin making a separate peace with Germany; we're trying to persuade him to enter the war against Japan; and we're trying to coax him into the United Nations. Every time certain Senators hear that Russians are spying on us, they try to cut off our military aid to Russia. And if we're going to sell the American people on getting into the UN with Russia, we can't always be exposing Russia as our enemy. There are all sorts of angles to this thing, Frank, and you and the scientists will have to be patient while I work everything out.'"

"What stupidity!" The doctor sighed. "Why didn't he arrest the scientist and Nelson before Nelson reached Ivanov and have them taken out to sea and shot? And he said he was afraid of exposing the bomb project!

Exposing it to whom! Everybody already knew about it except Congress and the American people!"

"Remember, Doctor," said Castleton, "the President hadn't yet met Stalin in September '43. He was going to meet him for the first time in November. He felt that if he could just keep the boat from being rocked until then, he could persuade Russia to do all that he wanted them to do."

"Madness!" said the doctor. "What else was said at the September meeting?"

"I took the risk of pressing the President on two other points," said Castleton. "I said, 'Mr. President, in about two weeks you're sending Mr. Hull to Moscow to confer further with Molotov and Stalin about the framework of the UN. Mr. Hull is taking me with him. Now, Molotov and Stalin know that we are making the bomb, but Mr. Hull does not know. So why not let Mr. Stimson tell him about the bomb? Then during the ocean voyage I could further inform him. In Moscow Mr. Hull could begin discussing our desire that all atomic weapons be placed under UN authority with Molotov and Stalin.' The President said he couldn't allow Mr. Hull to be told—not yet—because he himself wanted to be the first to mention the bomb to Stalin."

"Did he say he'd tell Stalin when they met in November?"

"Not in those words, no. So then I asked him, 'Well, Mr. President, since the scientists are terribly disappointed that you haven't yet proposed a bomb policy to Stalin, may I do this? May I tell them that from my conversations with you it is my impression that you will discuss bomb policy with Stalin when you meet him in the Middle East in November?' "

"What did he say to that?"

"He rubbed his chin, then said, 'All right, you do that. Since they know that Stalin knows we're making the bomb, tell them I'll begin talking about it at our first meeting.' "

"Did that satisfy you?" asked the doctor.

"No," said Castleton. "I left the President a few minutes later, and riding back to Washington I felt anxious and upset. For the first time I felt that the President was willing to use me to misinform the scientists. I didn't believe he'd tell Stalin, so when I went back to Los Alamos the following week I informed the scientists only that the President was moving as fast as he could."

Castleton got up, walked about the room, drank some water, then sat down in the chair facing Dr. Palkin. "Now tell me about the Moscow conference," said the doctor.

208

"It was a great triumph for Mr. Hull, and a great disappointment for me. At times it seemed unreal, even ridiculous. Mr. Hull was seventy-two and in poor health. Since he'd be the highest-ranking official of the United States ever to visit Moscow, he traveled in style. The War Department provided a four-engine transport plane and two colonels as liaison officers; the Navy provided a doctor and a lieutenant-commander to supervise the oxygen to be given the old Secretary every time the plane flew above eight thousand feet; and the Secretary took with him a dozen assistants from the State Department. We left the Washington National Airport with great ceremony at noon on October 7, 1943, and traveled in stages so as not to tire the Secretary, who had never before been in an airplane. The first day we flew to West Palm Beach, where we spent the night, then flew to San Juan, Puerto Rico, where Mr. Hull, the doctor, the lieutenant-commander and I boarded the cruiser *Phoenix* while the rest of the party went on to North Africa on the plane. A sea voyage to Casablanca had been ordered by the President to let Mr. Hull rest before his encounter with the Russians. Can you imagine! A sea voyage. It seemed ridiculous to me—in the middle of a war, a cruiser and two destroyers crossing an ocean so that an old man could rest! Bloody battles being fought in the distance, and I sat in a deck chair in the sunshine reading *Sohrab and Rustum* aloud to the Secretary of State! Or else I was playing his favorite tunes on the wardroom piano: 'Galway Bay' and 'The End of a Perfect Day.' Or I was strumming a guitar while he and I and several Navy officers sang 'The Blue-Tail Fly.' "

"Was there any serious talk during the voyage?"

"Some—Mr. Hull liked to talk about Churchill. He said that Churchill had the hardest role of any of the wartime leaders, because he knew he was losing while he was winning. After the war Stalin would be more powerful than he'd ever been, and Roosevelt could win another term in office and be the most powerful man on earth. But Churchill was like Woodrow Wilson: He'd lead his nation to victory, then be defeated in the post-war election."

"Had Mr. Hull quit satirizing the President?"

"Sure . . . for the moment," said Castleton. "After all, the President was sending Tough Old Cordell to Moscow to begin *handling* Stalin. So Mr. Hull was on top of the world, utterly devoted to the President. At Casablanca all the aides, assistants and liaison officers were lined up to meet us, our plane was ready and we took off for Algiers, where General Eisenhower and then General de Gaulle were waiting to report to the Secretary of State. At the end of the day Mr. Hull radioed a most enthusiastic report

209

to the President; then we made a night flight to Cairo, with the Secretary trying to sleep in a berth that was too short for him. Alexander Kirk, our Minister to Egypt, met us at the Cairo airport and escorted us to his palace near the Pyramids, where the Secretary received King Farouk of Egypt, King George of Greece and King Peter of Yugoslavia. Next morning, en route to Teheran, we flew low over Jerusalem, Bethlehem and Nazareth, so the Secretary could tell us how his mother used to read the Bible every night to him and his brothers, and how they passed the Good Book from one to the other, reading and reciting verses. From the Holy Land on to Teheran Mr. Hull couldn't talk, because the doctor made him wear the oxygen mask. Our new ambassador to Moscow, Mr. Harriman, met us at Teheran and took the Secretary for a courtesy call on the Shah of Iran at his Alabaster Palace. Two Russian navigators boarded the plane for the flight to Moscow, where we arrived late in the afternoon of October eighteenth—eleven days after leaving Washington—and we were met by a party headed by Molotov and Litvinov. They greeted us like old friends, nodding, laughing, handshaking. Molotov startled me by calling me by name. Then we drove to the American Embassy, Spasso House, and an informal meeting of the foreign ministers of Britain, Russia and the United States was held that evening."

"And I take it the conflict began there?" asked the doctor.

"No," said Castleton. "Everything went perfectly. The Moscow Conference was an uninterrupted triumph for Mr. Hull. The first formal meeting was in the Spiridonovka Palace. Each of the three foreign ministers was present with his staff, making a total of about forty men. Litvinov was interpreting for the Russians and Mr. Bohlen for us and the British. The first question was how to punish the leaders of the German government when they were captured. 'Hang them summarily,' said Mr. Hull. 'In no case should they live to see another sunrise after capture.' When Mr. Bohlen hesitated to express this in Russian, Mr. Hull gestured impatiently to him. As Mr. Bohlen spoke, the Russians looked at one another, doubting their own ears, until Litvinov repeated the statement, accenting the Russian phrase meaning 'summarily.' Then the Russians exploded with glee. Several of them jumped to their feet, yelling and applauding. Molotov was laughing as he rushed over and shook Mr. Hull's hand—the only time I ever saw him laugh. A Russian general rushed to embrace Mr. Hull, and since Mr. Hull was too frail to accept a Russian embrace, I jumped up and returned the general's embrace, and we did a furious dance as everybody laughed and applauded. Apparently I was the only active folk dancer in the

American delegation. After the merriment subsided Mr. Hull added, 'These Axis outlaws have crucified millions of persons, so they should be executed summarily by the troops which capture them.' "

"Was that suggestion taken seriously?"

"Very seriously," said Castleton. "It was later overruled by Roosevelt and Churchill, who wanted the Nuremberg trials. But Mr. Hull's plea for summary justice won him the admiration of the Russians, and they bent over backward trying to please him at all other sessions. I slept in the room with Mr. Hull, and every night he was so elated that he had trouble sleeping. He talked to me for hours about how reasonable and friendly and communicative Molotov had become. During intermissions at the Spirido-novka Palace when the weather was good we walked in the courtyard and drank tea or vodka and ate from tables of food. Mr. Hull always walked with Molotov, and he told me that during those walks he'd broken down all the old suspicions that had made Molotov so reserved during our first meetings in Washington. He repeated again and again how he'd always known that he could make friends with Stalin and Molotov when the chance came, and how he was going to devote the rest of his life to breaking down the last barriers between Americans and Russians, who were, after all, so much alike."

"Didn't you protest at all?" asked the doctor.

"No, I did not," said Castleton. "The old man was my godfather. I had no right to spoil his dreams. I did nothing but commend him for his triumphant *handling* of Molotov and Stalin."

"You saw Stalin?"

"Twice," said Castleton. "First, for an hour in the conference room adjoining his office. Mr. Hull took Mr. Bohlen, Mr. Harriman and me with him. We sat across the table from Stalin, Pavlov and Molotov. Mr. Hull, like the President, always tried to open discussion on what he called a personal note. So he began by observing that he and Stalin must have had similar boyhoods because they both came from mountainous areas, he from the Cumberlands and Stalin from the Caucasus. He wondered if Stalin ever planted any wheat. Stalin said he knew a little about wheat. Mr. Hull said that he had heard that wheat production in Russia was low, and he sus-pected that the Russians weren't planting deep enough. He said he and his father planted wheat as much as five, even six inches deep. Did Stalin do it that way? Stalin said his impression was that they didn't plant that deep. During the tedious interpretations Stalin and I were both drawing on the pads we had had placed before us at the start of the meeting. Mr. Hull now

211

wanted to know if Stalin had ever rafted any logs. Stalin said he hadn't done it himself but he had seen them rafted. Mr. Hull explained that the trick in rafting logs was to bind them together with hickory walings, and he wanted to know if the Russians used the same method. Mr. Bohlen and Pavlov had trouble expressing 'walings' in Russian. At the first mention of the word 'raft' I had begun drawing one, so now I indicated the walings and passed the drawing to Mr. Bohlen, who passed it to Pavlov, who gave it to Stalin. He looked at the drawing and turned to me and said it was good, particularly since I had drawn it so rapidly. I nodded my thanks, and Stalin replied to Mr. Hull that he didn't believe the Russians used walings, he thought they used vines to tie the logs together. Mr. Hull said walings were better than vines, and Stalin conceded they might be. And then, at last, they got down to business. Mr. Hull and Stalin discussed arrangements for the upcoming meeting between Roosevelt and Stalin, after which Stalin rose, signifying that the meeting was over. All during the meeting I had watched him draw, but I couldn't make out what he had been sketching. During the handshaking I asked Pavlov if the Prime Minister would give me his drawing—that since I was an artist I'd treasure it. When Pavlov mentioned it to Stalin he seemed pleased. He nodded, and Pavlov got the pad, tore off the page and handed it to me. I gestured to ask Stalin if he'd sign it. He understood and signed 'J. Stalin' under the sketch."

"Yes," said the doctor, "your father showed me the framed drawing in your home. I must say, very revealing—as a psychiatrist I found it interesting: a competent pencil drawing of the heads of three snarling wolves."

Castleton continued. "At any rate, the banquet came at the end of the conference . . . after the triumphant joint communiqué had been issued and while Mr. Hull was being acclaimed throughout the Free World for his success with Molotov and Stalin. The banquet was given by Stalin in the Catherine the Great Hall of the Kremlin. Mr. Hull sat on Stalin's right on the dais, and I sat below the dais with two other State Department men and three of our Russian counterparts. There was much eating, drinking, toasting and entertainment by musicians and dancers, but what really gave the evening a warm glow was the warm friendship that Mr. Hull felt had developed between him and Stalin. They were together for five hours, and he told Stalin that with both the United States and Russia emerging from isolationism and joining hands to create international authority to assure peace, the world was entering a new era in which the people of all nations, relieved of the burden of armament, could progress toward order, freedom and abundance."

"After hearing such talk," said the doctor, "what do you suppose Stalin thought of Hull?"

"Well, he thought what Mr. Hull was saying was nonsense," said Castleton. "But Stalin liked Mr. Hull as a person. In fact, Mr. Hull was the only American he ever liked. He held Hopkins and Roosevelt in contempt, but he really liked Hull. There were two interesting things that evening—two reactions I noticed which indicated that."

"What were they?"

"One of Mr. Hull's extravagant statements to Stalin was 'All human progress has been due to a few leaders. You have demonstrated that you are such a leader. So you must use your great talents for leadership to help rid the world of war.' In reply, as if on a sudden impulse, Stalin told Mr. Hull that after the Allies defeated Germany the Soviet Union would join in defeating Japan. He said that Mr. Hull could so inform Roosevelt. This, of course, was exactly what Roosevelt wanted most to hear, and no one else had been able to pry it out of Stalin, so it was a great triumph for Mr. Hull. Despite the fact that we were scheduled to leave Moscow at five A.M., Mr. Hull stayed until the end of the banquet . . . about two A.M. And when he and Stalin parted, the Russian did something which impressed all of us, Russians as well as Americans. Stalin and Mr. Hull stood shaking hands, making the usual courteous remarks, with Pavlov interpreting. Stalin said good-bye and walked away. But then he stopped, turned around, came back, took Mr. Hull's hand and stood there, looking into Mr. Hull's eyes for what became a noticeable length of time. Then Stalin left the room, without saying a word, and appearing to be deeply moved. Several Russians who saw it told us they had never seen him do anything like that before."

For the first time during this conversation Castleton's voice broke and tears came into his eyes. "Cordell Hull," he said, "belonged to the natural aristocracy of men. Stalin sensed this and respected him. And in the years since then, in my bitterness and despair, I have woken up more than one night with a terrible impulse to shout, 'My God! My God! If only the President had told Mr. Hull about the bomb and allowed him to tell Stalin in the fall of '43. If only he'd insisted that such bombs *must* be monopolized by the United Nations!' "

"You believe it would have made a difference?"

"Oh, God, yes," said Castleton. "I believe it would have meant the achievement of American purpose. It would have meant everything. But to complete the story. We didn't leave Moscow on schedule. A snowstorm delayed our departure for four days, and that brought complications. We had expected to cross the Atlantic again on the *Phoenix*. But the President was to leave Washington on November eleventh for his first meeting with Stalin, and before he left he wanted Mr. Hull to brief him on how to handle Stalin. So Mr. Hull, against the doctor's advice, decided to fly the Atlantic. And that we did, with overnight stops at Teheran, Cairo, Algiers, Marrakesh, Dakar, Fortaleza and San Juan. I kept Mr. Hull's spirits high on the trip by reading him cabled reports of acclaim for him. He even started crying a bit when I read him Churchill's statement to Parliament on how 'that gallant old eagle, Mr. Hull' had flown on strong wings and established with the Russians an alliance in mutual respect and faithful comradeship for the rebuilding of this tormented world. Even more satisfying to Mr. Hull was the report I read to him when we reached Marrakesh on November sixth. I distinctly recall it—how it read:

" 'The United States Senate today passed the Connally Resolution, resolving that the United States of America join with free and sovereign nations in the establishment and maintenance of international authority with power to prevent aggression and to preserve the peace of the world.'

" 'That's what Wilson wanted, Cap'n,' I said to him. 'It took you and twenty-five years and another war to get it.' When we landed at Washington National Airport on the afternoon of November tenth, Mr. Hull was overcome with emotion. There was a cheering crowd to meet him, including delegations from both Houses of Congress and the President of the United States.

"And the best was still to come," continued Castleton. "Never in the history of the United States had a Secretary of State been invited to address a joint session of Congress. But Cordell Hull was asked, and on November the eighteenth he spoke to both houses in what he regarded to his death as the moment of supreme satisfaction in his life. He said:

" 'At the Moscow Conference a new spirit of understanding among nations was born . . . I found in Marshal Stalin one of the great statesmen of this age. . . . As the provisions of the Four-Nation Declaration are carried into effect, there will no longer be need for spheres of influence, for alliances, for balance of power, or any other of the special arrangements through which, in the unhappy past, nations strove for security . . . Today, my fellow Americans, we have reason to believe that the end of war and of preparations for war among nations is in sight.' "

Castleton now looked tired and melancholy, but in possession of himself. He said, "That's the story of '43, Doctor. Except to add that at Teheran the President didn't mention the bomb to Stalin, and the meeting resulted only in another windy declaration. I still felt hopeful, but I also felt guilty, ashamed and afraid."

"I understand," said the doctor. "All right, thank you—that's enough for this session."

"No, wait a second," Castleton protested. "You promised to answer some questions for me at the end of this session."

"Yes, I did. So ask."

"Had you known what I knew at the end of 1943, and had every other American known it, do you believe that the situation in the world today would be better? Yes or no."

Dr. Palkin thought a moment and answered, "Yes."

"All right," said Castleton. "Now that you know what I knew at the end of 1943, would you say that I was justified in feeling that if the President would inform the world during 1944 that the bomb was being made, action would be taken to prevent an atomic-arms race between the United States and the Soviet Union, or between any other two nations?"

"Yes," said the doctor, "I think you had a right to believe that."

"Well, that belief sustained me at the end of '43, and it also kept the world's greatest scientists at work on the bomb in the Jemez Mountains of New Mexico. We believed that before any atomic bomb was ever used against a human target, Franklin Roosevelt would act to place all atomic bombs under UN control for the purpose of ending war among nations."

"I understand, Frank," said the doctor. "Now go rest and have your lunch, and spend the afternoon and evening with Mary. Tomorrow you can tell me what happened in '44."

Dr. Palkin walked to the window and stood looking out into the garden. Frank Castleton is an honest man, he thought. God, how he has suffered! I too am emotionally involved with him now. God help him, and God help me!

DIANE Castleton sat at her breakfast table in her suite at the Shoreham reading the *Washington Post*, smoking, drinking coffee, and reflecting. She wondered: Shouldn't I accept as a probability the fact that I'll divorce Frank after he leaves the hospital and becomes able to care for himself? And since I never want to live alone, and I need to be the wanted wife of *some* man, shouldn't I begin thinking of myself as some *other* man's wife, perhaps as Stumpy's wife? At forty-four am I capable of changing my identity from that of Mrs. Thomas Francis Castleton to that of Mrs. Clark Keith McDowell? Am I capable of leaving my hillside home in East Tennessee in which so much is invested and beginning to invest in a new sort of home in Washington? And since I've never lain naked with, copulated with, slept with or loved any man but Frank Castleton, am I capable at my age of learning to live intimately with another man?

These questions still frightened her, although she had been considering some of them for four months. Until a year ago she had assumed that she would be Mrs. Thomas Francis Castleton, of Norris, Tennessee, as long as she lived. So the questions also made her feel more resentful of Frank, for it was his obsession which had crippled him, driven them apart and compelled her to consider changing her life.

The Bertrand Russell story in the *Post* puzzled her. She had always thought of Bertrand Russell as a pacifist—one of those unrealistic people who insist that one nation can end war among nations by disarming itself. Frank was no pacifist! Frank believed that only collective force could end war among nations. But now apparently Russell had become a warmonger, advocating war against Russia unless Russia agreed not to make nuclear weapons. And now Russell was coming to Washington to try to "free" Frank so that Frank could aid in persuading the United States to make war on Russia. To Diane the Russell story was only more evidence that Frank was unlikely ever to be able to go home and be happy again.

She felt grateful to the ringing telephone for jarring her out of her reverie. "This is the real Clark Keith McDowell speaking," said Stumpy on the other end.

"Good morning, real Clark Keith," she said.

"Hear this proposal. Since this is the brightest happiest and most exciting third day of May that ever dawned, I propose a picnic."

"A what?"

"A communion with Nature. I have a majestic parcel of Mother Earth to show you in the country. I've ordered a picnic lunch for two. Now all I need is Jemmy Castleton dressed to frolic over hill and dale and to lie with me under the fig tree."

"Are you serious? Who'll be the public watchdog while you play hooky?"

"Today the public must watch out for itself."

She couldn't help responding to his exuberance. Why shouldn't she be merry? "But I've nothing to wear," she said. "I hardly expected to go picnicking on this trip."

"No problem," he said. "The tog shop downstairs will rush you a selection of skirts and blouses and a pair of oxfords. In sixty minutes you can be ready to chase sunbeams."

She hesitated, then said, "All right, Nature Boy. But I'll need ninety minutes."

"I'll be under the marquee," he said.

In an hour and a half Diane shed ten years of her age and became almost as pretty and lighthearted as she was on that June day in 1925 when she found Frank Castleton in the Smoky Mountains. She wore socks instead of stockings. She selected a crisp white cotton skirt, a red belt, a white blouse with red piping, a white cap, white-and-red oxfords and a white-and-red wicker handbag. As she walked briskly through the lobby toward Stumpy's car, she looked marvelous—excited, happy and ready for a day in the country. She was also equipped for sexual adventure, since she had decided to take along her too-long-unused diaphragm in that new wicker bag.

It was the first time she had seen Stumpy so thinly clad—he wore a purple open-necked T-shirt and tight-fitting gold slacks—so she noted the physical differences between him and Frank more than ever. Stumpy's sandy hair was much lighter than Frank's, and with his massive forearms and thighs he looked something like a blond bear.

But Stumpy, for all his buoyancy, had no time for aimless leisure. The goal of this picnic was to move further toward making Diane his wife, and the more he thought of the idea, the better he liked it. While telling her how nice she looked and how good she made him feel, he drove to River Road, where he turned and drove past the Congressional Country Club and into the Maryland countryside. On each side of the road were expensive estates, the houses sitting far back from the road on plots of from ten to forty acres. Many of these estates belonged to political lawyers who had made fortunes during the war obtaining government contracts and favorable rulings for corporate clients. As he passed each grand home, Stumpy told Diane who owned it and what maneuver had enabled him to buy it.

"It's pretty country," she said. "I miss the mountains. But the pastures, the lakes, the wooded areas and the white fences are certainly lovely."

"We're coming to the prettiest part," he said. He turned left on a narrow gravel road, stopped to unlock a gate, then drove along what was little more than a pathway across grassland, through a wooded area and out onto high ground overlooking a lake. "Here it is, Jemmy," he said. He got out of the car and helped her out. "Here's where you and I are going to build our Monticello."

"But you already have a home in Georgetown."

"That's an office and a place for trading entertainment for leaks. I'll keep it for that. Right here we're going to build a private home where Jemmy and the real Clark Keith will live in beauty, serenity and loving comfort. Only the few most interesting people in the world will be invited here. An invitation to come here for dinner or a weekend will be the most coveted offer in Washington."

He took a roll of architect's drawings from the car and spread them across the trunk. They showed a rambling ranch-style house, a pool, two guest cottages, a horse barn and a garage. Diane was astounded at how quickly he'd decided, but it made her admire this fast-talking, fast-thinking man all the more. "It'll all look dark red, green and gold," he said, "with a little French blue sprinkled in. Flowers will be everywhere. There'll be paths for walking and cycling, and forty acres for riding."

"Not even Jefferson had all that," she said.

"We'll have it all. Now let's walk over it and talk about us." He took her by the hand.

"During the next twenty years, Jemmy, I'm going to be the most important journalist in the world. Washington has become Imperial Rome —where the money is. As the government gets bigger and bigger, and the bureaucracy proliferates, only adversary journalism can be important, you see. I'm going to be big government's most persistent and effective adversary . . . exposing arrogance, hypocrisy, corruption and waste."

"Won't there be any goodness and greatness to report?"

"No," he said. "There can be no more great Presidents, not even successful ones, for no President can change the direction in which the avalanche is moving. Presidents will lie, cheat, bribe and extort to get reelected. But, dammit, I'll work at exposing them."

"Will you advocate *anything?*"

"What, for instance? Peace and brotherhood? Liberty, fraternity and equality? Back to the Bible? Back to the land? A balanced budget? Revolution? There'll be revolutions in the world; they'll result only in new despotisms."

Diane stopped by the lake, turned and looked directly at Stumpy. "What a strange creature you are. Do you *believe* in anything?"

"I'll surprise you by saying yes," he answered. "A difference between me and Frank is that I believe in God, while he believes in man. After Frank left Arcady he went home, back to his roots, where his father was solid as a rock—am I right? I went home too. I was going to study law and become my father's law partner. But on the Fourth of July he killed himself, and I went to Washington as a Congressman's assistant. During years when Frank was piping in the hills and loving you, I was clawing my way up the dunghill, loving no one and being despised instead of loved. Frank's now a broken-hearted worshipper of Wilson and Roosevelt, while I'm a confident tough-minded respected and feared realistic reporter of facts. I believe that beauty, truth, love and order, et cetera, must be sought privately and individually. That's why you're so important to me now, Jemmy. I'm

219

depending on you to help me privately achieve our haven. And we'll find it all together—beauty, order, grace, love and comfort."

He pulled her to him and kissed her. Then he laid his cheek against hers and held her until he felt her relax. He kissed her again, and she responded lovingly. Then they walked again, saying nothing for a long while. She turned to him at last. "What makes you so sure that I'm the woman you want to help you create this haven?"

He chuckled happily. "You're Sewanee-trained. That means I can trust you. You were loyal, loving and helpful to Frank; you'll be the same way with me. And you're a natural-born homemaker. You know how to make guests feel good."

"You mean," she asked, "that after building a successful home with Frank, you now want me to come here and build a successful home with you?"

"Yes, that's exactly it," he said. "You belonged with Frank during his best twenty years. You'll belong with me during what will be my best twenty years."

She winced. "That sounds selfish, doesn't it? A woman taking the twenty best years from two men?"

"It's being realistic," he said. "Some men, like Frank, have their best years between twenty-five and forty-five. Other men, like me, have their best years between forty-five and sixty-five. A smart woman, like you, knows when to switch men so she can have forty good years."

For a moment this realism disturbed Diane, but she relaxed when she remembered something she had read: *A smart woman always finds her second husband before she leaves her first one.* She asked, "Why don't you want a younger woman who could have a son for you?"

"I don't want a son. I only want you."

They went to the car, got the basket, and spread the lunch under an oak tree. Smoked salmon and champagne . . . pumpernickel, corned beef, butter, pickles, cole slaw . . . and more champagne with cheese and grapes. They toasted each other and the home to be built, then began laughing as they recalled reunions at Sewanee. Several times while they ate and drank and laughed they stopped to kiss, and after one such kiss Stumpy said, "You know, Jemmy, I value the traditions of Arcady just as much as Frank does. I'm trying to help the United States and thereby help mankind. And my way is effective, you see? We've got to expose the bastards who shame it. You can help me become the man in the Class of '22 who did most toward preserving freedom in this country."

220

"You think you'll succeed where Frank failed?"

"Frank never had a chance to succeed, because he never had a voice. He was bound in secrecy to Roosevelt, then to Truman. While he watched them fail all he could do was suffer in silence and fail with them."

After the lunch they both knew what the next step in their prospecting would be. "But," she said, "I'm past the age for al-fresco lovemaking."

"So am I," he said. "So let's visit the friendly neighborhood motel."

During the five-minute drive to the motel they scarcely spoke. Both of them realized they were now prospecting seriously. Never before had Stumpy moved toward a bed with a woman he wanted to love and whose love he wanted. He was a veteran fucker, but from Diane he wanted more —he wanted enduring affection. It was an unprecedented situation for him, and he experienced a touch of anxiety.

For Diane, however, the situation reminded her of a June day in 1925 when she had bedded down with an insistent young man whom she wanted. She had succeeded. Now on a May day in 1948 she was going to bed with an insistent middle-aged man whom she wanted. Having succeeded once, she expected to succeed again; she thought she knew how to convert fuckers into lovers. So as she moved into the bedroom, undressed and went to bed with Stumpy, it was she who gave the more confident and affective performance.

"God!" he exclaimed in admiration. "You sure know how to handle me!"

She complimented and caressed him, slept an hour with him, then began teaching him the difference between fucking and loving. "Goddamn, Jemmy," he said, "I'm going to love you as no man ever loved a woman!"

Driving back to the Shoreham, both of them sobered by sunshine and sexual release, they discussed realities. Stumpy said, "As for me, Jemmy, the prospecting is over. I want to marry you as soon as possible. Will you marry me?"

"I'll need time to answer that," she said. "Please don't rush me, Stumpy. I must get Frank back home, where I can talk with him. He knows I need a new life away from him. He'll give me a divorce and a fair property settlement. I must also talk with Frank's parents. They've been good to me. For me to leave them won't be easy. And of course I can't leave until after Susan's wedding."

"But you *will* leave?"

"I must leave," she said.

"Meanwhile we'll be together as often as possible?"

"Yes. But look, Stumpy, two people can't love each other just because they want to. They can't will themselves into love. The miracle must happen."

"It has already happened for me," he said. "You and I were destined to be married in the year 1948. Frank failed you just when I became able to marry you."

"We'll see," she said. "I have to fly home tomorrow for three days, then when I get back, we'll see." She then told him of the interest in Frank's paintings, how, at Frank's insistence, she was going to destroy his work since 1945, then show all his earlier work to the dealer and critic.

"God, what irony!" Stumpy exclaimed. "Had Frank begun showing his work in New York twenty years ago, he might have been called just another provincial artist. Now, with all the publicity, every art collector is going to be interested in the work of Thomas Francis Castleton."

"You think there'll be a demand for his paintings?"

"They'll be clamoring at your door," said Stumpy. "Truman has created the demand, and with Bertrand Russell, Henry Wallace and me, along with *Time, Life* and the rest of the press calling the paintings remarkable, how can there not be a big demand? How many painters are there who've been jailed by the President of the United States for going crazy from guilt over Hiroshima?"

Diane shook her head. "Poor Frank! He'll understand why he's suddenly so successful as a painter, and instead of feeling gratified and proud he'll feel even more ashamed of his situation."

"I suppose he will," said Stumpy. "Roosevelt made him rich with TVA and the bomb; now Truman makes him richer by creating a demand for his paintings! If only Frank could regain his sense of humor and bust out laughing about it all! That's his trouble, Diane—he can't accept the fact that life is also a big fucking joke to be laughed at."

After a pause, Diane asked, "Stumpy, what do you think about this Bertrand Russell thing—is it going to make it harder for us to get Frank out of the hospital?"

"Yes," Stumpy replied. "Russell wants the United States to attack Russia to keep Russia from making the bomb. Truman, who has been reducing defense expenditures, is determined not to risk war. That's not going to make it any easier for Truman to risk Frank's being free. I've talked with Thurmond Arnold about it. He's the best lawyer in Washington, and he wants to represent Frank against the government. If Frank isn't released next week, you've got to get Arnold."

When they parted at the Shoreham entrance, and Diane walked through the lobby and into the elevator, her feelings were a mixture of relief and melancholy. On her road toward freedom, she had burned a bridge behind her, but she wasn't sure whether the occasion should be celebrated or mourned. Stumpy, however, as he drove away, felt elated. His marrying Diane would add grace and affection to the most satisfying years of his combative and successful life.

At about the time when Stumpy and Diane left each other at the Shoreham, Castleton and Mary Sullivan were drinking iced tea in her apartment after a tennis game. Mary sat on the couch next to him. "Frank," she said, "this is sort of a touchy subject— but I think it's important. Dr. Palkin asked me to question you about the possibility that your having become rich may have contributed to your psychic distress. Do you mind my asking what you and your father are worth today? To put it quite bluntly."

"About five million 1948 dollars," said Castleton, smiling. "I don't mind talking about it. It's divided among all of us . . . my mother and father, my sisters and their children, and my wife, our children and myself. Incredible, isn't it? It's the total capital accumulated after eighty-three years of work and thrift by three generations."

"But that's not all, right? That accumulated capital has been made much larger by government spending, I take it."

"Yes, my dear, you're right. If there had been no TVA, no war, no bomb and no inflation, our wealth might now amount to five hundred thousand 1931 dollars. An acre of land near Oak Ridge is now worth—oh, I guess twenty times what it was worth in 1939 and forty times what it was worth in 1931."

"I wanted to ask you about Muscle Shoals. The first dam was built there, if I remember correctly. Did you and your father speculate in land values there?"

"Well, no, not at first, anyway. When the government began building the dam in 1917, land values in the Muscle Shoals area naturally jumped up. My father wasn't involved; as a matter of fact, he'd never been to Muscle Shoals. When the war ended and the Republican Congress halted work on the dam, land values dropped. Then, during the Panic of 1920–21, the land values hit bottom. My God, how I recall the summer of 1920. I paddled a canoe the length of the Tennessee River then, and looked over the unfinished dam at Muscle Shoals. I just took my time, walking over many acres of nearby land which had been divided into lots and sold to speculators in 1917 but which by 1920 were thigh-high in Johnson grass and almost worthless. I remembered that the Army Engineers had told me in 1917 that Muscle Shoals had the greatest power-generating potential of any spot on earth. So I figured we couldn't go wrong. When I got home I urged my father to invest in it."

"Did he take your advice?"

"No, he didn't. Muscle Shoals was two hundred miles away, and he thought we should invest nearer home. So I turned to Mother and Grandfather, and they agreed to lend me ten thousand dollars. I mean, I was determined, Mary. Since I was only eighteen, Dad had to go with me and help me, and we went to Muscle Shoals together and bought ten thousand dollars' worth of three-year options to purchase at very low prices."

"That was before you met Senator Norris?"

"Yes. But not long before. A few months after we bought the options, I met him in Washington. He told me that within a year or two he believed he could persuade Congress to resume work on the dam. So then I had some ammunition. I went back home and persuaded Mother to lend me another five thousand, then Dad agreed to lend me five thousand, and he and I went back to Muscle Shoals and bought another ten thousand dollars' worth of options. And you know, that twenty thousand dollars we had invested was quite something for a panic year . . . and we hadn't acquired any deeds or mortgages for it, only options to purchase within three years. Unless that land could be sold or the options renewed, all the money would be lost."

"You were gambling that work would be resumed on the dam?"

"Uh huh. But you know things never turn out as you plan. Something unexpected happened. Henry Ford offered to lease the unfinished dam from the government, complete the dam and build a big manufacturing center. The offer set off a land boom and quadrupled the value of my options. I guess I felt I was sitting on top of something really big. So the question for us became: While Congress is considering the Ford offer, should we sell the options for a profit, or should we wait and bet that Congress will accept the offer, then sell for a larger profit? Dad wanted to wait. He had gotten the Ford agency for Clinch County, so he was for going all the way with Ford. Mother and Grandfather wanted me to make the decision, and I suppose, for a guy of my age, that was a pretty tough responsibility. So I went back to see Senator Norris. He said he didn't think the Ford deal would be good for the government *or* the Tennessee Valley;

that he wanted the government to keep the dam and eventually transfer it to the agency which would build other dams; that he intended to oppose the Ford deal and believed he could kill it. So Dad and I sold our options at Muscle Shoals for a profit of sixty thousand dollars. And what do you think? A year later Senator Norris had killed the Ford deal, the reaction sent land values at Muscle Shoals lower than ever, and speculators around the country lost millions of dollars."

"But you were a winner?"

"I sure was," said Castleton, smiling. "Mother and Dad and Grandfather insisted that all the profit was mine, so on the day I graduated from Sewanee in 1922 I had a net worth of sixty thousand dollars. That was quite a feeling. You know, the last time I went to see Bess Foshee I gave her two thousand dollars. I mean, that woman had a lot to do with my personal success and my confidence. And then I began planning my home."

"Now think about this, Frank. Have you ever felt guilty about making that money?"

"No," said Castleton, without hesitating. "I didn't make it at the expense of poor people, after all—I sold those options to a New York banker."

"Do you think you took advantage of your friendship with Senator Norris?"

"Oh, but listen, it wasn't an unfair advantage. He said nothing to me he didn't say to the press. But, see, the difference was, I believed him. When he said he could kill the Ford deal I believed he could. Other speculators thought the pressure on Congress to lease the dam to Ford would be so strong Norris couldn't stop it. But I bet on Norris."

Mary nodded; then she got up and freshened the drinks. She had noticed a marvelous change in Castleton. He was beginning to act like a normal man. He sat at ease on her sofa; the rigidity had gone from his neck. His eyes are still too bright, she thought, but they are no longer watering. It was evident that reliving his disappointments of 1943 with Dr. Palkin had helped him. And then, the doctor had agreed with him that his hopes at the end of 1943 had not been extravagant, and that was supportive. Moreover, Mary could see that his relaxing with her was good for him.

"After you made money at Muscle Shoals, Frank," she asked as she came back to the sofa with the glasses, "did you and your father speculate at the sites where other dams might be built?"

"Yes," he said. "It was eleven years between the time I finished at Sewanee and the day President Roosevelt signed the Norris Act creating

TVA. During all those years both my father and I believed TVA would come. Even in the darkest moments, when President Coolidge and President Hoover vetoed Norris acts creating TVA, we believed the dams would be built. And beyond that, I knew where the likely sites were. By then, things were really moving—we were selling Standard Oil products and Ford cars and Coca-Cola. It was our business to get favorable locations for future filling stations. So we sought well-located land along the trails to the dam sites. When the dams were built, of course we made money."

"And what about your idealism, then? You don't feel that you were doing wrong in making money that way? Did you ever think you were selling out?"

"Why should I?" he answered quickly. "Oh, Mary, my father and I weren't spoiling land. We had strong competition. We weren't the only ones who knew where those dam sites were, as a matter of fact. The men who knew most about the sites were the engineers of the Aluminum Corporation of America. Alcoa was building power dams to generate electricity to smelt aluminum ore. They built three dams which later were taken into the TVA system, and owned the most valuable site on any of the tributary rivers, one which had to be acquired by the TVA before TVA could build Fontana Dam. What my father and I were doing was peanuts compared to Alcoa—we were only two small capitalists investing in the future of our region. Look, what *are* you getting at? How can you suggest that we may have been doing wrong?"

"I'm not suggesting that your father was doing wrong," she said quietly. "I'm asking if *you* might have been doing wrong. You know perfectly well that what makes an action right or wrong for a man depends on what he feels, what he believes. Action comes from feeling strongly about something, I think, and from feeling comes belief. Conflicts of belief in a man's mind can lead to neurosis, if you'll pardon my getting technical about it."

"Oh, I see—you think I'm suffering from conflicts of belief?"

"Well, I don't know," she said, looking straight into his eyes. "Dr. Palkin can discuss this with you better than I can. But, Frank, you're the only man we know who had prior knowledge of Hiroshima who is now suffering from shame and guilt and who's terribly depressed. Why only you? Now, it just has to stem from a really crippling conflict of belief, doesn't it? You believe that you're a humanitarian, and a rough dictionary definition of that rare species might be someone whose belief consists of faith in man and devotion to human well-being. Well, look at it logically—a humanitarian who believes that war is the greatest evil, and also believes

226

that a hundred thousand civilians should be incinerated at Hiroshima for the very purpose of trying to end war—he could wind up screaming hysterically on a mountainside, couldn't he? So could a humanitarian who believes that he has worked only for himself and his family. Whom have you worked for—humanity or yourself?"

"Oh, Mary, for everyone! I've worked for myself, my family, my county, my region, my country and for humanity. Maybe I spread myself too thin, but I don't see any conflict there."

"Yes, but the benefits, if you look at them closely, still seem to be basically yours. Have you ever given away anything?"

"Well," said Castleton, "ten years before TVA came to help us we were maintaining a demonstration farm to show farmers how to combat erosion, you know, and restore fertility to their land. We bought pine seedlings by the million and gave them to farmers to set out. We kept purebred bulls for free use among dairy and beef herds. And not only that—we gave agricultural-college scholarships to boys and girls who wanted to work at improving farm life. My grandfather's motto was 'Take care of the land and the land will take care of you.' We supported Hull, Norris and Roosevelt because they wanted to preserve the land as a way of life."

"But think about it, Frank. Aren't buying pine seedlings and bulls and scholarships . . . aren't those ordinary public-relations activities for banks in rural counties? Be honest with me, now. Doesn't every bank with mortgages on land want land to be improved?"

Castleton put down his glass and began rubbing his face and neck nervously, and his eyes began watering. With a deep sigh he said, "Perhaps you'll accept this as evidence of unselfishness? There is no commercial coal mining in Clinch County, although there is in several other counties of East Tennessee. There's a commercial quantity of coal in our county, but the Castletons own it. Well, actually, we own some of the coal land outright, and we own the mineral rights on the rest of it. On our coal seams there are three wagon mines, and any citizen of Clinch County is welcome to go there and dig all the coal he needs to heat his home and pay us nothing. But we have refused all offers from commercial coal operators, you understand. We don't want commercial coal mining, because it's not good for the land or for the people who work in the mines. We wanted our county to remain agrarian, with most every man knowing how to grow food for his family, and we wanted our industries to be small and related to the produce of the land. That was Senator Norris's dream. What can I tell you? My father and I at this moment are under pressure to sell our mineral rights to TVA for three million dollars so that the coal can be strip-mined for TVA steam plants. But, Mary, as long as I live there will be no coal mining in Clinch County. Would you call that a humanitarian attitude or action?"

"No good, Frank. You protest too much. That's an attitude that Mussolini, Hitler and Stalin would approve," she said. "Let me keep control of the land, for I know what's best for the people."

Castleton was now in deep distress. His chin began to tremble; it was evident that he was upset, anxious. Mary took his hand and drew him to her. "A man can free himself from a neurosis," she said softly, "only by being helped to understand what caused it. Hey, let's just worry about something else for a while. A change of mood. I'll put on the records and we'll dance. Listen, I am absolutely the most desirable thing around— literally." She smiled. "Try interesting yourself in your woman for a while."

He shook his head. "Hold on, Mary. You know I can't shift gears that fast."

"But you've got to learn to shift gears again," she said with determination. "Damn it, men stay sane only by shifting gears. We all live under the volcano. For a while each day we confront the volcano, then we shift gears and dance and make love. That's what normalcy is, okay?"

"You'll have to give me more time."

"Oh, all right. Back to neutral, then. Just for a while. I'll ask another question," she said, a little exasperated. "After you made your first money at Muscle Shoals, did you contribute to Senator Norris's campaign funds whenever he was up for reelection?"

"Sure, I contributed gladly," said Castleton, happy to be discussing what he considered crucial. "I persuaded other people to contribute. Let's see, I gave three thousand dollars to his campaign in 1924, again in 1930 and again in 1936. Then, in 1942, when he was old and facing defeat, the whole family chipped in—my father, my mother, my two sisters, my wife, my children and I, we each contributed three thousand dollars . . . a total of twenty-four thousand dollars to show him how much we appreciated him. In 1944 I was privileged to help bury him. Being his friend was a great honor, because he was a great human being."

"Come off it, for God's sake, Frank! You were making money out of him!" Mary exclaimed. "He was your bet to establish TVA, from which you stood to make much more money. You were gambling money on him . . . entertaining him, transporting him, helping to keep him in a position of power so that you could quadruple your investments. Don't you see now that it might have been wrong? Admit it."

228

"I can't believe it was wrong," said Castleton, shaking his head. "Private utilities spent money heavily to try to defeat him in each of those elections. Wendell Willkie raised a huge sum to defeat him. Men like my father and me had to come to his aid. I know I was right, Mary. You can't convince me otherwise."

For a while she said nothing, but just sat holding his right hand in both of hers. Then she stood up. "Come on. I'll take you to your room so you can shower and change before dinner." Frank looked at her, saying nothing, but he got up and followed her.

At dinner he was silent until at last she asked him, "Tell me something else. The other people in Clinch County—do they regard the Castletons as unselfish humanitarians or as selfish profit-makers?"

"Oh, I don't know. As both. There used to be a saying that the man the Castletons loved most was a farmer whose farm was mortgaged to our bank, who hewed cross ties and sold them to us, who bought Ford cars or trucks which he financed at our bank and insured at our insurance agency and who bought his gasoline at a Standard station where he drank a Coke each time his tank was filled. Obviously, we made a profit on everything he did, except when he comforted his wife. But folks chuckled when they repeated that saying. And I haven't told you about our competition. Until 1936 ours was the only bank in Clinch County, but there were banks in Knoxville. There were other insurance agencies. As many Chevrolets as Fords were sold in our county; there were other brands of gasoline; hell, even Coca-Cola had competitors. People in Clinch County like my mother and my wife better than they like my father and me. And then they like my father better than they like me, because I'm said to be more of a loner and not as good a mixer. But don't get me wrong, we're not a disliked family, and we've never done anything that could even be considered against the best interests of Clinch County."

"How about redistribution of wealth and privilege? Wouldn't you say that poor men at least have to try for it once in a while?"

"Yes, obviously I concede that," he answered. "The Castletons supported Cordell Hull and Woodrow Wilson because we favored the income tax, the inheritance tax and free trade. We also supported the New Deal, and God knows that was a revolt against the rich. We're for all the right things, Mary—the liberal things: trust-busting, social security, full employment and more TVAs. And it goes without saying that we want a continuous national commitment to conservation of land and water."

"But the bomb multiplied your wealth?"

"The bomb multiplied the number of dollars I control," he said evenly, "but it ended a way of life I valued so much more than dollars. I'm a victim, don't you understand, not a beneficiary of the bomb. I wanted Clinch County to remain agrarian. The bomb converted the county to industry, and most of its people now serve the bomb, or at least servants of the bomb. They've forgotten how to raise food and care for the land. Whatever the bomb may have added to my dollar worth I'd gladly give back to the government if I could have Clinch County as it was in 1939. Oh, how I would love that to happen! My sickness isn't the result of my financial gain; it's the result of my loss of home and community and of my part in the failure to use the bomb to end war and to end preparation for war among nations. Mary, really, I believed in the things I worked for. And they crumbled around me."

T HAT night, in the canteen, Castleton refused to dance or to play the piano or the cello. He sat silently, often by himself, as Mary danced with other men. When she took him upstairs and gave him his injection, she sat on the side of the bed and held his hand. "Frank, listen to me. In spite of what you said this afternoon, you must become aware of the fact that you're suffering from unconscious guilt. Conscious guilt, which is little more than remorse, couldn't cause a life-loving man like you more than temporary despair. Only unconscious guilt could have broken you down."

"Are you by any chance referring to original sin?"

"Well, if you like—that's the Christian term for it," she said. "Dr. Palkin describes it as neither rational nor conscious. It's—let me put it this way—it's the guilt which a civilized man unconsciously feels for his natural instincts. It comes out as anxiety and self-criticism. When a civilized man does wrong his conscience reprimands him. However, when he does *no* wrong his unconscious guilt may torture his ego."

"Blake's worm at the root of the rose-tree," he said. "Then, Preacher, what can I do to be saved?"

"Well . . ." She shook her head sadly. "Christ is widely believed to have died to save men from it. But I think you know how I feel about Him. If Christ can't save you, you can think about one of the Oriental disciplines which promise relief. Or you can turn to art, you gifted man. I know you can find relief and new purpose in painting courage and dignity into the faces of men who must live, struggle, dream, endure and die without hope."

Then she went out and closed the door behind her.

W<small>HEN</small> Castleton walked into Dr. Palkin's office the next morning, he looked well-groomed and physically healthy, but his breathing was shallow and rapid. Nearly every tenth breath was deep, like a sigh, to compensate for the nine shallow breaths preceding it. "How do you feel?" the doctor asked.

"Lonely . . . disturbed . . . insignificant . . . tired," Castleton replied. "But I'm ready to tell you all that happened in 1944."

"We'll get to that in a moment," the doctor said. "Since you feel tired, lie on the couch, stretch out, get comfortable and relax." When Castleton had settled himself the doctor added, "Mary was rough on you yesterday?"

"She was following your instructions, I suppose. A man in my position must go into everything he has ever done and think about every opinion he has ever held. I see the need for that."

"It's the only way we can hope to help you, Frank," the doctor said. "We must probe into your hurting psyche as persistently as a dentist probes into a hurting tooth. And we have to be particularly persistent with you,

231

because your case is so unusual. Severe depressions aren't usually caused by disappointments in public affairs, you realize. Public disorders and reverses, the failure of a promising public leader, riots, panics, breakdowns in law and order, even a nation's military defeat—they only provide the atmosphere in which crippling depression develops in certain individuals. Men adjust to public mistakes, but not always to conflicts within themselves. So—we keep searching for the cause of your neurosis."

"You can end that search today," Castleton said firmly. "For by the time we finish the session, I believe you'll agree that my depression is not the result of conflicting beliefs. In my opinion, it's the result of my having been present at and party to the most tragic betrayal of humanity in all human history."

"Then let's get into it," said the doctor. "We ended yesterday at the end of 1943. You were deeply disappointed that Hull hadn't been allowed to discuss the bomb with Stalin in Moscow, and that Roosevelt had failed to mention the bomb to Stalin at Teheran. All right, on to 1944. Whenever you're ready, I'm listening."

Castleton began speaking slowly, with frequent pauses to take deep breaths. "The situation was that the world's most powerful leader—the hope of mankind, Franklin Roosevelt—was physically sick and mentally out of touch with reality. He had returned from Teheran with a cold, and throughout the winter and spring of 1944 he was a wreck. I remember his face—it was ashen, with dark-brown splotches around his eyes. He had severe headaches; he felt exhausted before lunch; he would nod and fall asleep as he tried to listen to Mr. Hull or Mr. Stimson. Several times he blacked out completely. In February he summoned me to the White House late one afternoon. When I entered his office my heart sank. He looked like death . . . so weak and trembling . . ."

Castleton stopped and sighed deeply. The doctor said, "Take your time. Try to make each breath a little fuller."

After a moment Castleton went on. "I felt terribly frustrated as I stood there looking at him. It was vital that he be told that the Russians had achieved a slow-neutron reaction in a pile similar to Fermi's. He needed to know that the Russian espionage effort against us had been stepped up. He simply had to understand that the atomic-arms race between the Soviet Union and the United States had already begun, and that it must be stopped. But I could discuss none of this with him. He was too weak to comprehend or even care, Doctor. When I approached him he greeted me wearily, and when I took his hand I could feel it trembling. He said he was sorry he hadn't been able to summon the energy to receive a report from me but that I was to carry on the good work and as soon as he could recover his strength we'd get up to date."

"How long did you stay with him?"

"Three or four minutes. I was so appalled that I told him frantically, 'Mr. President, you *must* go to a hospital! Forget the war . . . the war is won. Now it's crucial that you gather your strength to make the peace. Only you with your immense moral power and prestige can achieve our aim of ending war among nations. You *must* recover your health!' "

"What did he say?"

"Nothing . . . he only nodded. He tried to listen to me, but he didn't hear me. A few days later he went to the hospital. The doctors found his heart dangerously enlarged, and he was suffering from bronchitis, hypertensive heart disease and cardiac failure."

"He should have resigned the Presidency and lived like an invalid with heart disease. I thought that then, and I think it now."

"I didn't think then that he should resign," said Castleton. "You see, I thought he was irreplaceable—the only man who could persuade the American people and Congress to give the bomb to a supra-national authority. His world prestige was immense, unmatched by that of any man in history, greater even than Wilson's in 1918. I thought he was the only man who could confront the Soviet Union with enough power, moral and military, to compel Stalin not to make the bomb and to accept constant inspection by supra-national authority. In any case, the doctors knew he wouldn't resign, so they prescribed a regimen they hoped he'd follow. They put him on digitalis and ordered much less daily activity, fewer cigarettes, a one-hour rest after all meals, no swimming and ten hours sleep every night."

"When did he begin mental withdrawal, do you recall?"

"Early in April. He was back in the hospital for a week, and when he returned to the White House he had lost all interest in public life. He told Mr. Hull that he had decided to 'let the world go hang.' He talked only about his youth, about sailing at Campobello, and he'd spend hours digging mementos out of old trunks and attaching notes to them for his children and grandchildren. Worst of all, he didn't ask the doctors anything about his condition, and none of them told him. He didn't even ask what the green tablets—the digitalis—was or what it was for. In May he agreed to go to South Carolina, to Hobcaw Barony, a remote country estate owned by Bernard Baruch, for a long vacation in the sun. He thought at that point

233

he was suffering from nothing more serious than the flu. Before he left Washington he sent me word by Mr. Hull that as soon as he felt better he'd want me to come to Hobcaw."

"Did you go?"

"Yes," said Castleton, "but before I get to Hobcaw I want to tell you about the rest of the situation in that winter and spring. With the President out of touch, there literally was no one in the higher echelons of our government who cared much about the bomb or paid much attention to it."

"That's a very shocking statement," said the doctor. "Surely you must be exaggerating."

"I'm not," insisted Castleton. "Paul Blanton prepared a weekly progress report on the bomb and delivered it to the White House, the Secretary of War and the four members of the Joint Chiefs of Staff, who were Admirals Leahy and King and Generals Marshall and Arnold. But Mr. Stimson, the only member of the Cabinet who knew about the bomb, was seventy-seven years old then, and he was overworked. His principal concern was the upcoming D-Day landing in France. Hopkins, who had always been curious about the bomb, was in the Mayo Clinic and was finished. His duties had been assumed by Admiral Leahy, whose office was in the White House and who received all war reports sent to the President, including Blanton's reports on the bomb."

"And the admiral ignored Blanton's reports?"

"Of course he did. He was sure the bomb would never amount to anything, so why should he bother with it? The other members of the Joint Chiefs ignored the bomb because it wasn't in the operational plans of the war they were fighting and winning."

"Did Blanton worry about the bomb being ignored?"

"No," said Castleton. "He worked hard preparing his reports, but he wasn't in the least concerned that no one bothered to read them. He went sailing on Long Island Sound or skiing in the Sangre de Cristo Mountains or horseback riding in the Smokies."

"So that left only you and the scientists to worry about Roosevelt's inaction?"

"One scientist in particular," said Castleton. "Niels Bohr—winner of the Nobel Prize in 1922, the year I left Sewanee. The venerated genius of nuclear science, who brought the news of fission to America in 1939, then went home to Denmark. Late in '43, living under Nazi occupation had become dangerous for him, because of his Jewish mother, so British Intelligence smuggled him in a fishing boat to Sweden. From there he was flown to England in the bomb bay of a Mosquito bomber. The flight was almost fatal to him, because the oxygen mask the RAF gave him to wear during the flight was too small for his broad face. They found him unconscious when they opened the bomb bay after landing near London. At any rate, thank God he got to America—his arrival in Los Alamos early in '44 made every scientist there feel certain of success. He helped solve the final problems of initiating and intensifying the fast-neutron chain reaction. And he was the unanimous choice of the scientists to lead the effort to try to persuade Roosevelt and Churchill to tell the world about the bomb and to begin creation of the supra-national authority to monopolize it. I went to meet him in Los Alamos the week he arrived."

As he recalled his first meeting with Professor Bohr, Castleton felt he was in the scientist's presence at Los Alamos. Only when questioned did he look directly at Dr. Palkin.

AFTER landing at the Army airfield at Albuquerque in the early evening, Castleton drove through a snowstorm in an Army car to the La Fonda Hotel in Santa Fe. Next morning he hurried over a snow-clogged road to Los Alamos, and after calling briefly on Dr. Oppenheimer he was shown to one of the old adobe buildings which had belonged to a boys' boarding school. He found Professor Bohr in a room which must once have been a master's office.

"You bear a heavy responsibility to mankind, Mr. Castleton," said Bohr, shaking hands. "You have the ear of the President."

Castleton thought the scientist looked like Goethe might have while on a winter holiday in the Alps: a stocky body . . . the clipped graying mustache, like that of H. G. Wells . . . the thick graying hair . . . the massive brow and the dark darting eyes of an impassioned man . . . the Old World–cut gray tweed suit and thick-soled high-topped shoes. They sat down in chairs facing each other before a fireplace in which birch logs were burning.

"You mustn't exaggerate my importance, sir," said Castleton. "I'm only a reporter who is questioned infrequently by the President about work on the bomb."

"You have known the President many years?"

"Yes, sir. But only as a supporter. I happen to be the godson of the Secretary of State, Mr. Hull, and officially now I'm listed as his aide."

"Then you also report on the bomb to Mr. Hull?"

"No, sir," said Castleton. "No one reports on the bomb to Mr. Hull. He doesn't know it's being made."

Professor Bohr gasped in amazement. "Are you saying that the man who is organizing the United Nations does not know in 1944 that he is living in the nuclear age?"

"No," said Castleton evenly. "The only man in the Cabinet who knows is Mr. Stimson."

"God in Heaven!" Bohr exclaimed. "We scientists must try to change that situation quickly. Mankind must not be compelled to stumble blindly into the nuclear age. We must have time to inform Congresses and Parliaments and the people themselves. The secrecy must be ended. Do you not agree?"

"Yes, sir, I agree," said Castleton. "But the President does not agree. Nor does Mr. Churchill."

"Then we must appeal to them—strongly and at once," said Bohr. "As spokesman for the scientists, I must see them both. Will you help arrange the meetings?"

"I'll do what I can," said Castleton. "But the men who must arrange for you to see the President are Dr. Conant and Dr. Bush, since they happen to be the scientists who have the most influence with him."

"They will help, of course," said Bohr. "They believe as I do . . . as we all do."

"Then I must tell you this, sir," said Castleton. "Even with the help of Dr. Conant, Dr. Bush and Mr. Stimson, you can't hope to see the President for weeks, perhaps months. He is very ill."

"But we are told that he has only a cold . . . what you call the flu!"

"That's unfortunately not true. The extent of the President's illness is also secret."

Castleton then told Professor Bohr about the President's condition, both physical and mental. "My God!" said Bohr. "So much depends on him! What if he dies!" Castleton replied only by shaking his head, and they sat for some time gazing into the fire, saying nothing.

They spent most of the day together, with Professor Bohr talking about what nuclear energy would accomplish for mankind. At one point he told Castleton slowly and emphatically, "Here in these mountains, the greatest assemblage of human intellect ever gathered in one place is producing the first of an arsenal of fission and fusion weapons. But under no circumstances must one of these weapons ever be allowed to become a national weapon!

Roosevelt and Churchill must agree to this." He paused, repeated the imperative, then asked, "Do I make myself clear to you?"

"I believe I understand you, sir," said Castleton. "We have in the United States a great theologian, Reinhold Niebuhr. In his book *Moral Man and Immoral Society* he makes clear the limitations of nations—that they will act selfishly and immorally; that therefore they cannot serve the highest interests of mankind. You want nuclear weapons to be monopolized by a supra-national authority which can serve the highest interests of mankind by ending war and preparation for war among nations."

Professor Bohr's broad face lit up with a smile. "That is it exactly," he said.

"But you want more," Castleton said. "After war, famine is the most tragic ill of mankind. So you want the supra-national authority to use nuclear energy to desalt sea water and make deserts grow food, to manufacture fertilizers to assure abundant food, and to preserve the food."

"Yes, yes," said Bohr. "How is it that you understand so clearly?"

"I was part of Roosevelt's proudest achievement to date," said Castleton. "The Tennessee Valley Authority. To create this supra-state authority we had to fight for ten years to overcome the selfishness of seven states and the resistance to such change in the rest of our nation. But with that supra-state authority we developed hydroelectric power to revitalize land and grow more food and forests. It seems to me only logical that what you want to do with nuclear power is only a vast extension of what we have done with hydroelectric power."

"Yes, yes," said Bohr. "And do most Americans now feel as you do about using supra-authorities to serve the best interests of mankind?"

"In my opinion," said Castleton, "when our people are given knowledge of nuclear power, yes, most of them will support the action you want taken. For in effect you want no more than the achievement of our national purpose. Tom Paine said the cause of America is the cause of mankind. In his youth Mr. Hull dedicated his life to the achievement of world democracy, and Roosevelt has proclaimed that the purpose of America is to achieve for mankind the elimination of the use of armed force between nations. For Americans not to support you, Professor Bohr, would be to disavow something we've all been taught to believe in since childhood, you see."

"Certainly! Certainly!" said Bohr, his voice rising and his hands chopping the air. "What was my first thought when I learned fission had been achieved? To rush to America! I saw in a flash that if Europe was overrun by Hitler, America, with nuclear weapons, could liberate us. I cursed the slowness of the *Drottningholm* that brought me to New York. On the dock I embraced Fermi and told him the wonderful news. Then I went to Columbia University and to the Institute of Advanced Studies at Princeton and spread the news. Ever since Wilson men have known that America is a nation capable of unselfish action. Only America can be trusted to manufacture an arsenal of nuclear weapons, then to create the supra-national authority and deliver the arsenal to it."

Professor Bohr, very excited now, got up and gestured toward the windows. "Here—this magnificent assemblage of human intellect—is the proof that good men everywhere trust America to act only in the highest interest of mankind."

W HEN Castleton paused Dr. Palkin asked him, "Your only problem, then, was Roosevelt: his heart and mind, his procrastination, and his insistence on secrecy?"

"Yes," said Castleton. "Well, actually, both Roosevelt and Churchill. Professor Bohr and I were joined by Fermi and Johnny von Neumann at lunch, and I remember how astounded I was to realize I was listening to no fewer than three geniuses. I'll never forget their attitudes. They assumed that Germany would surrender within twelve months and Japan within fifteen. And since the first bomb would not be ready for sixteen months, they assumed that no nuclear weapon would ever be used against human beings."

"They expected to demonstrate on animals?"

"No, they never expected to kill any living thing. They thought they would be demonstrating in deserts or underground and prove the destruc-tiveness of nuclear heat and radiation with instruments. They didn't believe any nation would ever want to possess nuclear weapons, because that would imply competition between powers and thereby create an unbearable threat to all people. They foresaw a small but decisive air-atomic force, controlled by the UN, which would allow no national possession of nuclear weapons or of a menacing number of any other offensive weapons."

"And they saw continued secrecy as irrational?"

Castleton replied, "Well, they didn't object to wartime secrecy on methods of enriching uranium or producing plutonium or triggering a chain reaction in a bomb. But they wanted the world to know the joyful news that the nuclear age had arrived. That nuclear weapons would be monopolized by the UN and would end war among nations. That nuclear power would help feed the hungry. Why should such wonderful news be withheld any longer from a war-weary half-starving world?"

"Did you explain usurpation to them? That if the revelation that we were making the bomb would no longer endanger our national security, then Roosevelt's keeping it secret was an impeachable offense?"

"Yes, of course I did." Castleton sounded exasperated, frustrated. "I made them understand that the President no longer had the right to keep secret our vast investment in nuclear energy."

"Which brings us back to Roosevelt," said Dr. Palkin, "and to your trip to see him in May at Hobcaw Barony. Tell me about that."

O$_N$ a Friday morning in May, 1944, less than a month before the D-Day landing in Normandy, Castleton received word in Washington that he was to be at Hobcaw in time for lunch on the following Wednesday. He left immediately for Oak Ridge to prepare for the trip. On Tuesday he made the trip from Oak Ridge to Georgetown, South Carolina, traveling with film and a film technician to operate the projector, and with a security officer and six men to guard the station wagons around the clock. At 11:30 A.M. on Wednesday Castleton arrived with his caravan at Hobcaw. The Marine guards admitted him to the grounds, and Castleton entered the main house and met Grace Tully, the President's secretary. Miss Tully said that the President had suffered a painful gall-bladder attack on Sunday, but he was recovering and he wanted to see Castleton after the lunch hour, since he couldn't eat. Miss Tully said that luncheon on trays would be served to Castleton and the men with him at the pool house.

At 2 P.M. Castleton reported back to Miss Tully, who directed him to a rose garden and told him to wait there. In a few minutes the President in his wheelchair was rolled into the garden by his Negro valet. The President wore blue cotton pajamas and slippers, and he smiled and waved to Castleton. His color was better; much of the gray had left his face; the brown splotches around his eyes were less obvious; and he seemed cheerful. "It's so *good* to see you, Frank," he said, and when they shook hands Castleton noted that the President's hand didn't tremble. "Sit down," the President said, "and let's have a good talk right here in the sunshine. It's been seven months since we've talked, so you must have a great deal to tell me and show me."

239

"Yes, sir, I have," said Castleton. "But first tell me about your health."

"Oh, I'm coming along. This plaguey gall bladder set me back, but it's better now. I'm going to be all right . . . ready to win another election. How are you and your family?"

"We're all fine, sir," said Castleton, "but . . ."

"But you're worried."

"Yes, sir, I am. I'm sorry to do it, but this time I must report concern as well as progress. I've brought films and models to show you the progress, and I can tell you about my concerns. Where shall I begin?"

"The bad news first," said the President. "I can't go inside and look at films now—they make me dizzy. I want to sit here in the sun. So tell me what worries you."

"All right, sir. A hundred and fifty thousand people are now employed on the Manhattan Project," said Castleton. "And the great majority of them are satisfied. They know only that they are making a Secret Something which will save lives. The military supervisors of the Project are perfectly content. Their job is to get the bomb made, and they're succeeding. The only people on the Project who are dissatisfied are the top scientists—the men I talk with."

"So they and you worry about secrecy and me procrastinating."

"Yes, sir," said Castleton, "exactly. And I must say, I'm relieved you're aware of this. We were disappointed when you didn't mention the bomb to Stalin at Teheran. We know Russian scientists are working on the bomb and that Stalin knows we're working on the bomb. We know Russian agents are working to penetrate our security net, and to some degree they are succeeding. So for you and Churchill to meet Stalin, as pretended allies, and not mention the bomb . . . well, you've got to see why we find that disturbing. But there's something else, Mr. President—something worse. What worries us more is that, as late as May, 1944, your Secretary of State is organizing the United Nations and he doesn't know the atomic age has begun!"

The President's face was somber, but it betrayed no emotion as Castleton scanned it for a hint of what Roosevelt was feeling. "You mustn't think, Frank, that you and the scientists are the only ones concerned about bomb policy. I've worried myself sick over it. I know that at the end of this war the United States and Britain must deliver our atomic arsenal to international authority, and that the Russians will have to abandon their ambitions to possess atomic weapons and submit to international inspection. The question is when to move to achieve all this. Now, at Teheran I met Stalin for the first time. His job and mine for this year is to win the battle for Europe. I have the additional job of winning reelection. Then I'll meet Stalin again. I've had to cultivate the man gradually, carefully, and I shall have to bring him under international control gradually as well, you see. I think I'm in a better position to know how to accomplish this than you and the scientists at Los Alamos."

"We grant that, sir," said Castleton. "But consider this. Mr. Hull is working to establish an international organization in which he designates Four Policemen—Britain, China, Russia and the United States—who will police the other nations and prevent international war. Mr. Hull believes that this is what you want. But the Four Policemen organization will have no power to police the Policemen. It can't prevent an atomic-arms race between the United States and Russia. Now, on the other hand—please consider this alternative, sir—the scientists want an international organization which will itself be the one and only policeman. This One Policeman, with forces supplied to it by all nations, will have the world's only arsenal of atomic weapons, which it can use against any nation which threatens other nations. Now, which organization do you want? Four Policemen or One Policeman?"

The President lighted a cigarette, inhaled, then exhaled. "I don't have to decide today, do I?"

"Well, sir," said Castleton, "the State Department is preparing *today* for the Dumbarton Oaks Conference, which begins in ninety days. The purpose of that conference is to reach further agreement with the Russians on the Four Policemen organization. So why can't we allow Professor Bohr to present to Mr. Hull the case for One Policeman next week? And when the Dumbarton Oaks Conference begins, why can't Mr. Hull be flanked by Bohr, Fermi, Conant and Bush? And why can't Molotov be flanked by Russia's nuclear scientists?"

The President shook his head. "You'll have to give me more time," he said. "Let's agree on Four Policemen this year, then maybe we can agree on One Policeman next year . . . after we've had a cataclysmic demonstration of the bomb. The way to get agreement on One Policeman is to start with consensus on Four Policemen."

Castleton fought to hide his disappointment. "Then let me tell you this, sir," he said wearily. "The scientists at Los Alamos want to present their case directly to you and to Churchill. They've selected Professor Bohr as their spokesman, and he'd like to go to London to try to persuade Churchill to help convince you that the One Policeman plan is best. Then he wants to come back to Washington and present his case to you. Do you want him stopped? Or do you want him to go ahead?"

"Don't stop him," said the President, "help him. I want you to go back to Los Alamos and tell the scientists that I completely agree with them—the only question is timing. We can't move too fast on this, you see. Tell Bohr he can't go to London for the next six or seven weeks, and tell him why: Winston's mind and heart will be in the English Channel. But as soon as the smoke clears over the Channel, you take Bohr to London. Help him. Support him . . . as in fact you do. See that he gets plenty of time to present his case to Winston. Then bring Bohr to Washington to see me."

Castleton began to feel cautiously optimistic, but he wanted to let the President know everything he had intended to tell him. "After you listen to Bohr, you'll have to listen to everyone else on this subject—Conant, Bush, Stimson and Mackenzie King of Canada are also in support of Bohr. So is Justice Frankfurter. We all feel that nations must never own atomic bombs—that the United States must be only the temporary custodian of bombs, and that eventually such control should be transferred to the UN. And we are all opposed to continued secrecy. Justice Frankfurter feels, as a matter of fact, that it's your Constitutional duty to inform Congress and the people of our vast investment in nuclear power. You are our pathfinder and our hope, sir, so we're going to be awfully persistent. We're going to keep hammering at you to persuade you to act."

The President smiled. "I'll listen to all of you," he said. "I've spent quite a few years listening to men trying to persuade me to act."

"You know, I've just got to say that you're still leaving me in an uncomfortable position." Castleton weighed his words carefully. "When I'm not listening to the scientists, I'm working with Mr. Hull on the Four Policemen plan. I don't believe in Four Policemen, and the two of us are perfectly aware of the fact that Mr. Hull wouldn't believe in them either if he knew about the bomb. So I feel terribly guilty for not telling him."

"I didn't give you this job to make you comfortable," said the President impatiently. "You can endure feeling guilty a while longer. When you get to feeling upset with me, remember this. I'm only sixty-two years old. Six months from now I'll win reelection, and eight months from now I'll begin a new term. By then our armies will be in Berlin and our fleets will be bombarding Tokyo. I'll have plenty of time to organize the world like you and the scientists want it. Just hold on. Not even I can build Rome in a day."

Castleton winced. "But that's just it, sir—Rome is what you must *not* build," he said. "You don't want our armies spread around the earth, with much of our industry wasted on defense. You want One Policeman for the world, his cost shared by all nations, so that America can disarm and use nuclear energy to build more TVAs."

The President chuckled. "That's well said, Frank." He extended his hand, signaling the end of the conversation. "Now go and enjoy Hobcaw for a few hours. Maybe do a little horseback riding, and we'll put you and your men up for the night. Tomorrow morning I'll look at your films and your models and see what's going on at Oak Ridge, Hanford and Los Alamos."

"Thank you, sir," said Castleton.

"And how was Hobcaw?" asked Dr. Palkin.

"Not very enjoyable," said Castleton. "I don't like live oaks or Spanish moss or camellias or the odor of magnolias. I don't like the smell of lowlands and swamps. The Waccamaw River looked dismal to me. I'm a mountain man, and Hobcaw is the sick old slave South which I've always disliked— the society which could produce no artists, only bigots and drunkards and demagogues and blowhards and war lovers and Ku Klux, and college men like those who looked down on my father because he had never had a Negro servant."

"Yes, all right, but let's get to the real reason for your discomfort—you figured Roosevelt would continue to stall during the rest of that year?"

"I thought he might, yes," said Castleton. "I feared he'd use the political conventions and the campaign as an excuse to continue the secrecy. Even more disturbing was the fact that he had used the words 'cataclysmic demonstration' to me for the first time. It seemed to me that he'd decided only a cataclysm could politically justify our expenditure on the bomb . . . or his advocating transference of our bombs to a supra-national authority."

"And by cataclysm you feared he meant killing a very large number of people?"

"Erasing a large city from the face of the earth was what occurred to me. Wiping it out. I knew how much the President liked to make sudden dramatic disclosures, so I feared he had begun thinking that the way to inform Congress, the American people and all mankind of the arrival of the nuclear age was with a horrifying event like that. However, I took hope

243

from the fact that he was willing to talk with Professor Bohr, and that he would arrange for Bohr to talk with Churchill."

"Did he show any interest in your films next morning?"

"Very little," said Castleton. "He tried to watch them and listen to me and ask questions, but he kept falling asleep. After about half an hour he told me to stop, so we packed up and drove back to Oak Ridge. The following week I flew to New Mexico and told the scientists at Los Alamos that the President agreed with them on all points, that all he wanted was a little more time to cultivate Stalin and that both he and Churchill would listen to their arguments. On the second Monday in July Professor Bohr and I took off from Washington National Airport in an Army transport plane for London."

"Tell me about that."

T HE Army C-54 transport plane was filled with men in uniform. Only Castleton and Professor Bohr wore civilian suits. They sat near the front of the plane, on the port side, away from the ascending sun. Professor Bohr was at the window, and Castleton often stood as he identified for Bohr places along the coasts of New Jersey, Long Island, then Massachusetts and Maine. It was a sunny morning, and the plane was flying northeast toward Gander, Newfoundland. Castleton was pleased when Bohr began asking questions about him.

"Curiously, Professor," said Castleton, "the year in which you received the Nobel Prize for physics and spoke in Stockholm, I received my academic degree in fine arts from Sewanee and made the valedictory address for my class."

"I'm sure that was a hopeful address, Mr. Castleton."

"Very hopeful. As freshmen, every member of my class had felt disappointed when the United States did not join the League of Nations in 1919. So in my address I told my classmates that 1922, with Harding President, was a dismal year to be young in America. Our nation, cowering in protectionism and isolationism, had refused to lead or even join the effort to end war among nations. But I insisted that this was a temporary refusal. We who were coming of age in 1922 would pick up the torch fallen from Wilson's hands and persuade America to accept the responsibilities of power."

"Do you think you knew what that would mean?"

"I didn't foresee nuclear power, as you did, sir," answered Castleton.

"But I remember saying that ours would be the age when instant communication and air travel would make the world smaller and more comprehensible; and in this smaller world, with weapons ever more expensive and destructive, the abolition of international war was imperative if humanity was not to be impoverished, perhaps annihilated. I said that the right of a people to revolt against their own rulers should never be opposed by an America which was itself created by violent revolt, but that prevention of war between nations was an attainable goal."

"It's attainable only at this moment in human history," said Bohr. "Nuclear power is the ultimate force in the universe. If two, then three, four and a dozen nations use it for military purposes, then the earth will one day be a cinder like the moon."

After being serviced at Gander, the plane flew through darkness to the Azores, and the flight from the Azores to Prestwick, Scotland, was also made in morning sunshine. Castleton forewarned Professor Bohr about the situation they would find in London. "Unfortunately," he said, "the Prime Minister will probably be in a black mood."

"Because of the delay in Normandy?"

"No, sir," said Castleton. "Our buildup in Normandy has been completed. We've taken Cherbourg, and our armies will break out within the next few days. No, it's Stalin who's infuriating Churchill. As soon as we established the Normandy beachhead, Stalin changed tactics. He halted the Red Army's advance toward Berlin and sent armies south to establish Communist regimes in Roumania, Bulgaria and Hungary. Here's a statement Churchill made last week."

Professor Bohr read from a sheet of paper which Castleton handed him: "Good God, the Russians are spreading across Europe like a tide! There is nothing to prevent them from marching into Turkey and Greece. Stalin will get what he wants: the Americans have seen to that. I have a strong feeling that my work is done. I once had a message: now I have no message. Now I can only say FIGHT THE DAMNED RUSSIANS!"

Castleton withdrew another document from his file. "Here's a statement made day before yesterday by Churchill's physician." Bohr read: "Winston never talks of Hitler any more; he's always harping on the dangers of Communism. He dreams of the Red Army spreading like a cancer from one country to another. It has become an obsession, and he seems to think of little else. The advance of the Red Army has taken possession of his mind."

Castleton expected Bohr to be dismayed by these reports. Instead he was pleased. "This is most fortunate for us!" he said. "In this mood and position, how can the Prime Minister refuse to support the only proposed action by which Stalin can be compelled to halt, to disarm, to allow constant and thorough inspection of his arms by supra-national authority and to abandon all hope of ever using armed force to intimidate any other nation, including Britain?"

"But, you see, sir, Churchill's bitter about something else as well, and it complicates the situation. The V-1 blitz is killing far more people in London each day than is being officially admitted. And having survived the blitz of 1940, then had three years of relative freedom from air attack, the British people, who know that the war is nearly over, are finding the V-1 blitz hard to bear."

"The victims have my sympathy, of course," said Bohr, "but I'm sorry to say their deaths can serve humanity. I shall explain to the Prime Minister Hitler's mistake, for which all mankind can be thankful. In 1939, while I was in America urging Roosevelt to begin work on nuclear weapons, Hitler was being similarly urged by German scientists. By moving quickly and concentrating on such weapons, Hitler could have had them by now. Instead he compelled nuclear physicists to go to Peenemunde and work on rocketry, and now he has his first. But they can't save him, for they can be armed only with TNT. Oh, they can kill a few hundred people each day, but they can't win a war. Surely the Prime Minister can be made to foresee the marriage of rockets and nuclear explosives! Surely he can be persuaded to concede that the only question worthy of his consideration now is 'How can I make sure that British people never have to live with Russian nuclear-armed rockets aimed at them?' "

At Prestwick Bohr and Castleton were met by two British Intelligence officers, flown to London in a small plane, and lodged in the Connaught Hotel, only a block from Grosvenor Square and the U.S. Embassy. On the afternoon of their fourth day there, when the waiting was getting to seem interminable, they were told to be ready to "complete their mission" sometime that evening. At 10 P.M. they were driven by the Intelligence officers to Number 10 Downing Street. There they were ushered into the office of the Prime Minister, who had with him Sir John Anderson, the brawny black-eyed Scottish chemist who headed the British uranium effort. The Prime Minister was at ease in a blue denim coverall suit, with cigar and brandy glass, while Sir John, Bohr and Castleton wore civilian suits and didn't smoke or drink. Sir John, who knew Bohr well and had met Castleton at Los Alamos, introduced them to the Prime Minister. Churchill, without smiling or offering his hand, nodded, sat down and said, "Professor Bohr, you may proceed."

For twenty minutes Bohr was allowed to plead his case without interruption. He asked that Churchill and Roosevelt immediately inform Stalin of the work being done on nuclear weapons, and that Churchill and Roosevelt propose to Stalin that for the safety of the earth and mankind all such weapons manufactured by Britain, Russia, and the United States be transferred to a supra-national authority. Bohr also asked that the people of the world be told at once of the effort to build nuclear weapons, and to create a monopoly of such weapons to end war among nations.

Sir John Anderson then said, "Mr. Prime Minister, I, too, support the views expressed by Professor Bohr. I believe we must confront Stalin with the problem now—we must prevent nuclear weapons from becoming national weapons—for there can be no hope for anyone in a nuclear-arms race between nations after the present war is ended. I also believe that Parliaments, Congresses and people should be told now that the nuclear age has dawned."

Castleton searched Churchill's face for some sign of agreement. Without raising his eyes from his desk, Churchill asked, "Professor Bohr, do you, sir, have personal knowledge that the Soviet Union is at this moment trying to make atomic bombs?"

"Yes, sir, I have."

"I'd be obliged if you'd tell me how you acquired such knowledge?"

"After my return from America in 1939," said Bohr, "I went back to Copenhagen until late last year, when I was brought here by British Intelligence. In September, 1943, I was visited by scientists who were agents of the Soviet Union. They had knowledge of the British-American effort to make the bomb and told me that a chain reaction had been achieved in Moscow. They urged me to come to Moscow and assist the Russian effort, assuring me they could transport me safely."

"You declined, obviously, but did you discuss the bomb with them?"

"Yes, sir," said Bohr. "Of course, I didn't reveal processes being used in America, but I did discuss fission with them. One of them had once studied with me in Copenhagen, and both had read the American magazine *Physical Review*, which published my views on fission in February, 1939, including my opinion that it was the U-235 atom which was fissionable."

"It was a friendly discussion?"

"Very friendly. And they agreed that after the war, whatever nations

247

had made nuclear weapons would have to allow them to be monopolized by a supra-national authority."

Churchill leaned back in his chair and chomped hard on his cigar. "You have just come from Los Alamos, where you have spent several months. In your opinion, when will the first British-American bomb be ready for military use?"

"In about twelve months," said Bohr. "Too late to be used against either Germany or Japan. But this bomb will have been made by Hungarians, Italians, Germans, Russians and Danes, as well as by Britons and Americans. The fissionable material will have come from the Congo. It will therefore be a weapon that should be owned by mankind, sir, as should all its fission and fusion successors, and my hope is that it will be employed only in the highest interests of mankind."

Churchill was becoming impatient. "Then call it mankind's bomb, if you will, Professor. If Stalin chooses to make bombs for Russia and not for mankind, how soon thereafter will there be a Russian atomic bomb?"

"Within four years," said Bohr without hesitating. "But once the war ends, Russian scientists and engineers will no longer need to make a bomb."

"If I approached Stalin next week," said Churchill, "and discussed the bomb with him, do you honestly believe that he'd agree to allow one authority to monopolize nuclear weapons? And do you believe he'd agree to allow international inspection inside the Soviet Union?"

"My answer is yes to both questions," said Bohr. "I've no doubt that Stalin would not *want* to make such concessions, but you can present the proposal so that he'll have no choice. First, if I may suggest, sir, you and President Roosevelt should present your proposal to Stalin *now*. Second, you should inform him of your intention to deliver all such weapons and means to use them to a collective authority. And finally you should ask Stalin to join you in simultaneously announcing to the world a British-Russian-American agreement on the internationalization of the bomb. If you proceed in this manner, world opinion, including opinion inside Russia, will so strongly favor such action that Stalin cannot oppose it."

"But if he does oppose it," asked Churchill, "and still insists on making nuclear weapons for his own use, what then?"

"Then," answered Bohr, "mankind will have no choice but to destroy the Stalin regime. Certainly, the war against his forces would be short, because his own people would revolt. Mankind would be justified in using nuclear weapons against Stalin's supporters."

Churchill put aside his cigar and drank from his glass of brandy. He looked at Sir John, then at Castleton, then back at Bohr. "That brings us to a final question," he said. "Present policy in regard to this matter is strict secrecy. Only the President and I, by joint agreement, can change the policy. Suppose, when we next discuss this matter, we decide to continue the secrecy. Can we depend on you, Professor Bohr, and on your fellow scientists at Los Alamos to respect our policy? Or will you commit treason and attempt to inform the world in spite of us?"

No one spoke for a moment. Bohr was amazed. Castleton fought to restrain his anger. Sir John's black eyes flashed, and it was he was answered first. "I can see no cause to suggest the possibility of treason, sir."

Then Bohr reacted. "I can't believe, sir, that you and the President will insist on secrecy much longer. Britain is presently suffering under a crude but cruel rocket attack. Next to Japan, Britain is the most vulnerable target to nuclear attack on earth. I can't believe that the great leader who saved Britain in 1940 will continue a policy which can only assure that the British people will soon begin living with Stalin's nuclear-armed rockets aimed at their homes and hearts."

Churchill persisted stubbornly. "You have not answered the question, gentlemen. Will you defy us?" Churchill turned directly to Sir John.

"No, sir" was the response. "You know I can't defy the Secrets Act."

Churchill turned to Bohr, who was struggling to keep his composure. "I can't answer that, Mr. Prime Minister," Bohr said. "I have a duty to mankind which transcends my duty to any nation."

"And what about you, Mr. Castleton?" asked Churchill.

"It isn't a relevant question for me, sir," said Castleton. "The President of the United States will not tolerate secrecy much longer. Had he not been ill most of this year, the policy already would have been changed."

"He can't change it alone," said Churchill. "Only if I agree."

"Then, sir," said Castleton, "if you continue to demand secrecy, in my opinion the President will defy you."

"And if he doesn't defy me," asked Churchill, "will you defy him?"

"It will depend on the President's mental condition," said Castleton. "If he is unbalanced and ill, as he has been much of this year, I may tell the Secretary of State and key members of Congress about the bomb."

"Quite a defiant note for the meeting to end on," commented Dr. Palkin.

"Yes," said Castleton. "Sir John was embarrassed. Professor Bohr was deeply offended, and I was furious. Churchill was so sick with despair that he could only strike out at anyone who talked sense. He could think of the bomb only as a weapon with which he might drive the Red Army from the Balkans and Central Europe. Next day Sir John came to the hotel and apologized to us for the Prime Minister's behavior. 'He hasn't been himself for weeks,' Sir John said. 'He broods . . . the thought of Stalin seizing Central Europe enrages him . . . he sees his whole wartime experience as a bitter failure.' Sir John also showed us a cablegram to Churchill from Lord Halifax, British ambassador in Washington, urging Churchill to consider Bohr's views favorably."

"I take it you then went to see the President in Washington?"

"Yes," said Castleton. "Bohr and I reached the Shoreham on a Friday morning. Within an hour I received a call telling me to be at the White House at four P.M. I went there and told the President exactly what had happened in London. He was leaving for Shangri-la for the weekend, so he told me that a limousine would pick up Bohr and me next day to bring us there."

"That news must have made Bohr feel better, yes?"

"His spirits soared," said Castleton. "It was the beginning of a week of triumph for him. I remember how he enjoyed the drive to the mountains on Saturday, and of course he was delighted that the President was so full of charm and good humor. Roosevelt chuckled and told Bohr to forget the rude treatment in London—that Churchill often reacted to new ideas by belligerently rejecting them. Then the President listened to Bohr for an hour, not once showing impatience or dropping off to sleep, and agreeing with everything the scientist said. He assured Bohr that after his next conference with Churchill in September, Stalin would be asked to join in internationalizing all atomic weapons and the secrecy would end."

"Did you feel that the President was lying?"

"Let's say—well—stretching the truth. I thought he was lying as to the time schedule," said Castleton. "He would see Churchill four or five weeks before election day, and I didn't think American voters were going to be told anything until after the President had been reelected. But after that I believed he'd discuss the bomb with Stalin and end the secrecy. He then told the two of us to go back to Los Alamos and make sure that every scientist understood the promises he had made to Bohr."

"Everybody there must have been delighted."

"They certainly were," said Castleton. "Every scientist wanted to hear that the bombs would not be used for mass slaughter, but instead to insure peace among all nations."

"What was the next development?" asked the doctor.

"Well," said Castleton, "of course Justice Frankfurter had known about the bomb project since 1939, when Einstein and Bohr used him to first inform the President of the military potential of uranium. So, early in September, knowing that Churchill would soon arrive and urge continued secrecy, Frankfurter called on the President in support of Bohr's plan. Frankfurter also warned the President that with the war nearing an end, and with the United States under no danger of atomic attack from either Germany or Japan, the President had no Constitutional right to continue keeping secret the nation's four-billion-dollar investment in atomic energy from Congress and the people." Castleton's voice had raised in pitch. He sounded suddenly nervous and excited.

"Frankfurter really laid it on the line?"

"He did indeed." Castleton now raised himself and sat on the side of the couch. He was having difficulty breathing and swallowing, and the doctor handed him a glass of water. After taking a quick swallow, he continued. "A week later Drs. Bush and Conant called on the President and told him flatly that secrecy could not prevent Russia from having atomic bombs within three or four years, and that the President must proceed at once to bring Russia into an international control agency. The very next day Mr. Stimson gave the President the same advice."

Castleton turned his face to the doctor. His eyes were watering, and his jaw was quivering. "You see, Doctor . . . every civilian who knew about the bomb . . . all the scientists . . . all of us . . . we were doing everything in our power to prevent the President from yielding to what we knew Churchill would demand."

"And you failed?"

Castleton nodded. "I learned about our failure on September twenty-ninth. The bitterest day of my life up to that point. The first of a succession of bitter days which destroyed everything—my hope, my confidence. Oh, God, if only it hadn't happened!" He tried to compose himself. "Churchill left Hyde Park on September twenty-eighth, and that night, as ordered by the President, I went by train to New York, then to Hyde Park. The moment I walked into the President's office I sensed that here was a man I had never met before. For the first time in my life I feared him. I felt that if I opposed him he wouldn't hesitate to imprison me without trial or have me killed."

GRIM-FACED, without offering his
hand, the Commander-in-Chief ordered Castleton to sit down in a chair
near him. "Frank," he said, "I'm handing you a document to read. It's an
aide-mémoire signed by me and Churchill for the eyes of all persons holding
a Q-clearance in atomic energy. I'm ordering you not to comment on it.
After you've read it, I'll give you a series of orders which you are to carry
out *to the letter!"*

The President handed him the one-page document, and Castleton
began reading:

> 1. The suggestion that the world should be informed regarding the
> atomic bomb, with a view to an international agreement regarding
> its control and use, is not accepted. The matter must continue to be
> regarded as of the utmost secrecy, but when a bomb is finally avail-
> able, it might perhaps, after mature consideration, be used against
> the Japanese, who will be warned that this bombardment will be
> repeated until they surrender.
> 2. Full collaboration between the United States and the British
> Government in developing atomic power for military and commer-
> cial purposes will continue after the defeat of Japan unless and until
> terminated by joint agreement.
> 3. Enquiries should be made regarding all activities of Professor
> Bohr and steps taken to ensure that he is responsible for no leakage
> of information to the Russians.

When Castleton finished reading and raised his face to the President,
he was crying.

"Spare me your tears, Frank," the Commander-in-Chief ordered. "This
is war, and you are being given orders involving life and death. Listen
carefully to every word I say. You are never in your lifetime to tell anyone
about this conversation. Without revealing that I told you to do it, you are
to go first to Los Alamos, then to Oak Ridge and Hanford, and talk with
Bohr and other scientists who will have received or otherwise learned about
this *mémoire.* You will tell Bohr and the others that this is a meaningless
and temporary concession by the President to Churchill—that while he's
involved in an election campaign is no time for him to fight battles with
Churchill and Stalin, that the time for the President to assert himself will
be after he has been inaugurated for his final term. After Hitler is finished,
and when the armies of Britain, Canada and the United States stand face

to face with the Red Army in Central Europe, then it will be appropriate."

The Commander-in-Chief paused while Castleton agonized in silent rage. He felt stunned, dizzy even, as if the floor were shifting beneath his feet. The gratuitous insult to Professor Bohr, who had rushed to America with the news of fission, who had lodged his hope in Roosevelt, was almost too much for Castleton to bear. The President continued, "You will say that in his inaugural address the President will explain to all mankind that the age of nuclear bombs and rocketry has arrived and demands a limited world government. Then, step by step, month by month, the President will end the war and build the sort of supra-national authority which Niels Bohr and Frank Castleton want. Now, you go tell that to Bohr and the other scientists, and make them believe it. Start by believing it yourself. A year from now, if you still want to wring my neck, as you do now, I'll let you do it."

"Did you say anything?" asked Dr. Palkin.

"Not a word," said Castleton. "I knew if I began speaking I wouldn't stop until I had spoken myself into prison and ended any chance I might have to help change the policy. Moreover, the President was still our only hope, and he was still promising to act. I walked out of his office and did what he had ordered me to do."

"But of course now you felt you were a different man . . . a heavy-hearted disturbed man?"

"Yes, sir, I was," said Castleton. "After three years in Washington, and after two years with the bomb, I was tortured by my total impotence to effect any change. I worried about the President's health: I was afraid he'd die before he could do what he seemed destined to do. I worried about Mr. Hull's health and about how my relationship with him had grown shameful and secretive. Senator Norris died, a disappointed and unnoticed man, in 1944. TVA was his monument—he had wanted it to be an adornment to agrarian life—and now Oak Ridge was using more electricity than all the TVA dams combined could generate."

"Then Mr. Hull had to retire?"

"Yes. He was in the Navy hospital in Bethesda. The President accepted his resignation the day after the election and appointed Mr. Stettinius Secretary of State. I felt deeply ashamed of my last year with Mr. Hull, with my godfather—the man who had so encouraged me and helped me. All

253

during 1944 I was supposed to be promoting his effort to create the UN: informing Senators and Congressmen, building support among them for Mr. Hull's concept of the UN. But because he didn't know there was to be a bomb, Mr. Hull's concept was inadequate. *I* knew he was in a ridiculous position, but he didn't know he was, and I was so ashamed of this, I began trying to avoid Mr. Hull. I could have prevented his taking positions and making statements which were wrong and would later appear ridiculous, and I wasn't doing it."

"You felt tempted to tell him there was to be a bomb?"

"Oh, God, yes," said Castleton. "I began feeling afraid to be alone with him, afraid I'd tell him. I felt the same temptation when I was alone with a Senator or a Congressman, especially those I had known for a long time, who had supported TVA and whom I deeply respected. They all needed to know there was to be a bomb, and their constituents, their nation, all mankind needed for them to know, and the press as well. But I couldn't do anything—I couldn't . . ."

"Why didn't you do it?"

"Because I couldn't tell them effectively. In the United States we had the worst sort of censorship—voluntary censorship. If I went to *The New York Times* or to one of the radio networks and told them everything, they wouldn't use it. Moreover, the President had promised that he would tell it all on January 20th, 1945."

"Did you see the President again in 1944?"

"Yes," said Castleton. "I saw him during the week after the election, and then again two days before Christmas. There were developments he needed to know about, so I telephoned the White House, and each time he invited me there for a meeting that evening. After we landed in Normandy, the Manhattan Project sent scientists into Europe with our armies to learn what the European nuclear scientists had done during the war. When these scientific intelligence agents—the effort was called 'Alsos'—when they reached Paris they hurried to the laboratory of Joliot-Curie, who told them the Germans had not tried to make the bomb, but that the Russians had begun their effort."

"Did he know about the American bomb effort?"

"Of course he did," said Castleton. "He grinned and spoke the words 'Oak Ridge,' 'Hanford' and 'Los Alamos.' When I saw the President just before Christmas I told him what was going on via Alsos, and then he stopped me dead by saying that he would not keep his promise to announce the bomb in his inaugural address. But before I could protest, he explained that immediately after his inauguration he was meeting Stalin. The first subject for discussion would be the bomb. They'd work out and announce a Russian-British-American agreement on supra-national control of nuclear weapons when they announced that such weapons were now possible and were being made."

"That was what Bohr wanted, wasn't it?"

"Exactly," said Castleton. "The President then said that to prepare for negotiations in depth with the Russians on the bomb, and also to be able to make necessary changes in the charter of the UN, the Secretary of State, for the first time, must know about the bomb. Accordingly, on January second I was to begin informing Mr. Stettinius. I was even to escort him to Los Alamos if there was time for him to go, but in any case I was to go to Los Alamos and inform Dr. Oppenheimer, Bohr and other key scientists of the actions the President was taking."

"That was quite a Christmas present the President gave you, yes?"

"I was overjoyed. Doctor, I felt he'd given me my life back—my hope. I suddenly felt that the President may have been right in the way he had handled the bomb, and that Bohr and the rest of us may have been too impatient. I said something like that to the President, and he chuckled. He was feeling good, and since he was leaving next day for Christmas at Hyde Park, and he knew I was going to Tennessee, he ordered two glasses of wine. He became his old warm friendly wonderful self. 'We've had a hard year in '44, Frank,' he said. 'Next year we'll have victory and peace. You've been one of my cherished right arms for many years. God bless you and your family and give you a merry Christmas and a happy New Year.' I replied, 'God bless you, sir. In 1945, under your leadership, armed rivalry between nations will end.' He said fervently, 'God grant it.' "

"He restored your faith, did he?" asked the doctor.

"He gave me the last good Christmas of my life," said Castleton. "I went home and celebrated. I played the piano and the cello and the organ at our church. I danced and sang and drank wine and made love to my wife —I was just delirious. I told everyone that 1945 would be the best year of our lives. On the last day of 1944 Diane and I piled into a Ford pickup, pulling two horses in a horse trailer, and drove up into the Smokies. Where the road ended we left the pickup and rode the horses to the cabin we had built at the spot where we first found each other. The air was crisp, and snow began falling before dark. I sheltered the horses under an overhanging bluff, and we built a log fire in the cabin and cooked steaks and drank wine and talked and remembered and made love. At midnight we went outside and stood together, feeling the snow-blanketed forest around us. There wasn't another human being within ten miles. We toasted the New Year and clung to each other, and I said, 'This will be the most hopeful year in human history. Roosevelt will make it so. He has the power and the prestige to do it, and God will give him the will.' Diane said, 'I hope great things happen, darling. But I'll be satisfied with little things . . . like peace and you coming home so we can live normal lives again.' "

"OKAY, Frank," said Dr. Palkin. "Let's take a break for a minute. Get up and drink some water. Take it easy—you're doing beautifully, and I think you're getting an awareness of how your past expectations crippled you. So—that was 1944. Tomorrow you'll relive 1945. But I think a more immediate question now is how you'll live the rest of this day of May 4th, 1948."

The doctor moved to his desk, lighted a cigarette, and sat down, while Castleton stood at the window. "You'll be here only a few more days, so we can do some more talking, and I've decided one or two electroshock treatments will be helpful to make those past disappointments seem more remote and less painful. Joe Bramwell's going to have a few words with you, also; then you'll leave and simply resume a normal life."

When Castleton said nothing, the doctor asked quietly, "Of all the men who had prior knowledge of the bomb, why are you the only one who has suffered psychic distress to the point of hysteria?"

"I'm the one who expected too much."

"But that's natural for you. That's your life purpose. You're an artist . . . a man in whom the urge toward perfection is stronger than in others. When you look at a face or a landscape you see something which makes you yearn to create perfection. When you consider ideals expressed by Lincoln or Wilson, you yearn to realize them. If I recall correctly, Proust said, 'The pleasure an artist gives us is to make us know an additional universe.' You must always strive to give man a dimension he doesn't have."

Castleton asked, "Just curious—how much faith do you have in my recovery, Doctor? Do you really believe I can create, celebrate, feel exaltation again?"

"I'm certain you can," said the doctor. "This afternoon with Mary I want you to talk only about the times you have felt ecstasy. Relive those times with her. Make her feel their jubilation. And this evening I want you to do me a special favor."

"What?"

"My wife's a music lover," said the doctor. "This evening she and I are bringing a few friends to the canteen to listen to you play music. We'd be honored if you could affect us, help us get beyond ourselves, make us know an additional universe."

Castleton nodded. "I'll do my best," he said.

At 3 p.m. that day, Castleton and Mary Sullivan walked from the hospital dressed for tennis. "Today," she said, "I want you to beat me."

"I don't think I can," he said. "You play better than I do."

"Not true," she said. "Each time we've played you've held back—given me a good game and allowed me to beat you."

"I was taught that a man should play that way against a woman."

"I know you were," she said. "But today we'll play by other rules. I'm going to play harder than you have ever seen me play. I'm going to do my best to beat you. If you don't win, I'll confine you to your room for the next two days."

"What's the point, Mary?"

"A Navy nurse is judged by how quickly she returns a man to duty. I can't get you back to work until I teach you to be more aggressive."

What followed was a three-set tennis match so fever-pitched that it attracted spectators. When it began Castleton seemed amused, but when he saw that Mary was determined to beat him his attitude changed. He quit playing defensively and began attacking. Wildness, however, cost him the first set. His overhead smashes were too hard, and therefore too often out, and several times he double-faulted as he increased the speed of his serves. His control improved enough for him to win the second set, and in the third set he blew her off the court. Twice he smashed her lobs so hard that the balls bounced over the backstop and were retrieved by spectators. When he ended the match with an ace she couldn't lay her racquet on, the spectators cheered.

As they walked together toward Mary's apartment, he waited for her to speak. In the heat of battle before spectators she had forgotten about wanting him to win. She had wanted to win, and she wasn't happy about losing.

"You wanted me to win, didn't you?" he asked.

"You didn't have to make it look so easy," she said. Only then did she manage a smile.

At the apartment Castleton mixed the drinks and selected three records for dancing, all polkas. They drank, danced and kissed, then went to bed and made tender satisfying love. When it was over he asked, "I believe you have promised to continue this relationship after I leave here? In places like Virginia Beach, Hot Springs, or Sea Island?"

"That depends on how hard you work," she said. "If you continue to waste your talents whimpering over Roosevelt's and Truman's mistakes, I really have no interest in continuing to see you. But if you'll quit whimpering, and get back to what you do best—if you'll strive in your paintings to give human life a significance it really doesn't have, for instance—I'll come running every time you whistle."

At dinner Castleton confided, "I haven't been able to complete a painting since 1944. Everything I started began looking like *Wheat Field With Crows* or *Raft of the Medusa.*"

"Explain that to me," she said. "I don't know those paintings."

Castleton then described van Gogh's dim paths crossing and leading nowhere . . . the storm-blown wheat at war with an enraged sky . . . crows flapping over the tumult, swarming toward the artist . . . the whole angry canvas rolling relentlessly forward . . . earth and sky coming together, blocking all paths of escape, determined to destroy the artist. And Gericault's vast canvas which compels emotional participation of the viewer in a political crime . . . men lost at sea after a shipwreck the government could have prevented . . . four men still reaching toward the sail of a rescue ship now distant beyond reach, while other men collapse in lassitude, resignation and death . . . an unforgettable expression of the artist's materialistic and pessimistic outlook.

"Of course," said Castleton, "it was Hiroshima and the political crimes of Roosevelt and Truman that made me try to express myself like that. But that's over for me. Now I'm going to paint new hymns to the earth as it might have been if the dreams of George Norris could have been realized. And I'm going to paint a new sort of courage into the faces of men and women—the courage which enables a human being to strive after both hope of Heaven and the American dream have faded. The courage which enables a man to fantasize when he knows that human life can be no more than a dreary round of habitual actions to satisfy primary needs."

"It takes more guts to live without hope than it does with hope, doesn't it?"

"A different sort of courage. It's—well, I guess it's really no more than a persistent longing for significance in the face of impending nothingness."

The two of them looked at each other with a kind of quiet determination.

THAT evening in the canteen Castleton played more effectively than he had played in years. The presence of Dr. Palkin, his wife and their party attracted an unusually large number of patients and volunteers. Castleton played the requested popular piano favorites, and for the music lovers he played several Chopin waltzes and one movement of Beethoven's "Appassionata." On the cello he played the loudly requested "Deep River," "Shenandoah," "The Old Refrain," and "The World Is Waiting for the Sunrise." The crowd stood on their chairs and yelled and applauded, and the doctor's wife and her friends came and shook Castleton's hands and thanked him.

So when Castleton and Mary went upstairs at 9 P.M., they were both feeling intensely emotional. When they closed the door to his room Castleton reached for her and kissed her and said, "Are you going to tell me to put on my pajamas while you go get the needle? Or are you going to let me give you an injection before you give me one?"

She smiled and did what she had never done before or even imagined herself doing. Minus only her shoes and step-ins, she allowed a patient to take her across a hospital bed. The sex was brief, but intensely pleasurable for both of them. Then she collected herself and said, "Now get on your pajamas while I go get your medication. You'll need an extra c.c. to calm you down tonight."

"If you'll stay with me," he said, "I won't need any other medication. I'll hold on to you, every time the walls start closing in."

"Not here." She touched his face gently.

In ten minutes she returned, and he was in his pajamas, lying on the bed. She sat down beside him, gave him the injection and sat rubbing the spot with cotton. He reached up and touched her cheek, then raised up and kissed her tenderly. "What is it your creed says?" he asked. "A man must love a woman tenderly and potently to stay sane?"

"That's what it says," she said. "Chant it before you go to sleep." Then she went out and locked the door behind her.

W̲ʜᴇɴ he greeted the doctor next morning Castleton was particularly well-groomed and -dressed. "How are you feeling?" the doctor asked, as he asked every patient he saw every day.

"I don't feel quite so insignificant today," answered Castleton. "I'm going to be able to get back to work. I know it now."

"Fine," said the doctor. "Let's move into 1945. Do you want to lie down, as you did yesterday?"

"I'd rather sit today," said Castleton. They took their customary places facing each other, and Castleton began the story.

I̲ɴᴀᴜɢᴜʀᴀᴛɪᴏɴ Day, January 20, 1945, was cold and gray in Washington, and a thin layer of snow covered the Capitol grounds. While President Roosevelt was delivering his Inaugural Address, he trembled repeatedly. It was not only his hands or his chin —his entire body trembled. From the day after Christmas his health had deteriorated rapidly. But his voice was clear as he spoke of how, during 1945, "we shall perform a service of historic importance which men and women and children will honor throughout all time."

The day after his inauguration the President boarded the cruiser *Quincy* for a voyage across the Atlantic and into the Mediterranean to the island of Malta. He believed that the voyage, with ten hours of sleep every night, would restore his strength. During the dark early-morning hours of February 2, the *Quincy* dropped anchor at Malta, where five hundred other

Americans and Churchill with two hundred other Britons were waiting to accompany the President on a flight to the Black Sea resort of Yalta. A contingent of Churchill's party boarded the *Quincy* at 1 P.M. for lunch with the President. Churchill's physician, Lord Moran, wrote in his diary that evening: "Everyone was shocked by the President's appearance. He looks old and thin and drawn, and he sits looking straight ahead with his mouth open as if he is not taking things in. He has all the symptoms of hardening of the arteries of the brain in an advanced stage. I give him only a few months to live. But the Americans here can't bring themselves to believe he is finished."

The seven hundred conferees traveled the 1,375 miles from Malta to the Crimea in twenty-five four-engined transport planes—twenty American DC-4s and five British Yorks. Before midnight on February 2 the planes began taking off at ten-minute intervals for the seven-hour non-stop flight. They landed in daylight during the morning of February 3 on an icy newly built concrete-block airstrip at Saki, which was a ninety-mile drive from Yalta. The President and Churchill left Malta in separate planes at 3:30 and 3:40 A.M. and landed at Saki about noon. A Red Army band played, and soldiers stood at twenty-foot intervals around the perimeter of the airfield. The welcoming Russian delegation was headed by Molotov, who apologized for the absence of Stalin, who refused to fly and wouldn't arrive from Moscow by train until next day. The President and Churchill were led into one of three nearby tents, where the other seven hundred visitors who arrived earlier had waited, drinking hot tea, vodka, brandy and champagne, and eating caviar, smoked sturgeon, salmon, black bread with butter, cheese and boiled eggs. A guarded caravan of more than three hundred cars and trucks traveled the narrow graveled mountain road from Saki down to Yalta.

The last cars of the caravan reached Yalta at 6 P.M. The President and two hundred members of the American party were lodged in Czar Nicholas's three-story summer palace, Livadia, where plenary sessions of the conference were to be held. The other Americans, the British and the Russians were lodged in a dozen smaller palaces and villas scattered along ten miles of coast. Livadia, built in 1910 of marble and limestone, stood on a shelf two hundred feet above the Black Sea, with forested mountains rising behind it. Livadia had been a German headquarters, and the departing Germans, who had driven into the Crimea in 1942 and left six months later, had wrecked it, as they had wrecked the other palaces and villas. To prepare for the conference, Stalin had sent carpenters, painters, stonemasons, plumbers, plasterers and electricians from Moscow, along with train-loads of furniture, fixtures, carpets and draperies from three Moscow hotels. The US Navy communications ship *Catoctin* had sent seamen to extermi-nate the vermin.

"WHERE were you quartered?" asked Dr. Palkin.

"I was lucky," replied Castleton, "because of the close relationship that had developed between Mr. Stettinius and me. It began—oh, I guess back in Washington. On January second I had begun telling him about the bomb, and his reaction had been a tonic to me and to every scientist on the project. He was only six years older than I—a graduate of the University of Virginia—we quickly began calling each other by our first names. He had been an executive with United States Steel, and was accustomed to dealing with scientists, and after he had listened to me twenty minutes he ordered an Army transport plane, and he and I left that evening on a whirlwind trip to Oak Ridge, Hanford and Los Alamos. During long hours in the air with him I told him everything that I had so long wanted to tell Mr. Hull. His appetite for information was insatiable. The scientists at Los Alamos, especially Bohr, hailed him as a godsend. He recognized at once that he must organize the UN so it could monopolize nuclear weapons, and he was impatient to begin negotiations with Molotov and Stalin. At Yalta he saw that I was quartered in Livadia near him, since he and I were the only members of the State Department delegation who knew about the bomb, and since he assumed that by the second or third day we would be negotiat-ing with Molotov for control of the bomb."

"What was it like at Livadia?"

"An experience. I'd never want to repeat it, I assure you," said Castle-ton. "Only the President, Mr. Stimson and the ranking admirals and generals were on the first floor. The President had the only private bath-room in the palace. I shared a bedroom on the second floor with only five other State Department men, so I was fortunate. I shared a bathroom with only twenty-five other men, so I had to stand in line usually no longer than an hour, while men on the third floor were lodged ten in a room and had to wait two hours to get into a bathroom. And the bedbugs were more ravenous on the third floor than on the second and first. You see, the seamen from the *Catoctin* had killed most of the rats and other vermin, but the bedbugs of Yalta thrived on DDT. The conference lasted nine days, and by the third day every conferee wore the wounds of nocturnal battle with bedbugs. Churchill said his feet were eaten up."

"Madness!" Dr. Palkin was horrified.

"The size of the American delegation was shameful. Three weeks before the President left Washington, he set a limit of thirty-five on the size of his party. Then, weak as he was, he gave way to all the junketeers and allowed the party to grow to five hundred, including his sons and daughter, and Hopkins's son, and Harriman's daughter, and Bronx political boss Ed Flynn and his daughter. All these picnickers were a shameful imposition on the Russian people. With Russian armies still forty miles from Berlin, with millions of Russians homeless and hungry, hundreds of Russian artisans had worked around the clock for six weeks trying to make these dirty old palaces comfortable for all those overfed Americans who took no part in the conference and who only gorged themselves on extravagant food and drink! Why hadn't the President taken his thirty-five needed aides to the American Embassy in Moscow for a week of work without ceremony or conspicuous consumption or constipation or bedbugs!"

Again Castleton's breathing had become too shallow and too rapid, so Dr. Palkin asked him to stop and sip some water to calm down. After a few minutes, Castleton went on. "Doctor, as the days passed, with all the bedbugs, crowded living, drinking and feasting, you cannot imagine how desperately restless and depressed I became! Through session after session I sat there with Stettinius, endured all those hours of talk and translation, waiting for the President to mention the bomb. He said nothing! Half the time he didn't know where he was! All we did was consent to Russian conquest of all of Eastern Europe and much of Central Europe and the Balkans. We agreed to a provision in the UN charter whereby the UN was forbidden to take any action against Russia, Britain or the United States. I needed exercise desperately between those awful sessions, but I couldn't go rowing on the Black Sea or hiking in the mountains, because German mines were still killing people. I could only walk or jog in the palace garden. I often walked with Stettinius and listened to his expressions of frustration. Every day he asked the President to allow him to begin discussing the bomb, and the President waved his hand and said, 'Not yet, not yet.' "

Dr. Palkin asked, "How do you account for the optimism Hopkins expressed about Yalta? He called Yalta 'the first great victory of the peace,' didn't he?"

"Hopkins had come back briefly from the grave to be at Yalta. Oh, when he was in Washington his judgment was often sound. But when he was in the Kremlin or the Livadia Palace, he was so busy marveling over how he, the son of an Iowa harness maker, managed to get there that he lost his balance. Whenever he was in the company of famous men he assumed that something great was happening. One afternoon in the garden at Livadia he rushed up to Stettinius and me and said, 'Now don't forget! We're here to win Stalin's confidence! Allies trusting one another, building a free and peaceful world—that's the spirit of Yalta!' "

"What did you say?"

"Nothing," said Castleton. Stettinius stared at him contemptuously and said, 'Horseshit, Harry!' Then we walked away and left Hopkins standing there."

"Was any action taken which pleased you or Stettinius?"

"None. Yalta was an unrelieved disaster for the United States and for all mankind. As the conferees were preparing to leave Yalta, Stettinius delivered this message to me: 'The President wants you to cross the Atlantic with him on the *Quincy*. He's leaving now to fly to Ismailia and board the *Quincy* in Great Bitter Lake and receive visits from Farouk, Haile Selassie and Ibn Saud (monarchs of Egypt, Ethiopia and Saudi Arabia). Then the *Quincy* will sail for Newport News, stopping en route at Algiers. You are to fly to Algiers and stand by and board the *Quincy* when it arrives.' And so I went."

DURING the gray wet afternoon of February 16, 1945, a U.S. Navy launch left the dock at Algiers and headed out into the harbor toward the battle cruiser *Quincy*. In the launch were two civilians. One was Judge Samuel Rosenman, who had flown from New York to make the return voyage with the President and help him write his report to Congress on Yalta. The other was Frank Castleton. The two men, who knew each other slightly, exchanged pleasantries during the ride, but when they reached the *Quincy*, they stopped chatting, so disheartening was the dismal atmosphere. On the deck they met a pale unsteady Harry Hopkins, who had become ill and was leaving the ship for treatment at Marrakech. It was evident he was near death. The President too was ill, exhausted and depressed. His cough and chills had returned, and he was in bed most of every day, seeing only his doctors and his daughter Anna. Even worse, the President's aide, Pa Watson, lay critically ill of congestion in the ship's hospital. As Hopkins was assisted down the gangway to the launch, Judge Rosenman and Castleton were shown to their quarters.

Five depressing days passed as the *Quincy*, flanked by destroyers, moved through the Straits of Gibraltar and into a cold stormy Atlantic. On the second night out of Algiers Pa Watson died, and the ship became a floating hearse. The President's gloom deepened, and, just as he had done a year earlier, he tried to withdraw and let the world go hang. He'd talk to no one but his daughter, and he didn't talk much to her; he sat with her with his head bowed and his mouth open. Judge Rosenman couldn't persuade him to begin work on the Yalta report, so the judge and Castleton read and talked and played poker with the ship's officers in the wardroom. Castleton shuddered every time he thought of how much depended on the frail body of Franklin Roosevelt. The battle for Iwo Jima was being fought, Russian and Allied armies were crushing Germany between them, at Hanford and Oak Ridge the pounds of plutonium and U-235 were accumulating—and the President was unable to think or act! On the sixth day the President called in Judge Rosenman and began work on the report, and on the seventh day a Marine sergeant came to Castleton and told him he was to present himself at the President's quarters at 3 P.M.

Roosevelt was propped up in bed, chain-smoking cigarettes as the ship rolled on waves twenty feet high. He didn't smile when Castleton entered, but he extended a weak hand and said he was feeling better. He continued, "I suppose you've been lying in your bunk cussing Roosevelt for not saving the world?"

"I've been depressed as you have been, sir," said Castleton. "But I'm still clinging to the hope that you'll do what you've promised to do."

"The trouble is that what you and Bohr and the others want may be impossible. What you want is world government—one world—and you want me to persuade Congress and the people of the United States to accept that and to be willing to make war if necessary to impose it on the British Empire and the Soviet Union. Isn't that right?"

"In a sense, it is," said Castleton. "We want a world authority strong enough to allow the United States, Britain and Russia to disarm, and strong enough to compel any nation to disarm which refuses to do so willingly. Nations can manufacture such of these weapons—nuclear weapons, rockets, long-range bombers, aircraft carriers and submarines—as the world authority that's created needs, and it, having a monopoly on these weapons, won't need many of them. Then each nation can choose its own form of government—it can indulge in civil war if it becomes necessary—but it can't threaten war against any other nation."

"That sounds good—just fine," said the President. "But the United

States won't accept it now. Remember Willkie? He's dead. He became a one-worlder, and when nobody would listen to him he died. Cordell Hull put you to work preparing Senators to accept a UN like he started building in Moscow in 1943, like he continued building at Dumbarton Oaks in 1944 and we continued building at Yalta. But you don't like Cordell's UN, because it can't impose its will on the United States or on Russia and it can't own any bombs. What you can't see, Frank, is that it's the only beginning we can make. If we can get Congress to accept it, then in time, after we see what nuclear weapons can do, we can amend the charter of the UN and give it more power. But if I presented a plan for world government next week requiring the United States to surrender one iota of its sovereignty to the UN, it wouldn't have a ghost of a chance in Congress. What you want is impossible until . . . until . . ."

"Until when, sir?" asked Castleton. "It's impossible until you tell Congress and the people that bombs are being made which can end human life on earth. The sooner you tell Congress and the people we are making this bomb, the better will be our chance to persuade all Americans to take the risks necessary to create world authority and to compel the Stalin regime to accept it."

The President lighted another cigarette. "I've thought a lot about this announcement I promised the scientists I'd make. I've even practiced a speech telling the world about the atomic bomb. If I made that speech next week, not enough people would believe me. How do I explain the atomic bomb to the average American over the radio? Despite all your efforts to explain it to me, I don't know how an atomic bomb works. If I bumble on about it over the air, my enemies will shout that Roosevelt is trying to scare Americans into giving up their freedoms and accepting world government, that Oak Ridge and Hanford and Los Alamos are another four-billion-dollar Roosevelt boondoggle. Stories about super-weapons are always discounted, so who's going to believe me when I say that one bomb can level a city? At this moment I don't know that the bomb is going to be any more destructive than a hundred B-29s dropping blockbusters. Yes, certainly, the scientists tell us they'll get a big release of energy, but they aren't sure how destructive it'll be. And of this you can be damn sure: Unless that bomb can wipe a big city off the map, it won't be destructive enough to make Americans risk world government. So let me ask you: Are you convinced beyond doubt that one bomb can wipe a big city off the map?"

"Yes, sir," said Castleton. "Last month Ed Stettinius saw one of those reactors at Hanford in operation. He studied the dials which show the awesome amount of heat and radiation. He was convinced, and so would you be if you had been there. Now let me ask you a question: Do you and Churchill feel the demonstration of the bomb can be convincing only if we actually wipe a big city off the map?"

"I'm afraid that's how it must be, Frank," said the President. "People are hard to convince. Only a cataclysm will persuade Americans of the fact that the atomic bomb was worth four billion dollars. And *most certainly* only a cataclysm will convince Americans that they should risk war with Stalin to achieve world government."

The President's body shook as he suffered a hard coughing spell. "All right, suppose I accept as a fact the destructive power of the bomb. And suppose you and Stettinius and the scientists accept the fact that we can move people toward world government only with a cataclysmic demonstration. What then?"

"Well," said Castleton, "I hope this means that next week, along with your report on Yalta, you'll report to Congress and the people that we are making the bomb and instruct Harriman in Moscow to begin discussing the bomb with Molotov and Stalin. That'll give us time to promote some understanding before the demonstration. I can take key members of Congress to Hanford, and maybe they'll be so impressed that destroying a city won't be necessary to move them. But I'm afraid you seem decided about sticking with your *aide-mémoire* and not breaking secrecy until after the explosion. Am I right?"

"I haven't decided yet," said the President. "I'll make up my mind before we reach Newport News and tell you when I talk with you again." He held out his hand, signaling Castleton to get up, shake his hand and leave, but this time Castleton ignored the signal.

"One more suggestion, sir," he said. "While you're thinking about that, will you consider three related questions? First, about the German surrender, which can come any day. At Yalta you told Stalin that, except for small occupation forces, our Army will be withdrawn from Europe after the German surrender. Now, Mr. President, mankind will never forgive you if you withdraw one American soldier from Europe before you settle the bomb question with Stalin. You know that. Second, the meeting to organize the UN is to be held in San Francisco in May. Are you going to allow those organizers to meet without telling them that they must organize for an atomic age? And third, at this moment U.S. Marines are dying to secure Iwo Jima. Our fighter aircraft will escort our bombers in massive daylight firebomb raids on Japanese cities from there. Japan can't defend against those raids because she produces no oil, her tankers have all been sunk and her fighter planes will soon be out of gas. So Japan will lie helpless under our firebombs long before we can have the first atomic bomb ready to demonstrate. And if I know your mind, sir, it seems to me you would be thinking of using a Japanese city for the cataclysmic demonstration you say we must have in order to convince Americans to risk international control of atomic weapons. Suppose Japan surrenders first? Must we incinerate Japanese people who have conceded our victory?"

Castleton then rose and offered his hand to the President, who took it and held it for a moment. Then the President said, "I'll give you my decision and my orders before we reach Newport News."

T HREE days out of Newport News the *Quincy* ran into a storm which lasted until the cruiser entered the harbor. Through the storm the President tried to work with Judge Rosenman, and during the last afternoon out he talked again with Castleton.

"I know what I must do, Frank. Again you won't like it, but you'll have to be patient with me a little longer. You heard me tell Bohr that I agreed with him, and I tell you now that I still do. But the problem of timing remains. Next week in my report on Yalta I'll sell Congress on the UN as presently proposed. While I'm doing that I want you to go back to Oak Ridge and Hanford and Los Alamos and tell the scientists that I'm carefully preparing to move in their direction. And tell them to hurry up with the cataclysmic demonstration! If only they had worked a little faster and given it to me by now! And tell them it mustn't be a small city nobody ever heard of—it must be a big city . . . *wiped clean off the map!* And we must do it soon, before the Japanese have a chance to surrender."

When Castleton seemed unable to speak, the President asked, "Did you think it was going to be easy to persuade the people of the United States to entrust the protection of this great rich nation to a supra-national nuclear armed force?"

Instead of answering, Castleton said, "Mr. President, if you are going to continue secrecy until you can end it by wiping a large Japanese city off the map, I must ask you to relieve me of this duty."

"Request denied," said the President. "You enlisted for the duration, so you must stay at your post."

"Then I have to reveal a personal problem," said Castleton. "I'm deeply depressed. Sometimes I feel that I am drifting hopelessly in space—that

I am spinning and whirling—and when this feeling becomes intense I'm terrified. The terror constricts my chest, and I have to fight to breathe or to swallow. So if I must continue in this duty, I must request that you allow me to have psychiatric assistance and to take drugs to help me sleep."

"Impossible! You know I can't allow any psychiatrist to probe around in your conscious or unconscious. And I can't allow you to take drugs under the influence of which you might make revelations which could endanger national security."

"What if I crack up? Many men have broken in this war under less pressure than I've been under for almost three years."

"You aren't going to crack up. You're twenty years younger than I am —you can endure whatever I can endure. All you need is a brief vacation. After you finish at Los Alamos, take a week off and go to the mountains with your wife or with some other woman. Enjoy living. You'll be all right."

"Did you take the vacation?" asked Dr. Palkin.

"Yes," said Castleton, trying hard to get a full breath. "I went up into the Jemez Mountains of New Mexico with a woman I'd met in Santa Fe. We rode horseback and cooked over campfires as we sat under that big star-filled sky at night. We held each other inside the sleeping bag, and I fucked her every time I felt scared."

"Did that help?"

"Yes, a bit."

"When did you see the President again?"

"I saw him two more times before he died," said Castleton. "Late in March, after I had returned to Washington from New Mexico, we talked in the Oval Study one evening. I told him I'd come to inform him on three matters which disturbed the scientists. The first was Oranienburg."

"Where's that?"

"It's a city fifteen miles north of Berlin. On March fifteenth the Russians were approaching it. It was in the zone which had been assigned to Russia at Yalta. There was a new factory in the town, and the Russians intended to move it intact to Moscow. In effect, on March fifteenth, that factory was valuable Russian property, so recognized by the United States at Yalta. But our Alsos agents had learned that this plant was refining thorium and uranium metals from which fissionable atoms could be obtained. So the Alsos agents persuaded General Carl Spaatz, who commanded our Strategic Air Forces, to destroy the building to prevent the

Russians from possessing it. During the afternoon of March fifteenth six hundred Flying Fortresses dropped fifteen hundred and six tons of demolition bombs and one hundred seventy-eight tons of firebombs and ruined the factory. This raid was a blow struck, not against Germany, you understand, but against the Soviet Union. The Russians knew but didn't protest because they didn't want to reveal their interest in atomic energy. I explained this to the President and showed him the Oranienburg photos. 'Mr. President,' I said, 'Americans and Russians are now fighting each other for possession of German factories which can help make atomic bombs. So why can't we move now to halt this atomic-arms race?' "

"What was his answer?"

"He asked me if the scientists thought we should have allowed the Russians to have the Oranienburg plant. I answered yes—that we should help Russia and all other nations produce atomic energy. I told him that a pound of plutonium could do the work of fifteen million pounds of coal, and that the world authority should monopolize only weapons utilizing atomic energy, not atomic energy itself. Then I told the President about one of the German nuclear physicists who was at the Kaiser Wilhelm Institute when fission was achieved, and knew that Bohr, Fermi and von Neumann had gone to the United States to escape Hitler. In March, 1945, he had assumed that the United States had the bomb. 'What a pity Germany didn't get the bomb first!' he told an Alsos agent. 'We would have conquered Russia with it. The United States will only waste it. Instead of using it to prevent Stalin from getting it, the United States will either give it to Stalin or do nothing while he gets it. And after Stalin gets it, what hope will there be?' "

"Did the President respond to that?"

"No," said Castleton. "He didn't bat an eye. Then I showed him photos of Tokyo taken before and after the first big firebomb raid on March eighth. The raid had incinerated a hundred and ten thousand people and made a wasteland of a large area of Tokyo. It was the most destructive single blow ever struck by one nation against another—many times as destructive as Pearl Harbor, and far more so than Hiroshima. The Air Force could repeat it every few days until Japan surrendered or until there were no more large densely populated areas to justify so destructive an attack. The firebomb thus threatened to dissipate the impact of the atomic bomb. The napalm bomb, as the scientists had foreseen, could gut all of Japan's big cities and not leave a big undamaged densely populated city for the atomic bomb to wipe off the face of the earth."

"Let's go back over that," said the doctor. "I must be certain I understand what you're saying. You were worried over the fact that there might not be a human target on which to demonstrate the atomic bomb?"

"No, no, of course not," said Castleton. "Like most of the scientists, I didn't believe that a cataclysmic demonstration of the bomb was a political necessity, that we had to wipe a big city off the face of the earth to demonstrate convincingly that the bomb could demolish a big city. I thought we could detonate the bomb over desert or water or underground, and let the instruments measuring heat and radiation prove to all mankind that nuclear weapons could end all human life on earth. But the President didn't agree. He wasn't a scientist but a politician."

Castleton dropped his voice. "Before we go on, Doctor, I must tell you that you can be secretly court-martialed and secretly imprisoned or shot for revealing what I'm going to explain to you now."

Dr. Palkin extended his right hand, studied the back of it, then said, "Go ahead."

"The atomic bomb," said Castleton, "was dropped on Hiroshima for several complex reasons, none of which had anything to do with persuading the Japanese to surrender or with saving American and Japanese lives. Churchill wanted to use the bomb, or the threat of the bomb, to drive the Russians out of Central Europe. So he wanted the bomb dropped for a military reason."

"And Roosevelt's reasons were political?"

"Yes," said Castleton. "Actually, he had three political reasons. The President believed he needed to justify his secretly spending four billion dollars on it. He couldn't risk being charged with getting *only another weapon* for four billion dollars, you see, and demolishing a city would be justification. He also needed to justify his unlawfully keeping the project secret from Congress for three years. Finally, the President sincerely believed that any hope for using the bomb to end war among nations depended on horror. He thought that only a thoroughly horrified and terrified Congress would ever consider giving our atomic weapons to a world authority."

"Do you suppose he was right?"

"He may have been," said Castleton, looking down at his tightly clenched hands. "In any case, when I showed him that firebombs could gut all of Japan's big cities before the atomic bomb would be ready for use, he took prompt action, and ordered the Air Force not to attack either Kyoto or Hiroshima."

"You mean he acted to preserve those two cities from being incinerated by napalm so they could be destroyed by atomic heat?"

"Yes, and that was almost five months before the bomb was dropped on Hiroshima. The President's choice for the atomic bomb was Kyoto."

"But Kyoto was the old cultural capital of Japan. The residence of priests, painters, poets and philosophers."

"The president knew that, naturally he knew it. That was the basis of his belief that man's best hope in 1945 lay in horror. The most horrifying act in the ancient world was the burning of the great library at Alexandria. All right, Kyoto was a city of a million people filled with shrines, colleges, museums and libraries—very old and beautiful—pitifully vulnerable to fire. So there you are—the colossal horrifying act for the modern world. He wanted to frighten the people of the United States so they'd follow him through whatever was necessary to create a form of world government."

"What did you think of that?"

"I was appalled by it. For almost five months I lived with the nightmare that we'd have to choose between Hiroshima and Kyoto. We'd have to decide whether to incinerate carpenters and fishermen and their wives and children, or to incinerate priests, painters, poets and philosophers."

"Good God!"

"The President then told me he was tired. He couldn't talk any longer, and he was going to Warm Springs in a few days for a long rest. He wanted me to visit him there, and he'd let me know when to come. Meanwhile, I was to continue assuring the scientists that very soon he would confront Stalin and demand agreement on a plan for a world authority to control atomic weapons."

ON the morning of Tuesday, April 10, 1945, Frank Castleton left his home in Norris, Tennessee, for the three-hundred-mile drive to Warm Springs, Georgia. He was alone, driving a dark blue 1941-model Ford sedan. He'd spend the night in a motel and arrive at the President's cottage at 2:30 P.M. on Wednesday.

Despite his anxieties, Castleton felt rested. He had just come from five nights at home, living like a man should live: enjoying his wife in their big luxurious bed, talking with her over hour-long breakfasts with many cups of coffee, walking with her and watching another spring come to the trees and flowers of their wooded hillside. On Friday afternoon he had run twelve miles through a forest. On Saturday he had gone horseback riding with his wife and their eleven-year-old son. On early Saturday evening they had telephoned their daughter in Baltimore, and the three of them at home had taken turns talking to her and telling her how much she was missed. Then he and his wife and son had danced for an hour with their neighbors in the Norris community house. On Sunday they all had gone to church, and afterward they had enjoyed Sunday dinner at his father's house, for which they were joined by one of his sisters and her family. Later on Sunday afternoon he and his wife and son had taken their power boat out of its berth on Lake Norris and run it ten miles upstream. On Sunday evening he had played the piano for his wife and his son. Not until Monday had he let the war intrude on him. Then he had driven the twelve miles down to Oak Ridge—to another world—where forty-five thousand people were involved in separating the two kinds of uranium atoms. He talked with scientists, he read the Alsos reports, and he read the report that by June 15 there would be enough plutonium at Hanford for the first test in the New Mexico desert, and by July 15 there would be enough U-235 at Oak Ridge for the event which would wipe either Kyoto or Hiroshima off the map.

Before he stopped for lunch at Rome, Georgia, Castleton turned on the radio. In response to the American invasion of Okinawa, the Japanese Cabinet had fallen. There had been another big napalm raid on Tokyo. Americans were within forty miles of Berlin, and the Russians were within ten miles. The war was rushing to a close, and all but a few Americans were anticipating celebrations of V-E and V-J Days and "bringing the boys home."

At 2:20 P.M. on Wednesday, April 11, Castleton approached the President's cottage. A Secret Service agent admitted him to the grounds and showed him where to park his car. The President had been at Warm Springs since March 30: sleeping ten hours every night, driving his Ford around the countryside, sitting in the sun, swimming in the therapeutic pool. Five women, his comforters, were in constant attendance on him: his cousins, Margaret Suckley and Laura Delano; his friend, Lucy Mercer Rutherford; his secretary, Grace Tully; and his two-hundred-pound Negro cook, Lizzie McDuffie, who came in to joke with him several times each day. (His wife was not with him; she was his critic, not his comforter.) The men nearest him were his Negro valet; his doctor, Howard G. Bruenn; and his aide, William D. Hassett. Other aides, Secret Service men, and a platoon of reporters stayed in nearby cottages. The President was sitting on the porch in his leather arm chair when Castleton approached. He was dictating to Miss Tully, and he waved to Castleton and shouted for him to come on up.

The President's appearance was heartening. His color was better; his voice stronger; he seemed more alert than he had seemed since 1943. He had been dictating a speech he expected to make on Jefferson's birthday, and he was so pleased with it that he told Miss Tully to read portions of it aloud: ". . . The work, my friends, is peace. More than an end of this war . . . an end to the beginnings of all wars . . . yes, an end, forever, to this impractical, unrealistic settlement of the differences between governments by the mass killing of peoples."

The President went on, "We've got a lot of traveling to do, Frank. Next month I'll be in San Francisco opening the organization meeting of the United Nations. We've got to get that charter agreed to, and approved by Congress, because we'll want to amend it after the demonstration of the bomb. I expect to be in Berlin in July for the peace conference, and I want to be back in time to go to Manila in August. Despite the war, we're giving the Philippines their independence right on schedule. We're going to end colonialism in this world, and we're going to show our British buddies how to get on with it in Manila. You'll be with me on all these trips."

"I'm thankful you feel strong enough to do all that traveling," Castleton said, but his mind still dwelled on the decision about the bomb.

"I'm going to be in top shape," said the President, "don't worry. I want you to read the latest exchange of cables between Churchill and me. During the past three weeks Stalin has been sending me insulting messages, and I've replied firmly. He's afraid the Germans will help us occupy Berlin before the Russians can get there, but none of this worries me much. I've told you all along that I'll handle Stalin at the showdown. Now read this."

On April 5 Churchill had cabled Roosevelt: "I am astounded that Stalin should have addressed you in so insulting a manner . . . This makes it imperative that we join hands with the Russian armies as far to the east as possible . . . If the Russians are ever convinced that we can be bullied into submission, I should despair of our future relations with them and much else."

On April 6 Roosevelt had replied to Churchill: "I am pleased with your very strong messages to Stalin . . . Our Armies will in a very few days be in a position that will permit us to become tougher than has heretofore appeared advantageous to the war effort."

Cautiously Castleton asked, "What does this mean, sir?"

"It means," said the President, "that you and Bohr have been too impatient. You haven't understood that we had to destroy Hitler before we could afford to get tough with Stalin. We had to bring Tokyo under our bombs, cut off Japan's oil supply and make sure we didn't need Russian armies to help defeat Japan. We had to wait until our armies were standing face to face with the Reds before we told Stalin that he isn't going to have any atomic bombs—that when this war is over we're all going out of the war business, and we're all going to depend on one exceedingly well-armed policeman, based in Alaska and Greenland, to guarantee every peaceful nation against armed attack by any other nation."

Castleton had been disappointed too often to believe what he was hearing. "Won't Churchill still be a problem?"

"No, he's finished," said the President. "He can't survive a post-war election. The British people don't want to be a world power any more. No, Frank, the only two nations left in the world business will be us and the Soviet Union. The governors of Russia do not govern with the consent of the governed, so their chief concern is not the welfare of their people but the extension of their own privilege and power. When this war is over, if allowed to do so, Stalin would repress the people he has in his grasp while he concentrated on an all-out effort to outstrip the United States in armed might. He'd have great advantages over us, a country whose elected representatives govern only with the consent of the governed, and whose first concern must be the freedom and welfare of the people. Nobody understands better than I the drawbacks of a free government in any protracted arms race with a Communist power. So you can be sure that I'll never allow Stalin to hold those advantages over us. The United States is never going to have to become another Rome and neglect and repress its own people in order to keep up with the Soviet Union in a nuclear and rocket arms race. You can relax and depend on that, and tell the scientists at Los Alamos to do likewise."

"That's wonderfully reassuring, Mr. President," said Castleton. "When will you confront Stalin on the bomb issue?"

"The day after the German surrender is signed."

"And you won't start withdrawing our forces from Europe?"

"Not a man, not a tank, not a plane," said the President. "We'll do it bilaterally, step by step. We'll withdraw and demobilize an army; they'll withdraw and demobilize an army. They'll inspect us; we'll inspect them. Step by step we'll build the UN. The United States will cede Alaska to the UN. Then the UN will inspect the Soviet Union and the United States and install permanent inspection teams in both countries. We'll deliver our atomic bombs to the UN in Alaska and help the Russians build themselves an Oak Ridge and a Hanford for the production of atomic energy. We'll give land-based and carrier-based bombers to the UN, and submarines and carriers, and begin junking our own. We'll abolish our Navy, Army and Air Force, and maintain only our National Guard and Coast Guard. Britain and Russia will do the same. Over a period of years, with security for everybody at every step, you understand, we'll liquidate three gigantic war machines and create one small efficient awesomely powerful UN-controlled strike force which no nation can hope to defy and live, and the cost of which will be shared by all nations."

Castleton was still afraid to believe the President. "What about the UN meeting in San Francisco? It's scheduled to open before the Germans are likely to surrender. Shouldn't that meeting be postponed until after you've confronted Stalin on the bomb issue?"

"No," said Roosevelt. "In my Yalta report I told the Congress that the original UN charter would need amending. So, let the UN be organized as we agreed at Yalta. Then, step by step, we can change it."

"Have you told Mr. Stettinius all that you are now telling me, sir?"

"Not yet," said the President. "But I'll tell him this weekend when he'll be down here."

"I'm very pleased, of course, sir, but one thing still troubles me," said Castleton. "In the light of all you've said, must we still have the cataclysmic demonstration of the atomic bomb?"

"Indeed we must."

"But what about Rotterdam and Dresden and London and Berlin and Tokyo? Hasn't conventional bombing already been terrible enough to convince most people of the necessity for one supra-national authority? Why can't we explode the atomic bomb over the desert and use instruments to measure the heat and radiation?"

The President shook his head. "Frank," he said, "you're an expert persuader of Congressmen. That's what Norris, Hull and I have used you for. So you know that persuading them to abolish the U.S. Army, Navy and Air Force, and to depend on an international force which we don't command to defend this great rich nation from a lot of hungry nations—that's going to be the hardest job we've ever attempted. We'll begin by showing Congressmen that either we give the bomb to the UN or we must risk being destroyed by it. Either we abolish our armed forces or we must sacrifice the freedom and welfare of our people in a perpetual arms race with the Soviet Union. We must be able to show Congressmen that atomic bombs can end human life in this world. That's the cold fact that you and I and the scientists must accept. So we must wipe Kyoto off the map with one bomb. And we must do that quickly!"

Castleton sensed that the President wanted to end the conversation when Roosevelt changed the subject to discuss lighter matters. "Frank, tomorrow afternoon we're having a barbecue on Pine Mountain for my friends and my staff and the reporters. I'd like you to come—you know, I'm really looking forward to it. The dogwood and wisteria and wild violets are blooming, and from up there we can look down on this whole greening coming-to-life valley. So why not stay over and go with me? We won't talk about bombs and war . . . just about sailing and canoeing and improving land and water and mountains and valleys and sea coasts. Can you stay?"

"I'd love to," said Castleton. "But I—no, I'm sorry. There are some good men at Oak Ridge and Hanford and Los Alamos who are anxious to hear what you have said this afternoon. They are anxious to believe that the bomb they are making will end international war."

"I've shared their anxiety," said the President. "That's why I've kept you flying between me and them, trying to reassure them. I too am responsible for making that bomb, so I'm as anxious as any scientist for the bomb to preserve peace."

The President held out his hand, and Castleton rose and took it. For fifteen years he had been rising from a chair and taking that hand. For fifteen years every hope he had held for America and for mankind had been invested in Franklin Roosevelt. For two years he had suffered from doubt; now he felt relieved. So Castleton, on leaving the President this time, wanted to say something in which he could take pride when remembering he had said it. He smiled, and with a lump in his throat he said, "Sir, I'll paraphrase what my grandfather once said to you. You're a great and good man. What Wilson dreamed, you will realize. I thank God that I have been privileged to serve you."

"He made you trust in him again," said Dr. Palkin.

"Yes," said Castleton. "When I drove away from his cottage that afternoon, I believed he'd do all he said he would."

"And do you believe now that had he lived we'd be on our way toward accomplishing what he said he would accomplish?"

"Yes, I believe that," said Castleton. "He certainly had the power to accomplish it. I believe he would have had the will."

278

A<small>T</small> 3:55 P.M. on Thursday, April 12, 1945, friends of Franklin Roosevelt's were gathering atop Pine Mountain for the barbecue. They had placed an arm chair at the President's favorite spot, under an oak tree surrounded by wisteria, where he could look out over the valley. Frank Castleton was then on an American Airlines DC-4 en route from Knoxville, Tennessee, to El Paso, Texas, where he would change for Albuquerque, New Mexico. At 3:55 P.M. the American Airlines plane was flying at eighteen thousand feet over the Mississippi River near Memphis.

At 4:10 P.M. a Georgia state trooper arrived at the barbecue site and told the reporters to hurry back to the President's cottage. At 4:30 P.M. the pilot of the American Airlines plane switched on the speaker in the passengers cabin. "This is the captain speaking," he said. "We have just been informed that . . . that the President of the United States is . . . is dead. He died at three fifty-five P.M., Eastern time, at his cottage in Warm Springs, Georgia." The speaker was abruptly turned off.

Frank Castleton slumped in his seat and put his hands to his face. "My God," he said, "where does that leave us now? With a new President who has never heard of the atomic bomb!"

H<small>ARRY</small> S Truman, as Vice-President of the United States from January 20 to April 12, 1945, was ignored by President Roosevelt. During most of this period Roosevelt was either at sea or at Yalta or at Warm Springs, and during the four weeks in March when he was in or near Washington, Truman was not invited to confer with him. Then Truman became President, thirteen days before the opening of the San Francisco conference to organize the UN, twenty-six days before the German surrender, eighty-five days before he left for his month at Potsdam, one hundred sixteen days before Hiroshima and one hundred twenty days before the Japanese surrender. Thus, during the four months when the United States of America was at the zenith of its power to act for mankind, it was hampered by having a President who was a hastily informed tragically ignorant man.

At 5 P.M. on the day before Roosevelt died, Frank Castleton had called Ed Stettinius, the Secretary of State, from a public telephone in La Grange,

Georgia. "Wonderful news, Ed! He's going to do everything we've hoped for!"

"Has he finally decided to act?"

"I'm convinced of it. He'll tell you about it this weekend."

"Thank God!"

"I'm driving home tonight. I'll tell the people there, and tomorrow afternoon I'll fly west and tell the others."

The next day, after hearing of Roosevelt's death, Castleton called Stettinius again. "I'm at the Dallas airport, Ed," he said.

"Get here as soon as you can," said Stettinius. "The problem now will be how to get enough time with Truman to educate him. He's caught in a whirlwind."

"You and Mr. Stimson must get us time," Castleton insisted.

Truman took the oath at 7:09 P.M., then met with members of Roosevelt's Cabinet and asked them to serve temporarily. After that meeting Stimson and Stettinius had five minutes alone with Truman, and began trying to tell him about the bomb. Stimson asked Truman to find time so that he could be properly informed.

Later that evening Truman asked Admiral Leahy to continue serving as the President's closest military adviser. "Admiral," he asked him then, "what do you know about this terrible secret bomb that Stimson and Stettinius have just mentioned to me?"

"Don't waste any time on it," said Leahy. "That thing's the biggest fool mistake we've ever made."

During his first day in office Truman, aware of how suddenly he had become President, acted on the Presidential succession. If he died under existing law, the Secretary of State would succeed him. That was Stettinius—a man who had never been elected to public office and who therefore should not be allowed to succeed to the Presidency, in Truman's opinion. He wanted Stettinius's resignation that day. But because the Secretary had handled all preparations for the San Francisco conference, Truman accepted his resignation as of the day the conference ended and appointed James F. Byrnes to become Secretary of State. He brought Byrnes into the White House immediately to sit with him in all important meetings.

"THAT meant," said Dr. Palkin, "that the President, who knew nothing about the bomb, had fired a Secretary of State who understood the bomb and replaced him with a politician who knew nothing about the bomb?"

"That's right," said Castleton. "Mr. Stimson said to me, 'Now *we* have a troika. Truman, with Byrnes on his right and Leahy on his left, will face Stalin at the peace conference. God help us!' After Roosevelt's burial service, Mr. Stimson was allowed time to tell Truman and Byrnes a little about how the bomb was being made, and how plane crews were being trained to drop the first bomb on either Kyoto or Hiroshima. 'All policy has been made by Roosevelt and Churchill,' Stimson said. 'The most recent written expression of policy is this *aide-mémoire* signed at Hyde Park in September, 1944.' Truman and Byrnes read this document and noted the rejection of any suggestion of international control and use of the bomb. Truman said, 'This leaves nothing for me to do. The decisions have been made. We'll wait and see.' Mr. Stimson then persuaded them to question me about policy decisions Roosevelt had talked about to me the day before he died."

"But you no longer had any official position, did you? You'd been on Roosevelt's Advisory Council, and he was dead. You'd been an assistant to Stettinius, and he was out. So what what was your situation?"

"Null and void," said Castleton wearily. "I was nothing but a mentally ill man who was still burdened with a Q-clearance in atomic energy. I had to wait until I could see Truman or Byrnes to learn what, if anything, was expected of me."

"How long was that?"

"God, an eternity! Twelve days in which I feared I was going insane. I withdrew completely. I had all my meals in my rooms at the Shoreham. I saw no one, returned no calls. I talked with Diane briefly every evening. She wanted to come to me but I said no—I was afraid they'd arrest me while she was with me. I spent much of each day wandering in Rock Creek Park, in the zoo or along the trails. I could hear my heart pounding and my pulse beating in my temples. I'd suddenly find tears streaming down my cheeks, and I'd experience sudden chills and fits of shaking. At night my breathing would become so shallow and rapid that I'd feel I was suffocating, and I'd hold both hands over my mouth to muffle my moans. Sleep was an impossibility. Of course, I couldn't go to a hospital without their permission. And I was afraid if I went they'd never let me out. I was terrified that they'd become afraid of me, of what I had been . . . what I knew."

"You didn't see anyone at all for twelve days?"

"Only Mr. Hull," said Castleton. "He had been in the Bethesda Hospital six months. I had learned that he was to receive the Nobel Peace Prize, so I had to pull myself together and go tell him how proud of him my father and I were, and what a privilege it had been to serve him. I loved that man. Knowing I'd have to fight to keep from revealing my own condition to him, I went to see him."

"Did talking with him make you feel better?"

"Jesus, it was a nightmare. It made me feel worse. He still didn't know about the bomb, so he was still talking about how Four Policemen could end arms races. He doubted that Byrnes and Truman could handle Stalin as adroitly as he and Roosevelt had handled him. As I sat there listening to him I remembered how I had once hoped that George Norris would die before he learned that the power from Norris Dam was helping make the atomic bomb. Now I hoped Cordell Hull would die before he learned that Roosevelt hadn't trusted him with the bomb secret . . . and that I hadn't told him."

"When did you finally see Byrnes and Truman?"

"On the morning of April twenty-fifth a Marine sergeant knocked on my door at the Shoreham and handed me a written order from Truman to be at the White House at three P.M."

"Did you feel able to go?"

"I had no choice," said Castleton. "I had to show them I was mentally stable. I had met them both several times before when I was working for Mr. Hull. They knew how I looked when I was normal. Now I had to face them and show them that I hadn't become a fanatic or a security risk."

AT the White House Castleton was ushered into the Cabinet room, where he sat alone for several minutes. He was wearing a blue suit, and he had on his college ring, and on his watch chain was his Phi Beta Kappa key. He appeared calm, his eyes were clear, his breathing was regular. Byrnes came in, and they shook hands and talked about the bedbugs and overcrowded bathrooms at Yalta. When Truman came in—brisk, dapper, wearing his bow tie—Castleton noted how strange it seemed that the President of the United States could walk. Truman smiled, shook hands with Castleton, then waved him to one side of the long table while he and Byrnes sat on the other side.

"Frank," said the President, "Mr. Stimson has told me how you served President Roosevelt in the matter of the bomb. So we need your help. We want you to tell us, as briefly as you can, what the President said to you about bomb policy on the afternoon before his death."

Castleton began speaking slowly and calmly. "Throughout the war the

President never once took an uncompromising position with Stalin, not even at Yalta. This was because he didn't want to risk a separate peace between Stalin and Hitler, and he couldn't be sure that we wouldn't need the Red Army to help us defeat Japan. But on April eleventh the President believed that by July first, when he assumed the peace conference would begin, he could safely take one uncompromising position with Stalin. The Germans would have surrendered. The United States would be far stronger militarily than Russia. The Red Army was strong but the nation behind it was exhausted, while behind our armed forces was a nation untouched by war and at the zenith of its power. Moreover the President felt certain that by July first Japan would lie blockaded under our bombs, and there would be no reason for the United States to seek the assistance of the Red Army in compelling Japan to surrender."

"What uncompromising position did the President say he'd take with Stalin?" asked Truman.

"He would insist that no nation be allowed to own nuclear weapons," said Castleton. "That all nuclear weapons and means to deliver them be monopolized by a world authority, based in Alaska and Greenland, powerful enough to compel all nations to disarm, and to compel the opening of all nations to international inspection."

"Did he expect Stalin to agree to that?" asked Byrnes.

"He didn't propose to give him any choice," said Castleton. "He expected to keep our armed forces in Europe—every man, every tank, every plane, he said to me—and confront Stalin with superior power, including nuclear power, gentlemen, until step by step the world authority was created and armed. Then the United States and Russia, bilaterally, would withdraw, demobilize and disarm."

"Had the President decided not to drop the atomic bomb on Japan?" asked Truman.

"On the contrary," said Castleton. "He knew that the Congress and people of the United States would be resisting delivery of our nuclear weapons to a supra-national agency. So to help him persuade Congress and our people to take the risks of limited world government, he was determined to use the first bomb to demolish the entire city of Kyoto—off the map."

"My Lord, what a thing to have to tell them," said Dr. Palkin. "How did they react?"

"Like they were dealing with a fanatic," said Castleton. "Since neither of them had the vision or the will to do what I had said Roosevelt intended to do, they had to prove that both Roosevelt and I were mental incompetents."

"And while they were proving it," said the doctor, "you had to try not to reveal any symptoms which would justify their arresting you?"

Since he was a lawyer and Truman was not, Byrnes conducted the cross-examination to expose the mental incompetency. "Frank, you don't really believe that Roosevelt intended to do any of that, do you? Except to drop the bomb on Kyoto?"

"He most certainly did. All of it," said Castleton. "He understood that a nuclear-arms race between the United States and Russia had to be prevented at all cost."

"Do you know the cause of the President's death?"

"I've seen the autopsy report."

"Then you concede that the medical evidence is that Roosevelt could not possibly have been thinking clearly on April 11, 1945? That the arteries supplying blood to his brain were so indurated that he was incapable of clear thought? That he was fantasizing in whatever he may have said to you on that date?"

"In my opinion the President was thinking very clearly on April 11."

Byrnes then opened a volume on the desk in front of him, into which several markers had been inserted. "You were aware, were you not, of the expert internal security service which protected and still protects the Manhattan Project?"

"Yes, sir."

"You knew it used and still uses the most sophisticated devices for overhearing and recording conversations?"

"Yes, sir."

Byrnes turned the pages and flipped to one of the markers. "On the evening of October 20, 1942, when the President assigned you to the Manhattan Project and gave you your Q-clearance, isn't it true that he warned you that you were regarded as a poor security risk by the intelligence community?"

"Yes, sir."

"Isn't it true that you were apprehended that very evening running and weeping along Connecticut Avenue in the vicinity of the Shoreham Hotel?"

"I wasn't apprehended," said Castleton. "I was only halted and questioned."

"But you *were* running and weeping?"

"My eyes were watering, and I was wiping them with a handkerchief."

"Indicating what? Bizarre behavior? Emotional disturbance?"

"Indicating that I felt sad," said Castleton. "The President had just told me how the bomb would affect my home and TVA."

"Oh, yes, the TVA," said Byrnes. "You will recall that I was a staunch supporter of TVA?"

"Yes, sir, you were. I've always highly regarded you for it."

"And I've so regarded you, Frank," said Byrnes. "You know there's nothing personal in our differences here." He picked up the *aide-mémoire*. "You are aware that last summer, after your trip to London with Professor Bohr, the President and Churchill found it necessary to order very strict surveillance of Bohr?"

"Yes, sir, I know that. Let it also be noted that Professor Bohr's views were supported by Drs. Conant and Bush, by Sir John Anderson and by Mackenzie King and Lord Halifax. Except for the secrecy, Professor Bohr would have been supported by most of the people of the world."

"Be that as it may," said Byrnes, "you are also aware that because you were and still are a supporter of Bohr's, the same very strict surveillance was ordered for you?"

"Yes, sir."

Byrnes turned to another marker in the volume. "Is it true that on the battle cruiser *Quincy* about two months ago, you asked the President to relieve you of your duty of reporting to him on the bomb?"

"Yes, sir."

"And when he denied your request you revealed a personal problem to him? You said you suffered from feelings that you were drifting hopelessly in space, that you were spinning and whirling and that you often became so terrified that you had to fight to breathe and swallow? Did you tell the President that?"

"Yes, sir."

"Was it the truth?"

"Yes, sir."

"And he denied you permission to seek psychiatric treatment?"

"Yes, sir."

"I'll come back to this," said Byrnes. "You, President Truman, and I —we all knew and served President Roosevelt for many years. Don't you agree that invariably President Roosevelt tried to appear to be saying that

285

he agreed with almost every visitor he had? He tried to send everyone away feeling that he agreed with him? Isn't that a fair judgment of Roosevelt?"

"Yes, sir," said Castleton.

"Then isn't it fair to assume that on the afternoon of April eleventh, sitting down there on his porch in Warm Springs, relaxing with a man who had carried water for him for fifteen years, the President indulged in his lifelong practice of telling you what he knew you wanted to hear?"

"In my opinion, Senator," said Castleton, attempting to keep his voice calm and steady, "he didn't do that with me on that occasion. On April eleventh this war was nearing an end, so it was too late for him to do that. The showdown between him and Stalin was at hand. In my best judgment, he told me the truth about what he intended to do."

"Then, reluctantly, I must examine this matter of your best judgment," said Byrnes. "Where have you been for the past ten days?"

"Most of the time I have been in my hotel room. The rest of the time I have been in Rock Creek Park."

"Is it fair to say that you have been mentally ill?"

"I've been despondent, because I know how the scientists who are creating the bomb are feeling." Castleton fixed his gaze on Truman. "Mr. President, you say you are a Wilsonian, so you should understand that the men of genius who came to America to help us make this bomb came here because of Wilson. The man who brought us the uranium ore did so because of Wilson. They all came here to give us first use of the bomb because Wilson had led them to believe that America would use it wisely. The scientists believed that Roosevelt, at the showdown, would continue toward the goal of ending war among nations."

"And they don't believe I'll use the bomb for that purpose?" asked Truman.

"No, sir," said Castleton. "They believe you'll go to the peace conference, not to make a demand on Stalin, but to implore him to make war on Japan. They don't believe you'll even mention the bomb to him. And the day after V-E Day they believe you'll start bringing the troops home, or transferring them from Europe to the Pacific to fight Japan."

"Is that what you believe President Truman will do?" asked Byrnes.

"Yes, sir."

"And you are unalterably opposed to that course of action?"

"Yes, sir, I am. President Roosevelt was unalterably opposed to it."

When Byrnes delayed his next question and Truman said nothing, Castleton continued. "I'm not out of my mind, Senator. I'm only sick at heart. I haven't violated security, and my record shows that I am not a poor security risk. If you have no more questions for me, I'll ask you and the President to relieve me of whatever duties I may now have, to cancel my Q-clearance and allow me to go home."

"BUT that they wouldn't do," said Dr. Palkin.

"Of course they wouldn't," said Castleton. "They had a recording of what Roosevelt said to me on April eleventh, so they knew I'd told them the truth. They were afraid of me. They hastily assured me that we were all friends—that I was still a valued member of the President's Advisory Council, that my Q-clearance would be renewed, that I'd continue to serve them just as I had served Roosevelt and Hull and Stettinius, that I could go home but I must be on call. Truman said when the bomb was tested in July he'd expect a prompt report from me."

"That was some spot to be in—they could jail you or shoot you secretly."

"Yes. And the security men based at Oak Ridge could watch every move I made and record every word I spoke."

"Then you witnessed the test at Alamogordo?"

"Yes," said Castleton. "You've read all about the test . . . how Nobel Prize–winners waited before dawn in concrete bunkers in red desert sand to witness the birth of the atomic age. The blinding white light, the earth-shaking release of energy, the awesome rise of the mushroom cloud. And you've read about how, after witnessing the miracle, we all jumped for joy—we yelled and wept and hugged each other. Now, Doctor, you want to know, why were we so goddamn happy? Were we jumping for joy because we could now incinerate a hundred thousand Japanese fishermen with their wives and children and old folks? Were we hugging each other because we had proved that Admiral Leahy was no expert on explosives? No—my God, we were joyful because we felt that this magnificent human achievement had made every human being on earth a little taller, a little more worthy of concern and respect, a little more significant. We felt that somehow this achievement must lift the burden of armament from the shoulders of mankind."

Castleton sniffed, and his jaw trembled slightly, but he shed no tears. He continued. "The scientists worked furiously, assembling results of the test, believing that they would influence the conferees at Potsdam. I flew the report to Washington, and Mr. Stimson, in spite of his seventy-eight years, joined me in flying the report on to Berlin to Truman, Byrnes and

Leahy. We hoped Truman would be moved by the report—that he'd
convene an emergency meeting with Stalin and show him that the world
had changed, that the war with Japan could be considered ended and that
the compelling business of the Potsdam Conference was now to consider
how to prevent an atomic-arms race between the United States and the
Soviet Union."

"But Truman wasn't impressed?"

Castleton's jaw hardened, and he replied angrily. "The unbelievable
truth, Doctor, is that the report of the bomb test didn't move anybody at
Potsdam! It changed nothing! It wasn't even important enough to be put
on the agenda! By his own account Truman on July twenty-fourth 'casually
mentioned to Stalin that we had a new weapon of unusual destructive force.
Stalin showed no special interest . . . I never forgot for a moment that the
most urgent reason for my going to Potsdam was to get from Stalin a
personal reaffirmation of Russia's entry into the war against Japan. This I
was able to get, so the conference was a success.' "

"How degrading!" exclaimed Dr. Palkin.

"By 'casually mentioning' the bomb to Stalin," said Castleton, "Truman degraded the Presidency, the United States and Bohr and Fermi and
Neumann and Oppenheimer and all the others whose genius had gone into
producing the bomb. He degraded all of us who had witnessed Alamogordo."

"Imagine the contempt Stalin must have felt for Truman!"

"Yes," said Castleton. "At the moment when Stalin was 'showing no
special interest' to Truman—Jesus, every time I say these words my hair
stands on end—well, even then, war-exhausted Russian people were slaving
under the whip of Beria to make atomic bombs. Stalin knew Truman
commanded the power to halt this effort, to compel international control
of the bomb and to compel the Soviet Union to submit to inspection. Stalin
respected such power, and when he saw that Truman lacked the vision to
use it, he dismissed him with a contemptuous shrug!"

"Poor Stimson!" said Dr. Palkin. "That must have been a long bitter
plane ride back from Potsdam for you and him! He had flown five thousand
miles with information which merited only casual mention!"

"I talked with him several times on the flight," said Castleton. "I think
it's important for me to tell you about it."

DURING the long hop from the Azores
to Gander, Mr. Stimson lay in the bunk reserved for high-ranking passen-

gers and slept off and on. Castleton stood for a while, looking down at him, and they talked.

"Chief," said Castleton, calling him by the title that many of his close friends used, "don't you think the President may decide now not to drop the bomb? He knows the Japanese are trying to surrender."

"He's going to drop it," said Stimson. "I have his order with me."

"But why?" asked Castleton. "Roosevelt had what he felt was a high purpose for dropping it. Since Truman isn't dropping the bomb in the hope of ending all war, why does he want to do it?"

Stimson replied, "For his own high purpose—getting the Presidency off the hook for spending four billion dollars in un-Constitutional secrecy."

"The target is Kyoto?"

"Not on your life," said Stimson. "The President has left selection of the target to me. I've been to Kyoto and know it well. It's beautiful and inspiring. If I do nothing else that I'll want to remember in this war, I'll remember that I saved Kyoto. The target will be Hiroshima. It's a city without distinction."

"I'm glad you had to make that choice and not me," said Castleton. "If I had been ordered to choose between incinerating poets, priests and philosophers or carpenters, cobblers and fishermen, well, I don't know . . ."

"From Washington you flew on to Tinian?" asked the doctor.

"Yes," said Castleton. "On the exhausting forty-eight-hour flight from Washington to Guam, I spent most of the time on the floor of the DC-4 transport, wrapped in a blanket, trying to sleep. On the afternoon of August fourth I flew from Tinian up to Iwo Jima with several officers, and we were there about four hours. I walked through the cemetery and noted that half of the four thousand Marine dead were born in 1927—the year my daughter was born—so they had died before they reached their eighteenth birthdays. Later I joined the ten thousand men who were sitting in that red volcanic dust at the foot of Mount Suribachi listening to a woman sing. She was Helen Traubel, and she sang without accompaniment, her back to the dead—the cemetery—and her face to the living. I'll never forget how she affected those men as she sang 'Shenandoah,' 'Deep River' and 'The World Is Waiting for the Sunrise.' "

"Is that why you played those same numbers on the cello yesterday evening?"

289

"Yes. I hoped I could move the men listening to me just as she did on Iwo Jima.

"On Tinian," continued Castleton, "among the handful of officers who knew about the bomb, there were two expressed views. The B-29 crewmen who had been trained to drop the bomb were proud of their role. They said they had been chosen 'to end the war and save all those lives we'd lose if we had to invade Japan.' The only ones who knew that the Japanese government had already asked Stalin to act in its behalf in arranging surrender to the United States were one general and an admiral. The general told me we were dropping the bomb 'to show Stalin who's boss.' The admiral said we were dropping it 'to help us keep the Russkies in their place.' "

"Tell me about August the sixth," said the doctor.

"Well," said Castleton, "the B-29 flying time from Tinian to Hiroshima was about six hours. The bomb was to fall at eight A.M., so it was past midnight when the *Enola Gay* took off. As I watched it roar down that long runway I prayed: for the victims, for the men in the plane, for all mankind. Three hours later, when the *Enola Gay* was over Iwo Jima, I was in a B-29 which took off from Tinian and flew to Hiroshima three hours behind the bomb. We heard all the radio reports to and from the *Enola Gay*. What to me was unforgivable about this bombing mission was that we knew it would be unopposed. We could have sent three hundred fighter planes from Iwo Jima and from carriers to protect the *Enola Gay* as it found and attacked its target. We didn't send one protective fighter. Normally a B-29 carried eight guns in four power turrets for protection, but all the turrets and guns had been removed from the *Enola Gay*. To deliver a bomb which had cost the people of the United States four billion dollars, we were sending one unescorted unarmed bomber!"

"But you say we were taking no risk?"

"No risk at all," said Castleton. "We knew the Japanese no longer had any means to attack a plane flying at thirty thousand feet. Oh, they had a few fighter planes left, but they didn't have enough fuel to send them up to thirty thousand feet. Their antiaircraft guns were so worn that they were ineffective above ten thousand feet. They just didn't have the steel to replace them. The *Enola Gay*, carrying the equivalent of twenty thousand tons of TNT, could fly over the Japanese islands on a clear August morning in bright sunshine, deliberately find its target, make a level straight-line run to the bombing point and release its terror on utterly defenseless people. So the mission of the *Enola Gay* was not an act of war, let alone an act of hope, Doctor. It was only an atrocity."

Castleton paused, then said, "When I got off the plane at Tinian I saw men clustered around a radio. They were listening to Truman tell the world that we'd dropped the bomb on Hiroshima to compel the Japanese to surrender, and that we'd keep our secrets and thereby monopolize the bomb 'pending further examination of possible methods of protecting us and the rest of the world from the danger of sudden destruction.' "

"Why did you go back to Hiroshima with the Evaluation Team in October, 1945?" asked the doctor.

"I went to try to tell the mutilated ones how it all went wrong," said Castleton sadly. "How the bomb was made by men of genius who hoped it would end war among nations, and how hope was defeated by politicians with no vision. I was stopped from saying this and forced to leave Japan ahead of the other members of the Evaluation Team. During the last months of '45 and all of '46 I talked with a few Senators and Congressmen whom I've known for years, but I was watched and repeatedly warned. As soon as the war ended, Truman became even more afraid of me, so since then I've been watched, opposed and slandered. Congressmen have been told that I'm a fanatic. Last year I began to give up, and I lost more and more self-respect as I began seeing myself as just another demented voice crying in the wilderness—another lean-faced luminous-eyed Jeremiah standing on a mountaintop crying, 'Madness! Madness!' "

Dr. Palkin got up. "That's enough for today, Frank," he said. "These are hard facts to hear as well as repeat, you know. Now you get your lunch and rest. Tomorrow we'll talk some more, and I'll have some suggestions for you."

"Thank you, Doctor," said Castleton. Palkin watched him leave the room, and sat quietly in his office for a long while afterward.

"Mrs. Castleton, after examining a hundred of your husband's paintings and drawings, I can tell you that they are valuable. Many people will want to purchase them." The art dealer from New York was named Roberto Palmieri, a frail white-haired Italian-American wearing thick spectacles who talked rapidly and gestured with his entire body.

"Are the paintings and drawings valuable because they are good?" asked Diane. "Or because of the amount and nature of the publicity my husband has received?"

Mr. Palmieri raised his brows and spread his hands. "I never discount the value of publicity. Art is also a business. Without the publicity, how could I have learned of the existence of Thomas Francis Castleton? But if I had examined this work without knowing who the artist was, I still would have responded to its/lyrical appreciation of nature. There is both vigor and poetry. Your husband has talent for perceiving, for framing, for using color and light."

"But you do feel there are flaws in his work?"

"Well," said Mr. Palmieri, "his most obvious shortcoming is a common one. He can perceive more than he can express on canvas. There is evidence of offhandedness, of too-easy execution. Some of the sensuality borders on sentimentality."

The *Time* magazine man added, "He has more talent for conception than he has patience for execution. But everything he does is exciting . . . and salable."

"I can wish," said Mr. Palmieri, "that this artist had been subjected to expert criticism from childhood . . . that he had had to paint for a living and therefore been subjected to the disciplines of the marketplace. He would have worked harder and been more accomplished than he is now. But I view his experience in a mental hospital as a possible blessing in disguise. He may now be ready to strive for excellence in art as he has never striven before."

"He may need to strive for excellence in art," said the *Time* man, "in order to find reason for being."

"Well, what's the next step?" asked Diane. "Do you want to show his work in New York?"

"I'll do more than that," said Mr. Palmieri. "I'll not only arrange shows, but I'm also prepared to advance fifty thousand dollars against sales, less my commissions."

"That sounds all right," said Diane. "I'm flying back to Washington this evening. I'll tell my husband how you feel, and I'll telephone you next week."

"Please convey my compliments and best wishes to him," said Mr. Palmieri. "Tell him that if he is now ready to concentrate and work hard on his paintings, I have no doubt that he can make a satisfying place for himself in the art world. He can also earn a substantial living."

W<small>HEN</small> Castleton entered Dr. Palkin's office that Thursday morning, both the doctor and Mary Sullivan were waiting for him. "How are you feeling?" asked the doctor.

"Ready to complete the story and discuss getting out of here," said Castleton firmly.

"Fine," said the doctor. "Today we'll change the routine. Since the weather is good, let's all three of us walk around the grounds and talk."

The doctor put on a light coat, and they went out the back of the building. Mary moved to Castleton's left so both she and the doctor could hear him better.

"The one question remaining, Frank," said the doctor, "is why did you crack up *now?* If you didn't crack in 1945, why in 1948?"

"Well, I think you'll agree I'm a pretty strong person—I mean, emotionally I've always been more or less on top of things. But each year since 1945," said Castleton, "I've felt a little more guilty and ashamed. Passage of the National Security Act of 1947 was a crushing blow to me. The CIA can spend a billion dollars a year bribing, torturing and murdering this government's opponents—that's some free hand for any agency. The act was copied by Admiral Potter from Roman and British laws which protected empires. And now that Truman faces possible political defeat, he's harassing me intolerably. And believe me, this is not paranoia . . . this is fact."

"How does he harass you?"

"By assigning more security agents to watch me and threaten me."

"He's afraid you'll give his opponents information damaging to him?"

"Certainly," Castleton replied. "He's running on the claim that he has stood up to the Russians in Greece and Turkey . . . the Truman Doctrine. So when a prominent Democrat like Adlai Stevenson says, 'The year 1945 seems to have been an extraordinary moment in history. It seems to have been a time when we should have gambled and established some sort of world agency powerful enough to restrict the kind of arms nations may maintain' . . . well, naturally a statement like that causes Truman to send more agents to search for evidence that I have violated security and Executive Privilege. He wants to prove I told Stevenson what Roosevelt told me on April 11, 1945."

"Did you tell him?"

For the first time Castleton ignored one of the doctor's questions. As if he had not been asked, he went on, "And when Douglas MacArthur writes, 'The only safe course now lies in construction of a new world order in which armies can be reduced to the minimum required for internal order and international police,' Truman assumes I've been unlawfully in touch with MacArthur also, you see."

"Well, have you?"

"Let me finish answering your first question, Doctor," said Castleton. "About why I cracked now instead of three years ago. After Potsdam and Hiroshima—after the scientists saw that Truman was not going to use the bomb to end war—many of them quit the Manhattan Project feeling betrayed. Some of the security agents who had protected the Manhattan Project left in disgust. And a month ago a Top Secret piece of information disappeared—the wire recording of Roosevelt's conversation with me on April 11, 1945. That recording is still missing, and I'm suspected of having it."

"Do you have it?"

"Again," said Castleton firmly, "let me finish what I was saying. Bear with me, all right—I've got to talk this out. Truman is also running for election on the claim that the Russians won't have atomic weapons for twenty years. But that's absurd, because the Russians will test their first bomb within months, perhaps before election day, and, damn it, Truman knows this. The most secret operation we are now conducting is called 'air sampling.' We know where the Russians are likely to test their bomb, we know the direction of the air currents, so every day the CIA is sending planes to collect air samples at various altitudes from secret air bases in Turkey. So these samples are going to tell us, to the day, when the first Russian bomb is tested."

"You're saying," said the doctor, "that if you should reveal that we are now sampling air on the Russian border because we know they're about to test their first bomb, the President would be in a much more difficult political position?"

"I'm saying," said Castleton, "that whenever the Russian bomb explodes and ends the period during which we monopolized the bomb, the American people are going to understand what Stevenson and MacArthur are telling them. That 1945 was indeed an extraordinary moment in human history—the United States was stronger vis-à-vis the Soviet Union than we will ever be again and could have established 'some sort of world agency powerful enough to restrict the kind of arms nations may maintain.' We could have constructed 'a new world order in which armies could be reduced to the minimum' and achieved our national purpose, keeping faith with Lincoln, Wilson, Hull and Roosevelt. And the American people are going to understand that this precious opportunity was lost by a deaf and blind man named Truman. He was told and he wouldn't listen; he was shown and he couldn't see."

After that emotional release, the three walked in silence for a while. Then the doctor turned toward a bench and indicated that they all sit. Castleton remained in the middle, and the doctor decided it was a good moment to go back to the painful subject his patient had been avoiding.

"Frank, let's complete your answer to my first question. Why did you become demoralized to the point of hysteria during the night of Monday, April 26, 1948?"

Castleton sighed, then began. "I had endured almost six years of being watched. Jesus, you can't know how it feels—being watched, suspected, distrusted, having your mail intercepted, your conversations recorded! That's got to have a cumulative effect on a man who believes he inherited freedom. During the third year after Hiroshima I was being watched more relentlessly than ever—oh, not out of fear that I'd reveal bomb secrets, since Truman knew the Russians knew the secrets, and not because I had knowledge that if made public would embarrass the President—many other men had such knowledge—but because I was the one man who had such knowledge who was so upset about it and who was therefore distrusted by the President and his supporters."

"You were still aware that you were mentally disturbed?"

"My Lord, I hadn't been unaware of it since Yalta," said Castleton. "And since I wasn't allowed to seek the help of a white psychiatrist, I sought help from Indians."

"You mean Indian medicine men?"

"No, no, my friends—two ordinary Cherokee Indian farmers," said Castleton. "Long John Cotton and Billy Birdsong. You see, a white psychiatrist tries to help you by talking with you; Indians try to help you by being silent with you. By hiking with you along a trail, by dancing, chanting or running with you, or sleeping near you around a campfire. Making you feel they trust you and value you as their brother."

"And that's what you were doing up in the mountains when the breakdown occurred. The Indians were trying to help you?"

"Yes," said Castleton, "but we realized some men were following us. So that evening after Long John and Billy were in their sleeping bags, I went back and confronted the white men."

"Were they unfriendly?"

"Oh, no," said Castleton. "I know them both. They've eaten meals at my home—Dave Parker and Chris Townsend are good men. Both are graduates of the University of Georgia law school. Dave went with me on my first trip to Hyde Park with bomb information, as a matter of fact. Chris went with me to Hobcaw Barony. To keep from startling them, as I approached their campfire I called out, 'A friend is approaching.' "

Dᴀᴠᴇ Parker looked up and said, "Welcome, friend." Chris Townsend patted a spot on the blanket next to him. "Come and have some coffee and whiskey with us." Castleton accepted the empty tin cup and half-empty whiskey bottle and sat down. Parker poured coffee into the cup from a pot, and Castleton added the whiskey.

"Hope we're not bothering you too much, Frank," said Parker.

"Just following orders," said Townsend.

"I know," said Castleton wearily. "Just give me a break, will you? When will it stop?"

"You know when," said Parker. "You stop giving aid and comfort to Truman's enemies—then all your problems are over, friend."

"But I don't know any enemies of Truman," said Castleton. "Only a few of his opponents. There's a difference, isn't there?"

"Not in your case," said Townsend. "You're an adviser to Presidents. Now, when you talk to somebody who wants to Dump Truman, you can talk about the bomb and what Roosevelt might'a done with it that Truman didn't. Powerful material. That's dangerous talk."

"That's why we have to trail you," said Parker, "and report on everybody you communicate with."

"You keep making reckless statements, Frank," said Townsend. "Like 'If only Roosevelt had lived.' Now, coming from you, that's improper talk, to say the least. To folks in Washington, that sounds like treason."

Castleton sipped his coffee and looked at the two men. They all look alike, he thought. They all travel in pairs, and they all look alike. Whether FBI men, or CIA men, or special security men assigned to safeguard the bomb. They all look neat and clean and trustworthy, and they are all good honest educated well-meaning God-fearing red-blooded Americans.

"Why don't you quit worrying 'em, Frank?" asked Parker. "Just make your peace and enjoy living. Hell, you got everything in the world a man could want!"

"Not quite everything." Castleton sipped his coffee thoughtfully.

"Well, you got everything you ought'a want. Just put it all out'a your mind and your troubles are at an end. Think about it, friend."

"Quit worrying them, and they'll quit worrying you."

They all sipped their coffee for a while, and looked up at the rising moon. Then Parker said, "You're gonna have to give us that wire recording, Frank."

"I haven't got it."

"Maybe you haven't, but they think you have. They think you're the only man who'd want it—"

"Certainly," Townsend interrupted, "they think you're the only man who'd want it bad enough to pay twenty-five thousand dollars for it."

"And you might be hiding it up here in the mountains somewhere. Or maybe letting one of your Indian boys hide it."

"Ridiculous."

"They don't think it's ridiculous," said Townsend. "They think you're a fanatic, so there's no telling what you might do."

"You're gonna have to give us that thing, Frank," said Parker. "If you don't have it, you'll have to help us find it. We'll just have to keep after you till you do. It's too bad, but there you are. Just doing our job, you understand."

Castleton got up and set the cup on a rock. "Thanks for your hospitality."

"Remember," said Townsend, "we have the authority to search you and your gear any time. And we have the authority to search those Indians too."

"You'd better not try that," said Castleton.

"You threatening us?"

"Only advising you."

"WELL, Doctor," said Castleton, "as I walked away from them, up the trail, under trees, through patches of moonlight, I felt like the last straw had been added to a burden which was about to crush the last breath out of me. It all hit me at once. I remember fighting for breath. I trembled and was suddenly soaked with icy sweat. Blood beat like a hammer inside my head, and I screamed to let it out— to escape from that godawful pain in me. Several times I think I fell down, and once I must have lost consciousness. When I finally stumbled back to Long John and Billy, they built up the fire, wrapped me in a sleeping bag and rubbed and pounded my body. I was suffocating. Somehow they got me to the pickup truck and then home, where the doctor quieted me with morphine."

"That was a hard night. But it's something you'll never have to experience again. All right, Frank. I guess that completes your story down to the present. Now, come on, will you answer the questions you evaded? Did you contact Stevenson and MacArthur, and do you have knowledge of how the recording disappeared and of where it is now? I'm your doctor—this information is confidential. Please trust me."

"Before I answer," said Castleton, "you tell me a couple of things. Why did you choose today to walk and sit out here? Were you trying to make sure that what I've told you wasn't overheard? And why did you choose today to have Mary with us? Are the two of you expecting to support each other in reporting what the suspect said?"

"Listen, Frank," said Dr. Palkin. "You know that neither Mary nor I wanted this assignment. What you have revealed to us will now disturb us . . . not to the extent that it has disturbed you, of course, that goes without saying, but I won't lie to you—our lives could have been more pleasant if we could have avoided hearing it. You've put monkeys on our backs, and we've got to try to be loyal to you and also survive in the United States Navy. I don't think any of our conversations . . . I certainly hope they haven't been recorded, but I wanted to make damn sure that today's wasn't recorded. And yes, Mary and I will confer as to what we answer when we're interrogated."

"Those are honest answers," said Castleton, "so I'll respond in kind. No, I've never communicated with either Adlai Stevenson or Douglas MacArthur. They reached their conclusions without advice from me. And why shouldn't they have? I don't see how any intelligent American, if he'll stop to reflect on it, can fail to see that 1945 was the extraordinary moment when the United States could have done something constructive about working toward peace. And I have no knowledge of how the recording of my conversation with Roosevelt disappeared or where it is now."

"I believe you," said the doctor.

"So do I," said Mary.

"Well, that's just fine, but how sad—my telling the truth and your believing it will not change what they believe," said Castleton. "They believe I bought the recording, and that my Indian friends have hidden it in the Smoky Mountains. That's their truth, and *their* truth is *the* truth."

"Maybe their truth won't always be the truth," said the doctor. "Now, you rest and have your lunch. Enjoy your afternoon and evening. Tomorrow we'll talk about shock treatment, and about your going home."

THAT afternoon Admiral Potter again came to the hospital and conferred with Captain Palkin. "You have completed interrogating Castleton?" he asked.

"Yes, sir," said the captain. "He told us all he knows."

"Did you learn anything I should know that I don't know?"

"I doubt it, sir. He denies any knowledge of the missing wire recording."

"He's lying. He's a fanatic, Palkin, so he thinks he has the right to lie in support of a cause. Under hypnosis you can get the truth from him."

"There was a great deal of other interesting material, sir—he revealed much that surprised me and Lieutenant Sullivan."

"For instance?"

"Air sampling, and that the Russians will soon have the bomb."

"The sooner they test it, the better for us," said the admiral. "We can then get adequate appropriations for national defense. With ample funds, we can stay ahead of them."

"Then," asked Captain Palkin, "the publicity about Castleton being dangerous because of secrets he might reveal to the Russians . . . ?"

"Useful. It creates and sustains a public demand that we keep Castleton locked up."

Captain Palkin breathed deeply, exhaled slowly and decided to ask no more questions. He'd confine himself to answering the admiral.

"What else surprised you, Captain?" asked Potter.

"Well, sir, we were surprised that despite the strict secrecy Professor Bohr's views gained so much support while we were making the bomb. Lord Halifax, Mackenzie King, Sir John Anderson, Drs. Bush and Conant, Justice Frankfurter."

"That shows you how dangerous a fanatic Bohr was," said Admiral Potter. "Why Roosevelt and Churchill had to issue special orders against him. Bohr infected Castleton."

"I'm afraid, sir," said the captain, "that Castleton was infected long before he met Bohr. My interrogation revealed that Castleton was infected by men such as Tom Paine, Lincoln, Wilson, Hull and Franklin Roosevelt."

"Yes, the campaign oratory," said the admiral. "I know all that—the rhetoric about freeing mankind. It has always been a dangerous threat to this nation. That's why Castleton must be kept here indefinitely, and why you must help us retrieve that missing recording."

"Kept here indefinitely?"

"By all means. With Russians blockading Berlin, and with Democrats trying to Dump Truman, we can't risk Castleton being exploited by the likes of Bertrand Russell. And we can't risk him being questioned by the Joint Congressional Committee on Atomic Energy."

"But he's recovering rapidly!" said the doctor, who was shocked at his superior's appraisal of the situation and yet dared not show it. "He's coming to terms with his disappointments. He has regained sexual potency. He's ready to put politics out of his mind and work hard as a painter. He's expecting to leave here within a few days."

"Then it's up to you to prescribe treatments that will take weeks . . . months."

"But he'll insist on leaving! He's regaining self-confidence. He'll initiate legal action."

"As an incompetent he can do that only through his wife," said the admiral.

"Well, she'll certainly—"

"She'll initiate nothing," said the admiral. "She's taken up with Stumpy McDowell, and we have very clear photos of her visiting a motel and entering a room with him. After Paul Blanton shows her those photos, she won't risk having them shown to her son and daughter . . . let alone to her sick husband."

Captain Palkin was now breathing rapidly. "You'd resort to that?"

"Resort? Resort?" said the admiral. "That's a strange question coming from the author of the Palkin Doctrine for motivating our infantrymen against the Japanese. In defense of our nation, Captain, we resort to whatever we must. You never forget that—especially not if you are to become the first Jewish admiral in the United States Navy."

Admiral Potter stood up to leave. Mechanically Captain Palkin stood with him, but he said nothing.

"Captain Palkin," the admiral ordered, "you and Lieutenant Sullivan will now prepare Thomas Francis Castleton to be your guest until after the November election. He can put politics out of his mind and concentrate on his painting here instead of at his home."

The admiral turned to leave, and when Captain Palkin still remained silent, the admiral said, "I'm waiting to hear your reply to my order, Captain."

"Aye, aye, sir," replied the captain.

P$_{AUL}$ Blanton had spent the morning raising money for President Truman's campaign. It was hard work, since most everyone believed the President would lose in November to Governor Dewey. Only executives of the corporations which did much of their business with the government, or which could be hurt by an adverse ruling of some government agency, were contributing, and Blanton hadn't been able to get more than fifty thousand dollars from any of them. At 3 P.M. Admiral Potter, whose aide had called for an appointment, came in, shook hands and sat down.

"I just came from the hospital," said the admiral. "Captain Palkin has completed his interrogation."

"I don't recall asking you to go to the hospital today, Admiral," Blanton said sternly. "By what authority did you go?"

"Well, Mr. Secretary," said the admiral, "since you asked me last week to instruct Captain Palkin in the rules under which he and his nurse would be allowed to conduct the interrogation, I assumed you'd want me to make certain that the rules were followed."

"I'd like to point out to you," said Blanton, "that Captain Palkin and Lieutenant Sullivan have not been *interrogating* Castleton. He is neither a prisoner nor a criminal suspect. He is a respected aide of this government. Captain Palkin has been treating him with psychotherapy to restore him to health as quickly as possible. Do you understand?"

"Yes, sir."

"All right," said Blanton. "Just remember I'm a civilian Cabinet Member, and I'm the one ordered by the President to handle this case. Your only function is to assist me when and if I ask for your help. I'm going to the hospital tomorrow and talk with the doctor, and with Diane and Frank. The moment Frank's morale has improved to where he is reasonably stable, he'll walk out of that hospital. Is that clear?"

"Quite clear, sir," said the admiral.

"All right. Now tell me—I assume the doctor learned nothing from Frank that we don't already know about?"

"That's correct, sir. Castleton denies any knowledge of the theft of the missing recording."

"Well, you have no evidence that he was involved in any way?"

"No hard evidence," said the admiral. "But we feel that he must have knowledge of the present whereabouts of the recording."

"Feelings!" sneered Blanton. "From the moment Roosevelt gave Frank Castleton a Q-clearance, you intelligence people have *felt* he was a poor security risk. Yet in all those years, even while he was associating with Bohr, even though he's been bitterly disappointed, there hasn't been a shred of evidence that he ever violated security in any way."

"He has never been under any pressure to violate security," said the admiral. "But if he's released now, with all the publicity he has had and will continue to get, and this being an election year, the pressure against him will be more than an unstable man can be expected to resist. I don't have to remind you, sir, that the Joint Congressional Committee on Atomic Energy is now headed by a Republican—U.S. Senator Bourke Hickenlooper. Hickenlooper is preparing to move heaven and earth to bring Castleton before his committee."

"We can prevent that," said Blanton. "Frank is a confidential adviser to the President. The right of Executive Privilege will prevent him from appearing before any Congressional committee."

"Then what about Bertrand Russell? He's coming here to try to use Frank in his effort to compel the President to make war on Russia. The fact that Russell is a world-famous pacifist makes him dangerous when he advocates war."

"I'll see that Frank stays away from Russell, don't worry. I'm sorry to have to oppose you so bluntly on this, Admiral. But we're dealing with people I know much better than you do. I've spent a lot of time in Frank Castleton's home. I respect him. You heard Diane say she was allowing her husband to be brought to Washington only because she trusted me. Well, I'm not going to betray that trust. I'm going to bend over backward trying to help. The Castletons are fine people."

"I understand how you feel, Mr. Secretary. I'm sorry I moved out of turn. I have just one more thing to say, then I'll leave this matter entirely to you. When you talk with Mrs. Castleton tomorrow, you may find that she is in no hurry to take her husband out of the hospital."

"Why do you say that?"

"She's decided to divorce Castleton and marry another man."

This surprised Blanton, though he remembered that he himself had told Diane that it was widely assumed she would soon be looking for another husband. "Who is it?"

Admiral Potter opened his briefcase and pushed three enlarged photos across Blanton's desk. The first was a long shot of a motel with a Cadillac Coupe de Ville standing at the office entrance. The second photo was a closer shot of the car parked at the door of a motel room with Diane and Stumpy getting out. The third photo, made with a long lens, was a close shot of Diane and Stumpy entering the room.

Blanton studied the photos, then grunted in disgust. "That son of a bitch, huh!"

"Apparently they're supposed to spend tomorrow night at Stumpy's cottage on Chesapeake Bay," said the admiral. "The caretaker told us Stumpy'll be there, and our assumption is that she'll be with him. She has a reservation on the flight to Washington which leaves Knoxville a few minutes from now. Stumpy'll probably meet her at National Airport."

Blanton couldn't take his eyes off Diane's face in the third photo. It was a profile shot—her best angle—and she looked seductive and eager. Blanton remembered evenings in Tennessee, with Frank in New Mexico, when he himself had felt tempted to make a pass at Diane. He had never tried anything, believing she'd reject him. Now he wondered. With her husband locked up in a nut house, he thought, she's romping in a motel bed with that cynical grinning lying humper of other men's wives!

Admiral Potter left Blanton's office satisfied with his visit. He had taken a chewing out, but he had accomplished his mission. He had neutralized Castleton's only powerful friend. Blanton wouldn't be so concerned about betraying a trust. He might still go to the hospital and try to help Frank. But he wouldn't try hard. He wouldn't bend over backward.

CASTLETON and Mary were playing tennis when Sam, the attendant, came and delivered a message to Mary, ordering her to leave Castleton on the grounds with Sam and report to Dr. Palkin at once. When she reached the doctor's office, he led her to a small treatment room down the hall, and they went in and closed the door. Quickly he told her about Admiral Potter's visit. They looked at each other helplessly. "I saw this coming," said Palkin. "But I confess I didn't want to think about it—try to do anything. Now, how do we protect our patient, and how do we protect ourselves?"

"Oh, God." Mary sighed. "Frank thinks he's going to leave here this weekend."

"We've got to play for time, that's all," said the doctor. "We can't allow him to begin suspecting he's a prisoner, and we've got to convince him—so it's his choice—to stay here and take electroshock treatments. If you start guiding him toward that choice, tomorrow I'll clinch it with him."

Mary went back to the tennis court feeling like a hypocrite, a betrayer, but she calmly finished the set. Then they went to her apartment, showered, made love, slept in each other's arms for half an hour. Then they lay in bed and talked.

"You have become important to me, Mary."

"You're important to me too."

"After I leave here you're going to remain a significant part of my life, you know that?"

"Like your father and Miss Edna?"

"Much more than that."

"But you'll always be married to Diane?"

"Yes," he said. "I want to tell it to you straight, Mary. I don't believe in divorce, and she doesn't either. We're a family. Whatever its shortcomings, the family must endure. Especially now. When there's no God and no country to sustain a man, what else can sustain him but his family? Self-gratification can never be enough."

"For people like me, self-gratification has to be enough, doesn't it?"

"You have your work," he said. "You can be sustained by being able to restore men to duty. And you'll have me. From me you can get affection, respect, loyalty and money."

"Speaking of my work," she said, "there's a further step in your therapy. Dr. Palkin and I have thought it would be very helpful—so I hope you won't insist on leaving here until you've had several electroshock treatments."

"You want to send charges of electricity through my brain?"

"That's right. It's a therapy that's been used successfully for ten years. It helps nine out of every ten patients suffering from depression."

"Can it be harmful?"

"Never. Hey, what do you think I am, anyway? Would I want to hurt you, ever?" She touched his face gently and felt his closeness as well as his need for her supportiveness. She went on. "We put the patient to sleep with a general anesthetic and inject a relaxant to prevent any bones being broken during the convulsion. We attach electrodes to the temples and pass a weak charge of electricity through the brain. There's a momentary convulsion, after which the patient regains consciousness within a few minutes. Memory is the only function of the brain which is affected."

"There *is* loss of memory?" he asked.

"But that's only temporary," she said. "Then gradually the patient remembers everything he remembered before the shock."

"If the shock doesn't erase any memories," asked Castleton, "how does it do the patient any good?"

"Well, it's interesting—it seems to make disturbing memories a little less so. And it makes disappointments a little easier to live with. In your case, Frank, I believe there'd be another benefit. Shock usually makes the patient more amenable to counseling. Your principal problem, as we've discovered, is that your hopes for humanity have been too high. Between shock treatments you can talk with the Reverend Bramwell and Dr. Palkin about—well, to sound sort of grand about it—about human limitations. What men working together can actually accomplish and what they can only dream of. You'll begin to feel more tolerant and comfortable, I think. You've become more reasonable about lots of things—I think you might be about this."

"You think the treatments might insure that I'd never have to come back here again?"

"I believe they would," she said. "After shock treatments patients feel either euphoric or lethargic. Knowing you, I believe you'd feel euphoric. The euphoria wouldn't be permanent, of course. You'd experience periods of down, followed by more periods of up. But there would be enough good times to help you conclude that life under the volcano must be endured during depression in order to be enjoyed during euphoria."

They fixed scrambled eggs, listened to music, danced and talked and made love again. Around 8:30 they left Mary's apartment and walked back to the main building. They held hands as they walked, and Castleton looked down at her and felt how close she was to him and how much he had come to depend on her. In his room they went through their ritual. He undressed and put on his pajamas while she went for the needle. Then she sat on the side of the bed, gave him the needle, caressed and encouraged him.

"This is the most hopeless part of my situation here," he said, looking around him. "During the day, while I'm with the doctor and with you, I feel that I really can work and love and believe again. Then night comes, and I've got to have the needle to sleep in a padded cell behind a locked door which I can't unlock. This is it—this is what I must change, Mary. All right, I'll think about the shock treatments. Maybe I'll decide to take them. But I have to get out of here—be free. I must go home."

"You'll soon be free, and you'll soon be home," Mary said as she went out.

As she rode from the airport with Stumpy, Diane told him what the art dealer had said about Frank's paintings.

"That's my column for tomorrow morning and my lead item for Sunday's broadcast," said Stumpy. "Everybody in Washington and most everybody in the United States will know that the man who advised Truman on the bomb and who now feels ashamed of Truman and Hiroshima, is a painter of considerable achievement and great promise. That'll grind Truman's guts and send Paul Blanton, Admiral Potter and Jack Hardwick into another emergency session."

"I have to get Frank out," said Diane, "get him out and take him home."

DURING the four-day period between Friday, May 7, and Monday, May 10, 1948, these reports appeared in the *Washington Post:* Congresswoman Helen Gahagan Douglas denounced the rising cost of living, pointing out that steak which had sold for 33 cents a pound in 1940 was now selling for 79 cents in Washington supermarkets . . . American Airlines announced that it had cut the non-stop flying time between Washington and Chicago to 3 hours, 35 minutes . . . the Carnes Barber Shop on Massachusetts Avenue became the first shop in Washington to ever charge more than $1 for a haircut; it raised its price to $1.25 . . . Pulitzer prizes went to Tennessee Williams for *A Streetcar Named Desire* and to W. H. Auden for *Age of Anxiety* . . . General Eisenhower took his farewell salute from the Army at Fort Myer, and next day he was pictured in a freshman cap and called "Columbia's New Freshman" . . . Taft was winning over Stassen in Ohio, and Dewey was winning over Stassen in Oregon . . . John Mason Brown lectured at the Mayflower and said the competition of horror realism in world affairs was making creative writing more difficult . . . furnishings worth more than $800,000 were sold at auction at Friendship House, home of the late Evalyn Walsh McLean . . . Walter Masterson pitched a four-hit shutout and broke a Nats losing streak . . . construction began on an auto underpass at Dupont Circle . . . there was a radio debate on "Will the third party bring peace and prosperity?" Participants were Dorothy Thompson, Dwight MacDonald, Glen Taylor and James Stewart Martin . . . and Mrs. Agnes Meyer, owner of the *Post*, objected to public sale of the Kinsey report.

But what attracted most attention in the paper was the continuing campaign by Stumpy McDowell to "free" Frank Castleton from "Truman's Lubianka." This one man who knew most about atomic bomb policy —this godson of Cordell Hull, trusted by both Roosevelt and Truman to report to them on the bomb—why shouldn't he be allowed to appear before the Senate Foreign Relations Committee and answer the unanswered questions about bomb policy? This talented man whose paintings would soon be shown in New York—why shouldn't he be allowed to explain what he meant by his anguished cry, "If only Roosevelt had lived?" His cry must mean that Roosevelt intended doing *something* with the bomb that Truman had failed to do. What was it? Indeed, what *was* Truman's atomic bomb policy?

Over and over Stumpy repeated Truman's words after Hiroshima: "We'll keep our secrets pending further examination of possible methods of protecting us and the rest of the world from the danger of sudden destruction." And: "I shall make recommendations to the Congress as to how atomic power can become a forceful influence towards the maintenance of world peace." Then Stumpy asked, Where is Truman's policy for protecting the world from the danger of sudden destruction? Where is his recommendation as to how atomic power could maintain world peace?

On Friday morning, May 7, Stumpy ended his column with the words "Frank Castleton, under the expert care of Capt. Arthur Palkin and Lieut. Mary Sullivan, has recovered his equilibrium. So the question for every American is: When Castleton and his wife ask that he be allowed to leave the hospital, will Truman allow him to leave?"

At 9:30 A.M. on Friday, looking stylishly attractive in a burnt-orange linen suit, Diane Castleton entered Dr. Palkin's office, greeted him and sat down opposite him.

"I've learned from the morning paper that the experts were impressed with Frank's paintings, and I want you to tell me more about what was said. But first, let me just say, we've completed our examination of Frank, we think we understand his problem, and I'm—well, I'm quite pleased. I'd like to recommend some further treatment, but that's just—it's to be expected in Frank's case. Your husband's experience during his first forty years didn't condition him for the tension-building anxiety-producing situation in which he found himself after forty. He lived too simply; he met too little resistance. He wasn't born rich, but he was born comfortable, without social grievance, into a non-competitive agrarian society in which most people were satisfied to subsist. When he left home to be educated, he merely moved into another sort of Arcadia. His fellow students had satisfactory places in society waiting for them no matter how poorly they did in college, so in that environment Frank had the advantage of being the one with reason to strive . . . he was the one whose mother worked like a nigger and whose father had been treated badly at Sewanee. He had to prove he and his family weren't white trash. So Frank made himself valedictorian—he was a striver without much competition. Life might have been different for Frank if he'd had some other people around him determined to move up in society."

"If he was a striver," asked Diane, "why didn't he work for distinction as a painter or a musician?"

"He wasn't that much of a striver. Arcadia doesn't produce great painters or musicians. Trying to achieve individual distinction in the arts is a tension-filled activity which only the driven few can endure."

"Interesting. That's what the art dealer said," said Diane. "Frank has more talent for perception than he has patience for execution."

"Of course," said the doctor. "Frank is a man of intense imagination, but he quickly loses patience with things as they are and sees only things as they could be. However, he lacks the talent to put into a narrow frame the values and meanings that a great painter puts in."

"Is that why he expended so much of himself on politics?"

"Yes," said the doctor. "Well, of course it's much easier to seek purpose in common cause than to strive for artistic distinction. That's why the movement for TVA attracted Frank. He could dig into that without risking more than temporary disappointments. All he had to do was entertain Congressmen and his fellow bankers while he jogged through forests with Indians, made music, folk danced, painted pictures, acquired an attractive wife, sired children and accumulated wealth. And look how easy sex was for him! For many boys sexual intercourse, particularly their first feeble effort, is an anxiety-producing experience. But not for Frank Castleton. Bess Foshee wanted something from him, managed his first time with her so he'd feel exultant, then relieved him of sexual tension throughout his college years. All without emotional investment, without risk and at little cost to him."

"And of course," said Diane caustically, "you're going to point out how easy I was for him? How quickly I relieved his tension?"

"That's not a bad thing at all—for either of you," said the doctor. "You were easy for him because you decided he was what you wanted. You had your university degree, you wanted a home and a husband, you found Frank Castleton. So you fastened yourself to him in a hurry."

"Have I been bad for Frank? Have I been demanding enough?"

"No, you haven't been bad for him, and if you ever had been he would have left you. You were what he wanted—feminine, attractive and expert in the art of making life easy. That extraordinary home of yours—Frank Castleton may have envisioned it, built it and decorated it with his paintings, but it was Diane Jemison Castleton who made life easy in it, gave it order and charm and reared the children while Frank was leading his euphoric outdoor life and helping improve the world."

"We've both contributed to our home and enjoyed it."

The doctor nodded. "Yes, all right, enjoyment. A human creature living a life of ease, pleasure. And with the feeling that he was helping improve the world. When he left his Arcadia for Washington in 1941, Frank wasn't aggressive, repressive or competitive. He was a runner but not a racer. And of course he accepted only a dollar a year and travel expenses from the government for his position. He wasn't rich enough to afford that."

"That wasn't his fault," said Diane. "His parents wanted him to do it. They don't think an American who has a living should accept payment for serving the nation in wartime."

"So he had only one conceit," said the doctor. "A few people would have admired him for wanting to feel he was improving the world. Others would have scorned him for it. And I have to tell you, I don't agree with you that he should have gone into the Army. As Hull told him, he would have wound up managing the officers' club, and he would have hated that. I think his staying in Washington was correct for him. With Hull he could indulge his conceit and feel he was working for a better world."

"You think Mr. Hull was right in what he was trying to do?"

"I think so, yes," said Dr. Palkin. "By 1941 he was a vain ill-tempered old Tennessee mountain feudist who thought he should be the President's foreign minister in conducting the war. But Roosevelt rejected him and gave the job to Hopkins. Hull worked so hard to win the peace only because Roosevelt wouldn't let him help win the war. If Frank had done no more than help Hull, then in May, 1945, he could have gone with Stettinius to San Francisco as Hull's mantle-bearer, and he could have felt pride in helping organize the UN. By August, 1945, he could have been at home with you, his war service honorably ended, resuming his easy life. When the bomb hit Hiroshima he could have been as surprised as any other American, and no more affected by it."

"As long as we're on the subject, tell me, shouldn't Mr. Hull have been told about the bomb?"

"I don't know. Knowledge of the bomb wouldn't have made Hull support a powerful UN. Hull believed that the UN should never be granted the power to take any action, or even consider taking action, against the United States. That's why he agreed with the Russians when they demanded that the UN have no power to consider moving against them. Hull wanted the UN to be the agency through which Britain, the United States, the Soviet Union and China, while living peacefully among themselves, policed all the other nations. The knowledge that Russia and China, along with Britain and the United States, would soon have atomic bombs would have meant to Hull only that all Four Policemen would be better armed for their work. He would never have agreed with Frank that the Four Policemen should arm the UN, then disarm themselves and rely on the UN for protection. He felt convinced that the Four Policemen, in their common interest, would choose not to indulge in arms races with each other."

"Then was it his association with the scientists that hurt Frank?"

Dr. Palkin paused noticeably. Then he said, "Here, Mrs. Castleton, I'll have to be very careful. Frank has now told me much that I didn't know before and that is still classified secret. But I believe I can safely tell you this: After atomic fission was achieved in 1938, the first concern of most of the nuclear physicists in Europe was to prevent Hitler from getting a fission bomb. This group, led by Niels Bohr and Joliot-Curie, jointly agreed that none of them would do any research which might help Hitler get the bomb. Next, fearing that Hitler might overrun Europe from Scotland to the Urals, they wanted to make the bomb somewhere outside Europe and use it to destroy Nazi military power. Joliot-Curie proposed making it in the Belgian Congo with Britain and Canada supplying the money and materials. Bohr, Fermi and the Hungarians believed that Roosevelt was the

312

best bet for the project. That's why Bohr and the others came here, and through Einstein and Frankfurter persuaded the President to finance the effort. The purpose was clearly understood: The bomb was to be made in the United States and used to destroy the Hitler war machine. You see, this is why so many Nobel Prize–winning geniuses were willing to work at bomb-making . . . willing to live and work hard and secretly in the boondocks of Tennessee, New Mexico and Washington State."

"Then, you would say, they lost their purpose?"

"Well, I'd say the Russians appropriated it," said the doctor. "With only conventional help from Britain and the United States, the Russians were going to destroy the Hitler machine. By 1943 the scientists knew their bomb would never incinerate a single Nazi. Japan was too weak an enemy to justify an atomic bomb, too poor in oil and steel, too easily blockaded. The United States would defeat Japan before the bomb could be ready, so why should scientific geniuses continue trying to make bombs? To add to the power of the Pentagon and the profits of Dupont, Union Carbide and Tennessee Eastman? It was then that Bohr hurried back to the United States and proposed an even better purpose for continued bomb-making. The bomb could end all war! Forever! The bomb would be the world's policeman under whose protection all nations would disarm and devote themselves to enriching individual human life. Bohr converted many scientists and a few politicians, and unfortunately he converted Frank Castleton."

"But Frank was so vulnerable. He so wanted to believe that an arms race between the United States and the Soviet Union could be prevented."

"But as long as man exists there will be armed rivalry. That's where Frank remained totally blind. That's why the proposal to use the bomb to end war among nations was a conceit. A man becomes a fanatic when he begins insisting that a conceit can be realized. Roosevelt, the practical politician, needed a cataclysmic demonstration of the bomb to justify the vast secret expenditure of money and materials. Frank objected, but when he couldn't prevent the bombing, he rationalized by lodging all his hope in it. Of those with prior knowledge of Hiroshima, only Frank went there and tried to keep faith with the bomb's victims. He had hoped they would die worthy deaths—that they would be the last human sacrifices necessary for mankind to achieve an end to war between nations. When he saw that those sacrifices would not be enough to achieve the goal, when he confronted the truth that Hiroshima was only an atrocity, he felt guilty and ashamed. He lost hope, then self-confidence, then equilibrium, and at last

313

he could think of no one but himself. He neglected you; you resented his neglect; you could no longer comfort each other. Frank became so consumed by anxiety that he simply lost all ability to love, to enjoy, and to rationalize. His descent into his very private torment inevitably led him to panic."

Dr. Palkin paused, examined the back of his hand and added, "That, Mrs. Castleton, is my diagnosis of your husband's disorder. That's why he is now suffering from severe depression and incipient hysteria."

"Have you been able to help him?" asked Diane.

"Yes, I think we have," said the doctor. "By listening to him sympathetically we've guided him toward acceptance and adjustment. The antidepressants have been useful, of course, but the self-awareness he's gaining is far more beneficial. Most helpful of all, I must tell you, we have restored his sexual self-confidence."

Diane parted her lips to speak, but she was too surprised to do more than stammer, "You . . . what?"

"I don't mean to shock you," said the doctor. "No man in your husband's condition can ever initially regain sexual confidence with his wife. She has simply witnessed too many humiliations. When he moves toward the sex act with her, he knows he's going to fail. He can hope to succeed only with a woman who hasn't seen him fail—an uncomplicated male-and-female situation without emotional involvement. He needs a boost—some skillful reinforcing."

"Mary Sullivan is his reinforcer?"

"Yes. He now enjoys normal sexual relations with her."

"That means he'll never be capable of normal intercourse with me again?"

"It may mean that," said the doctor. "Many wives of severely depressed men choose divorce. You've been contemplating divorce, and it's true, isn't it, that you have at least one prospective new husband in mind?"

Diane didn't blush or falter. Inside she felt suddenly afraid, but she looked hard at the doctor for a moment, then said, "Yes. Have they been watching me?"

"You should have anticipated that they would," replied the doctor. "McDowell, of all people, should have expected it. In this town, whenever you are annoying the President you're likely to be watched, overheard and photographed."

"They can't force me to hurt Frank," said Diane fiercely. "They can publish their pictures and I'll still do whatever is necessary to get Frank out of here whenever he wants out."

"I don't doubt that," said the doctor. "And with that sort of devotion to him, the two of you may be able to save your marriage and resume normal sexual relations."

After a moment Diane said, "I understand your diagnosis. Is there anything else you can do? What's the rest of his treatment?"

"Two electroconvulsive shock treatments a week for four weeks." The doctor explained how such therapy was given and the benefits to be expected from it. "In addition to the shock treatments," he added, "I advise daily counseling toward helping Frank decide that the goal which he believes was achievable was, in fact, quite beyond the reach of nations and of mankind. He's got to see that the world just isn't ready for his dream —maybe it never will be."

"How do you propose to convince Frank of that? This has been his dream for—for as long as I can remember."

"By destroying Roosevelt's credibility," said the doctor. "The most damaging day in Frank's life was April 11, 1945, when Roosevelt told him the United States would compel creation of the world authority to monopolize the bomb. I want to go over the autopsy report with Frank again. It shows that on that date the President couldn't have known what he was saying. I'll bring in one of Roosevelt's biographers to prove that Roosevelt was a calculating liar—a procrastinator whose reaction to new ideas was always to agree with the proponent. He was a cold lonely man who used other men, and who wasn't close to anyone, not even his wife or his children. I'll use Secretary Blanton to convince Frank that had Roosevelt lived he would have taken about the same actions Truman has taken. Then I'll call in the Reverend Bramwell."

"What will you use Joe for?"

"To help me convince Frank that man is incapable of achieving world disarmament. Frank isn't going to concede *that* without a struggle, I'm sure. But as a Christian minister, an expert on man's incapacities, Bramwell can throw the whole weight of the Scriptures against Frank's belief in the capacities of man. I can throw the whole weight of Freud. As part of our bibliotherapy, I've asked Frank to study *Civilization and Its Discontents*. And God knows Freud will remind him that man by nature is a hunter and must forever feel uneasy without weapons at hand, that the more power man achieves over his natural environment the more anxious he becomes, that man's communal life will always be threatened by his twin instincts of aggression and self-destruction. The shock treatments will also make him more and more amenable to counseling."

Diane looked away from the doctor, toward the window. As he had talked she had begun to feel closer to Frank than she had felt for two years. She had begun to understand him, and to understand is to forgive. "Tell me, Doctor," she asked, "either here or in Tennessee, can Frank be treated with shock as an outpatient?"

"No," he said. "He must be hospitalized."

Again Diane hesitated while she thought. Then she said, "I came here this morning with my mind made up to tell you that tomorrow I would take Frank back to Tennessee. All the publicity about his being brought here in handcuffs—about how he must be confined here to protect the nation, how he's queer and should never have been trusted with the bomb secrets, how he's a pinko who was party to the sellout at Yalta—all this is going to make life much more difficult for him than it was before he panicked. If he's given shock treatment that too will be publicized, and it's got to be another blow to his remaining self-confidence. I want him a whole man again, Doctor. So my inclination is to reject your advice and take him home, where he can live in seclusion but still feel free. But now you tell me that shock treatments could help him. I'd like to discuss the decision with him."

"Of course," said the doctor. "I can't treat him with shock without both your and his written permission."

Diane rose from her chair. "May I talk with Frank now?"

The doctor nodded. "I'll have him brought to you out on the grounds."

"No," she said. "I want to talk with him in his cell."

"But you'll embarrass him," objected the doctor. "He feels so diminished behind a locked door. He doesn't want you to see him in confinement."

"I'll share his confinement," she said. "If I can, I . . . I'll relieve his embarrassment. Perhaps I, too, can reinforce him."

"You mean go to bed with him . . . here?"

"If he wants it," she said. "On every other morning of his life when he has been with me in Washington behind a locked door, he has wanted it and had it. It never failed to make him feel euphoric. Well, during the past three years he's been alone in Washington. I haven't been with him in body, or in spirit, for that matter. I've been his critic and housekeeper rather than his supporter and traveling companion. Now I'll rejoin him . . . and we'll see what happens."

"I'll have you shown to his room," said the doctor.

"See that we aren't disturbed for an hour," she said.

IN THE HOURS OF NIGHT

O<small>NE</small> of the experiences which separates human beings is confinement. The child who has been locked in a closet by a parent is forever separated from the child who has never been locked in a closet. The man who has been locked in a closet by authority, compelled to wait hours, days or years for someone outside to come and unlock the door, is forever separated from the man who has never lived behind a door which he couldn't unlock. Confinement in either a penal or a mental institution reduces a man's self-respect, and others' respect for him as well.

As Diane walked along the corridors of the hospital with Sam, smelling the institutional odor, looking through glass into the vacuous faces of inadequate men, she tried hard not to feel humiliated. She wanted to greet Frank lovingly. She wanted to make him feel better, so she hoped they could smile, touch each other, talk easily and decide what they should do together. I must not make him feel that he is to blame for his mental illness, she thought.

Frank was reading, waiting for Sam to come and take him for his session. He felt apprehensive, for the attendant was late in coming for him. When the door opened and he saw Diane, he swallowed hard and was momentarily embarrassed. But when she came in smiling, her eyes twinkling, looking happy and pretty, and came and hugged him and kissed him on the lips, he managed a smile and hugged her tighter than he had in a long time. She surprised him by telling the attendant, "Don't come back here for me until noon! You understand?" When she took off her hat and shook her head to loosen her hair, he helped her out of her jacket and put her things in the chair by the bed.

"Now show me this luxurious suite," she said jokingly.

"Not quite up to the Shoreham." Frank looked at her, trying to fathom what she was thinking.

"Oh, I don't know," she said, looking around. "I've seen worse. No drawers or closets in which to forget things."

"Everything's in full view," he said.

"Well," she said, "it's not quite the Willard, where we used to set lovemaking records between visits to the Great White Father and the National Theater. And it's not quite the Shoreham during the war, when you used to meet me at Union Station about this time in the morning and we'd rush to the hotel to make love before lunch."

She came to him, reached up and fastened her hands behind his neck and said, "The long dark night is over for us. Hallelujah!" She pulled him down and kissed him on the mouth, and he responded. "Let's break out the champagne," she said.

They sat at the table, and he poured two paper cups of orange juice from a cardboard carton in the refrigerator. They touched the cups in a toast, drank, and kissed again. Then he said, "They want to keep me here and treat me with convulsive shock."

"Is that what you want?"

"I'm considering it, Jemmy. I hate being locked up in this torture chamber. At night when that door is locked on me, I want to scream. But when I go home this time I must be able to love you and quit hurting you. If shock treatments will help me do that, I must take them."

"Dr. Palkin says you are much better. You seem fine—really well. Are you?"

"Yes," he said. "As a matter of fact, I haven't felt as well in years. So the question is, do I go home now, taking my Ritalin and Demerol with me, and try to make it? Or do I stay here four more weeks and take shock treatments in the hope I'll be even better able to make it? What do you think?"

"I want you to decide," she said. "Me, personally? I'd like to take you out of here now and take you home."

"Now, why did you say that," he said sharply. "I don't need you to *take* me. I'm no invalid. I didn't need to be *brought* here . . . certainly not by Potter's Task Force. I could have come here alone. When I leave here, I'll leave alone."

"I'm sorry about the choice of words," she said. "I know you can travel alone."

"There's something else I want to get straight between us, Jemmy," he said. "Of the thousand other men in this hospital, every one of them is blamed by his family for being here. Do you blame me? Do Susan and Cord and my father and mother blame me?"

His eyes began to water, and she felt so helpless that she began struggling to keep from crying. She took his hand and said, "Remember, Frank, I'm not a therapist. So in answering you, I may . . . choose the wrong words. Look, we haven't blamed you as if you had done something cruel or evil or illegal. We've felt desperately depressed at not being able to help you. And know this, dear: You're a loved talented and educated man. You and the rest of us have been taught that such a man, if he wants to and tries

318

hard enough, can put things out of his mind that disturb him and hurt him and his family. So, well, naturally we've been disappointed that you haven't been able to get rid of what bothers you."

"I tried to put it out of my mind and couldn't," he said. "If that means I'm weakwilled, then I am. What about neglecting the rest of my life—the painting and music—you blame me for that?"

"Well, again, Frank," she said, "blame isn't what we've felt. The President involved you with the bomb, and you wanted it used to end war. No one blames you for wanting that. But when it wasn't done we wanted you to come home and work at developing your talents. We wanted it for you as well as for us."

"All right, another problem. You began hating me when I couldn't make love to you any more, right? Answer me, Jemmy."

Diane answered tearfully, "Not hate. It was only despair I felt. I knew how disappointed you were. But lovemaking for a husband and wife can sometimes be an antidote for disappointment and despair and loneliness and the fear of growing old. It's a way for a man and woman to find repose. And I was terribly depressed, after twenty years of feeling proud to give and receive such joy, to suddenly find myself unable to excite you."

He decided. He picked her up, carried her to the bed and helped her out of her clothes. Then he slipped out of his own clothes and took her as affectively as he ever had.

She was standing in the bathroom repairing her make-up when she told him what the art dealer said about his paintings and drawings.

"I've always known that they weren't as good as I was capable of making them," he said. "That's why I've never offered them for sale. Tell the art dealer to come to see me as soon as I get home."

"He says there is already a strong demand for your paintings—that they're valuable and good—and that if you really work now, you can be an important artist."

"That's what I'm going to do," said Frank. "Work. Concentrate. I'm going to work harder at painting than I have ever worked at anything. From now on I won't be trying to improve anything but my own talents."

When Diane came out of the bathroom Frank said, "Sit down a minute, honey, while I tell you what I want you to do. Go to Dr. Palkin and give him your written permission for me to be treated with convulsive shock. Then go to the Shoreham, check out and go home. Neither you nor I will ever be back in Washington again, I promise you that. This government will never again do anything hopeful enough to attract us. You and

319

I are going to build a cottage on the Domain at Sewanee, and we're going to live and love each other at home, at our cottage in the Smokies and at our cottage at Sewanee. Over the weekend I'll be talking with Paul Blanton, Joe Bramwell, the doctor and Mary, and I'll phone you on Monday morning. If I decide not to take the shock treatments, I'll fly home Monday or Tuesday afternoon. Otherwise I'll be home about four weeks from today."

"Suppose they—now, I think you ought to consider this, Frank— suppose they try to keep you here against your will?" she asked. "Before I leave, shouldn't I retain a lawyer for you?"

"If I need one, I'll get one," he said. "And if I stay here beyond next Tuesday, I'll be speaking to you often. What I need most to know is that you, our family and our home are safe—they're all that will matter to me from now on. You are dearer to me now, Jemmy, than you have ever been. You're everything I have."

He was hugging her tenderly when Sam came for her.

At 3 P.M. that day Paul Blanton, in a chauffeur-driven limousine, arrived at the hospital and conferred with Dr. Palkin. Then Castleton was brought to the doctor's office, and the doctor withdrew, leaving Blanton and Castleton alone.

"I'm glad to see you looking so much better, Frank," Blanton said, taking off his coat.

"I appreciate your helping me, Paul. Not to mention the President's allowing me to be helped. Please express my thanks to him."

Blanton pushed up his sleeves, sat down on the couch and began filling his pipe. "The doctor says you're now able to talk about anything we need to discuss, so I want to do whatever else I can to help you."

"Help me make peace with the President," said Castleton. "I want to go home, live quietly and not be watched any more."

Blanton lighted his pipe, sucking on it several times, creating a cloud of smoke. "You can have peace with the President. He's giving you the treatment you need; now you must give him what he needs."

"All I can give him is silence," said Castleton.

Blanton chewed on his pipestem, then said, "You haven't read any newspapers or listened to the radio since you got in here. Our bringing you to a hospital resulted in an enormous amount of publicity."

"What do you mean?"

"Damaging to the President. When we arrived here reporters wanted me to say you had broken with him, but I denied it—said you were a valued adviser to the President, that you would remain so, that your Q-clearance would be renewed and that you would contribute to Truman's campaign, just as you did to Roosevelt's."

"If I'm a Truman supporter," asked Castleton, "how has my illness been used to hurt him?"

"People worry about the bomb," said Blanton. "So they wonder why you got sick. Some say you're suffering from guilt over Hiroshima. Remember, Frank, while you were hysterical you moaned, 'If only Roosevelt had lived.' That must mean that you think Roosevelt intended to do something with the bomb Truman hasn't done. And Diane told reporters you believe the Russians will have the bomb in months, maybe weeks."

"Look, what more can I say? I'm sorry I got sick," said Castleton. "I'm sorry I mentioned Roosevelt . . . or the Russians. From now on I'll try to stay sane and silent."

"Can you silence Stumpy McDowell? Every day he charges that Truman has mishandled the bomb. Since he was your classmate, the assumption is he gets information from you."

"He doesn't," said Castleton. "But he's a free man. Not even the President can shut him up."

"When you leave this hospital," said Blanton, "an effort will be made to bring you before a Congressional committee and question you under oath about how Roosevelt intended to handle the bomb."

"Truman can use Executive Privilege to defeat such an effort."

"But if you force him to do that, the papers will say he's afraid of what you can reveal."

Castleton's eyes began to water. "Are you trying to tell me, Paul, that I can have peace with the President only by staying here?"

Blanton avoided a direct answer. "I'm only trying to explain the gravity of your situation, Frank. You too have been hurt by the publicity. The American people are now afraid of you. They want you locked up or guarded to keep you from spilling information to the Russians on how to make the bomb."

Castleton rubbed the back of his neck and began to breathe rapidly. "The people—if they were told that the Russians already know how to make the bomb—they wouldn't fear me."

"Well, they won't be told that," said Blanton. "And I hope to God the Russians don't test a bomb before election day. It would defeat Truman, and that would be a catastrophe for the Free World. The breakup of the

French and British empires has left a vacuum which the United States must fill to keep the Russians from stepping in. Only Truman has the guts to fill it."

As Castleton looked at Blanton through tears, the Secretary frowned and shifted his heavy body on the couch. Both men were conscious of the change in their relationship. They had become friends when Blanton was a frequent guest in Castleton's home . . . when Castleton could look down on Blanton . . . when Castleton was an assistant to Hull and Roosevelt while Blanton was only an assistant to Stimson . . . when Blanton envied Castleton his graceful way of life, his secure place in a community and his attractive wife. Now the situation had changed. Blanton was the most powerful member of Truman's Cabinet, and Castleton was—well, what the hell was he? A nut in a nut house. Moreover, Blanton knew Castleton had been cuckolded, and the cuckold has always been a contemptible figure. So while at one moment the Secretary remembered his friendship and regard for Castleton, the next moment he saw him only as a troublesome fool, brought from his cell to plead for favors from the government.

As if he knew what Blanton was thinking, Castleton said, "Tell me, Paul—back in '43 and '44, when we talked about the bomb at my home and in the La Fonda Hotel in Santa Fe—didn't you hope, just as I did, that the bomb would end arms races among nations?"

"Yes. I shared your hopes, but I didn't share your expectations. I hoped the bomb would end war, but I didn't expect it. As I see it, unrealized hopes don't hurt men much. But unrealized expectations can leave men gasping, weeping and defeated. That's why you're unbalanced now, while I'm still balanced."

When Castleton didn't respond, Blanton continued. "Now, I sincerely want to help you, Frank. And I can if you'll listen to me."

"Go on," said Castleton.

"Well, first," said Blanton, "you must admit you've been unfair to Truman. When he went to Potsdam you advised him to compel Stalin to accept a UN powerful enough to monopolize nuclear weapons. But George Marshall advised him to go to Potsdam only to persuade Stalin to enter the war against Japan. Now, whose advice could you reasonably expect Truman to follow? Yours or Marshall's?"

"I didn't presume to advise him," said Castleton. "I told him what Roosevelt intended to do. That's what Truman should have done."

"You really think Truman could have believed Roosevelt would have done it? Frank, that's just unreasonable," said Blanton. "And after Hiroshima you expected Truman to amend the UN charter so the UN could take custody of our bombs. But Truman knew the Senate would never help create an international authority more powerful than the United States. He'd served in the Senate, after all. So again, what you expected was out of line."

"Paul," said Castleton wearily, "just tell me what I can do now to find peace."

"All right," said Blanton. "On Monday we'll hold a press conference here. The doctor will report on your recovery, and you'll read a statement. You'll denounce all the criticism of the President resulting from your illness. You'll say that Truman has handled the bomb just as Roosevelt intended to. You'll say that Truman's election this fall is an imperative for the Free World, and that you and your family are contributing fifty thousand dollars to the Truman campaign."

Castleton got up, drank some water and walked to the window. After a moment he asked, "If I tell those lies and pay the ransom, will the President restore all my civil rights? Will he allow me to leave this hospital, then will he cancel my Q-clearance, accept my resignation from the advisory council and quit having me watched?"

"All in due course. After you make your statement to the press, the story will begin to die down. After you've had your shock treatments I'll take you back to Tennessee. I'll post an unobtrusive guard to guarantee your privacy for a few more weeks. Meanwhile I'll cancel the Q-clearance, replace you on the advisory council, and you'll be relatively free again."

"Relatively free?"

"Well, hell, Frank, you can never be free of your obligations! You can never reveal your conversations with two Presidents, or any dealings you had with them!"

Both men realized they had reached the end of their bargaining. Whatever they eventually got out of the deal, neither would be entirely satisfied.

"I'll give you my decision Monday morning," said Castleton. "Now tell me—suppose I decide not to tell the lies or pay the ransom or take the shock treatments? Suppose I decide just to walk out of here, take a taxi to the airport, get on a plane and go home? Will you try to hold me here?"

"You and I are friends. We have to work something out."

"Suppose we can't. Will the President try to hold me?"

"Well, it's absurd to discuss it, but yes, under the National Security Act, the President has the authority to hold you."

"No, he doesn't," said Castleton. "He knows the Russians already know how to make the bomb. There's no way I can jeopardize national security. All I can mess up is Truman's election—and that doesn't make me a potential danger to the nation. Truman can't try to hold me here by saying my case involves national security."

"You're wrong there, Frank," said Blanton. "Any case involves national security if the President says it does. Members of Congress and the people think we're still the only ones who know how the bomb is made, and they're afraid you'll hurt the United States by revealing it. The President has the right to consider the fears of those who haven't yet been given knowledge."

"What about you, Paul?" asked Castleton. "You know that any effort to hold me here implies I'm a political prisoner. Will you be a party to that?"

Blanton dropped his eyes and reflected. Then he answered, "No, I won't. I believe you'll decide to do as I have suggested. It is in your best interest. But if you decide otherwise, all I ask is this: Give me your word that you'll notify me twenty-four hours before you try to leave. That's to give me time to arrange for you to get out in a way that will be best for you and for the country."

"You have my word on that," said Castleton. "Now, let me ask two favors of you."

"What are they?"

"Give me the right of a common criminal to talk to members of my family on the telephone."

"I'll arrange that," said Blanton. "Just do your talking in the presence of the doctor or the nurse. What else?"

"Most patients here," said Castleton, "have some freedom of movement without escort. I'm lodged in a cell designed for a maniac, and I can't leave it without an escort. I want to be moved to a room where things aren't bolted down and where I have a key to the lock. And I want some freedom of movement."

"I've already discussed that with the doctor," said Blanton. "You're getting a new room. It'll still be in the closed area of the hospital, but you'll have some freedom."

Blanton looked at his watch and got up to go. He could still reach Chevy Chase Country Club in time for nine holes of golf, and after devoting an hour to a cuckolded fanatic in a nut house, he needed to get out on the course. He put on his coat and shook Castleton's hand.

"You're going to be okay, Frank," he said. "Just cooperate with me and your troubles will soon be over."

O_N Saturday, May 8, Frank Castleton became a relatively free patient in the hospital. His private room with bath on the fourteenth floor was furnished about like one in a hospital for physically ill patients. The bed, chair and chest of drawers were movable; there was a closet in which to hang clothes; and there was a seat on the toilet. He had a door key, but at all times, even when he was inside the room with the door locked, the nurses and attendants could open the door from the outside. He was free to move unescorted through the "closed" section of the hospital, which included a dining room, barber shop, gymnasium, swimming pool, library and an outdoor exercise area the size of a football field. This outdoor area was enclosed by a wire fence topped with barbed wire too high to get over. To go to the doctor's office or the canteen, to play golf or tennis, to walk in the wooded area or visit Mary Sullivan's apartment, he had to be escorted. He had not gained the freedom of the "open" area—he couldn't leave the hospital without permission—but he had gained the maximum freedom allowed to patients who had been brought to the hospital by authority. As a special concession, he was to be allowed to use a telephone in the presence of either Dr. Palkin or Mary Sullivan.

During the morning he stayed in his room, weighing his options. To appear with Blanton at a press conference, pledge his support to Truman and contribute fifty thousand dollars to his campaign, after which Blanton would eventually take him home, cancel his Q-clearance and allow him to resign from the Advisory Council, and gradually reduce surveillance. Or to reject Blanton's plan but agree to remain in the hospital four more weeks while taking shock treatments. Or to demand on Monday that he be allowed to go home on the next day, bound only to continued secrecy as to the bomb and his service to the Presidency.

Before Diane had left Washington Friday afternoon, she had called Stumpy and told him she couldn't go with him to his beach house. Then on Saturday morning they again talked on the telephone. She mentioned that Frank had told her about the possibility of his coming home Tuesday.

"They won't let him leave that soon," said Stumpy. "If he leaves they must refuse to let him talk with Bertrand Russell, and they must invoke Executive Privilege to keep him from being brought before a Congressional committee. They don't want to be put in that position, so they're going to hold Frank as long as they can."

"But won't they be criticized for trying to hold him against his will?" asked Diane.

"How can anyone know what his will is?" replied Stumpy. "They have drugs to control his will."

"Susan's going to see him Sunday afternoon," said Diane anxiously. "She'll report to me on what he wants to do. On Monday I'll telephone Dr. Palkin, and if I suspect they're trying to hold Frank, I'll ask Mr. Arnold to begin an effort to free him. Does that sound like a reasonable course of action?"

"It's all you can do," said Stumpy. "It'll get a big play in the papers and on the air."

"Well, won't all that adverse publicity be worse for them than allowing Frank to come home and be quiet?"

"All the publicity won't be against them, my dear, keep that in mind," said Stumpy. "If they try to hold Frank, they'll have a lot of support. They might even win in the courts. Truman can do almost anything in the name of national security, so God knows what they'll do."

"What a mess!" sighed Diane. "I wonder if Frank can ever have a good life again!"

"But you can have a good one . . . with me," said Stumpy. "When do I see you again?"

She replied hesitantly. "I . . . don't know. If Frank is to stay in the hospital, I'll probably fly back to Washington next Friday."

"Then we can go to my beach place, can't we?"

"I'll . . . I'll have to call you one night next week after I've talked further with Dr. Palkin."

ON Saturday afternoon Joe Bramwell came to the hospital and talked first with Palkin. He was briefed on Frank's diagnosis and recommended treatment. "I've been worrying about that man," said Bramwell. "I'm afraid life can't mean much to him from now on."

"I'd say the cure lies in turning to subjectivism," said the doctor, "as other men have done when their national self-respect and community have been lost. Frenchmen did it after the shameful fall of France . . . an individual feeling of revulsion, oddly enough, can be sustaining."

Bramwell shook his head. "I can't see Frank ever becoming an existentialist. Since he was fifteen he has been a sucker for Wilson's, then Roosevelt's rhetoric. So at forty-six how can you expect him to find comfort in Kierkegaard and Sartre?"

"Do you think he might be able to consider one of the Oriental philosophies?"

"Not any subjective philosophy, no," said Bramwell. "I know the man. He can never believe that the chief purpose of life is to experience some sort of subjective feeling."

"I don't know. He's also an artist—he evidently finds purpose there."

"He can work at art," said Bramwell, "but it can't be his sole purpose. Art is an expression of individual yearnings, but Frank wants more. Somehow, impossible as it may seem, he's always wanted to express collective yearnings of men to rise above collective limitations."

"Well," said Dr. Palkin, "to more down-to-earth matters. We agree that convulsive shock can help him feel less distressed. So as you talk to him I hope you'll urge him to remain here and take the treatments."

"I'll do more than that, Doctor," said Bramwell. "I'll support you in urging him to think seriously about subjectivism. Then, and God knows how I'll manage it, I'll urge him to continue to have faith in the United States."

Castleton was then brought in to join the doctor and minister. Bramwell congratulated him on his recovery, and Castleton smiled thoughtfully. "Yes, Joe, I think I can work now. I'm going home to concentrate on my painting and let the world go hang."

"That can be your salvation," said Bramwell. "A man should never allow his spiritual health to become dependent on a nation or a society. They're such sums of parts, Frank. Nations wax, wane and die. In human society there's always struggle, destruction and rebirth. Now, you got sick because you believed that to fulfill yourself personally you had to help end war among nations. Once you start seeking fulfillment only in yourself, you'll find it."

"The individual search seems selfish and lonely," said Castleton. "The Greeks believed that the acceptance of hopelessness for mankind is the beginning of wisdom. What do you think about that, Joe?"

"Sure, I agree with it," said Bramwell. "In both Buddhist and Christian doctrine a searching man starts gaining wisdom only when he accepts the fact that all life on earth is filled with sadness. For you to find comfort you're going to have to accept that human life in the future will be no less sorrowful than it has been in the past."

"That's hard for me to accept," said Castleton. "I've always needed to believe that men, acting together under wise and inspiring leaders, can make human life better."

"And I've always warned you," said Bramwell, "of the limitations of all human effort. Oh, of course collective effort can produce better food, clothing, shelter, schools, roads and medical care. But it can't end envy, hate, fear, anxiety or war, Frank."

Castleton sighed, then said, "A sad situation, isn't it? A man seeking to fulfill himself after he has lost faith in his nation!"

"Nevertheless, you can find fulfillment," said Bramwell. "Throughout history men have flourished creatively after their country had failed them. Just keep remembering that all nations fail but all men don't. A man has a mind, both conscious and unconscious, that unconscious, in Christian terms, being the soul. A man can use his mind and soul to create a painting or a symphony or a poem or a sculpture. A man can find within his own mind and soul comforts to sustain his life."

"Then what about the Redeemer? Man doesn't need Him?"

"Man needs Him desperately," said Bramwell, "but some of us can't accept Him. Most human beings find help in the explanations which have comforted the religious through the ages. We Christians have our way of looking at it: The Hebrew myths explain the beginning, validate the moral order and give us rites of passage, and the Redeemer gives us victory over death. Christianity comforts so many human beings—I minister it, and you, being a compassionate man, profess it and support it. But Christianity can't comfort you and me, for we are scientific men. For us there must be the unending search through the unconscious. We must suffer our own Gethsemanes and Calvarys, and be our own Redeemers."

"You too, Joe?"

"Yes, me too," said Bramwell. "Being a minister doesn't exempt me from the search. We're very similar, you realize."

"With one exception," said Castleton. "I had prior knowledge of Hiroshima. When I couldn't prevent it, I hoped at least that the horror of such an event would lead to some good, some change."

"That was misplaced hope," said Bramwell. "You forgot what Niebuhr calls 'the brutal character of the behavior of *all* human collectives.' The larger the collective, the more immoral it will become. To try to end war among nations, you were willing to create a super-collective which, inevitably corrupted by its super-power, would have become a super-evil."

That statement shook Castleton. He looked for a moment as if he would burst into tears. Then he asked, "Do you mean, Joe, that you prefer an atomic-arms race between the United States and the Soviet Union to the risk of making the UN strong enough to prevent such a race?"

"I certainly do," said Bramwell. "I'd rather risk atomic war among nations than risk the creation of a totalitarian tyranny which would enslave all mankind."

Castleton, breathing hard, was gripping the end of the desk with both hands. "If Roosevelt had lived . . . and had tried to put our atomic weapons under UN control . . . and had been willing to go to war to compel Stalin to do the same . . . would you have opposed Roosevelt?"

Bramwell replied quickly. "Yes, I would have. So would have Cordell Hull and the Christian Church. So would have most Americans."

"Then, my God," gasped Castleton, "are you saying that Truman was right and I've been wrong?"

Bramwell hesitated, then looked at Dr. Palkin, who nodded. "Yes, I'm saying that, Frank," said Bramwell. "Think about it a moment."

Castleton got up, drank water, then walked around the room rubbing his neck and wiping his eyes. Gradually he began to breathe evenly. When he sat down, Bramwell said, "Frank, for you to live a healthy life from now on you must love the United States of America for what good remains in it. You come from an old family of men, all of whom have been fiercely political. You're the godson of a fierce politician. You're a proud inheritor of the United States, and you must love and support your inheritance. The political choice in the United States in 1948 is between Truman and Dewey. Remember how you wept when Coolidge, then Hoover vetoed Norris Acts to create TVA? Dewey would even try to roll back the clock on TVA!"

"He couldn't do that," said Castleton. "TVA's biggest customer now is Oak Ridge."

"But Dewey would have to try it," said Bramwell, "so why don't you put your misplaced hopes behind you and leave this hospital as a Truman supporter?"

Castleton turned to Palkin. "Doctor, do you believe I should go along with Truman?"

"Yes, Frank," said the doctor, "I do."

Castleton hit the table with his fist. "Then, goddammit, you've mistreated me! After I told you what I knew at the end of 1943 I asked you whether I was justified in feeling that if the President would inform the world in 1944 that the bomb was being made, action would be taken to prevent an atomic-arms race between the United States and the Soviet Union. To which you replied yes. Now you say I should support the President who refused to take action to prevent such an arms race—Truman! You haven't been honest with me!"

"If I've confused you, I'm sorry," said the doctor. "I said yes, you had reason to hope in 1943 and 1944. Now I'm saying that in 1948 you must accept your disappointments and make the choices which are left to you."

Castleton then turned on Bramwell. "And you, Joe. First you say I should concentrate on my painting . . . 'a man should never allow his spiritual health to become dependent on a nation.' Now you say I must remain a political activist."

"That isn't conflicting advice," said Bramwell. "At Sewanee you were taught both to develop your individual talents and to be political."

"Then, firmly and finally, I say to both of you," said Castleton, "I can never support Truman. Like Douglas MacArthur, Adlai Stevenson and Niels Bohr, I believe that in 1945 the United States of America could have begun the process of saving mankind from the burden of war. When we failed to do that, we lost our national soul, and we'll never recover it. So help me God, I'll believe that until I die."

CASTLETON asked Mary Sullivan to leave him alone in his room for the rest of the day. He said he wanted to think, read and make some notes, so she brought him a new tablet and a pencil. At dinner time Sam brought him a cheese sandwich and hot tea.

He sat in the chair and read his favorite selections from Browning and Yeats. He read of a man he deeply identified with—a sixteenth-century painter named Andrea del Sarto, who could have been another Raphael or Leonardo. He had the talent for it, but he failed because of a "certain want of force in his nature." Castleton also read and re-read "The Second Coming" . . . "the blood-dimmed tide is loosed, and everywhere the ceremony of innocence is drowned."

When Mary came in with his medication she found him pensive but calm. He was in his pajamas, ready for bed. He asked her to delay giving him the narcotic for a few minutes. He had torn twenty pages from the tablet and folded them into a packet. "Hide this in your clothing," he said, "and read it when you get to your apartment. We'll talk about it tomorrow." They lay across the bed, and he held her and kissed her several times, but he didn't move to possess her. She got up, sat on the side of the bed and gave him his injection. "You'll feel much better after you begin taking the shock treatments," she said. Then she went out, locking the door behind her.

He waited for her to walk down the hall and enter the elevator. Then he jumped up, grabbed the chair and battered the screen out of the window. He picked up the Yeats and Browning books and put them under his right arm. For a few seconds he stood at the window, looking toward the sky. "God help the United States of America! God help all nations which in the future may depend on the United States! And God forgive me!" Then he dived head-first through the window and fell fourteen stories into a flower garden.

SINCE he had died at 9:10 P.M., there was time for the wire photo of his shattered body lying among rose bushes to appear on the front page of every Sunday newspaper in America. It was the disturbing end of a disturbing story.

He was buried near his grandfather, on a hillside in Clinch County, on a sunny May afternoon. Joe Bramwell conducted the service; Paul Blanton spoke for President Truman; and the pallbearers were six full-blooded

Cherokee Indians. Five thousand people stood on the hillside listening to the service through loudspeakers. Among the mourners were all the Castletons and their kin, Stumpy McDowell, Dr. Palkin, Mary Sullivan and delegations from the Sewanee Class of '48, the State Department, the TVA and the Atomic Energy Commission.

The day after the burial, Mary Sullivan came to the Castleton home to meet with Diane, Susan and Cord. The four of them sat in the music room, and Mary took from her handbag the packet Frank had given her. "Frank wrote this letter in the last hours before his death. He gave it to me to read and then deliver to the three of you. It's addressed to 'my daughter and my son' and it is to be read by Cordell to his mother, his sister and me, and to no one else . . . *ever.*"

Cordell Hull Castleton took the handwritten letter and began reading aloud:

Dear Susan and Cord:

I have hurt both of you, as well as your mother, by becoming too disturbed by the sorrows of the world. So tonight I will die. After my death I want you to have this brief explanation.

When I was seventeen, President Wilson, with tears in his eyes, begged the Senate to accept the League of Nations. He said:

"Prior to the great war just ended, the people of the world were told that fleets and armies, which they toiled to sustain, meant peace. The people know now that they were lied to: that fleets and armies mean war. They know that no old policy means anything else but war . . . war . . . always war. And they know that this is intolerable.

"Every true heart in the world, every enlightened judgment demands that, at whatever cost of independent action, every government that takes thought for its people or for justice or for ordered freedom should now lend itself to a new purpose, and utterly destroy the old order of international politics. Statesmen may see difficulties, but the people see none.

"A war in which the people have been bled white to beat the terror that lies concealed in every Balance of Power must not end in a mere victory of arms and a new balance. The monster that is war must be put in chains that cannot be broken."

When I was alone in the mountains I used to recite those words and weep. They are the most moving expression of hope for humanity I have ever found in any language.

That sorrowful scene—a weeping Wilson begging for an end to international war—lived in my mind, and I came to believe that whenever the United States of America reached the zenith of its power, Wilson's dream would be realized. In my heart I felt that it was America's destiny to lift the burden of armament from the shoulders of mankind.

In the summer of 1945 America had reached the zenith of its power. The towering geniuses of Europe—Bohr, Fermi and the four great Hungarians—had come here and placed in our hands the atomic bomb and asked only that we use it to realize Wilson's dream.

You will be told that we who believed that war between nations could be ended were fanatics. But no one accused General MacArthur of fanaticism when he told President Truman: "The only course for us now is construction of a new world order in which arms can be reduced to the minimum required for internal order and for international police."

To construct a new world order, the United States had to take two actions. It had to compel the Soviet bureaucracy to disarm, to concede the right of international search and seizure within its borders, to agree not to manufacture atomic weapons and to depend on international police to protect it from external attack. And the people of the United States had to agree to disarm, to transfer our atomic arsenal to the international force and to depend on this force for protection.

I believed that all this could be done. Particularly since the best and bravest of the Russian people, many of them in prison camps, were praying that it would be done. In New Mexico, after visiting the scientists at Los Alamos, I used to ride horseback into the mountains, and I felt that the Creator Himself was arming the United States with the bomb so that we could utterly destroy the old order of international politics, and construct a new order.

Now comes the crushing disappointment which will shadow your lives and which has tormented me to death. The United States failed to fulfill its destiny. We committed the unforgiveable sin among nations: We failed to use for good the power which Providence had given us. At the pivotal moment when we possessed the power to end war among nations, we lacked the will to use it.

Don't make the mistake of hoping that America will get another chance. Thucydides understood that all men grow to despise a nation which does not live up to its capacities.

So I come to the saddest part of this letter: my admission that you, my children, are the first American generation to inherit a diminished nation. In your lifetimes America can only endure, trying to make the best of its bad situation, trying to offer both welfare and freedom to its citizens, while it bears an ever-heavier burden of arms, and fights wars in which freedom cannot win.

I'll not advise you how to live in such a situation. I'll only express

333

the hope that you will turn to simplicity, solitude, books, ritual, art, music and metaphysics.

I leave you with my prayers and one request. I will die believing that some day . . . decades, generations or centuries from now . . . men, acting together, will somehow make Wilson's dream come true on this planet. So I ask you to remember Wilson's plea to the Senate. Memorize it . . . recite it often when you are alone. Pass it on to your children, and ask them to tell their children . . . so that for poor, struggling, striving mankind Wilson's dream will never die.

POSTSCRIPT

IN 1949, after the Soviet Union tested its first atomic bomb, Henry Cabot Lodge proposed that the United States submit its nuclear weapons to UN control and be willing to go to war if necessary to compel the Soviet Union to do the same. This proposal was opposed and defeated by President Truman and Secretary of State Dean Acheson.